Praise for *New York Times* bestselling author Nalini Singh and the Guild Hunter series

'Nalini Singh is a major new talent'
#1 *New York Times* bestselling author Christine Feehan

'With the launch of a second paranormal series,
Singh provides incontrovertible evidence that she's an
unrivalled storyteller . . . This book should be at the top
of your must-buy list! Tremendous!'
Romantic Times (Top Pick)

'Terrifyingly, passionately awesome . . . you'll love it'
#1 *New York Times* bestselling author Patricia Briggs

'I loved every word, could picture every scene,
and cannot recommend this book highly enough.
It is amazing in every way!'
New York Times bestselling author Gena Showalter

'Ms Singh's books never fail to draw me in and keep me
enthralled until the very end'
Romance Junkies

'*Archangel's Consort* is a great novel that makes me want
to read everything that Nalini Singh has ever written'
Fresh Fiction

'A heart-pounding and strongly emotional read'
Publishers Weekly on *Archangel's Blade*

Also by Nalini Singh from Gollancz:

Archangel's Enigma

A GUILD HUNTER NOVEL

NALINI SINGH

Copyright © Nalini Singh 2015
Excerpt from *Slave to Sensation* copyright © Nalini Singh 2006
All rights reserved

The right of Nalini Singh to be identified as the author
of this work has been asserted by her in accordance
with the Copyright, Designs and Patents Act 1988.

First published in Great Britain in 2015 by
Gollancz
An imprint of the Orion Publishing Group
Carmelite House, 50 Victoria Embankment, London
EC4Y 0DZ
An Hachette UK Company

5 7 9 10 8 6

A CIP catalogue record for this book is available
from the British Library

ISBN 978 0 575 11259 9

Printed in Great Britain by Clays Ltd, St Ives plc

The Orion Publishing Group's policy is to use papers
that are natural, renewable and recyclable products
and made from wood grown in sustainable forests.
The logging and manufacturing processes are expected
to conform to the environmental regulations of the
country of origin.

www.nalinisingh.com
www.orionbooks.co.uk
www.gollancz.co.uk

Prophecy

Zhou Lijuan stared into the large metal disk that hung on the far wall opposite her throne. It was a piece of art given to her by an admirer long, long ago. The admirer was lost in the mists of her millennia-old memory, but she'd kept the gift—there was something about the sleek shine of the disk, the way the carvings on the edges had been done with such delicacy, that spoke to her.

Even after thousands of years of having it in the throne room of her innermost stronghold, she found it fascinating. Perhaps because that disk reflected her as clearly as any mirror, and yet was not fragile. The metal disk might dent but it would never break. It had reflected her strength and ambition as a young archangel, wisdom and power as she grew older. Today, it showed her the ravages of war.

Many in the world still thought her dead and it suited her to allow them to believe such, so long as they kept their hands off her territory. Her generals were taking care of security, though she didn't think even Michaela was arrogant enough to attempt an incursion. All feared her.

Good.

But for the fear to remain, they could not see the woman in the metal mirror. Not yet. That woman had hair of a familiar icy white; Zhou Lijuan had been born with hair as black as night, but the color had faded with the growth of her power, as if her strength had leached it all away. By the time she was a thousand years old, her hair was "white as snow."

Her mother had said that to her and if she tried very hard, Lijuan could sometimes recall the face of the woman who had given birth to her. Mostly because she had bequeathed Lijuan her fine facial bones. The reflection in the metal had dramatic cheekbones that pushed against delicately translucent skin so thin it appeared it might tear with a touch. Thin blue veins pulsed beneath, but it was the red blood vessels around the pearlescent shade of her irises that caught the attention.

It was as if her irises were swimming in blood.

And they were—Raphael had hurt her. Her rage at that knowledge was a violent cold deep inside her body. *No one* hurt Zhou Lijuan. She would annihilate the upstart Archangel of New York for the insult, but first, she would make him watch as she enslaved his mortal consort. And for that, she needed to have patience, needed to finish healing, needed to finish *becoming*.

Because not all of her had regenerated the same as before Raphael tried to obliterate her from existence.

Lifting her hand with muscles that were weak and quivering, she examined her nails. They had grown back a gleaming ruby red and hooked over her fingertips like the talons of a great bird of prey. The incisors in her mouth, too, weren't the same. Her other teeth were pure white, the incisors dark scarlet.

It was oddly beautiful. As befit a goddess.

Those incisors weren't functioning yet, however. She'd attempted to feed on the glowing lifeforce of loyal subjects who wished to sacrifice themselves so their goddess could heal quicker and with less pain, but while her incisors appeared strong, they weren't mature. She couldn't penetrate the skin, and even when she used a knife to make the cut, she could suck up only a little useless blood, not the lifeforce of the sacrifice.

Agony burned her nerve endings every instant of every day.

Her bones ached.

Her wings couldn't hold her aloft.

Only her mind was whole.

Laying down her fully regenerated right hand on the arm of the throne of jade carved with nightmares and dreams and considered a treasure among angelkind by those who had seen it, she focused on the kneeling form of the angel below the dais. He had his forehead to the floor, his wings held gracefully to his back. She couldn't remember how long he'd been sitting there and she couldn't quite make out his form with clarity.

Her bleeding eyes didn't always work as they should.

"Speak," she said, and the word came out through a ravaged throat, the sound a harsh whisper that nonetheless howled with screams.

Raising his head from the floor, the man . . . ah, it was the Scribe. Yes, she recognized that yellow hair down to the shoulders. The Scribe placed his hands on his thighs and kept his head respectfully bowed as he began to speak.

"I have finished my work on the prophecy, sire."

Her blood pulsed, her senses sharpening. She remembered assigning him this task in the months before the battle with Raphael, even remembered reading the prophecy in an old scroll when she'd been a mere angel. At the time, it had meant nothing and she'd forgotten it for an eon. Then had come her growing power, and with it, a faint whisper of memory that told her the scroll was important.

It had taken her scholars and trackers almost a year to rediscover the ancient text, and since the moment of rediscovery, the words had become an echo at the back of her head, a drumbeat she couldn't unhear.

Archangel of Death. Goddess of Nightmare. Wraith without a shadow.
Rise, rise, rise into your Reign of Death.
For your end will come.
Your end will come.
At the hands of the new and of the old.
An Archangel kissed by mortality.
A silver-winged Sleeper who wakes before his Sleep is done.
The broken dream with eyes of fire.
Shatter. Shatter. Shatter.

"Tell me," she ordered the Scribe.

The Scribe's voice was crystalline as he said, "I have traced the origins of the prophecy to the Archangel Cassandra."

Lijuan's hand curled over the armrest of the jade throne, the carvings cutting into her flesh as the tiny hairs on her nape rose in a primeval response. "You are certain?" Cassandra had gone to Sleep so long ago that she was more myth than memory, an Ancient among Ancients. But one thing about her legend had never changed: that on her ascension, she had gained the great and terrible gift of seeing the future.

Legend stated that she'd chosen to Sleep soon after she clawed out her own eyes in a vain effort to stop the visions. Her eyes had grown back within the day, and in the hour afterward, her dress still bloody, she'd disappeared. Most of her prophecies had been lost in time and the ones that remained were often disregarded as the scribblings of some unknown fantasist.

"Raphael is the one kissed by mortality." Lijuan didn't understand how such a weakened archangel had almost been able to bring her down, but she would not make the mistake of underestimating him again.

"I have no answers for the last-mentioned, for the broken dreams with eyes of fire," the Scribe responded. "But the silver-winged Sleeper can be only one."

Lijuan's grip on the armrest grew vicious as her back spasmed. Her wings had grown back after her brain and spinal column, as per the angelic hierarchy of what was important, but they were weak and prone to causing her torso to spasm, further exacerbating her remaining injuries.

Breathing through the vicious sensations, she stared into the metal disk that acted as her mirror, and spoke the name of the Sleeper who needed to die. "Alexander."

1

Seven *months* Naasir had been hunting. Seven months since he'd told Ashwini he was ready to find a mate. Seven months and still his mate hadn't made herself known to him. Didn't she *know* he was looking for her?

Crouched on the railing-less edge of a high Tower balcony, he growled.

A Legion fighter who'd just flown past turned to give him an appraising look. Naasir snapped his teeth at the bat-winged male and was pleased when the fighter changed direction to head to the Legion's new home. Naasir liked that home, even if it had walls. It was a high-rise that had been turned into a giant greenhouse, windows taken out to form balconies, walls replaced with massive sheets of glass where possible, and a flight tunnel created in the central core, a tunnel big enough to accommodate wings.

With fall now a blaze of red and orange and yellow across Central Park, the engineers had also added clever transparent "curtains" of what Illium had told Naasir was a high-tech material that allowed the Legion to fly in and out at will, but that maintained a warm, growing temperature within. Each time a fighter went through, the curtains fell automatically back in place, trapping the heat inside.

Naasir had snuck into the high-rise soon after he first returned to New York two weeks earlier. The inside was structured so that the remaining parts of the internal floors and ceilings jutted out at unusual angles; the distance between one and the next was often deep. Enjoying the lush greenery within, the vines climbing up the sides already starting to take strong hold and small trees digging in their roots as flowers bloomed, Naasir had made his way to the top regardless—without alerting the Legion he was in their territory.

He didn't think the Primary had been pleased when Naasir appeared on the glass of the roof, but the leader of the Legion was loyal to Raphael, and Naasir was one of Raphael's Seven, so they existed in a wary truce. Just thinking about the Legion made Naasir's skin prickle and muscles tense.

They were so old and so *other* that he often had to fight the compulsion to bite them.

Despite that, or perhaps because of it, he sometimes felt that the strange fighters who flew on wings devoid of feathers, were more like him than anyone else in the entire world. Naasir might not have wings, but he was as *other*. Except, where there were seven hundred and seventy-seven in the Legion, he was only one.

You are angry with us because we are many, but you know deep within that you are one of us. A child of the earth. Bitterly young in comparison to our eons-long existence, but with a connection to life that is primal.

The leader of the Legion had said that to Naasir with a straight face. The other man—though man didn't feel like the right description—truly believed his words. He didn't understand that Naasir wasn't anything natural. He hadn't been born of the earth; he'd been created by a monster.

A monster whose liver and heart Naasir had clawed out and eaten.

Teeth bared, he looked down at the balcony to his left and two floors below, noting that it was one of the rare ones with a railing. Dmitri had said he couldn't jump to the city streets because he'd end up flattened like a pancake, but this jump wasn't far and the wind, while brisk, wouldn't push him right to the edge. Muscles bunching a split second after his eye fell on the other balcony, he jumped.

Cold air rushed past his face, pasting his T-shirt to his body and stinging his eyes, and then his bare feet hit the hard surface of the balcony. Absorbing the impact through his entire body, having purposefully ended up in a feline crouch, he found the wind had pushed him farther than he'd expected—another couple of inches and he'd have hit the top of the railing, would've had to scrabble for purchase to keep from tumbling out into open air.

He was grinning at the close call when he became aware of someone rushing out onto the balcony. He didn't need to look behind him to know who it was; Honor's scent was as familiar to him as his own. Rising to his full height as he turned, he saw that her cheeks were pale beneath her gold-kissed skin, her green eyes huge.

"Naasir!" She ran across to him, frantically running her hands over his shoulders and down his arms. "Did you hurt yourself?"

Naasir suddenly realized he might be in trouble. "No," he reassured her. "It was only a short jump."

"A *short jump*?" Honor pressed one hand over her heart, her other hand gripping tight at his upper arm, as if she was afraid he'd fall off the balcony. "You scared me half to death!"

Moving slowly so as not to scare her any more, he wrapped her in his arms and nuzzled his cheek against her hair. "Don't tell Dmitri," he whispered.

"You are a person." The deadly vampire who was Honor's mate had said that to Naasir when he was only a feral child. *"You are* Naasir. *I'll lose a piece of me if you die and it's a piece I'll never get back."*

Until that instant forever seared into his memory, Naasir hadn't actually understood that anyone considered him a real person, a person who would be missed if he was gone, and who had the right to other people's love, affection, and care. That day, in Dmitri's dark eyes, he'd seen pain at the idea of a world without Naasir, as well as raw anger at the fact Naasir had once again endangered himself, and it had forever changed the boy he'd been.

In many ways, that moment marked his true birth. The birth of Naasir, the person.

Even today, though he was full-grown, Naasir didn't like making Dmitri scared for him, or angry with him—and he felt the same way about Honor. She was Dmitri's mate and part of

Naasir's family now. She treated him as if he were hers to care for, to spoil, and to touch as family touched. That should've been strange, but it wasn't. He had no trouble following Honor's orders, no matter that he was the far more dangerous predator.

Maybe because she belonged to Dmitri . . . and maybe because she made him feel safe and protected. It made no sense, but when he was with Honor, her soft scent in his every breath, he felt like he thought a cub must feel next to the comforting warmth of its mother. She *looked after* him and she didn't do it in a way that made his hackles rise.

Laughing a little raggedly now, she ran her hands down his back. "I won't tell on you," she promised, "but you can't go around doing things like that." She leaned back so she could hold his eyes with the jeweled brightness of her own. "What would I do if you hurt yourself?"

He hung his head, looking at her through his lashes. Like the choppily cut hair that slid around his face, they were a metallic, inhuman silver that marked him as different. "I'm sorry. Sometimes I forget to think like a human."

Shaking her head, Honor cupped his face in her hands. "You're perfect exactly as you are," she whispered with so much love that he felt as if he was being hugged. "I just don't want you hurt."

He smiled at the last, knowing he was forgiven for having scared her. Lifting her up in his arms and off her feet, he squeezed her tight. She laughed, silhouetted against a cloudless sky of chrome blue, and, when he put her back down, said, "Be on time for dinner. I asked Montgomery for the recipe for the spiced meat you like."

Making the promise, Naasir walked her back into the Tower and realized he'd jumped onto the balcony right outside her study. He was thinking about curling up in a sunny armchair in the corner and just napping when he felt the crashing wave, the biting, fresh touch of water, that was his archangel's voice in his head.

Naasir, I need to speak to you.

I'm on my way, sire. Leaving Honor with a rub of his cheek against hers that she permitted with a smile, he made his way to the room in the Tower from which Raphael ran his territory. Spearing through the Manhattan sky, the city's Archangel

Tower held countless rooms, all with a purpose. Above this floor were the private suites.

Naasir had one, but he preferred to stay with Honor and Dmitri.

Why would he want to be by himself when he could be with family?

Entering Raphael's office, he was disappointed to find that Elena wasn't there. He liked sparring with his sire's consort and they'd done it several times since Naasir had finally been released from long-term duty at Amanat, the city held by Raphael's mother, Caliane.

Caliane's forces had grown strong as more and more of those who remembered her rule returned to her and swore their allegiance once again. It was no longer necessary for Raphael to second one of the Seven to Amanat, though Naasir knew the sire would continue to assist his mother while she adapted to the modern world.

"Sire."

Raphael's wings were backlit by the sun where he stood behind his desk, his feathers sparking a white gold as metallic as Naasir's hair, and his gaze on an array of blades spread out over the polished volcanic stone of his desk. Even after all these centuries of being one of Raphael's most trusted men, part of Naasir always felt a punch of awe at the violent power embodied in the archangel in front of him. That punch came from the primal core of his nature, the part that had never been meant to be within such proximity to an archangel.

"Are you rested?" Glancing up, Raphael held his gaze with eyes of a blue so pure that as a child, Naasir had thought they must be made from actual gemstones.

Fascinated, he'd used to creep up on Raphael and try to touch them. It was to Raphael's credit that he'd dissuaded Naasir's persistent efforts without ever terrifying or hurting him. Only as an adult had Naasir understood just how tolerant and lenient Raphael had been with him.

Even before he'd become an archangel, the sire had been a *power*.

"Yes," he said in response to Raphael's question. "I'm glad to be here." He didn't mind the work at Amanat—he liked and respected his partner in the task, and it had been fun sneaking over into Lijuan's territory to check on the emotional pulse of it. But the posting had been distant from all his family.

If Venom, Raphael, Janvier, and Ashwini hadn't visited Amanat during the six months since he'd left New York, Naasir might have returned to his feral roots. As it was, he'd made Janvier and Ash stay for a week longer than they'd intended, delighted to have playmates who understood the way his mind worked. "I don't want to leave," he said to the archangel to whom he'd given his loyalty the day Raphael had found him.

Naasir had been a tiny boy then, and at that instant, he'd been feeding in the clawed open chest cavity of the Ancient angel who'd Made him. He must've looked like a small blood-covered monster, but instead of killing him, Raphael had lifted his growling, ferocious body into his arms and said, "Quiet. You don't want to eat that meat."

Naasir hadn't been sure what those words actually meant, since his Maker didn't talk to him like a human, but the tone had gotten through. He'd stilled and allowed Raphael to carry him into the clouds and to his home in the angelic stronghold of the Refuge. Not once since that day had Naasir felt the urge to challenge the male who'd taken him from the ice and from the evil.

Raphael was the alpha of his family and Dmitri was the alpha's second.

Naasir had been a cub, but he wasn't any longer.

Coming around the desk, his wings held off the floor with the unconscious strength and discipline of a warrior, Raphael met him in the center of the room. "I know you want to stay in New York," he said, the painful blue of his eyes continuing to hold Naasir's gaze. "But you're not built for this environment—you'll start to buck at the civilized skin you have to wear in the city."

Naasir felt his hands clench as a growl built up inside his chest. He wanted to lie, to tell Raphael that he could stay always in the city, but the lie wouldn't come. Already, his nature was starting to rebel, to ache for open spaces where he could run and climb and explore. "My family is here," he said instead. "I don't want an alone task."

"You also have family in the Refuge."

Interest sparked in his blood. "Am I to go there?" Honor wouldn't be there, but Jessamy would be—his relationship with her was different from the one he had with Honor, but he loved the angelic Historian and Teacher the same way he loved Honor. Venom and Galen, too, were currently based in the mountains of the Refuge.

"Your task will begin there," Raphael said, "and while you will have to leave the Refuge and your family for a time, the task is one I think you'll enjoy."

Since Raphael understood him, too, Naasir waited.

"I want you to discover where it is that Alexander Sleeps."

Naasir went motionless. The Sleeping place of an angel or archangel was a taboo thing. Even Naasir, who didn't have much respect for rules, hadn't broken that one. "Do you want to kill him?" If Raphael needed to kill Alexander, Naasir would help him. Because Raphael didn't, had never, smelled like bad meat. Once, before Elena, he'd started to smell disturbingly like cold and ice, but that was gone, too.

Now he smelled of himself and of touches of Elena.

Naasir wanted to smell like his mate, he thought with an inward snarl. Why was she *hiding* from him?

"No, I have no desire to kill Alexander." Raphael's tone chilled. "Jason has been in and out of Lijuan's territory this past month."

Naasir hissed at the sound of Lijuan's name. That one was bad meat through and through. As a child, he'd once thought he wanted to kill and eat her, but now he knew he wouldn't touch her even if he was starving. He still wanted her dead, however. "She's alive, isn't she?"

"Jason hasn't been able to glimpse her, but all signs point to that." Features grim, Raphael stretched out his wings before tucking them back into his body, the white fire that licked over his feathers appearing an illusion created by sunlight.

Naasir had been fascinated by angelic wings since childhood. When Raphael first found him, he'd gripped at the feathers hard, pulling off a large white one with golden filaments that he'd held possessively in his fist. He hadn't known he wasn't supposed to touch angelic wings, that it was an intimacy permitted only to friends and lovers, and even though he didn't have that excuse now, he did still sometimes touch one without asking.

Only of his friends and family, however. Only people who wouldn't look at him as if he'd done a terrible thing. Yesterday, he'd lain on the grass with Elena after a sparring session, and she'd put her wing across his chest so he could stroke the sleek beauty of it as much as he wanted. Black and indigo and midnight blue and dawn and white gold—Elena had such fascinating feathers that he'd been tempted to steal one of each shade, except the colors blended seamlessly into each other.

Then she'd fallen asleep on the grass beside him.

He'd thought about reminding her that he was dangerous, but since he wasn't ever going to hurt her, he'd let her sleep and played with her feathers instead. He was as fascinated by Raphael's wings, but he resisted the temptation to grab at them when Raphael turned to head to the balcony. He wasn't sure the unpredictable white fire wouldn't burn.

Naasir followed the sire, going to crouch at the edge in his favorite position. He could see a stream of tiny yellow cabs from here, flowing along the straight ribbon of the road. The scents this high were faint but he caught a hint of the river and of the green, growing things in the Legion's home. The green smells made him want to break free, to stretch out in a way he couldn't, even in Central Park. "Is Lijuan searching for Alexander?"

"Jason isn't certain, but he's seen hunting parties being dispatched from Lijuan's citadel. A member of one had a little too much to drink when they halted for the night, and Jason heard him boasting of how they were planning to find Alexander."

"He's not like Lijuan, is he?" Naasir had only been two hundred when Alexander went to Sleep, didn't remember much about the silver-winged angel with golden hair. He did, however, have one faded memory of a powerful being hunkering down in front of him when he was yet a boy, the silver eyes that met his gaze as near to Naasir's own eyes as he'd ever seen. "I think he gave me one of his feathers once. I wanted it because it was like my hair."

At the time, he'd been too young to understand the *why* behind the unusual echo.

"I can well imagine him doing that." Raphael's tone was difficult to judge. "He was never cruel or callous, certainly never to children. And you he kept an eye on until you were full grown."

Frowning, Naasir tried to bring the memory of his meeting with the Ancient into focus, but he'd been too young. "He was a good leader?"

"He was a great one," Raphael said quietly, so many layers to his voice that Naasir couldn't unravel them all. "He was also a viciously powerful archangel who preferred the old ways to the new, and who thought me an upstart. As a result, he almost started a war with me, but in the end, he chose to Sleep rather than indulge in violence."

Wings whispering as his feathers slid against one another, Raphael came to stand right beside Naasir. His power burned against Naasir's skin, but the pressure was familiar after so many centuries at his side.

"It's possible Lijuan believes he might be an ally because of his past aggression toward me," Raphael continued, "but given her delusions of godhood, it's far more likely that she wants to kill everyone who might have the power to oppose her."

Naasir's hunting instincts rose to the fore. "Is Alexander powerful enough to do that?" If he was, maybe this time Lijuan would stay dead.

"Unpredictable. He was stronger than her when he went to Sleep roughly four hundred years ago, but Lijuan's power has grown exponentially in that same period, while he's been in stasis."

Naasir knew that when angels Slept, they didn't change, but that wasn't his concern right now. "I need a scent to track and Alexander has been gone too long from the world." Even Naasir couldn't track a ghost.

That annoyed him; he didn't like not being able to find his prey.

Like his mate. Who was *hiding* from him.

"You'll have help," Raphael replied, then paused to watch a solitary squadron fighter do a number of intricate flight moves while practicing with a crossbow. "Jessamy has a scholar studying under her who has specialized in the Sleeping archangels. Your task is to keep her safe and explore the locations she suggests."

Naasir frowned. "Is her specialization known to others?"

"Yes." Raphael's voice was cold enough to frost the air. "It's unlikely even Lijuan would order the abduction of an angel right from the Refuge, but given her track record of breaking angelic taboos, I have Galen and Venom keeping an eye on Andromeda regardless."

"I'll look after her." Naasir could be a good guard dog when needed.

"You will also have to watch her," Raphael said. "She is Charisemnon's granddaughter."

Naasir bared his teeth at the name of the archangel who had caused the Falling, the terrible event that had hurt or killed so many angels. Charisemnon was also responsible for a deadly vampire disease. "Why are we working with her?"

"Jessamy assures me that Andromeda is a scholar right down to the bone, one who cut all ties to her family when she arrived at the Refuge, and who is horrified at the thought of the murder of a Sleeper. Galen backs Jessamy's judgment."

Naasir nodded. "Galen has good instincts." Jessamy was smart but with too tender a heart. "I'll be able to tell if the scholar lies." Immortal or mortal, liars had an unmistakable and sour scent. "But since Lijuan's people are searching without success, Galen and Jessamy seem to be right about her loyalties."

"Yes, close as Lijuan is to Charisemnon, he would've shared the knowledge if he had it. We will give this young scholar the benefit of the doubt and a chance to prove herself."

"Who'll watch over her when I need to explore the locations she suggests for Alexander's Sleeping place?"

"You'll take her with you."

Naasir looked up at Raphael.

Blinked.

Then snarled. "I can't be dragging around a historian. They *break*." As a boy, he'd once broken Jessamy's arm by jumping on her from a high shelf, he'd been so excited to see her. She'd told him not to worry, that she knew he hadn't done it on purpose and that she'd heal quickly, but he'd never forgotten her cry of shock and pain—or the horrible crunching sound her arm made as it snapped.

"It's your task to make sure she doesn't break, Naasir." The midnight of Raphael's hair whipped around his face as the wind rose in a sudden gust. "Andromeda is our greatest chance of reaching Alexander first—we can't forget Lijuan's age or the age of the scholars in her court. She may have access to information that gives her a head start."

Turning his attention back toward the metal and glass and glittering water of the city, Naasir tried to sound human as he spoke. He didn't wholly succeed, his words guttural. "How am I supposed to find my mate if I'm dragging around another woman?"

"You've survived six hundred years without a mate." A touch of amusement in Raphael's tone. "Why are you so impatient now?"

"Because it's time." Naasir lived according to the rhythms of his blood and of his soul, and that rhythm was now pounding a single beat. "Is this scholar wild and interesting?" he asked hopefully, because like his sire, he didn't judge a person on their bloodline, only on their actions.

"Not according to your definition. It appears Andromeda has taken a vow of celibacy."

Naasir groaned. "I think I should jump off into traffic. It'd be less painful than such torture."

Naasir liked sex, liked touching women's soft, warm bodies, liked driving his cock into their tight, wet sheaths as they screamed his name. He hadn't done it since the night he decided to go mate hunting, so he wasn't frustrated by the vow of celibacy because he planned to seduce the scholar—no, he was frustrated because that vow confirmed she wasn't his, and now he was going to be stuck with her for who knew how long.

No mate of his would ever be so ridiculous as to take a vow of *celibacy*. "What kind of strange person takes a vow like that?" Angelkind wasn't exactly known for its lack of excess.

Raphael laughed, the big, open sound one Naasir hadn't heard for a long time before Elena came into the sire's life. That was what Naasir wanted—a mate who'd play with him, who'd make him laugh, who'd challenge him. And who'd rut with him. Over and over. No idiotic vow of celibacy permitted.

"There are the odd few," Raphael said after his laughter faded. "Scholars sometimes believe cutting out physical distractions heightens the mind."

"In that case, I'd rather stay unenlightened." Rising to his feet, Naasir held Raphael's gaze. "I will go, sire." He'd miss dinner with Honor and Dmitri, but they would understand—and when he returned, he'd be welcome at their table.

Raphael shook his head, the inky strands of his hair crossing over the painful blue of his eyes as the gust returned. "Not tonight, Naasir. Tonight, you'll spend with family in New York."

2

Naasir hated traveling in the metal bucket of a jet, but it was the fastest way for a non-winged traveler to get most of the way to the Refuge. He paced the cabin the entire time and was out the door almost before it was fully open once they landed. The sun on his face, the kiss of wind, it was pure pleasure.

Breathing deep for the first time in hours, he shook himself to settle his skin back into proper place, then grabbed his duffel when the pilot threw it out. He grinned and saluted one of the two men—the other being the co-pilot—whom he'd driven crazy over the flight. The other vampire was used to him and flashed Naasir his fangs before disappearing back inside.

Naasir laughed and, duffel slung over his shoulder, loped to the private parking garage that housed his motorcycle. He could see mountains in the distance, clouds touching them, but they weren't of the Refuge. He was still far, for the angels had nothing of civilization close to them.

Any unauthorized vampire, or mortal who accidentally entered Refuge territory, soon forgot about it, the memory taken quietly away. The landscape itself was so forbidding that it kept most at bay, and the powerful angels who lived permanently in the Refuge were able to do something that swathed the approaches to the angelic haven in heavy fog.

The stubborn climbers who insisted on venturing farther found themselves in an icy, inhospitable region that equaled broken limbs a hundred percent of the time. Anyone who returned a second time didn't leave alive: angelkind did not play games when it came to protecting the place that sheltered their young.

Nodding at the mechanic on duty, Naasir went straight to his bike.

"She's ready to go," the vampire mechanic said in the local tongue, coming over to pat the electric-blue side panels. "I envy you the ride. The weather's perfect for it."

Naasir had learned to ride motorcycles with Janvier after the machines first became fast and exciting. They'd both fallen off more than once. Never during that time or afterward, had Naasir worn a helmet. He picked one up today, though—the last time Ashwini had seen him riding without a helmet, she'd gotten so angry that he'd apologized then gone out with her and bought a helmet.

Janvier's hunter mate had lost her brother and sister less than a year earlier; she'd been so sad for so long that it had hurt Naasir to see it. He wasn't going to be responsible for making her sad again by getting so damaged even his immortality couldn't save him—because unlike what the mortals believed, Naasir knew no one was *totally* immortal.

Then there was Lijuan.

The Archangel of China had a nasty habit of coming back from the dead.

Considering once again what might keep her dead, he put on the helmet then started up the bike. It came on with a silken roar. Gear stowed, he gave the mechanic a thumbs-up and headed out. He'd fed from bottled blood and cold meat on the jet, and it would fuel him for the next stage of the journey. The bike would also need fuel later on, but he, Janvier, and a few others who used this method of transport had hidden caches in a number of discreet locations.

For now, he could just ride the mountain pathways and glory in the wind pressing against him. It threatened to push him right off his bike and into a massive gorge halfway through. Teeth bared at the challenge, he bent lower over the bars and kept going. At one point, after he'd slowed down to admire a sparkling river, he saw a sign that warned of tigers in the area.

It reminded him of Elena's attempts to find out his origins.

Laughing so hard he almost fell off the bike, he gunned the engine and took off again. He didn't stop when the hard, clear sunlight turned to shadows, then to midnight, his night vision as good as his ordinary sight. Utilizing a fuel cache when necessary, he continued on. He had to stop and hunt a few hours later, but even if he hadn't found prey, he was in no danger of starving, old enough that his body didn't burn through as much fuel as a younger vampire.

Not that he was a vampire exactly, but it was the word most people used to describe him. Elena called him a "tiger creature" and had no idea how close to the truth she'd inadvertently come. He liked teasing her by making her guess, but what intrigued him most was that Raphael played the game, too. The sire refused to tell Elena, either.

Naasir had never seen Raphael play games. Not that way. *Secret rules between mates.*

Like the secrets he'd have with his own mate once he hunted her down and growled at her for hiding from him. Or maybe he wouldn't growl. He might just bite her instead.

Thoughts of his elusive mate in mind, he rode through the night and the next day, resting only when the sun was hot and uncomfortable. During that time, he found a tree, settled on a branch and went boneless. Dmitri had once discovered him in the same position as a child, called up to ask Naasir what he was doing.

"I was sleeping!" Naasir had scowled at being wakened from his nap.

Dressed in pants of a tough black material, boots, and with his upper body sweaty from a combat session against Raphael, Dmitri had raised an eyebrow. "Aren't you worried you'll fall?"

"No. That's why I sleep like this." He'd pointedly waved his arms and legs, which straddled the branch, hanging down below his prone body.

"In that case, rest well."

Naasir rested well today, too, and when he woke, found some water and drank it. Not as good as blood, but it was fine for now. Riding on through the afternoon, he finally brought the bike to a halt in another garage. This one was built into the side of a mountain and hidden so well that no one who didn't know it was there would ever see it.

Opening it using his palm print, he rolled the bike into the silence and parked it next to a number of rugged all-terrain vehicles and familiar bikes. Behind him, the mountain closed again, enclosing the garage in unrelieved darkness, as he hadn't activated the lights when he walked in. He tugged off his helmet and hung it carefully from the handlebar of his bike so others would know it was his, then grabbed his duffel and, running a hand through his hair, began to make his way to the back of the cavernous space.

He hated the tunnel part of the trip, but at least it was a wide tunnel.

Teeth gritted, he broke into a run to more quickly navigate the underground passageway. It was just over a mile, according to the records Jessamy had once looked up for him. Nothing really, not to Naasir, except that he hated being shut inside.

He stretched once he was finally outside, then began to lope across the landscape, his lungs expanding to cope with the thinner air. Having a strong dislike for the cold, he curled his lip at the ice and snow that covered the approaches to the Refuge—though the Refuge itself was generally kept clear of snow by means no one fully understood.

Once, when Naasir was very young, Raphael had answered his curious questions by telling him a story of the Ancestors who Slept below the Refuge. "The very first ones of our kind," he'd said, his muscular arms on either side of Naasir's body as he taught Naasir how to use a crossbow. "The ones from before recorded history, before all known Ancients, so old that they are almost another species."

Legend said it was the influence of the Sleeping Ancestors that kept the Refuge's weather mild, but for irregular seasons of snow and ice. "When winter comes," Raphael had murmured, "it's because an Ancestor is distracted by a dream. Or that's the story my mother told me when I was a babe."

No one knew if there was any truth to the legend, but *something* was different about the physics of the Refuge. Nothing at that high an altitude should be free of the icy lash of subzero temperatures.

Naasir's secret aerie was outside the Refuge proper, but Aodhan had put in heating for him, including underfloor heating, which kept it at the temperature he liked. All of it was powered by discreet solar panels placed some distance from the actual aerie so no one would discover it by accident.

Today, he avoided going up into the colder altitudes for as long as possible.

When it was no longer avoidable, he washed himself clean in a glacier-fed stream that made him hiss out a breath, then dried off and changed into fresh clothes. On top, he wore the black cashmere sweater he'd bought in New York, below that a dark gray shirt with silver studs that Honor had bought for him. Leaving the tails of the shirt hanging out over his jeans, he threw on the battered leather jacket Janvier had gifted him a decade earlier.

Thick socks, his scuffed and worn-in boots with their special ice-grip soles, and he was done.

It wasn't that he really *needed* any of it. He wasn't going to freeze, his blood too hot. But who said not freezing was the only thing? He fucking hated being cold. He hoped his mate wasn't someone who liked the cold and wanted to live in snow without heat to offset the natural temperature. That would be terrible. He'd have to persuade her to move to an in-between climate that was cold but not subzero, but if she didn't want to come, he'd stay. Of course he'd stay.

If he could ever *find* her.

Shoving his dirty clothes into the duffel, he saw a glint inside. When he tugged on the glint, he found it was a thick identity bracelet in brushed metal. Admiring the way his name scrolled across the bar, he tore off the little card attached to it.

Be careful and don't forget to wear your scarf. I also swapped out your socks for better ones and put gloves in the front pocket. ~ xo Honor

He smiled and put on the bracelet before tucking the card carefully into an inner pocket. One tug, two, and the lined black leather gloves were on. Flexing his toes inside the socks, he wrapped the dark green wool scarf around his neck and lower face, then slung the duffel over his shoulder again. "I'll be careful," he promised. "My mate is waiting for me."

He could almost hear Honor's laughter. The last time he'd said that to her, she'd asked him a question. "What if she's annoyed with you because you made her wait all this time? What then?"

Naasir had been stumped for a while—he'd never really thought about the fact that maybe his mate had lived longer than him, had been waiting for *him* to be ready. Things like that did happen. Honor was younger than Dmitri, but Jessamy was older than Galen.

"I'll court her," he'd said after careful thought. "I'll convince her the wait was worth it."

That in mind, he filled the remaining hours of his journey to the Refuge with courtship plans. It almost made him forget the brittle cold and the sheer danger of the ice, the jagged rocks around him not looming threats but familiar adversaries. Unlike the hapless climbers who, between them, had broken countless limbs before ever getting this far, Naasir knew how to navigate the sharp natural teeth that guarded the angelic stronghold. He didn't need to walk. He could run, his booted feet sure on the glaciers and ice sheets he preferred over the deep snow, and his eyes seeing every risk.

When the shadow of large wings swept over him as the sun was about to sink below the horizon, he looked up. Vivid red hair lit to scarlet brilliance by the final rays of the sun and dark gray wings striated with white, Galen dipped his wings to acknowledge Naasir's wave, then circled around to land not far away.

"Were you watching for me?" Naasir asked upon reaching the wide-shouldered male.

"I was expecting to have to go out to the foothills." The weapons-master embraced Naasir in a backslapping hug that almost knocked him off his feet, Galen was so strong. "You must've cut at least two hours off your previous time."

"I'm faster." He was growing in ways even Keir didn't understand and the healer understood many things; all anyone knew was that while Naasir was an adult full grown, his abilities and gifts hadn't yet settled into their final form.

You are the only one of your kind ever to survive to adulthood.

There is no blueprint for your development, no way of predicting your ultimate strength.

"When you have time, we'll have to test how much faster." Galen's voice broke into the echo of Keir's words. "Are you planning to run the entire way in?"

"Yes." Naasir had been carried by angels as a child and he'd liked it. No longer. Now he wanted the ground beneath his feet—he didn't even like riding in the baskets the squadrons utilized to ferry in non-winged guests. "Tell Jessamy I'm coming for dinner."

His smile reaching the unusually pale green of his eyes, Galen spread his wings. "She's been watching for you since dawn."

That delighted Naasir. Waiting until Galen had taken off in a powerful beat of wings that drew a flurry of snow up into the air, Naasir stepped up his pace even further, until to anyone watching, he'd have been a blur. More wings passed overhead an hour later, the aerial traffic increasing steadily until he began to hear the rush of landings, the beat of takeoffs, the laughter and conversation of people going about their lives.

The sky was a soft black broken only by several early stars when the snow suddenly ended, warmer air against his chilled face.

He went straight to Jessamy and Galen's house on the cliff.

"Naasir!" A vampire, his poison-green eyes slitted like those of a viper and his dark, dark brown hair having grown to touch the collar of his T-shirt, caught him in an embrace on the paved yard outside the house.

Slapping Venom on the back, Naasir dropped his duffel to the paving stones, the small yard edged with pots bursting with flowers. "I see Galen hasn't broken you yet." He took in the younger man's jeans and simple black T-shirt. "No more suits?" Venom was well known for his dangerously elegant appearance, his grace as liquid as it was lethal.

"Who cares about suits when I'm getting my ass handed to me in the training ring every day." Venom winced and pointed to a blue-black bruise on his jaw, the color vivid against the warm brown of his skin. "Sometimes I'm not sure if Galen's teaching me or trying to kill me."

Naasir bared his teeth. "If Galen was trying to kill you, you'd know." The weapons-master didn't fight like Naasir or Venom, his style heavier and more steady, but he was a brutal and deadly force. "He'll toughen you up." Venom was a dangerous cub who had the gift of deadly poison in his blood, but at just over three hundred and fifty, he was the youngest of the Seven.

He needed a little more tempering.

"There you are!" Jessamy ran out of the cottage, the misty yellow of her airy ankle-length gown frothing around her legs and the chestnut waves of her hair woven into a loose braid. Her lush brown eyes glowed with welcome against the cream of her skin, her smile luminous.

Grabbing her tall and delicately slender form up in his arms, his skin brushing the insides of her wings, Naasir spun her around and around until she protested. "Oh, I have *missed* you," she said with water shining in her eyes, before cupping his face and kissing him on both cheeks. "Come inside. I have a drink waiting for you."

His stomach rumbled right on cue, but he hadn't forgotten his mission. "The scholar, she's safe?"

"Yes, she's working in the Library. I thought you could rest and have a snack before I introduced you two—I'm planning on inviting her to dinner with us."

Walking with Jessamy and Venom into the cottage just as Galen landed behind them, Naasir released a quiet breath. It was good to be with family again.

Andromeda tried to focus on the illuminated manuscript she'd placed on a stand at the back of the Library, but all she could see were the words of the letter that had come for her an hour earlier.

In twenty-two days, you turn four hundred. You have had many years of indulgence. We have allowed you all of it— even when you chose to forsake your bloodline.

It is now time to return home and undertake your obligation to your family and to your archangel. We shall expect you for the start of the ceremonial celebrations six days prior to your day of birth, following which, you will go to your grandfather's court to take up your position by his side.

He has little use for scholars, but you are his sole grandchild, and as such, he is willing to overlook your failings as long as you conduct yourself as a princess of the court during your time of service. Do not disappoint him, Andromeda. Your grandfather's mercy is not endless.

She gripped the sides of the stand, the wooden edges digging into her palms. "Indulgence" her mother called Andromeda's centuries of learning, learning that had seen her offer help to countless immortals who came to the Library for assistance. She was a keeper of angelic histories and a teacher of their young. Yet after a bare three hundred and twenty-five years, give or take, she was a mere apprentice. There was *so* much more she had to learn.

And the journeys she'd taken . . . the world was ever changing and she wanted to continue to drink in every single part of it. But time had run out. She'd always known it would, always known that one day, no matter any other choice she'd made, she'd be four hundred years old and expected to return to the court of the Archangel Charisemnon—to fulfill the terms of a familial blood vow her parents had made on her behalf when she was a babe newborn.

Jessamy had asked her if she was bound by any such vows when Andromeda first came to the Refuge. Scared she wouldn't be accepted into an apprenticeship should she tell the truth, admit she'd have to stop her studies at four hundred, Andromeda had lied and said Charisemnon had forgiven her vow since she was so clearly unsuited to court life. As the years passed, the lie had become more and more difficult to put right.

None of it mattered now. Allowing one day for the journey, she had fifteen more of freedom before she had to return to the stunning, heartbreaking land she'd left as a girl not yet an adult. Any other action would be considered high treason, death the penalty.

No one, enemy or friend, would offer her safe harbor. "Stealing" children from another archangel's blood family was considered an act of quiet violence that could ripple out into war. She'd considered asking Raphael or Titus for sanctuary, since they were already at war with her grandfather, but she knew that even if they paid attention to the petition of a lowly apprentice, the two archangels could not give her what she wanted.

To do so would be to shock and disturb the more traditional archangels who were Raphael's and Titus's allies against the death and disease her grandfather and his own nightmare ally had spread across the world. And regardless, she'd be hunted to the end of her existence should she run. Far better to serve the five hundred years required of her and hope her soul was intact at the end of it.

As a princess of the court, she'd be expected to be a ruth-less and vicious arm of Charisemnon. Her grandfather might not kill her the first time she refused an order to torture or to humiliate, but he'd do everything in his power to break her, make her his puppet. Charisemnon did not suffer defiance.

Fifteen more days.

Taking a deep, shuddering breath, she was attempting to focus on the manuscript again in an effort to find stable ground, when the hairs rose on the back of her neck. All at once, she wished she didn't have her hair in a braid, that her nape wasn't so open, so vulnerable.

Throat dry, she turned in wary quiet, reaching at the same time for the razor-sharp blade strapped to her thigh and access-ible through a hole in the pocket of her gauzy raspberry-colored gown. When she saw it was only Jessamy heading toward her, she began to smile . . . then realized her mentor wasn't alone.

There was a shadow next to her.

A shadow with silver eyes that watched Andromeda with-out blinking.

Every hair on her body stood up this time, or that's what it felt like. She knew who he was—everyone knew Naasir, though like her, most had no idea of his origins or nature. He was one of a kind. Skin of a warm, deep brown that held golden undertones and that invited a caressing touch, eyes of silver and hair the same shade. *Silver*, not gray. It was as if his hair and his eyes had been formed out of the metal and pol-ished to a high shine.

He stood out, made you remember him.

Of course, she'd never before been so close to him. Naasir had passed through the Refuge many times in the three and a quarter centuries she'd lived here, but Andromeda had ensured

they never met. At first, she'd been too young and too determined to succeed at her studies to worry about anyone of the
male sex. But later . . . Naasir incited things inside her that
weren't right for a woman who had taken a vow of celibacy,
made the out-of-control animal within want to come out.

That didn't mean she hadn't watched him from afar.

He moved like a jungle cat, fed on blood and yet ate meat,
had eyes that saw through the darkness, and seduced mortals
and immortals alike with ease. Andromeda might not have
ever surrendered to the same primal urges, but she understood
that he was unique in his ability to entrance so many. Add in
his feral beauty, so compelling and hypnotic, as well as the
potent depth of his power, and he was a threat on many levels.

"Andromeda." Jessamy tilted her head a touch to the side. "Is
everything all right?"

Realizing she'd been standing frozen in place as she watched
the vampire who wasn't a vampire walk toward her, she forced
her stiff muscles to move. "Yes, of course," she managed to get
out. "Just lost in thought."

Jessamy took her words at face value, her concern segueing
into an affectionate smile as she touched her fingers to Naasir's
arm. "I wanted to introduce Naasir to you before dinner. You'll
eat with us?"

Heart pounding as if she'd flown a hard physical race,
Andromeda went to say that she'd rather be alone so she could
finish her last-minute research, when Naasir *moved*. He was less
than an inch from her before she knew what was happening.
Nostrils flaring and that impossible silver hair sliding forward
over his luscious skin, he lowered his face to her throat.

Her blood roared to that pulse point even as her hand closed
over the hilt of the blade.

3

Naasir drew in a long, deep breath and felt his mouth water. She smelled *right*, smelled like his mate should smell. He wasn't sure she was his mate yet, especially since she was so small and had such big, scared eyes, but he knew he wanted to lick her, taste her, bite her.

About to nuzzle at her, he heard Jessamy's voice. *"Naasir."*

Realizing he'd done something uncivilized in his excitement, he forced himself to step back, but he couldn't stop looking at the delicious-smelling angel. She had skin like honey. He liked honey. He had a feeling he'd like licking her skin just as much. Her eyes were a translucent brown with a bright golden starburst around the pupil.

Pretty.

Her wings, from what he could see of them, were a rich shade close to the dark chocolate Honor liked to eat.

And her hair, it was a thick, silky-looking golden brown. It was in a braid right now, but he could tell it would be curly if let out; he already had plans to undo the braid so he could play with it. Of course, first he'd have to convince her he wasn't planning to eat her. "Hello," he said, on his best behavior now. "I just wanted to smell you."

"Oh." Lines between her eyebrows, the tone of her voice making him want to close his eyes and just listen. "Do you sniff everyone you meet?"

Smiling inside at the curiosity she couldn't quite hide, he said, "No." He drew in her scent again, careful to make it appear he was simply breathing. "Only women."

"Why?"

"I'm hunting my mate."

A sudden, dazzling smile, all her fear erased in a single heart-beat. "I suppose that makes sense." Then she turned to Jessamy, as if everything was explained. As the two women spoke, he stood there confused. Nothing was explained. She smelled right, smelled delicious. He wanted to taste her.

Why didn't she consider him a threat any longer?

Vow of celibacy.

He scowled at the reminder. Just because she'd taken a vow didn't mean *he* was no threat. Only . . . He bit back a satisfied smile. The delicious-smelling angel thought she was safe so she'd probably allow him close to her, close enough that he could determine if she was or wasn't his mate.

In truth, enticing though she was, he couldn't see how she could be his—she looked very breakable and soft, but he wasn't about to give up without determining the truth. Perhaps he was meant to have a breakable mate, though that seemed ridiculous to him.

Or perhaps she was hiding her real self.

The idea his maybe-mate might have a secret side fascinated him.

Andromeda had intended to say no to the dinner invitation from Jessamy. It wasn't because she didn't enjoy eating with her mentor and the weapons-master—they were two of her most favorite people in the whole world and had accepted her for who she was, seeing the woman she'd become and not the bloodline that marked her.

As for Venom, the vampire having become a familiar sight at Jessamy's dinner table since his transfer to the Refuge, he had a biting sense of humor and a cool intelligence Andromeda appreciated.

It wasn't even because Naasir unsettled her.

It was because she knew Jessamy had been looking forward to Naasir's arrival, as had Galen and Venom. The four were old friends, with the three males allied to the same archangel, and she didn't want to intrude.

However, when she opened her mouth to say no, Naasir sniffed at her again, the masculine heat of his body pressing against her, and her words deserted her. "You can't do that," she said when she could speak again—by which time Jessamy had taken her silence for assent and the three of them were halfway to Jessamy and Galen's home.

Wild silver eyes looked at her in utter innocence. "What?"

"Sniff people."

Naasir shrugged . . . and sniffed her, heavy silver strands of his hair brushing her skin. "Sorry."

Narrowing her eyes, she pursed her lips. "You're not sorry in the least."

Jessamy's gentle laughter filled the air. "Don't let him tease you, Andromeda. He's an expert at it."

Andromeda decided to ignore the prowling vampire who wasn't a vampire by her side. Except it was all but impossible to ignore Naasir, especially when he was determined not to be ignored. He picked up her braid and tugged on it. When she pulled it away, he pinched the light fabric of her gown between his fingertips and rubbed.

Stepping away didn't stop him. He just stepped with her.

By the time Jessamy went on ahead, waving at Galen and Venom—who were waiting out in the courtyard—Andromeda wanted to snarl. Tugging away her braid one more time, she spun around to face the silver-eyed menace. "Can you not act civilized for a minute?"

He went eerily motionless, his expression altering in a way she couldn't describe except to say that the man who'd been teasing and annoying her was suddenly not the same man any longer. "Of course," he said, his deep voice resonant and cultured. "I apologize if I caused you any distress or offense."

Andromeda felt her stomach knot, a sudden sick feeling inside her, but they'd reached the courtyard now lit by the gentle glow of lanterns strung up in the trees.

"I thought we'd eat out here," Jessamy said and got a round of assent.

Hauling Jessamy close with one big hand on her nape, Galen planted a kiss on her mouth that left her breathless and flushed and smiling. A satisfied glint in his eye, the weapons-master said, "We'll bring out the table."

Andromeda had been startled when she'd first learned that her wise, educated, and quietly elegant mentor was madly in love with the barbarian of a man who was weapons-master to the Archangel Raphael. Two more disparate people she couldn't imagine. Then she'd seen the tenderness in Galen's expression when he looked at Jessamy, witnessed how Jessamy's eyes lit up at the sound of his powerful wings.

Her heart hurt at the beauty of their bond.

"Venom, Naasir," Galen said and the three men walked to get the table from a small building that Andromeda knew Galen used as a workshop when he didn't want to work in the weapons arena.

That table was scarred from countless weapons being placed on it, but buffed clean. Having gone inside to get a tablecloth, Andromeda draped it over the wooden surface, hyperaware of Naasir standing on the other side before he disappeared to bring out one of the two bench seats. Minutes later, the food was out, everything ready.

Since she knew Galen and Jessamy liked to sit next to each other, she went to the bench on the opposite side. Three sets of wings competing for the same space could get awkward. Venom slid in on one side of her, Naasir on the other. Both males were careful not to touch her wings.

"First, a toast," Galen said, splashing champagne into their glasses. "To having Naasir home with us."

Jessamy's face was radiant in the lamplight. "You've been deeply missed," she said, raising her glass. "Next time, don't be away so long."

Naasir bent his head slightly in acquiescence, his expression difficult to read from what Andromeda could see of his profile, but whatever it was Jessamy saw, it made her smile deepen as they clinked glasses and drank the toast. The bubbles fizzed on Andromeda's tongue, the taste of the champagne sunshine in a bottle.

Her homeland produced no such golden liquid, but it had a wild and heartbreaking beauty she'd missed desperately since her faux defection. At least when she returned to do her five hundred years of service, she'd be able to breathe the warm African air again, look up at the hazy blue of a sky unlike any other on this earth.

That would be her reward for each day of horror in her grandfather's court.

"Would you like some bread?"

It wasn't the words that startled her. It was how intensely polite they were, given the identity of the speaker. Taking the breadbasket from Naasir, she glanced up at his face and saw nothing but courteous interest. No feral glint as she'd seen earlier, certainly no attempts to annoy her.

The hairs rose on her nape again.

Disturbed by Naasir's sudden politeness in a way she couldn't articulate, she put a piece of the thick, warm bread on her plate and handed the woven basket to Venom. The vampire with the slitted eyes of a lethal snake and a dark sensuality that drew countless women to his bed, looked from her to Naasir but didn't say anything except, "Thank you."

"Here." Jessamy passed a small bowl to Naasir. "I made your favorite. Honor sent me Montgomery's recipe."

Naasir took the bowl of what seemed to be rare—or was it raw?—meat of some kind, his open grin making Andromeda's breath catch. However, the mask of civilization was firmly back on his face when he looked at her partway through the meal. "Do you require anything from this side of the table?"

Shaking her head, she took a bite of the food on her plate while Venom and Naasir sipped blood from small goblets. Venom nibbled on something here and there, but unlike Naasir, he didn't really eat any of the solid food.

It only highlighted the fact that Naasir was no ordinary vampire.

She ate slowly, listened to the others speak . . . and felt her skin chill each time Naasir said something polite to her. Catching Jessamy's frown at one point, she realized she was right to feel on edge. Logic told her that made no sense. People were normally polite to strangers . . . except Naasir was unlike any other person she'd ever met.

And he hadn't been polite to her before she snapped at him.

"So, you are to find Alexander," Galen said toward the end of the meal. "Where will you begin?"

Naasir's silver eyes landed on Andromeda. "I was told you have possibilities for us to explore."

"In a sense," she said, her skin tight with a kind of cold fear that had nothing to do with Naasir's unsettling behavior and everything to do with the fact that, unbeknownst to anyone at this table, she would soon be forced to have enemy loyalties, forced to be Charisemnon's bonded subordinate.

Not for fifteen more days, she reminded herself. Long enough to try to save the life of an Ancient. "I never studied Alexander with the intention of finding his Sleeping place." He had fascinated her because he was both a great statesman, and a warrior who had led his troops from the front till the day he chose to Sleep. "My suggestions are only educated guesses. I don't presume to know the mind of an Ancient."

"A hunt in the dark," Venom mused. "With Lijuan's people on your tail."

Galen's expression went flat, while beside Andromeda, Naasir's fingers clenched on his goblet. "When is she going to die? I've been trying to accomplish that since I was a child."

Andromeda felt her eyes widen. "Is the story true?" she asked impulsively. "That you once got into Lijuan's Refuge stronghold and pretended to eat her pet cat?"

A sideways glance that was so cool, she almost felt frost break out over her skin. "Yes," he said and turned back to his conversation with the others. "We also need to find out why she's suddenly decided to murder Alexander." A sip of blood. "Because I agree with the sire that this is far more apt to be about eliminating the competition than waking a possible ally."

Jessamy shook her head, her expression troubled. "I've seen Lijuan walking closer and closer to the darkness but this I didn't expect. To murder an Ancient in his Sleep? It's a horror too huge to be borne."

Andromeda could add nothing to that ugly truth.

Two hours after the dinner, Naasir shoved out of bed. He was meant to be resting so he and Andromeda could start the hunt tomorrow, but he was too wound up. She'd snapped at him to be *civilized*. Clearly, she wasn't his mate even if she smelled so delicious that he could scent her in spite of the walls that separated them. It didn't matter if she made his mouth water; his mate wouldn't tell him to be what he wasn't.

A woman who knows me, understands what I am, and who wants to have secret rules with me.

That's what he'd told Ashwini he wanted in a mate and he hadn't changed his mind. His mate wouldn't ask him to wear a different skin, wouldn't expect him to be "normal." He wasn't normal, not by any measure, but he was a person and people were allowed to have mates. *He* was allowed to have a mate.

Gritting his teeth against the urge to follow the beguiling scent of the woman who was clearly *not* his mate, he pulled on his jeans and headed to the small training arena behind the stronghold. It wasn't the main training ring, rather a walled courtyard on the edge of a cliff where those who had to work inside the stronghold could go spar, or stretch their muscles.

He would jump up on the wall, climb down to the cliff, and make his way to the very bottom of the gorge that bisected the Refuge, then back up. The trip was difficult enough that it should exhaust—

He growled inside his chest as *her* scent grew in depth and intensity the closer he got to the courtyard. There were no sleeping rooms at this end of the stronghold. What was her scent doing here?

Not that he cared.

He was going to ignore it.

Muscles bunched, he stepped out into the night and frowned at the diffuse light from the two lamps someone had lit at a low intensity. His eyes adjusted quickly enough, but he preferred full dark at night. The woman who was doing some kind of exercise in the center of the training arena, however, clearly couldn't see in the dark.

She was no longer dressed in the flowing gown the color of ripe raspberries in which he'd seen her earlier, but in black pants that hugged her curvaceous form. Her top was the same color and close to a T-shirt. The wing slits were closed off with discreet buttons, the soft fabric hugging her upper body while leaving most of her arms bare.

Light glinted off the threads of gold in her hair, her honeyed skin aglow.

When she moved, her wings rustled, but she kept them scrupulously off the ground. Galen must've been at her—the weapons-master was ferocious about teaching his students to maintain wing discipline. Dragging wings could not only get damaged, the habit created weak muscles. Andromeda's wing muscles were strong, her movements graceful.

Those wings flared out as she made a controlled turn and he felt his gut clench. Her wings weren't just chocolate dark, though that had been more than strokable enough. They were patterned with intricate gradations of color all the way to a pale golden brown, but the secret was only visible when she spread her wings.

They closed in a second later as she turned into another move.

He'd seen people practicing something like this in Lijuan's land. It was called tai chi. He much preferred the harder, faster martial arts like karate and tae kwon do. He could take those movements and make them his own. This type of patience would drive him insane.

Watching Andromeda do it, however . . .

"Oh." She came to a startled halt after her next turn left her facing him—and his glowing eyes.

Naasir could make them not reflect, could also shield them with his lashes when he didn't want to be seen, but he wasn't in a good mood right now. Scaring her with his predator's eyes made him feel momentarily better.

About to lunge onto the top of the wall so he could begin his climb down, he was stopped by a ridiculous feminine question. "Are you looking for a sparring partner?"

He stared at her. "Do you want to die?" Naasir was very, very, *very* good, and unless he held back his lethal side, he could easily kill someone of her soft nature.

"No," she said, doing another stretch in front of him.

The move pulled the fabric of her top taut over her breasts and bared a thin strip of her abdomen and he wondered if she was taunting him. His blood grew hot, his predatory instincts snarling. "You'll die if you spar with me," he said in warning, wanting to bite her so she'd know exactly who it was she was baiting.

"Your sire would be disappointed in you if you killed your partner."

She wasn't his partner. She was just someone he had to work with, but she was right: Raphael would not be happy if he killed their expert. "More reason for us not to spar." He shifted back toward the wall he intended to scale.

"Scared?"

Naasir froze, sheer incredulity holding him in place. When he turned, it was to prowl over to her until they stood toe-to-toe, both of them in bare feet. "What did you say?"

4

A smile of challenge from the small, soft scholar who was taunting him. "I asked if you were scared," she said, not backing off, though he could see the pulse thudding hard in her neck.

"Do you *want* me to bite you?" he asked seriously.

Scowling, she stepped back. "Fine, if you don't want to spar, I'll find someone else."

He barely held back his growl. She wanted him to act civilized? He'd wear the skin so well she'd never see the real Naasir again. "Rules for the session?" he asked. "Other than my not killing you."

"I get to have a sword as a weapon. You get bare hands."

He shrugged. "That's fair." What it was, was suicidal on her part. She could have ten swords and he'd still be inside her guard in a heartbeat. "Is that your sword in the corner?"

"How did you see that?" she asked. "It's in the shadows."

He didn't say anything, just watched her until she broke eye contact and walked to pick up the sword she'd propped up neatly against a wall. It was in its scabbard and when she drew it out, he saw it gleamed. Either Galen had drummed it into her to clean her weapons, or this weapon had never actually been used in any kind of serious combat. She probably just used it as part of her routine with the flowing, patient stretches.

He snorted under his breath.

"Ready?" she asked, taking a wide-legged stance across from him, enough distance between them that she probably thought herself safe.

"Yes."

"In that case, three, two, one!"

Naasir lunged, not holding back his speed or agility. All he had to do was put her on the ground and this ridiculous exercise would be done and he could leave and his mouth would stop watering at the intoxicating scent of her. The air whistled past his eyes, the world so slow in comparison to his speed, the stars blurring together—

"*Grr!*"

He snarled as he came down on his feet, looking in disbelief at his upper arm. There was a thin line of red across his biceps. Shaking his head, he looked again but it was still there. It healed before his eyes, the wound superficial, but the blood remained behind to mark the spot. "You *cut* me," he said to Andromeda.

Heart a racehorse and breath coming hard and fast, Andromeda wondered if she knew what the hell she was doing. She hadn't meant to challenge him, but he'd been so horribly, unnervingly polite that her mouth had opened and the words had tumbled out. He'd clearly decided he didn't like her, and for some reason that infuriated her.

Now he was looking at her through narrowed eyes of glowing silver, his hair hanging over his face before he shoved it back. "How did you cut me?" A demand.

She was the one who shrugged this time. "I cheated."

A long, slow blink. "Cheating's not allowed."

"Yes, it is. You're bigger, faster, and far better trained than I am. If I don't cheat, we'll have no fun."

Another slow blink . . . and she realized he was moving, and she was moving instinctively in response, the two of them circling one another. Going into that space inside her head where she was one with the blade, she reacted on instinct again when he moved, and scored him across the hard ridges of his abdomen. Only he didn't stop in surprise this time but kept going.

She'd never worked harder with the blade in her life.

He still pinned her to the ground in under three minutes, his body heat on her front a stark intimacy. Knees on either side of her hips and hands gripping her wrists above her head, rendering her sword useless, he leaned down until his breath kissed hers and she could look into those astonishing eyes at a proximity she'd never expected.

They were clear, so clear, and utterly beautiful. The silver glowed in the night, the striations within the irises a darker silver. "You cut me seven-and-a-half times," he said, his voice holding a gritty, growly undertone.

Chest heaving, she tried to shrug again, as if she wasn't trapped under an unfriendly predator. "Pretty good for a scholar."

He moved even closer, until his nose was a bare whisper above hers. "You have secrets," he said slowly. "You wear another skin, too."

Andromeda went motionless, the game suddenly dangerous. "No," she said through a hoarse throat. "I don't have secrets. I'm exactly what I seem." At least for her final fifteen days of freedom, fifteen days where the people she respected still believed in her, still trusted her.

"A scholar who wields a sword?"

"Have you never heard of a warrior-scholar?"

He continued to watch her with those clear silver eyes that made her imagine she could see galaxies within. "You have spots on your face."

"What? It must be dirt from when you took me down."

Shifting her wrists to one strong hand, he touched the rough-skinned pad of a finger to her nose and her cheeks on either side. "Spots."

She glared past the shiver that wanted to ripple through her. "Those are freckles!" A sprinkling of them across the bridge of her nose and on the tops of her cheeks that had only become more entrenched with time, until she'd given up all hope of ever pulling off cool elegance.

Ignoring her, the predator holding her captive began to count her "spots."

"*Naasir.*"

He looked up, expression suddenly dead serious. "Cutting me after fooling me with your outside skin wasn't nice. It wasn't civilized."

"I didn't promise to be civilized," she said, then wanted to clamp her mouth shut. She'd spent most of her immortal lifetime being civilized and well-behaved and not an addict of sensation driven by her base needs.

Naasir snapped his teeth at her.

When she jerked, he laughed and stretched out on top of her, one hand still gripping her wrists, and his warm, masculine scent in her every inhale. "Then I'm not going to be civilized either."

It was odd. She'd only met him hours earlier, and yet his words made something in her unknot, untwist. As if she'd lost something but managed to win it back again. "I only asked you to behave *for a minute*," she found herself saying when she should've been telling him to get off. "You were aggravating me."

His fingers flexed on her wrists but he didn't release her. "I wasn't hurting you," he said with a scowl.

"No," she admitted, the words from the letter stark against the landscape of her mind. "I was angry about something else and I yelled at you. I'm sorry."

Those astonishing eyes held hers again as he closed the distance between them. "I want to lick your skin."

That skin prickling with something that was very much not fear, she tried to buck him off. Of course she failed. He was significantly heavier. "I can't breathe."

"You're an immortal."

"My wings are squashed."

He raised himself off her. "Spread them out."

She did, easing the strain, but when she tugged at her wrists, he held on tighter and brought his body right back down on top of hers. "Now your wings aren't squashed anymore and we can talk."

Given that she could feel his arousal, hard and thick against her abdomen, Andromeda didn't think it was talking he had in mind. She had the idea that if she gave him a single ounce of encouragement, she'd be naked with him inside her in a matter of seconds. "No," she whispered, and for the first time in her existence, she felt regret for the choice she'd made.

He tilted his head to the side. "No?"

"I've sworn a vow of celibacy. It wasn't done on a whim, or without thought." It had been a hundred years in the making. "The vow is part of my honor, part of what makes me Andromeda." Not Charisemnon's grandchild. Not Lailah's daughter. Not just another jaded princess of the court. *Andromeda*. Scholar and warrior.

A low, rumbling sound in Naasir's chest, silver eyes burning above her. "Rutting isn't dishonorable."

Her cheeks burned from within. "It is for a woman who has vowed not to indulge in it."

He shifted to rub himself against the juncture of her thighs. Her breath caught, her inner muscles spasming on aching emptiness as the place between her thighs went damp. Nostrils flaring, Naasir leaned in close enough to nuzzle her throat. "You want me." It was a satisfied purr of sound.

Her throat was so dry it took her several attempts to get the words out. "That doesn't change my choice."

Squeezing her wrists but not hard enough to hurt, he snapped his teeth at her again. "What will change it?"

The words just fell out past her lips, as they had a way of doing around Naasir. "Finding the Star Grimoire." That was her escape clause—she'd be released from the vow should the Grimoire return to the world.

"What is a Star Grimoire?"

"A book." A book lost in the mysteries of time, the reason she'd chosen that as the key that would unlock her vow. "An ancient book no one has seen for thousands of years. An angelic treasure."

Naasir was quiet for a long time. "If I find this stupid Grimoire, will you rut with me?"

Her cheeks blazed hotter even as her nipples grew tight enough to throb. "You can't find the Grimoire."

"If I do?"

"If you do, you can do whatever you like to me," she said recklessly.

His smile was pure sin, the fangs that flashed in the muted light gleaming white. Rising off her, he held out a hand and, when she took it, hauled her to her feet. "Who taught you the blade? Your style is not Galen's."

"My other mentor." She saw him looking admiringly at her sword and passed it over so he could examine it.

Taking it, Naasir stepped away and sliced the sword through the air in a fast, dangerous rhythm. "Someone from Charisemnon's Refuge stronghold?"

"No. I don't have anything to do with my grandfather's people." Not yet. Not for fifteen more days. "It was Dahariel."

An icy cut of sound as he halted his swordplay. "Dahariel is Astaad's second."

"Teachers and scholars aren't tied to any one archangel unless they swear that allegiance." It was assumed Jessamy was more loyal to Raphael than to any other archangel because of her relationship with Galen, but even so, others of the Cadre still came to her for information.

As for Andromeda, she'd proven her loyalty to unbiased scholarship over more than three hundred years of hard work and unrelenting discipline. Most people had forgotten she was of Charisemnon's bloodline, seeing her as belonging only to the Archives.

Naasir bared his teeth at her. "Do you report to him?"

"No. I report to no one."

"For this task? To find Alexander?"

"In accepting the task, I have agreed to keep Raphael's confidence for the duration." *No one* could compel her to betray any of the secrets she learned during her remaining days of freedom. And instinct told her that by the day of her fourhundredth birthday, this task would be over, one way or another. Events were moving too fast for it to be otherwise.

Naasir handed back her sword. "Dahariel is not a good man." The words were harsh. "He hurts people. Sometimes he hurts people who aren't full-grown."

Andromeda flinched. "He may," she admitted, "but he saved me." She'd been a child who was a possession held jealously close yet rarely given any attention or nurturing. Dahariel alone had seen her as a person; the hawk-faced angel had put a blade in her hand and taught her what he knew best.

The blade will give you a way to earn your place in the world.

As it was, she hadn't had to sell her sword to find precious freedom. But when she'd broken away from her parents while still technically a child, it had given her the confidence to believe she could protect herself on the skyroads. Her sword and a small pack of belongings was all she'd had when she arrived in the Refuge and petitioned Jessamy for the learning so long denied her.

Charisemnon used scholars but didn't respect them. He respected only strength—and in his court, that meant cruelly hardened men and women who could mete out pain and torture and humiliation without blinking, who could make a living being beg and crawl and bleed. Lailah had learned that lesson at her father's knee, and she'd raised Andromeda in a home as filled with brutal violence . . . and as redolent with the smell of sex.

The more deviant the better.

Andromeda's parents were beyond jaded at this point.

I promise I will learn and I will treat the Library and the Archives with respect, she'd said to Jessamy that long-ago day. *I will not harm any of the volumes.* The last she'd had to add because it wasn't every would-be scholar who came from parents who'd been banned from the Archives. *I want to learn.* To have a chance to be more than a puppet driven by pain and obsessive sexual need. *Please, teach me. Please.*

Stepping far too close to her, his bare upper body a sensual temptation she had to gird herself to resist, Naasir said, "What does Dahariel ask in return?"

Andromeda's heart squeezed, the ache deep and old. "Nothing," she whispered, remembering what Dahariel had said to the girl she'd been.

Maybe you are my one good deed. But there is only so much good in me and I've spent it all on this—expect nothing more.

"We should get some rest," she said, to stop Naasir from following up on her answer. "We start the hunt tomorrow."

Naasir didn't get out of her way. Reaching out, he curled an escapee tendril of her hair around his fingers. "Tell me of the Grimoire."

Andromeda didn't back away. That would give the wrong signal to this vampire who wasn't a vampire. He was a predator and she did not want to become prey. "It is legend that the Grimoire was a record of secret things, beings, and treasures, all of which have been long lost in time."

Naasir tugged on the tendril he'd captured. "You like secrets?"

"I like hunting them."

A wicked, dangerous smile. "So do I."

Somehow, Andromeda didn't think he was talking about the kind of slow, methodical research that was her preferred method of the hunt.

Dawn came in soft washes of color on the horizon. After speaking to the guards on duty at Raphael's stronghold, where she was currently staying, Andromeda took a walk along the top of the cliffs that overlooked the gorge. Since she had no intention of being kidnapped by Lijuan's people, she stayed within sight of the stronghold and the guards.

Yes, she could defend herself with the knives she wore strapped to her thighs under her airy mint green gown, but she wouldn't win against a squadron of trained warriors. Better not to take the risk—and it was no hardship to keep her morning walk to this part of the Refuge. It was peaceful, few angels having yet left their homes or aeries, while none of the vampires in the Refuge seemed to be up and about.

In the calm, she found her center again.

Discipline. Serenity. Learning.

The three foundations on which she'd built her chosen life.

Wild silver eyes and a sword dance that still made her breath catch.

Andromeda shook her head, fisted her hands, and closing her eyes, drew deep of the crisp air of a mountain dawn. There was no room in her life for Naasir's brand of wildness; she only had two precious weeks to build emotional shields tough enough to survive five hundred years in hell. Those shields had to be created of absolute discipline and steel will.

Feeling the slap of wind against her cheek that signaled a nearby angelic landing, she opened her eyes. She was determined to be polite in spite of the rudeness of such a close landing, but her polite smile disappeared the instant she saw the razor-sharp cheekbones and red-streaked dark gray wings of the black-haired angel bare inches in front of her.

Xi. One of Lijuan's generals.

Andromeda didn't hesitate; she stepped backward off the cliff and snapped out her wings . . . but Xi hadn't come alone. Panic buffeted her as her wings were caught in the fine threads of the net that had been waiting for her. There was no chance to recover or to go for her blades. They had her tightly wrapped within heartbeats.

Then the entire team dropped to the bottom of the gorge at dangerous speed. She screamed the whole time not out of fear but in an effort to give the guards sounds to follow, though her pragmatic side told her it had all happened too fast. The guards probably hadn't even made it to the top of the cliff yet. And there was little chance of anyone else hearing her—almost no one flew this low in the gorge, so low that she could feel the spray of water from the thundering river beneath.

Xi's men and women had to have been watching her, had to have learned her habits.

Her hard-fought discipline and allegiance to order and routine had been used against her.

Face pressed uncomfortably against the netting, she managed to insinuate her hand down her side to her thigh and pulled out one of her two blades. It was viciously sharp but when she tried to hack at the netting, she made no progress. Metal filaments, she realized. That was why the strands felt like they were cutting into her skin. She wasn't getting out of this until Lijuan's people unwrapped her.

She worked to hide her knife again. Since she never practiced in the public training areas, Xi might not be aware that she wasn't a soft target. If they didn't search her on landing at Lijuan's Refuge stronghold, she could use the blades to help in her escape. While not as confident with them as with a sword, she'd been sparring with Venom since his arrival and he'd taught her a few sneaky tricks.

However, as the minutes passed and the terrain changed below her, she realized they were leaving the Refuge. Her heart chilled at the only possible explanation. She was being taken directly to Lijuan's citadel, a place where she had no friends, no allies, and that was reputedly far from all civilization.

A place where the living were sacrificed, and the dead walked.

5

Naasir caught Andromeda's scent on the breeze as he went outside, was about to follow it when he saw a small body flying frantically not far from him. Frowning because he knew the cub was far too young to be up so early and because he could smell the acrid bite of fear, he ran after the child and lunged up to catch one small ankle in his grip.

Sam cried out as Naasir drew him down, but then threw his arms around Naasir's neck, his glossy black curls atumble and his black-tipped brown wings drooping over Naasir's arm. "Naasir, Naasir, they took Andromeda!"

Naasir went motionless. "Who took her?" he asked the boy.

Chest heaving, Sam tried to get the words out. "An angel with gray and red wings," he said on a gasp. "I thought it was a game but the angel and his friends wrapped Andromeda up in a net and took her away!"

Naasir had been moving at high speed toward Sam's home even as he listened to the boy. "Which way did they go?" Only one angel had wings of red-streaked gray and that angel was allied to Lijuan.

Sam pointed, his brown eyes huge. "I could see them even

though they went all the way to the bottom where I can't go. I promise I saw them."

"I believe you." The direction taken by the enemy squadron didn't lead to Lijuan's Refuge stronghold. It led out of the Refuge altogether.

Blood hot with the need to hunt, to track, Naasir ran through the open door of Sam's home. The very small cub's mother was in the kitchen and her mouth fell open at seeing Naasir's tiny burden. "*Sameon!* I thought you were still in bed."

Sam dove into his mother's arms. "I was going to sit on the cliff and watch Galen's squadron but then I saw the bad angels take Andromeda. They were mean to her, Mama."

Hugging her trembling son close and rubbing his back, Sam's mother met Naasir's eyes, her own gaze dark with worry.

"I will find her." With that promise, Naasir raced out and followed Andromeda's scent to a point on the cliff where it disappeared without a trace. She'd either flown off in an effort to evade Xi and his squadron, or been pushed off.

A few steps to the left and he confirmed it had been Xi who little Sam had seen. The general's scent was familiar to Naasir after the years Naasir had spent in the Refuge. Xi's scent, too, disappeared without a trace.

Aware he was racing against time, Naasir ran to the weapons arena where Galen was readying his squadron for an early-morning drill. The weapons-master took his men and women immediately into the air on hearing Naasir's report, arrowing out on the flight path Sam had indicated.

Naasir didn't stop. He made his way to Astaad's Refuge territory and quickly located Dahariel. For the cruel, dangerous angel to have taught Andromeda to fight without ever making any demands on her pointed to a deeper emotional connection than Andromeda realized.

Dahariel was not known for his kindness.

The other man's gaze glittered with ice on hearing Naasir's report. "I'll take my squadron to join Galen's," he said, his tone as cold. "You're certain Sameon saw what he believes he saw? He is only a child."

"Yes." Sam didn't lie and he was clever. "I'll search the Refuge in case Xi doubled back and hid her here."

A sharp nod and Dahariel lifted off on powerful wings

patterned like those of an eagle, in shades of brown and black. It was possible the aerial pursuit would catch up to Xi and his men—had Illium been here, that would've been a certainty. But the blue-winged angel was in New York, his speed unavailable. And Xi had a head start. All he'd have to do to evade detection was take an atypical route or set down in a hidden area until nightfall.

Teeth gritted, Naasir snuck into Lijuan's Refuge territory. There was no sign of Andromeda. Neither was there any sign of her in the Refuge territories of any of the other archangels. Her scent was freshest at the clifftop and even that had faded by the time he completed his intensive ground search.

Galen's and Dahariel's squadrons didn't return until after the sun fell and the stars blazed.

They didn't have Andromeda.

Naasir knew she had to be halfway to China by this point. To find her, he'd have to penetrate the lair of nightmare.

6

Raphael was sweat-slicked after a practice session with the dual blades he liked to use in combat, when Montgomery came out into the yard of Raphael and Elena's Enclave home. It overlooked the Hudson, and across it, the steel and glass of Manhattan. *Yes, Montgomery?* he said without stopping the fury of the blades.

His consort would be bitterly disappointed to return home from her hunt to discover he'd taken time for a session. She loved to watch him, but even Elena, brave and brash and magnificent, didn't attempt to join him. "I can't so much as separate out your movements, you're so fast when you do that," she'd said the last time she watched him, her eyes sparking with unhidden appreciation. "And I'm quite fond of my head and would like to keep it attached to my body."

"As would I," he'd said before taking her to the grass for another kind of sweaty, heated battle.

The truth was that no one in his territory could do this particular exercise with him. Not even his deadly second. Of the archangels, Neha alone had the skill, speed, and strength. The others preferred different weapons, but the Archangel of India and Raphael had sparred together with dual blades once upon a time, Neha slender and fluid in combat leathers as she attacked and defended in equal measures.

Raphael didn't regret executing Neha's daughter for her crimes, but he did regret that it had so badly damaged his relationship with an archangel who, for all her stiffly traditional thinking and occasional cruelty, cared for her people and did not hesitate to share her knowledge with younger archangels.

Sire, Montgomery replied even as those thoughts passed through Raphael's mind in a matter of split seconds. *Galen wishes to speak with you. He says it's a matter of urgency.*

Raphael was already moving toward his study before Montgomery added that last. Galen only ever made contact if he had something to say. Entering the study, he saw Galen's face on the wall screen. "What is it?" he asked his weapons-master.

"Xi has taken Andromeda," Galen said, then told him the details.

Putting down his blades on his desk as he listened, Raphael wiped off his face using a towel Montgomery brought in. The chilled glass of water the butler offered was also welcome. The vampire left the room straight afterward, but even had he stayed, Raphael would've felt no concern.

Montgomery's loyalty was without question.

"Naasir's already on his way to China," Galen said, the harsh angles of his face set in grim lines. "He caught a ride with my squadron to the airport. The jet'll take him as far as Japan, after which he says he has his own methods of crossing undetected into Lijuan's territory." Galen shoved a hand through the deep red of his hair. "He refused backup, said anyone but Jason would get them both caught."

"Wait," Raphael said and, splitting the screen, contacted Jason. "Where are you?"

It turned out Raphael's spymaster was in Neha's territory, right next door to Lijuan's. "Mahiya isn't yet ready to return to her homeland and talk to her mother," the black-winged angel said, speaking of his mate. "But she asked me to check up on her."

"I need you to meet Naasir."

When Raphael laid out the reason why, Jason's skin pulled taut over his facial bones, the intricate Polynesian-inspired tattoo that covered the left side of his face suddenly stark against his brown skin. "There's a reason I've always told Naasir not to try and get into Lijuan's citadel."

Galen, able to hear the conversation since Raphael had looped him in, nodded. "He's too reckless, with no care for his life."

That wasn't quite true; Naasir did care for his life. He simply had no fear. As a result, he took far too many chances for Raphael to be certain he wouldn't be caught by Lijuan—and unlike when Naasir had been a child, Lijuan wouldn't forgive the trespass. "You've been in the citadel," he said to Jason. "Can Naasir get in?"

"Yes." Not in its usual queue today, strands of Jason's black hair blew across the curves and fine dots of the ink that marked him. "He's also stealthy enough to get away with it, *if* he doesn't allow his more primal instincts to take the lead."

"That might be a problem," Galen said, his hands on his hips and tone rough with concern. "He was adamant that Andromeda is his responsibility."

Galen had good cause to worry. Once Naasir took on such a task, he'd die before failing. "Go," Raphael ordered Jason. "Track him down, and help him break out the scholar." He knew Jessamy's apprentice wouldn't have been harmed . . . or not badly harmed in any case. Lijuan wanted the information Andromeda held in her head.

And her blood was that of Lijuan's closest ally.

"Sire." Jason signed off.

"Is the scholar likely to cooperate with Lijuan to save her skin?" Raphael asked Galen.

"No." A response that held not the slightest hesitation or doubt. "Every time I've spoken to her on the subject of Alexander, she's been adamant in her distaste for what we all believe Lijuan intends to do."

"Lijuan's Refuge stronghold?"

"It stands—she's left a full squadron there and they're bristling today."

Raphael had believed Lijuan understood the lines she'd crossed when she precipitated a battle in the Refuge, but clearly her arrogance left no room for the rules that bound their race.

"How long is Andromeda capable of surviving in Lijuan's citadel?"

"Not many know that she's a fully trained and capable warrior," his weapons-master told him. "So she'll survive—but I don't know if she'll survive whole. Lijuan's methods of persuasion can be horrific."

In Galen's pale green eyes was the knowledge that no one who experienced Lijuan's brand of "hospitality" ever came out the same.

7

Andromeda had forced herself to stop struggling during the journey. The futile action would only tire her out and leave her defenseless when they reached their destination.

Do not be stupid. That is the first lesson of battle. Think.

Repeating Dahariel's words silently in her mind, she lay painfully quiescent.

As it was, Xi's squadron did stop twice. The first time, it was in an ice-strewn cave only about an hour out from the Refuge. And though they stayed there until daylight had faded from the skies, Xi didn't release Andromeda, despite her repeated requests. She finally worked out that they wanted her tied up and ready to go should they have to make a rapid departure.

Stiff and cold after so many hours in such discomfort, she was almost grateful when they did finally take off again. At least this way, she had fresh air. The second stop came deep into the night, on a small island that was a dot in the ocean. She might have been tempted to fly off, but her wings were severely cramped from being crushed in the net, and she knew her speed in flight was nowhere close to Xi's. Better to bide her time, to be smart and wait for a better opportunity.

"I can fly," she said after the short rest period when she'd been given some water and trail bread to replenish herself. "There's no need to truss me up like a chicken."

Xi didn't answer, just threw a blindfold in her direction. "Or I can blind you," he said conversationally when she balked. "Given your age and the complexity of eyes, they'll probably take three months or so to grow back."

A trickle of cold sweat rolled down her spine. "I'm sure your archangel wouldn't be well pleased by such abuse." Lijuan needed her.

"You don't need eyes to tell my lady what she needs to know." The general stared at her, his own eyes as dark and hard as onyx. "Which will it be?"

She put on the blindfold, wondering once again why evil wasn't ugly. Her grandfather with his skin of deep gold and hair of richest brown, had been beautiful before the ravages of disease, would be again when his body healed. A mortal poet had once written of him, saying:

My heart's blood for but a single instant
My soul for the agonizing glory of his touch
Such beauty is not meant for mortal eyes
It maddens. It ravages. It murders.

Xi, too, was a very handsome angel and she knew he had no dearth of lovers. Long ago, before she'd realized the cold heart that beat in his chest, she'd admired his form in flight—he was a sleek and beautiful machine, his one-of-a-kind wings starkly beautiful.

Yet even as she thought of his nature, she knew that to his squadron, he wasn't evil. To them, he was simply a loyal general serving his lady. The fact his lady had proven she had little regard for the lives of the people she professed to rule, and yet Xi still followed her, *that* was what made him evil.

"How can you justify it?" she said to him when he hauled her up to her feet.

No answer as he lashed her wrists together.

Her blindness made her bold. "Giving your allegiance to an archangel who turned her people into the walking dead?" The reborn were nightmares given flesh and set free to feed, to infect, to murder. "If that alone is not crime enough, she feeds from the lifeforce of her subjects and leaves them dry husks."

As a scholar and apprentice teacher who worked under Jessamy, Andromeda had access to reports filed by both sides of the fierce battle above New York. Each had used different words, but neither disagreed on the basics: Raphael's side said Lijuan had fed on the lifeforce of her people until she was glutted with power.

Andromeda could still remember the line in the report that had made her skin chill: *Her mouth was rimmed with blood after she lifted it from the neck of her sacrifice.*

Lijuan's side had stated that her soldiers had volunteered in droves so their archangel could gain glory. In this, the soldiers had found honor beyond mortal or immortal ken, leaving a proud legacy for those of their bloodline.

In this case, Andromeda had a feeling both reports were equally true.

One side had seen horror, the other side honor.

She couldn't fault Xi for the reports he'd personally filed: he'd been brutally honest in terms of the wins and losses of battle. He also hadn't attempted to make it seem as if Lijuan had won—though he had softened her fall, as would any loyal general, saying that his lady had retreated from the field of battle so that she would be strong for the war to come.

His interpretation was strikingly different from the report filed by Illium. Raphael's lead aerial commander had stated that Raphael "blew Lijuan to smithereens," though Illium, too, had made a note that Lijuan may or may not be dead: *Zhou Lijuan is an archangel and they do not easily die.*

"I have served my lady for most of my nine hundred years on this earth," Xi said after another member of his squadron tied her ankles together. "You know nothing of her. Your task is to record, not to judge."

Andromeda inclined her head because in this, he was right. "But," she added, "some small judgment is required when we record the histories. We must often search for the truth amid grandiose claims, outright lies, and everything in between."

That, Jessamy had taught her, was why they so often put competing reports into the official history. Both Xi's and Illium's reports lay within the pages to do with the battle in New York, along with an overview written by Jessamy after she'd read, watched, and listened to all records of the battle. "If we record blindly, we are little better than machines."

"As I make no untrue claims in my reports," Xi responded, "you have nothing to say to me on that point." His fingers gripped her chin without warning, the hold firm but not painful. "I will give you one piece of advice, scholar."

Able to feel his power crashing against her, though it was more muted than she'd previously felt near Xi—testament to the statement in Illium's report that Lijuan fed her generals power—Andromeda went motionless.

"Do as you are told," Xi said in his cool, refined tone, "and you will not be harmed." He released her chin. "Unlike your grandsire, my lady has a soft spot for scholars."

"I appreciate the advice." It wasn't a lie. Xi's statement told her how she could play this until the opportunity rose to escape—because she didn't have the same faith in Lijuan as Xi. Badly injured angels were like any other injured creatures in their pain and frustration. They could strike out without warning.

The fact Lijuan had been unstable prior to her injuries only made the situation more volatile. Add in the fact that she was an archangel . . . No, Andromeda would never survive a confrontation should she anger Lijuan. No matter what she saw or heard or experienced, she had to act the meek scholar who was out of her depth.

Xi barked out an order at that instant and Andromeda found herself lifted up unceremoniously into a sling formed of the net. They did her the courtesy of allowing her to lie on her side this time, ensuring her wings weren't crushed, but the netting dug into her flesh nonetheless. As the salt wind whistled past her on takeoff, she found herself thinking of the wild creature with whom she'd sparred under lamplight.

Never had she fought with anyone who moved like Naasir. She wanted to do it again, wanted to watch his eyes flash in the darkness and that slow, dangerous smile wreath his face as he took open pleasure in the dance. There was something fascinating about the vampire who was not a vampire . . . fascinating and dangerous.

Andromeda wanted to escape for many reasons, but chief among them was the driving compulsion to dance with him again, to fly too close to the flame that, for the first time in her existence, made her question the rigid control and sensual discipline that defined her.

A vow of celibacy was easy to hold when there was no temptation.

8

Elena winced as she continued to hold the hover off the Tower roof, her mind going over her earlier conversation with a coldly furious Raphael.

"If Lijuan succeeds in tracking down and killing Alexander, it'll fracture angelkind at the core. In all our millennia of existence, such a crime has never been committed."

Elena didn't need her archangel to tell her that the fracture would lead to chaos and all-out war. Some would follow in Lijuan's twisted footsteps, while others would battle against it. Hundreds of thousands—*millions*—of mortals and immortals both would die, the world forever scarred.

"Stupid Cascade," she muttered on a huff of breath, sweat pasting her T-shirt to her skin.

"Did you say something, Ellie?" Aodhan asked from beside her, his mist-pale and diamond-bright hair glittering like faceted gemstones in the afternoon sunlight, and his extraordinary eyes of blue and green shards shattered outward from the pupil, afire.

Next to him, Elena's own near-white hair was nothing out of the ordinary.

"Cursing the Cascade," she got out, her muscles straining.

"Shit—I think I'm at my limit." She dropped down to the closest balcony. "How did I do?" she asked when Aodhan landed beside her.

His feathers caught the light, sending bright sparks in every direction.

"Two minutes longer than in our last test." Aodhan, his body having healed fully from his grievous battle injuries, pushed back the sleeves of his shirt. "You passed."

"I feel like I did on my first day at Guild Academy." Stretching out her stiff muscles, she took a seat on the edge of the balcony. "I need to get stronger." War boiled on the horizon—if not this year, then soon, and she had to be strong enough to fight at Raphael's side.

Aodhan took a seat next to her, his wings carefully folded to ensure they wouldn't touch hers. "There are some things you can't control. Like a child who grows to his adult strength, you have to grow into your immortality."

Elena knew that. It infuriated her. Taking out a throwing blade she'd honed to a deadly edge, she played it over and through her fingers in an effort to channel her frustration, and looked out at the city that no longer bore any scars of battle. It had taken brutally hard work to achieve that, but as the center of Raphael's territory, New York had to show an undaunted face to the world.

"I'm worried about Naasir." Alone, he was a ghost no one could catch, but if all went well, he wouldn't be alone on his way out. He'd be shepherding a scholar. It didn't matter if the scholar had warrior training—no one, and Elena included herself among that number, could move with as much stealth as the silver-eyed maybe-vampire who refused to tell her his origins, and who'd dug his way into her heart.

"I've learned never to underestimate him." Aodhan leaned forward, his forearms braced on his thighs and his gaze on the waters of the East River, the Hudson not visible from their current position. "Have you noticed the changes in Illium?"

"Hard to miss." The blue-winged angel's power had escalated in the months after the battle, until it burned in the gold of his eyes and pulsed in his skin.

He still teased Aodhan as wickedly, insisting on calling him Sparkle, still made Elena laugh with his open and unrepentant flirtation, but he was also growing away from them and it hurt. She couldn't bear to think of a New York without Illium, because while she respected all of the Seven, her relationship with Illium was different.

He'd been the first one she'd truly come to know, his humor and wit critical in helping her adjust to this new life. Even among the Seven, he seemed to hold a special place: no one was ever angry at Bluebell. The idea that power might change him, chill that joyous heart was even worse than the thought of losing him to it.

"He's too young." Aodhan's voice was quiet, his left hand fisting on his thigh. "Like you can't do certain things, he isn't physically old enough to control that much power."

Stomach knotting, Elena turned to look at Aodhan's flawless profile, his skin not white or cream but something other, alabaster kissed by sunshine. "The Cascade?"

A nod. "The sire believes it's accelerating Illium's natural development—only his body isn't catching up."

She gripped the edges of the balcony so hard her bones pressed up white against the dark gold skin she'd inherited from her Moroccan grandmother. "Is there anything we can do?"

Aodhan shook his head, the movement scattering shards of light in a brilliant, unexpected rain. "No one can stop the growth of an angel."

Ice cracking her heart, Elena went straight into Raphael's arms when he returned home from an offshore drill. "Why didn't you tell me about Illium?"

"Because he is your favorite and you would worry when there is nothing to be done." Wings of white gold licked with the cool flame that appeared and disappeared without warning, wrapped around her. "Your Bluebell's development can't be halted."

"Could he become an archangel?"

"One day far in the future, yes. If he ascends now . . . he's not ready." Raphael held her tight, his voice taut with a hard thread of unvarnished emotion as he said, "Illium's body will break apart from the power overload and he's not old enough to survive such total annihilation."

Elena wanted to squeeze her eyes shut and wipe away the horrific image. And if she felt that way, she couldn't imagine her archangel's grim anger and concern. He'd known Illium since Illium was a boy, and Illium's mother, Sharine—known among angelkind as the Hummingbird—held a special place in his powerful heart. That heart knew how to love, how to be loyal.

"What the hell is happening, Raphael?" she said, holding him as tightly as he was holding her. "One of our friends is heading right into the heart of that crazy bitch's territory, and another is on the verge of a catastrophic change."

Raphael's voice crashed into her mind, the bright sea and cold kiss of it intimately familiar. *The Cascade has no allegiance and it chooses no sides. No one is safe.*

9

Naasir crossed the border into Lijuan's territory just before dawn the next morning. He'd done it many times. Then, his task had been to take the temperature of the land, discern the mood of her people. He'd prowled in the shadows of villages and cities and he'd listened, then reported back.

Today, he was racing against time through a landscape lashed with the brilliant colors of fall. If Xi's squadron had flown straight from the Refuge to the citadel, Andromeda had already been in Lijuan's clutches for at least twelve hours.

Naasir didn't think she'd survive much longer than another forty-eight at most. She was a warrior and a scholar, but she wasn't sneaky. Okay, maybe a little sneaky since she'd fooled him with her civilized skin, but not deep-down sneaky—Naasir wasn't sure she'd be able to mislead Lijuan long enough for Naasir to get to her.

Because one thing he knew: Andromeda would not betray what she knew about Alexander. Others might doubt her allegiance because of her bloodline, but he'd seen the truth of her as he held her pinned to the earth. Her honor was an indelible part of her, embedded into her true skin in a way nothing could erase.

Winter storms and lightning.

He changed direction at the scent in the air, running through the long grasses without bothering to lower his body. The sun hadn't yet risen, the light dim and gray. Even had it been noon, no one saw Naasir in the grasses when he didn't want to be seen. He was a shadow, a striped mirage. The angel who waited for him beneath the spreading branches of a large tree dressed in leaves of scarlet and gold was another kind of shadow.

Wings of black held tight to his back and his body motionless, Naasir wouldn't have seen Jason if he hadn't caught his scent. He approved. To him, the spymaster had always been one of the most dangerous members of the Seven. It caused Naasir no surprise that Jason had found him. As Naasir could track by scent, Jason had methods of his own.

"You'll help me find Andromeda?" he asked on reaching the black-winged angel, because if Jason had another task, Naasir couldn't assist, not today.

But Jason nodded, his tattoo bared by the neat way he'd pulled his hair into a queue at his nape. Naasir had gone with Jason on one of Jason's trips to the Pacific Island home of the artist who'd done the work. Jason had walked alone for a long time, but sometimes he didn't seem to mind a curious Naasir tagging along.

Naasir felt the same way about pain as he did about cold: he could bear it, but he didn't choose it. However, he understood Jason's choice to go through the grueling process that meant the tattoo would "stick" to his immortal skin. The tattoo was like Naasir's stripes—an acknowledgment of the wildness inside Jason.

Now, Jason spread out the midnight of his wings to stretch them, then folded them back in, the smooth motion a wave of silent darkness. He was the only angel Naasir knew who could, when he wished, move his wings with zero sound. No susurration, no rustle, nothing but pure silence.

"I've confirmed the scholar has been taken to Lijuan's central citadel."

Naasir bit back a harsh, nonhuman sound at Jason's words. He had no argument with the spymaster's intelligence—Jason was never wrong about things like this. It was the idea of Andromeda shut up with Lijuan's ugliness that made his claws emerge, the curved blades gleaming even in the murky light.

"Can you get her out?" he asked, because getting Andromeda to safety was the important thing, not who did it, and the sky-road was faster than the ground.

Jason shook his head. "Not alone. Also, the fact she doesn't know me could cause a dangerous delay."

"Then we go in together, get her out."

"You'll need to practice patience for this, Naasir." Jason closed the short distance between them. "I know you can get in, but we have to get in and out with her without being seen and without alerting her guards."

"You're strong. You can kill them." He'd seen Jason's black fire ignite the sky. "I'll help you." Naasir could fight many men at once.

"We're not strong enough to defeat the sheer number of troops stationed in and around the citadel." Jason's voice was quiet but hard, demanding attention. "You must use the primal part of your nature in this. You must be cunning and stealthy and unseen."

Naasir flexed his fingers and thought about what Jason had said. "Can I kill some of them?" They had taken—and probably scared, maybe hurt—someone in his care; he wanted to mete out punishment.

"Only if it won't lead to us being exposed."

Forcing his claws back in, he stared at Jason. "All right," he said at last, trusting Jason's advice because Jason was one of his family and had stood with Naasir whenever it was necessary. "I can get in—but if I'm to get Andromeda out without Xi's forces being aware of it, you need to tell me the layout of the citadel."

Jason pulled out a map from a pocket, unfolded it.

For the next ten minutes, Naasir contained his impatience and listened and learned. He was smart. Dmitri had told him that as a child when he'd refused to go to Jessamy's school; the older vampire had found him sitting atop a high shelf in the stronghold library, arms folded and face set.

He'd pretended he was being stubborn because he didn't want to go, but really, he hadn't known how to be like the other children, how to understand the words he'd seen Jessamy write on the board when he'd snuck over there to peek through the windows.

"You're clever," Dmitri had said, hunkering down in front

of him after ordering him down. "You have more smarts than many an adult."

"Then why do I need to study?"

"Because it'll give you another weapon." Dmitri's dark eyes hadn't moved from his, the fact he was a far more dangerous predator calming to Naasir. No one could harm him or make him do bad things while he was in a family with Raphael and Dmitri.

"Else," Dmitri had continued, "others will be able to do things behind your back, have secrets you can't unravel."

Naasir hated the idea of being shut out, so he'd gone to school. It had been difficult for him to stay still for long periods, but Jessamy hadn't thrown him out, even when he climbed the wall to cling to the ceiling. She'd smiled instead and continued to teach and he'd learned his words. He'd even learned sums. And somewhere along the way, he'd made friends who liked to do wild, naughty things with him.

One parent had been so angry at a game he'd taught her son that she'd marched in and demanded "the savage brat" be removed from the school. Naasir had gone quiet that day. Dmitri wasn't there to protect him and the angel who'd marched to the school was powerful, much more powerful than thin, breakable Jessamy.

He'd been ready to claw the powerful angel if she dared hurt his gentle teacher, but to his shock, he'd seen Jessamy face down the other woman without once raising her voice. That was when he'd understood two fascinating things:

One—Jessamy didn't just tolerate him, she was willing to fight for him; she *liked* him.

Two—sometimes, you could win a fight without claws.

Today, it was the latter lesson that he kept at the forefront of his mind. "What if Andromeda is being held in one of these places?" He pointed out what Jason said was the central throne room, as well as several other public areas.

"You wait." Jason put away the map after confirming Naasir had memorized it. "Even if she's being hurt, even if she's screaming and begging, you *wait*."

Naasir's claws wanted to release again. "Would you wait if your princess was being hurt?" Naasir didn't yet know Jason's mate well, but he'd danced with her during a dinner at Elena and Raphael's home. She was young and sweet and not at all dangerous. Because he respected Jason, Naasir had been very careful not to scare her.

Jason's expression was unreadable, but Naasir had known him for centuries, felt the storm crackling in the air. "If I knew that to rush in would equal further torture for her, yes," Jason said at last. "If you go in, you'll die or be taken hostage. Lijuan will use you to make her talk, or to take revenge against Raphael. Either way, you'll be useless to Andromeda. So you wait. *Even if she bleeds.*"

Naasir flexed and unflexed his hands, a growl rumbling in his chest. "I want to hurt you right now."

"You know I speak the truth."

He forced himself to nod. "I'll wait." Because Jason was clever, too. Very, very clever. He'd been in and out of Lijuan's citadel without the archangel ever being the wiser. "Where will you be?"

"I'll go in with you and do whatever's necessary to divert attention from your escape route. You have a phone?" At Naasir's nod, he said, "Message me after you learn her location so I can cause a distraction away from it. And tell Andromeda not to fly once you're out—the sky is too heavily guarded."

"I won't leave you there alone." Naasir did not leave his family behind.

"I'll be behind you," Jason assured him. "If you can't send me a message to let me know your location, just keep going. I'll find you."

"Don't take too long or I'll come back for you."

Jason held his eyes and then he did something he hadn't done for a long time. He reached out to touch Naasir, closing his hand over Naasir's shoulder in a firm grip. "I know," he said. "Now, let's hunt."

Naasir bared his teeth again and twisted to continue his run through the grasses as Jason prepared to lift off. Perhaps, he thought, considering Jason's touch, there were more benefits to mating than he'd realized. Even with a soft, breakable mate, Jason was happy now. Jason hadn't been happy for hundreds of years. He'd been dark inside.

Naasir wasn't dark inside . . . but he was alone. The only one of his kind in the entire world. He had friends, had family, but he had no one who was like him. Mating wouldn't change that, but it would give him a person who belonged to him just as much as he belonged to her. And maybe one day, they'd have a cub and there would be another like him in the world.

He grinned at the thought of a naughty cub hanging upside down from a tree branch. No one knew if he could reproduce, but Keir said there was no reason he shouldn't be able to; he wasn't like Made vampires who were only fertile for about two centuries after their Making. He'd been born as well as Made . . . and he was mostly *not* a vampire.

What even Keir couldn't tell him was whether he was biologically compatible with a female, mortal or immortal, vampire or angel. He'd never tried to create a cub with anyone—he knew when he was in heat, could feel it, and he never took lovers during that time.

He didn't want his cub to have a mother who thought he—or she!—was a savage. He wanted someone he trusted to love their child. And he hadn't been old enough to be a father. Now, he was, and he'd found an angel who wore her own secret skin, but who'd shown her real self to him.

He wanted to play more with her, find out if she could be his mate. To do that, he first had to rescue her from hell.

Andromeda had actually fallen asleep during the last part of the journey to Lijuan's citadel. It wasn't by chance. Dahariel had taught her that skill over a hundred years of training. A warrior who could sleep where he or she had the chance, was a warrior who'd last longer in battle—or in enemy hands. While as an angel of almost four hundred, she didn't have to sleep every night, she couldn't last days or even weeks without sleep.

Sleep is a weapon. Dahariel's aquiline features in her vision. *It rejuvenates and heals. Use it like any other weapon at your disposal.*

She'd never appreciated the value of his training and advice more than she did today.

Her hours of sleep meant she was alert when they arrived at the citadel just before sunrise. Ordering her bonds cut off as soon as they landed, Xi allowed her to remove her blindfold herself. "Are you in any pain or discomfort?"

She wasn't surprised at the civility of his question. Xi was a general down to his bones. That didn't mean he wouldn't execute or torture her should it become necessary, but until then, he'd treat her with flawless courtesy.

"A little stiff," she said, stretching out her wings and wincing more than strictly required. "May I be permitted to do a low flight to ease my muscles?" It would give her an idea of the landscape at least.

Unfortunately, Xi was too smart to permit such a slip after keeping her blindfolded this long. "No," he said. "But you can spread your wings in this courtyard before we go in."

Andromeda took her time. She *was* stiff and she needed to move smoothly if she was to seize an escape opportunity when it arose. Going through some basic exercises taught to most angels in childhood, she did nothing to betray her training under Dahariel—or the fact she'd kept up her skill by sparring with Dahariel and Galen behind walls that protected her secret.

Both angels had agreed with her choice to keep a hidden skill in her arsenal. Galen helped her because she was one of Jessamy's apprentices, but Dahariel's motives were . . . complicated. Andromeda didn't like to think too much on those motives, but her training meant she had some kind of a chance in this hostile environment.

You have secrets.

Naasir's deep voice echoed in her head and she wondered what he'd done after discovering she'd gone missing. He would've joined in the search, but even a silver-eyed vampire who wasn't a vampire couldn't be expected to infiltrate this citadel. As far as she was aware, no one aside from Lijuan's people even knew its exact location.

If she was to survive this and escape, she'd have to rely on herself. Ironically, her bloodline might sway Lijuan enough to keep Andromeda alive, but Andromeda was no hypocrite. She wouldn't attempt to use a family name she'd chosen to forsake—and regardless, given the way she'd been abducted, Lijuan wasn't worried about offending Charisemnon.

"Thank you," she said to Xi after completing the stretching routine.

She'd taken the opportunity to note the armed guards atop the high turrets, as well as the squadrons overhead. For some reason, and despite having witnessed the exquisite beauty and stately elegance of the Forbidden City before its destruction, she'd expected Lijuan's citadel to be an ugly monstrosity full of despair—instead it was formed from a shimmering dark gray stone that the rising sun lit to glowing life.

Flowers in subtle shades bloomed in large planters situated around the courtyard, and she could see not only soldiers of both sexes moving about, but also maidens dressed in delicate silk cheongsams and ethereal gowns. There were pretty male court- iers, too, wearing embroidered silks and fashionable tunics.

Water glinted through one passageway out of the courtyard, along with flashes of green. A pond, Andromeda realized. Per- haps a garden created around that source of water. That had to be the true courtyard where Lijuan might walk amongst her courtiers. This was the more practical external one, and even it was paved with stones that glittered with flecks of sparkling minerals.

The parts of the roof she could see from here had sinuous dragons along the edges, while painstakingly carved stone bridges connected one section of the citadel to another. Those bridges endowed on the surely sprawling edifice an appear- ance of fragility. Impressive, given that it was hewn out of stone and could probably withstand a long-term siege.

"It's beautiful," she murmured. "I expected a more military-like structure."

"This is our lady's home," Xi said, a touch of censure in his tone, his posture military straight. "She has always loved and nurtured artists, though she has never flaunted it like Michaela. This citadel was designed by a gifted architect long ago."

"Ah." She ran her fingers over the stone, her bones aching from the sense of history embedded in the silky smoothness under her touch. As if so many hands had touched this stone over so many millennia, it had been worn down to its purest essence. "Suyin?" she asked in wonder.

A small incline of Xi's head. "She was born of Lady Lijuan's sister."

Andromeda felt her heart sigh. To be allowed to view, to touch one of Suyin's lost masterworks . . . It almost made her forget her circumstances. Craning her neck, she wished she could see the citadel from above—not for escape this time, but because her scholar's heart was aflutter at the idea of exploring what may well be the largest structure Suyin ever designed.

Xi allowed her time to admire the parts she could glimpse before nodding at her to walk with him into the citadel.

"The world lost a great artist on Suyin's death," Andromeda said, her hands itching for a sketchpad and a pencil.

"Yes."

Even as she continued to glory in the grace and splendor that shouted Suyin's touch—as embodied in the palace the architect had designed for Alexander—she was recalling the sad and mysterious circumstances of the other woman's death. "Since Suyin's body was never found, I've always hoped that perhaps her suicide note was a feint intended to allow her to go to Sleep on her own terms."

Xi's wings brushed hers on a tight corner. "My apologies," he said, immediately putting an inch between them. "I wasn't alive at the time Suyin created this citadel, but my lady may have further insights. We go to see her now."

Andromeda's blood chilled, wonder erased by ice-cold fear.

10

Swallowing to wet her dry throat, she said, "Is it possible for me to refresh myself prior to meeting the archangel? She is not known for her kindness to those who offend her." An undeniable truth. "I would rather go in looking my best."

"A wise and intelligent choice." Xi's near-black eyes skimmed her dusty form, but there was nothing derogatory in the glance.

No, it was more like a general taking stock of one of his men.

"You have fifteen minutes," he said. "I will speak to my lady in the interim and tell her I have given you time to recover." He made a small gesture and a short, sturdy-looking Chinese vampire appeared out of the woodwork to bow deeply toward him.

Andromeda's heart slammed hard against her rib cage. She hadn't seen the black-garbed vampire, hadn't even suspected he was hovering. She'd have to be far more alert if she intended to make it out of here. Following the vampire down the corridor, then another and another and another, she realized he was either deliberately taking her on a circuitous and confusing route, or this citadel was a maze. It didn't matter—a scholar's mind was her greatest weapon and Andromeda had long ago learned ways to memorize and retrieve information.

Reaching the room at last, the vampire waved her in. "I will wait for you, honored guest," he said in one of the major dialects spoken in Lijuan's territory, then began almost immediately to repeat the words in French.

Andromeda held up a hand. "I understand." Like most angels, even the youngest, she spoke multiple languages. However, as a scholar who wished to work at Jessamy's side, she was expected to learn every single one that might be used by mortals and immortals both, including those languages that had fallen slowly out of favor.

For how can a Historian keep a true record if she doesn't hear and understand all of the voices, even the quietest?

Jessamy's words the day she'd explained the importance of language studies to a young Andromeda who was a novice at scholarship but who wanted *so* desperately to learn. Andromeda's current retention rate was fifty-eight percent and included all the major world languages, as well as about a third of the minor ones.

Also remaining on her list were the subdialects, as well as certain languages spoken only in isolated pockets of the world, and the "dead" tongues. Of course that percentage would never hit a hundred—language was a living organism that changed from day to day, year to year, century to century.

Even Jessamy considered herself only ninety-eight percent proficient at any given time.

"I won't be long," she said to the vampire and closed the door behind herself.

The room she'd been given was elegantly appointed in dark gray with touches of jewel blue, and to her surprise, it had a window large enough to allow an angel to fly out. When she opened the latch, the window swung outward, letting in cool outside air that settled like a balm on her strained skin.

In front of her were rolling fields full of wildflowers that appeared undaunted by summer's absence, beyond them trees resplendent with fall foliage that glowed in the soft morning light. While Andromeda had no idea of her exact location, the fact that the landscape appeared mountainous, when added to the noticeable chill in the dawn air, suggested that this part of Lijuan's territory would turn snow white come winter.

It would be much more difficult to escape in snow, or icy, torrential rain.

The flowers beckoned at her to take a step, fly free.

The window was beautifully convenient.

It was as if Xi *wanted* her to fly out.

Leaning out with her hands tightly gripping the window-sill, she drew in a long breath, doing her best to make it seem that she was simply enjoying the view. As she did, she took in everything around her. Still, she'd have missed it if she hadn't trained under Dahariel, and later, under Jessamy.

Dahariel had taught her how to assess a threat situation.

The Historian had taught her not only to look, but to *see*.

What Andromeda saw was that the fields might be empty but the same couldn't be said for the sky. It wasn't that she spotted any wings or caught a glint off a sword strapped onto a body high above. No, what she saw was a single feather float down to land on the grass not far from her window. That feather was small, could've been of a bird except that it was a pale yellow streaked with blue.

A very distinctive coloration identical to that of Philomena, one of Lijuan's generals.

Only a fool would expect to beat Philomena and her squadron on their own terrain.

Pushing away from the window, Andromeda walked to the bed to see a change of clothes laid out for her. Had she given it any advance thought, she might've expected the garments to be delicate—and wholly impractical for escape purposes—courtier clothing, but the outfit was formed of tunic and pants, of a style she might have chosen herself. The hip-length tunic's design echoed that of a cheongsam, the fabric lush midnight blue silk hand-printed with tiny white flowers. The pants were loose and white and cuffed at the ankles.

Stark and lovely both—and clearly tailored for her body.

The underwear placed beside it in a discreet cloth bag was still in its packaging . . . and also of the correct size. It made her wonder exactly how long Xi's people had been watching her from the shadows, just waiting for the opportunity to grab her.

Feeling painfully vulnerable, she bathed quickly before getting into the new garments. A little fiddling and some creative use of strips of fabric torn from her dirty and already damaged gown and she managed to hide her blades along either side of her hips, under the waistband of the pants. She'd taken care to rip the gown along tears created by the net when she was first kidnapped, so there was no reason it should arouse suspicion.

As for this outfit, the pants were light enough that they wouldn't hamper her should she need to run, though she would've preferred a color other than white; her best chance of escape would be at night, when no one would expect a scholar to venture out into the unknown.

That, however, was a problem for later.

For now, she had to survive Lijuan.

Having washed her hair, she tamed it into a neat knot at her nape while it was still wet and manageable, then slipped her feet into the provided slippers of white silk before opening the door. "Thank you for waiting."

The vampire bowed again and turned to lead her onward. The corridors through which they walked were wide and, thanks to myriad windows, full of morning sunlight. Art lined the walls: fine pencil drawings and detailed paintings of parts of Lijuan's territory intermingled with small but intricate tapestries. Flowers sat fragrant and lovely in large porcelain vases almost as tall as Andromeda.

"Oh." She couldn't help herself when she saw one particular vase. Touching her fingers to the masterwork by an angel long lost, she felt her heart weep. Lijuan had lived *so* long, seen so much beauty, been a patron of it . . . how had she become this twisted nightmare?

"Honored guest."

Swallowing the sudden lump in her throat, Andromeda rejoined her escort.

The light-filled and gracious atmosphere of the citadel began to change in slow degrees the closer they got to the center. Darkness licked at the edges like a crawling beast, creating pools of shadow the leadlight lamps set into the walls seemed unable to penetrate. There was no longer any natural light. And the flowers . . . they were wrong.

Instinct told her they'd come from stock identical to the flowers she'd seen earlier, but a dark power had warped these blooms after they'd been picked, the same maleficent energy that made the hairs rise on Andromeda's arms and on the back of her neck and that caused nausea to churn in her gut.

Girding her stomach, she took care that no part of her touched the shadows . . . at least until they grew so thick not even a child could've avoided them. Cold whispered over her feathers and her skin where the shadows found purchase, and it was a cold that made her think not of winter, but of the grave and of dead, decaying things.

She tried to tell herself it was just her imagination, but the mute courtiers she passed in the corridors, their faces pinched and skittering fear in their eyes as they walked rapidly in the opposite direction, argued otherwise.

"We are here, honored guest." Her escort stopped in front of a set of large doors that had been opened outward. Two vampires stood guard, both dressed in dark gray combat uniforms embellished with a single stripe of red down the left side.

The same colors as those in Xi's wings.

As Lijuan had used these colors since her ascension, it made Andromeda wonder if the archangel had paid a young Xi particular attention because of his patriotic coloring. Had Xi's future been written the instant his wings settled into their final coloration?

If she survived this meeting, perhaps she'd ask Xi.

In front of her, the guards didn't so much as appear to breathe. One was a square-jawed and blue-eyed blond, the other dark-eyed and black-haired, his features angular, but they'd clearly been tempered in the same merciless crucible, their eyes without pity.

Walking past the two and leaving her guide outside, Andromeda found herself in a cavernous space that contained only a single piece of furniture. It was a throne carved of jade, the shades within spanning the spectrum from creamy white to a green so dark it was near black. Set atop a dais reached by five wide steps, it was spotlighted by the gentle golden light of the standing lamps set behind it. The soft lighting brought up the warmth in the jade, made the carvings glow.

Drawn to what was surely a treasure beyond price, she glanced around but saw no one else. She couldn't resist. Going up the steps, she didn't touch but bent to closely examine the carvings. Eerie, haunting, and disturbing in equal measures, they made her fingers itch once again for a pencil and a paper so she could record what she was seeing.

"Astonishing, is it not?"

The spectral voice was filled with a thousand echoes, with

endless screams. As if behind that voice stood countless trapped souls. Spine threatening to lock as her skin iced over, Andromeda shifted on her heel to look around, but the metal disk on the opposite wall reflected only her own image back at her.

That meant nothing. Not when it came to the Archangel of China.

Abdominal muscles clenched tight, she walked down the steps and, making the decision to face the throne, clasped her hands in front of her. "Yes, my Lady," she said. "I apologize if I overstepped."

"It is to a scholar's credit to be curious." A frigid rush of air and then Zhou Lijuan appeared on the throne in a whisper of light and shadow that Andromeda's mind struggled to comprehend.

Lijuan's wings had always been a glorious dove gray, beautiful and elegant. The color had suited her age and her power. Those wings spread out behind her, as elegant and as flawless as always, and for an instant, Andromeda thought Lijuan was back to who she'd been before the battle with Raphael.

Then she saw eyes swimming in blood . . . and she saw absence.

There was no evidence of legs under the gown of red silk that flowed from Lijuan's painfully thin shoulders. No indication of bones pushing against the skirt, nothing but emptiness. Her left sleeve hung equally hollow at her side.

Andromeda's stomach twisted.

If Lijuan's legs and arm—and possibly other parts of her that Andromeda couldn't see—hadn't yet grown back, then Raphael had done a kind of damage no one could've predicted when it came to a confrontation between an archangel who hadn't yet reached his second millennium, and a near-Ancient. It also meant Lijuan was far more dangerous than even Andromeda had anticipated.

A woman who believed herself a goddess would not appreciate the daily, and excruciatingly painful, reminder of weakness.

At least, but for her eyes and her thinness, the archangel's face seemed as it had always been. The same blade-sharp cheekbones, the same pearlescent eyes, the same ice-white hair. Her skin appeared fragile but that—

Andromeda choked back a scream.

Lijuan's face had turned into a skull, her eye sockets black hollows crawling with maggots that screamed. It lasted a split second before her face was normal again, but Andromeda would never forget the horror. Raphael's right temple now bore a vibrant and ancient mark in a wild blue lit with white fire, while the newest reports from Titus's territory said he was developing a stunning tattoo-like marking in deep gold across the mahogany of his broad chest, but none of the archangels had developed anything so macabre.

Of course, no one had seen Charisemnon in months. And Michaela . . . she'd been missing from public view as long, highly unusual for a woman known for her love of the camera. Andromeda could've asked Dahariel, who was reputed to be Michaela's lover, but Andromeda and Dahariel's relationship was a small, tightly defined thing. He taught her to fight and if she asked, he spoke to her about angelic politics and how to understand the complexity of it.

That was all. And it was all it would ever be.

Lijuan's face changed again, and this time Andromeda couldn't hold back her gasp. If the first change had been horrific, this was so far beyond beauty as to bring tears to the eye and make the heart hurt. The Archangel of China glowed from within, the light of her power a blinding white that made her luminous with a fierce, primal sense of life that reminded Andromeda of Naasir. Lijuan's features seemed softer, her eyes sparkling, her eyelashes deeper and thicker.

It was as if Andromeda was seeing a glimpse of the angel Lijuan had once been.

So perhaps . . . perhaps the other was who she would eventually become.

Naasir fed rather than rested. He didn't kill, didn't harm. He just made his way to the outskirts of a small, isolated village and smiled at a maiden out in her fields; she smiled back at him, her lips parting. When he walked up to her, she didn't run and he could hear her pulse thudding, her scent changing as her body readied itself for him.

"I am hungry."

Shivering at his words, she angled her neck and he drank,

one of his hands cradling her head as her breath came in harsh gasps and her eager body pumped more and more of her rich, hot blood into his mouth.

He was gentle, didn't gorge or take more than she could afford to give, and when he was done, he made sure she'd bear no marks. He always treated his food well, aware that without food, he'd die. "Thank you."

She gripped at his wrist, stars in her eyes. "Will you return?"

"No." Lying to his food wasn't good treatment, so he didn't do it. "Don't wait for me."

Two fat tears rolled down her face. Leaving her watching wet-eyed after him, he disappeared back into the woods, rejuvenated from her gift of blood. He'd had countless similar conversations in his lifetime. When he was a child, he'd fed from Dmitri or Raphael or Keir. At the time, he hadn't understood the depth of the honor he was being given. He'd known only that three men who were very definitely *not* food, were allowing him to feed from them—as a result, he'd been on his best behavior.

All three were also so powerful that he'd only needed a sip once every two days at most. It would've lasted even longer had he been able to feed more deeply, but he'd been small, only able to handle a tiny taste of such potent blood. Dmitri was the one he'd gone to most often. The older vampire had disciplined him more than anyone else, but Naasir liked that, liked knowing Dmitri cared enough to teach him things. When he'd needed to feed, he'd found Dmitri and Dmitri had held out his wrist.

Never once had he withheld it, not even when Naasir was in trouble.

The times when all three men were gone from the Refuge, he was meant to feed from Jessamy, but in his childish mind, he decided she was too weak to spare blood, and so forced himself to drink the bottled backup blood Dmitri stocked for him.

All that changed as he grew into a bigger boy, then almost a man. He'd discovered that girls liked him. And not just girls. Women, too. Vampires, angels, mortals when he snuck out into the world, women of all ages and races were drawn to him. Their scents melted when he neared.

Suddenly, he had more food than he could ever consume, even if he gorged.

Not that he hadn't tried.

11

After first discovering his sudden irresistibility to women, Naasir had taken advantage. Then, thinking about all the lessons he'd had from Jessamy, and what he'd learned of honor from watching Dmitri, he'd gone to Dmitri and confessed that it was possible he'd inadvertently been compelling women to him. He was unique—even he didn't know his own capabilities.

Dmitri had treated his worries seriously. Restricting him to bottled blood, Dmitri had gone out and spoken to over fifty women, all of whom had fed Naasir since he started finding his own food. At the end of his investigation, he'd come to Naasir with a lethally amused smile on his face.

"You aren't compelling anyone, Naasir. The women are all of sound mind and body and recall their encounter with you with pleasure." A raised eyebrow. "If they weren't so terrified of me, I think I'd have been bombarded with invitations for you to return any time you feel hungry."

Dmitri's laugh had held a vein of sensual cruelty that drew countless women to the man who was Naasir's father in all the ways it counted. "It appears you have the same effect as a jungle cat on certain women—they find you beautiful and want to pet you, tame you. Having a wild creature at their throats excites them."

Since Naasir couldn't be tamed, he wasn't angered by the women's thoughts. Their response to him *was* occasionally annoying though—it made the hunt too easy. Not only that, it was clear that they reacted to him on a purely physical level, without ever knowing anything about who he was as a person.

Andromeda hadn't liked him or melted for him. She'd fought with him.

He grinned.

He'd *make* her like him after he got her out of Lijuan's citadel. And when he fed from her, he'd feed her in turn, so she'd know she wasn't just food to him. He wondered what she liked to eat. He'd have to find out so he could court her properly and confirm she was his mate. He'd never courted anyone before, but he'd watched other people do it. He knew he was supposed to bring her gifts, do things that made her smile.

To accomplish that, he'd have to discover Andromeda's smaller secrets. Having watched others win and lose at courting, he knew the best gifts matched the person. Maybe he'd find her a knife. Elena liked the knife Raphael had given her, and Andromeda was a warrior, too. But he'd have to find the right knife. Or perhaps he'd get her something else.

Dmitri had given Honor jewels he'd held safe for centuries, as if part of him had known he was waiting for his mate to claim them. Honor's eyes went soft every time she touched her fingers to those jewels. Naasir hadn't seen Andromeda wearing jewels but he hadn't known her long. Maybe she liked sparkly things. Naasir liked them sometimes. He had a large cache he'd collected over the years. He hadn't even stolen most of them—he'd stopped stealing things even from people he didn't like four hundred years ago, after he grew up.

It had taken him longer than other immortals because he was different.

A growl sounded not far from him. He growled back and had a running companion for over an hour before the other runner rumbled a snarling good-bye and turned back into his territory. Continuing to run at the same relentless pace, Naasir looked up at the sky and tried to find Jason. He couldn't. The spymaster was too good.

When he saw a small truck parked up ahead on the far edge of a field—as if the owner had walked into the village in the distance—he got into it. Hot-wiring the ignition, he drove the truck until he'd exhausted the fuel, ran again until he found another ride. He was moving as fast as he could without causing his body to shut down, but Lijuan's territory was vast. It would take him at least another full day to reach Andromeda. Another twenty-four to thirty-six hours when she was alone with Zhou Lijuan.

Snarling, he reminded himself that the woman who smelled like his mate wasn't prey. She was smart. She had secrets. She would survive.

Andromeda's gasp was still hanging in the air when Lijuan smiled. "Ah, have you seen my faces?" She carried on speaking without waiting for an answer. "I am continuing to evolve. Soon, I will be more powerful than even the legends rumored to Sleep beneath the Refuge."

Andromeda had no doubts Lijuan was changing, but she wasn't sure she'd call it evolution. "Lady," she said instead, her tone respectful. "According to reports filed after the battle, you perished in the fighting." She needed to keep Lijuan talking. It would give her precious more time to think of a way out of this situation.

"I am not so easy to kill." Lijuan's voice echoed with screams again on the last two words, as if the souls she'd swallowed were fighting to get out. "I decided on a strategic retreat, decided to permit Raphael to live."

Andromeda allowed Lijuan's rewriting of history to stand. Discretion wasn't only the better part of valor at this instant, it might be her only chance at survival. "Will you rejoin the Cadre?"

"The Cadre is a weak construct." Lijuan flicked her hand as if brushing aside the idea. "It is time for a new world order." Leaning back in the throne, she smiled, her face continuing to fade in and out of its different forms. It was eerie and oddly compelling at the same time. "I will create a better world."

For the next hour, Andromeda listened to Lijuan speak of the world she planned to build. The archangel's words were rambling and disjointed, and at times, they faded off completely,

Lijuan's body phasing in and out at the same time. However, Andromeda knew it would be a fatal mistake to underestimate her. Zhou Lijuan had at least nine thousand years of life and experience behind her, likely more.

"You listen well, scholar."

Andromeda inclined her head. "It is my task to listen and to record."

Lijuan smiled right as her face changed into the skull avatar. It turned the smile into a grotesque grimace filled with agonized howls that made Andromeda want to clap her palms over her ears. Controlling her breathing with grim effort, she gripped her hand tighter in front of her.

"Then hear this," the archangel said in her sepulchral voice. "I have need to speak to Alexander."

"The Ancient Sleeps." Andromeda's response would be expected, shouldn't engender torture or violence. It remained a calculated risk nonetheless. "No one is meant to disturb an angel's Sleep." It was a taboo on par with that which forbade the abuse of children.

"I understand your qualms, but the world is changing and you must change with it." Lijuan's bloody eyes held her own. "Xi tells me you know where Alexander Sleeps."

"No, Lady. I do not," Andromeda said even as the crushing depth of Lijuan's power threatened to suffocate her. "Alexander was too good a general for it to be otherwise. I know only of a possible location where he might have gone to ground."

"Lying to me would not be a good idea." A strange chill infiltrated the air at Lijuan's words.

"I would not." Andromeda's breath felt like shards of ice in her lungs, stabbing and painful. "Alexander was an Ancient when he went to Sleep. He must have had the power to hide himself in the same way as Caliane." Raphael's mother had taken an entire city with her into Sleep, and when it rose after more than a thousand years, it was in a location far from its origins. "We cannot know whether he buried himself in the earth or under the seabed."

Lijuan nodded at last, the inhuman chill receding. "You speak the truth. I must not forget that Alexander was always a great tactician. The tales his peers told of him as a young fighter . . ." A shake of her head, her tone almost affectionate as she added, "He would neither confirm nor deny most of them when I asked."

Aware Lijuan's mood could turn in a heartbeat, Andromeda used grim focus to keep her voice steady, though fear was a cold intruder in her gut. "May this scholar importune you for such stories as have been lost in time?"

Lijuan laughed and for an instant Andromeda could see the archangel as she'd once been. The one who was old and arrogant, but also wise and a cool head on the Cadre. The one who had found amusement in a wild boy who'd pretended to eat her cat.

"So young and curious." Lijuan shook her head. "Yes, I will tell you stories, scholar, but first, you will give the possible location of Alexander's place of Sleep to Xi." It was an order. "He will mount the search."

Spine stiff from the relentless discipline it took to stand firm against Lijuan's power, Andromeda didn't crumple. "Lady, as a fledgling historian, I took certain inviolable oaths. I cannot reveal Alexander's possible location without compromising those oaths."

"Your qualms do you credit, but as I have said, the world has changed."

Though her flesh was icy from the renewed chill and her bones ached, Andromeda fought for courage, found it in the sudden memory of a sword dance with a silver-eyed vampire who wasn't a vampire. Naasir thought she had a secret skin. Today, she'd wear the skin of a troubled young scholar and it would be her mask and her shield.

"May I have a night to consider my decision?" she asked. "It is a difficult one, for while my oaths are sacrosanct to me, I know Alexander's strength is needed in this world."

Lijuan's face faded to almost nothing without warning, as did her body. "You are of the blood of an ally, so I will give you this chance." An echoing, screaming, horrifying voice. "Go. Consider." A wave of her hand as her body took form again.

Andromeda left before the archangel changed her mind. Her vampire escort was no longer outside the great doors, but Xi was on his way in. "General," she said calmly, fighting the pounding urge to run until she had no more breath and the sinuous, screaming shadows of Lijuan's throne room were far in the distance.

"Am I forbidden from exploring the citadel? I'm curious to see Suyin's creation."

"Go where you will," Xi told her. "If you need help to find your way, ask any of the people you meet." A curt nod. "I must attend my archangel."

Andromeda forced herself to walk away at a tempered pace, her heart beating so rapidly it was all she could hear. Xi's acquiescence confirmed Andromeda's suspicions that Lijuan didn't intend for her to leave. Ever.

Even as the harsh truth settled in Andromeda's stomach, she didn't panic. That would get her nowhere. Once out of the central part of the citadel, she noted the number of guards, tried to pinpoint possible exits she could use, but had to admit the complex was too big and sprawling for her to believe she'd seen even a tenth of it in her explorations.

She tried to imagine what Naasir, renowned for his stealth, would do. He was impossibly beautiful when he moved, an apex predator who feared nothing and no one, and who had a dark, deadly grace.

You have secrets. You wear another skin, too.

Hand fisting against her abdomen, Andromeda fought back a sudden surge of raw emotion. It was silly, foolish. She'd known him for a flicker of time. It shouldn't matter that she might never again see him, never again play games with him that threatened to unravel her hard-fought shell of civilized discipline.

But it did. It *mattered*.

Hours after that stabbing instant of loss, terror was a quiet tattoo in her head. Because this citadel was a fortress. She'd tired her feet to throbbing pain without discovering a single avenue of escape. Swallowing past the sour taste of fear and refusing to give up, she was padding down a quiet hallway when she heard it: a low, lyrical humming that caught at her heart, it was so evocative.

She followed the exquisite sound to a set of open doors at the far end of the hallway, knocked softly. "Hello?"

The humming trailed off. "Yes?" A gentle voice.

Entering, Andromeda found herself in a light-filled room decorated with white fabrics and colorful cushions. The angel who looked up at Andromeda from the sofa on which she sat, a sketchpad on her lap and her legs folded under her, had Lijuan's sharp cheekbones and ice-white hair against cool white skin, though her eyes were a rich obsidian. A tiny beauty spot dotted the delicate skin just below the far edge of her left eye.

You have spots on your face.

The mental echo of Naasir's growly, fascinated voice snapped her out of her stunned shock. Because this angel's distinctive features, when added to the arching snow-white wings with bronze primaries that Andromeda could see behind her, made her identity impossible to mistake. "*Suyin.*"

Lijuan's niece and one of the greatest architects the world had ever known.

The angel smiled, and it was startling to see such open, kind welcome on a face that could've been a duplicate of Lijuan's but for the color of Suyin's eyes and the beauty spot. "And who are you, youngling?"

Andromeda supposed she *was* young in comparison to an angel many thousands of years old. "Andromeda," she said. "A scholar."

"Ah." Returning her eyes to her sketchpad, Suyin motioned her head toward the opposite sofa. "Sit, Andromeda," she said in the same aged dialect she'd used earlier. "Tell me what you do here."

Andromeda saw no reason to lie.

Pencil motionless on her sketchpad, Suyin looked at her with sad eyes once she was done. "My aunt will not allow you to leave."

"I know." It was no longer Lijuan she saw when she looked at Suyin. The other woman's own spirit was too bright and too gentle both. "Have you been imprisoned here all this time?" It must've felt like living death to an angel who, according to the histories Andromeda had read, had loved to fly the world.

"I was given the choice to Sleep or to die. And in this, I was . . . lucky, for others who helped build this citadel and thus knew its secrets, were all executed." Sorrow in every part of her as she flipped a page and began to sketch again. "I chose to Sleep, but I wake every few hundred years to see if this prison I built has fallen and I can fly to freedom." The quiet horror of her pain made Andromeda's eyes sting. "Yet each time I wake, my aunt is more powerful, more a nightmare."

Andromeda wanted to trust this woman who appeared to be a fellow captive, but she couldn't. Not so quickly. Yet she risked asking, "Did you ever try to escape?"

Setting aside her sketchpad, Suyin rose to her feet and turned. Andromeda cried out, one trembling hand rising to her mouth. Suyin was missing most of the lower half of one wing, the exposed muscle and tendon of the bottom edge hot and red.

"I tried to escape the first time I woke," Suyin said after sitting back down, the faint breathlessness in her voice the only indication of what must be agonizing pain.

She nodded to the crossed swords mounted on the wall behind Andromeda. "The blades used to clip my wings each time I wake."

Andromeda couldn't imagine the endless horror. "How are you sane?" she whispered.

"I do not know myself." Suyin's fine-boned hand moved over the paper in confident strokes. "Perhaps because I was old enough before my imprisonment that I understand time passes like an inexorable river, bringing change with it."

Wise, sad eyes met Andromeda's once more and for an instant, her skin prickled with a dizzying sense of déjà vu. As if she was facing Lijuan again, only this Lijuan was who the archangel *should* have become.

"I have heard whispers of a change called the Cascade," Suyin said. "Is this true?"

There was no reason to hide the knowledge. "It's said to be a time when the archangels grow so viciously in power that the consequences could shatter the foundations of the world."

And the archangels were not who they should be, and bodies rotted in the streets and blood rained from the skies as empires burned.

Nothing could ever soften the grim impact of those words, the first specific mention of a previous Cascade that Jessamy had discovered in the Archives. "A small number of ordinary angels have also been affected."

Illium was the most dramatic example. All the older immortals had begun to notice the violent acceleration of the blue-winged angel's development. There were rumors that he might break away from Raphael's Seven and seek to rule a territory, but those who believed that had forgotten Dmitri. The vampire was one of the most powerful in the world and he chose to be Raphael's second.

"If the world is on the brink of catastrophic change," Suyin said softly, "then, perhaps the next time I wake I will be free . . . and the world will be a ruin. One nightmare to another."

Naasir ran under the moon after his latest truck ran out of fuel, his skin covered by a fine layer of sweat and his muscles straining, but he was still too far from Lijuan's citadel. *Be smart,* he thought to Andromeda. *Be sneaky. I'm coming.*

12

Andromeda woke knowing there was only one feasible course of action.

Bathing, she braided her hair while it was still wet. It was the only way to control it since she didn't have access to the modern tools that had made life so much easier of late. Before that, she'd simply made it a habit to wear her hair in a tight bun. Jessamy had commented on the hairstyle that didn't suit her youth, but Andromeda had shrugged and said it was convenient.

It was, but that wasn't why she did it.

Clean and fresh, she put on a robe and ate from the tray that had been brought in soon after she woke, then dressed in the clothes that had been delivered with the food: another cheongsam-style tunic, this one in a deep, intense pink with black accents, and black pants that hugged her legs. Lovely, but the cut of the pieces made it impossible for her to secrete her blades on her body.

Feeling naked without them, but aware she couldn't risk betraying her one small advantage, she hid the blades deep under the mattress, slid her feet into the black silk slippers that had come with the outfit, and opened the bedroom door. Her waiting escort was a female vampire this time, the other woman's skin creamy as fresh milk and her cheekbones wide and flat below eyes of dark hazel, her uniform the familiar formal black worn by the citadel's household attendants.

The trip to the throne room passed in silence.

On arrival, Andromeda discovered Lijuan speaking to Xi. She walked to the edge of the steps and waited politely for the two to finish. With an archangel as traditional as Lijuan, simple good manners might be enough to save her life at some point. No need to waste that chance when it cost her nothing.

It wasn't till a minute later that Lijuan looked at her, her face normal enough for the moment, though anger had darkened her expression. "Before you tell me your decision, scholar, I have a small matter with which I must deal."

Relieved at the reprieve, Andromeda stepped aside and away from the throne. An angel with wings of dirty cream was dragged into the room soon afterward. Dressed in the colorful silks of the courtiers, his broad face was pale, his brown eyes beseeching. "My Lady." Tears ran down his cheeks, his breath hiccupping. "I meant no betrayal."

"Yet you were feeding Michaela information about my court." Ice hung off each word.

Andromeda's chest squeezed at what was surely to come.

Prostrating himself at the foot of the stairs, the angel sobbed. "I was seduced by her beauty, my Lady. I was weak and she took advantage."

"You are a fool." Lijuan was pure regal goddess in that moment. "But I will be merciful because Michaela has a way of bewitching men. You will be permitted to live."

The angel began to blubber his thanks, but Andromeda, her gut twisting, knew he was speaking too soon. She'd seen the wooden frame that had been brought out of the shadows behind him. Two minutes later, the wild-eyed courtier was manacled to that frame in a spread-eagle position. He was still wearing his clothes, but they were slowly, methodically cut off him by the blond guard until he was totally naked.

Then the frame was turned horizontal by four guards, one on each corner, leaving the angel being punished facing the floor.

"Come," Xi said to Andromeda as the guards began to move the frame out of the throne room. "My lady believes you may find this edifying."

Bile burning her throat, Andromeda walked out with Lijuan's favored general. The guards took the frame to the courtyard and placed it on four posts that seemed to have been erected in the center of the open space for exactly this purpose. The angel now faced the cobblestones, held up about a foot from it, his spread-eagled body exposed to the air and to the pitying gaze of others.

Walking over to the sobbing angel, one of Xi's men began to slice him, the cuts relatively minor. Andromeda's stomach stopped lurching as she took her first real breath since the angel had been brought into the throne room. If this was his punishment for such a deep betrayal, he'd gotten off with nothing more than a rap over the knuckles in immortal terms. She hoped he understood the depth of his luck.

Perhaps he was a favorite of Lijuan's.

Then the guard with the blade backed off, and Andromeda heard the barking. "No," she whispered, stepping instinctively toward the helpless angel.

Xi caught her wrist in an unbreakable grip without taking his eyes from the brutal scene about to play out. "Do not intervene or the hounds will tear you to shreds."

Two seconds later, the first hound appeared. Drawn to the blood, the sleek black animal licked at the sobbing angel . . . and then it bit. The angel screamed. Andromeda closed her eyes but she couldn't close her ears to the horrific sounds. She forced her eyes open a heartbeat later. She *would* escape this place and when she did, she would record this horror.

Of course, the vast majority of angelkind would find nothing wrong with the punishment. Being immortal wasn't always a good thing. It meant the ones meting out the sentence had had centuries to think of suitable punishments . . . and that to fit the crime, sometimes that punishment was brutal. There was no point lashing an older angel when the wounds would heal within days.

Even Raphael, an archangel not known for cruelty, had once broken every bone in a treasonous vampire's body. The unfortunate vampire, his body hanging together by stringy tendons and shattered bone that stabbed through his skin, had been left on display in Times Square for three hours.

To betray an archangel was to make a mistake that could never be undone.

The angel who'd made that mistake in Lijuan's court was

covered in bites within minutes, his skin streaming liquid red. He was also missing pieces. The frenzy continued until his screams of terror and pain eventually died down to whimpers, then to silence. That didn't mean he was dead—Lijuan had given him her word that he'd live, and so he'd live.

Feathers flew into the air as the hounds began to rip at his wings for what appeared to be the fun of it, having already feasted on the flesh that had been their first target.

"How long?" she asked, her voice a rasp. "How long will his punishment last?"

"Until my goddess wills otherwise." Xi finally released her wrist. "You know his crime deserved no less. Why are you shocked?"

Andromeda swallowed. "It has been centuries since I witnessed such a punishment." Hundreds of years since she'd run from the terror-soaked home where she'd been born.

"Yes, you are a scholar," Xi said, as if that explained everything. "Come."

As they turned to reenter the citadel, Andromeda tried to temper her visceral response to what she'd seen, but she knew she was pale, her skin cold as frost. Not that Lijuan could be surprised by that. Fear, slick and choking, had been the archangel's intention when she made sure Andromeda witnessed the punishment. A thin scream rose into the air at that instant, as if the angel had found a final dreg of strength.

Andromeda's hands clenched. "He'll go mad," she said to Xi.

"An unavoidable side effect." The general stopped without warning. His eyes were unblinking when they met hers. "Any one of the Cadre would have meted out a punishment as severe for such betrayal. Heng was a trusted member of the inner court."

Thinking once again of the vampire in Times Square, Andromeda was forced to nod. And Raphael wasn't the only other archangel who'd delivered pitiless justice. Astaad had once staked a duplicitous angel in a pit filled with poisonous beetles whose bite caused flesh to necrotize, and left him there for an entire month. As for Michaela, she'd ordered every part of an angel flayed off piece by piece, including his eyelids . . . and by the time the task was done, the angel had started regenerating enough that the cycle could continue.

A shiver crawled up Andromeda's spine.

"I take your point," she said to Xi through teeth that wanted to chatter. "Our world is a harsh one."

Xi started walking again. "Immortality equals arrogance for many."

Andromeda wondered that he didn't see the irony of his own statement. Lijuan was unquestionably the most arrogant of all the archangels. She believed herself a goddess and perhaps she was: a goddess should be able to give life, and Lijuan had created a whole new entity.

Simply because the reborn were ugly mockeries of life didn't change the fact that Lijuan had the ability to alter the very nature of mortals and immortals both.

This time when Andromeda entered the throne room, the guards closed the doors behind her, cutting off all evidence of the outside world. Watching Andromeda and Xi walk toward her, Lijuan glanced at Xi, clearly speaking to him as an archangel could with those she chose.

Whatever his report, it seemed to satisfy the Archangel of China.

Andromeda had braced herself for Lijuan's attention, but the touch of those bloody eyes still caused her primitive, survival-driven hindbrain to attempt to take over.

"Now, scholar," Lijuan said. "You've had a night to sleep on your decision. Will you share your knowledge of Alexander?"

Unspoken was the silent threat that if she didn't, she'd suffer a fate similar to that of the unfortunate angel in the courtyard. "My Lady," she said, "it is difficult for me to break my vows when it comes to those who Sleep, but I believe you are right. The Sleeping ones need to wake to help steady the world."

"Tell us," Lijuan said.

Cold perspiration threatening to break out over her skin, Andromeda lowered her gaze, as if in deference. "All my research suggests that he would trust his Sleep to Titus." The friendship between the Ancient and an angel who had once been a child in Alexander's court was legendary.

Lijuan's eyes grew sharp. "*Yes.*"

Andromeda pushed on. "The difficulty is in pinpointing the exact location." Titus controlled the sprawling landscape of southern Africa, the line that separated his lands from

Charisemnon's cutting the continent in half. "However, after reading through all known records of their friendship, I believe he must lie beneath or within Mount Kilimanjaro."

Lijuan smiled right as her face took on that impossible, haunting beauty. And for a moment, she was piercingly young. "I remember the stories of what those two did on Kilimanjaro's peaks." Her laughter was light, carefree. "A young and headstrong Titus once challenged Alexander to a climbing contest and beat him. At which point, they challenged one another to climb down in the dark."

Andromeda was astonished at the warmth in Lijuan's tone. It was as if she was a different woman. And the history that was her memory . . . Andromeda would've been no kind of historian if she hadn't been drawn by it. "Did you know Titus as a youth, my Lady?"

"Yes. Always obstinate that one, but with such a huge heart that none could hold a grudge against him." Smile fading, youth fading, Lijuan herself faded and came back into focus in a way that seemed more . . . blurry than before. "I can see Alexander choosing to Sleep under the mountain he well loved, in the lands of a friend he trusted."

"Alexander was known for his attachment to his people," Xi said into the whispering quiet that had fallen. "And he left behind a son who even now resides in his palace."

"Rohan was an overconfident infant." Lijuan's features turned skeletal, the maggots crawling in her eye sockets making Andromeda's stomach turn. "Instead of alerting the Cadre after Alexander chose to Sleep, he attempted to hold his father's territory, almost caused a vampiric bloodbath."

"Regardless," Xi said, "he was deeply trusted by his father."

Lijuan gave a small nod. "Scholar, what say you on this?"

Biting her lip and hoping her voice wouldn't break and betray her, Andromeda shook her head. "I considered Alexander's attachment to his people and to his son," she said, "but as you yourself noted, he was a great tactician. I do not think he would make such an obvious choice."

"Emotions can blind," Lijuan said, before glancing at Xi. "However, it could also be said that Alexander would not place his son in danger by going to Sleep below his palace."

Xi inclined his head in acceptance of the point before

saying, "It could also be a double-bluff." He glanced at Andromeda. "Friendship alone isn't why you believe it's Kilimanjaro."

"No." Andromeda told them of the scrolls she'd read, the stories she'd found in the Archives, even requested a piece of paper and mapped out Alexander's possible location on the mountain. "A bare year before his disappearance, Alexander was seen on this exact spot by another angel, and yet it was later discovered that Titus knew nothing of the visit." Andromeda had been so excited when she'd discovered that piece of what had then been an intellectual mystery.

"I follow you," Xi said, examining her hand-drawn map. "No archangel would cross over into another's territory without permission unless the need was critical. And to not tell his friend, it suggests an attempt to protect Titus from the weight of the knowledge."

Andromeda's pulse pounded. "Yes, exactly."

"Head to Kilimanjaro," Lijuan ordered Xi. "I will decide our next course of action once you either find Alexander, or clear the region." Blood-drenched eyes held Andromeda's again. "While Xi is gone, you will write down every other possibility, no matter how small."

Only one answer was safe. "Yes, Lady Lijuan."

"I will send advance scouts today, make preparations to leave on the next dawn." Xi's wings caught the golden lamplight as he resettled them in what Andromeda knew wasn't a restless move but that of a warrior who wanted to ensure his wings didn't cramp. "We must take extreme care. Titus has ramped up his security since the rise in hostilities with Charisemnon."

The general glanced at Andromeda, the intensity of his gaze a glistening black blade. "You are certain Kilimanjaro heads your list?"

You have secrets. You wear another skin, too.

Andromeda clung to the memory of Naasir's words, to the skin of an intimidated and scared scholar that was her shield. "Yes."

Lijuan leaned back on her throne, her body translucent. "Remember this, scholar." Words that echoed with so many screams, Andromeda's eardrums threatened to bleed. "If I find you have lied to me, Heng's punishment among the hounds will appear as nothing."

Andromeda bowed her head. "Lady, you must understand I can offer no certainties." No one could. "I am but an apprentice."

No answer, and when she looked up, Lijuan was gone. As if she'd turned into her noncorporeal form. Even as Andromeda's breath caught at this evidence of Lijuan's "evolution," she wondered if the choice to become noncorporeal had been a conscious one. It seemed to her that Lijuan had simply been too tired to hold the physical manifestation of her form.

"I hope for your sake that you do not lie." Xi's voice was a scalpel.

"I would be a fool to lie." She was proud her voice didn't tremble. "There is nowhere I can go to escape punishment."

13

Naasir entered citadel territory after nightfall.

Jason's spies in the villages that lay directly below the flight paths to that citadel had confirmed that Xi and his squadron had flown in at dawn the previous day. They'd been carrying an unknown burden in a sling.

Andromeda.

A growl built in his throat at the idea of Andromeda trapped and treated like prey.

But his anger turned into a teeth-baring smile the next second. Because Andromeda wasn't prey. However, she was smart enough to fool Xi and Lijuan into believing such, so that she'd be left alone to think up an escape. Gritting his teeth at the realization she might try it before he was there to help watch her back, he continued to lope through forests in the shadow of mountains, just another shadow among shadows.

The sky hung low and sullen above him.

It was in the last patch of forest before the grasslands that Jason had told him surrounded the citadel that he caught the ugly, rotting scent that denoted the presence of the reborn. He hissed out a breath. The world believed Lijuan's infectious creations erased from the earth, but clearly, she'd managed to save this nest. To survive, the reborn must've been allowed to feed on mortal or immortal flesh—or had been fed.

Naasir wanted to kill each and every one, but Andromeda was waiting for him.

An angry, rumbling sound vibrating in his chest, he avoided the creatures—not difficult given their stench to his sensitive sense of smell—and made his way to the grasslands. Those grasslands were a good precaution by Lijuan's generals, ensuring a direct line of sight for the sentries.

Too bad the grasses had been allowed to grow to knee-high. That was plenty long enough to hide Naasir's form, such grasses an environment which part of his nature knew how to utilize instinctively. He reached the outer wall of the citadel without being spotted. From there, it wasn't difficult to avoid the vampiric guards, but it did take precise timing to make sure he remained unseen by the winged squadron.

He could smell rain on the winds. That could be an asset or it might be a threat. It would depend on the skills of the woman with secrets who smelled like his mate. The heavy cloud cover *was* an undisputed gift, hiding as it did the light of the moon. Naasir could use the moon's light to his advantage, his body a rippling ghost, but Andromeda's lickable, honeyed skin would've been spotlighted by it.

Prowling along the edges of the wall, he watched the guards, listened to their conversations, and when one of them went to answer the call of nature just as the sentry in the sky angled off in another direction, he slipped over the wall right under their noses.

Cunning and stealthy and unseen.

Reminding himself of Jason's words, he spilled no blood and left no trace of his presence as he went over the second wall and jumped down into the inner courtyard. He landed in an easy crouch on the cobblestones, his bare feet absorbing the impact through his entire body without giving him a hard jolt.

Slightly spoiled meat and blood and the ugly miasma of fear.

A predator at home in the moonless night, he made his way toward the tainted meat that must've been lying in the sun for hours. It was alive, he realized as he got closer. Alive and marked by the scents of multiple dogs. Feathers told him the meat had been an angel before being fed to the dogs. It was now in pieces, though the head remained attached to the gleaming, exposed spinal cord.

Either exhausted or simply weak, the meat was motionless but for a closed eyelid that flickered in a rapid pattern—as if the angel was dreaming. His other eye socket was a gaping hole clotted with viscous fluid that had either dried in the sun, or was a result of his body attempting to regenerate itself.

Brutality didn't interest Naasir; he'd seen more than one pitiless punishment over the centuries and he wasn't going to judge this one without having the details. What did interest him was the scent that lingered around the man.

Andromeda.

She'd been here recently. Why?

He looked at the meat again and had the thought that maybe the woman who smelled like his mate might have a soft heart. From the position of her scent, he could tell she'd stood or sat close by the head, possibly in an effort to provide what comfort she could.

Deciding he liked the idea of a mate who had a soft heart, he tracked her scent into the citadel. Seeing an angelic courtier up ahead, he jumped up to the ceiling and held himself there using his claws to hook into the ridged detail. He dropped down as soon as the courtier was out of earshot and continued to track the delicious, unique scent of his warrior-scholar.

There were many overlapping trails; Andromeda had clearly been exploring the citadel with a view to escaping. But Naasir's senses were acute and he had no trouble pinpointing which scent was the freshest.

Sliding behind a wall to avoid a guard, he found himself trapped between two oncoming individuals, one from either direction. He didn't waste time, went up to the ceiling again. No one ever looked up. You'd think angels would, but inside their homes, they never did. It was as if their wings blinded them to the fact that there were other ways of going high than just flying.

Moving across the ceiling using his clawed hands and feet to get a grip, he was careful not to dig so deep that his passage created dust or fine curls of whatever it was that made up the ceiling. It amused him to go right over Philomena's flame-red head. He wanted to pounce on her and go "Boo!" but he'd save that for another day.

Tonight, his priority was Andromeda.

Climbing the top part of a wall and around a corner, he froze in a pool of shadows.

Xi.

According to what they'd learned during the battle above and in the streets of New York, Xi was only violently powerful when Lijuan fed him power, but that didn't change his tactical mind and military training. He was dangerous and Naasir respected him as another predator. If Xi hadn't been fighting for the other side, Naasir would've invited him over for a drink and talked to him about tactics.

Now, he stayed motionless.

Xi paused right under where Naasir was hooked onto the wall, the general's attention caught by a vampire who'd emerged from another corridor. "Yes?"

The slender male bowed deeply. "The scholar has returned to her room. She sat with Heng until he lost consciousness again, and she told him stories of fantastical beings."

Naasir grinned. He'd been right; she had a soft heart.

"Such gentleness is to be expected of a scholar," Xi said at the same instant. "Do you have anything further to report?"

"It appears from her movements that she is searching for a way to escape the citadel."

"Unsurprising," Xi responded, no irritation or anger in his tone. "Show her to the library tomorrow. That will distract her and give her another outlet for her frustration." Xi paused. "Be careful with her."

Naasir heard the same thing that had the vampire bowing deeply again: a faint thread of possessiveness. It appeared Xi found Andromeda attractive. Naasir wanted to rip out the angel's throat for that, had to dig his claws deeper into the wall to keep from acting on his instincts. If Xi thought he could court Andromeda, he knew nothing.

The general was too civilized for her. Xi didn't understand secrets, didn't understand that Naasir's scholar was a sword dancer who liked fighting and whose blood ran hot. That secret truth in mind, he held his strained position for an entire minute until after the vampire and Xi both disappeared. Only then did he drop soundlessly to the stone floor and prowl along Andromeda's scent trail.

There were fewer guards in this wing. Naasir understood why—situated in one of the corners of the citadel, it gave the illusion of freedom because of the number of windows and doors, but the outside was heavily guarded. Andromeda was smart not to have tried to escape from this direction. If she'd gone to ground, she'd have been run to the earth by the hounds that Naasir scented below. If she'd gone up, she'd have been shot down by the squadrons above.

The dogs could prove a problem if the rain didn't come. Naasir could handle them, but it would be an annoying distraction, and there was a risk that someone paying attention would work out that the dogs were whimpering away from a certain point with their tails between their legs.

Reaching the door beyond which he could scent Andromeda, he listened carefully, heard nothing. He smiled and, instead of turning the knob, scratched lightly on the carved wooden panel. It was pulled open from within mere heartbeats later. Hauling him inside with a grip on his olive green T-shirt, Andromeda shut the door with conscious quietness.

Her cheeks were marked by hot red spots when she turned to face him. "What are you *doing* here?" she said, the pulse in her neck thumping.

He wanted to kiss her, but he satisfied himself with what was left on the tray of food placed on a side table. "Rescuing you."

Andromeda's mouth fell open, her brain struggling to comprehend what she was hearing. Naasir had come after her. Right into the heart of the most dangerous territory in the world. "Did Raphael send you?"

Naasir finished off the meat she'd left on her plate and shoved back the silver hair that had fallen over his face while he ate. "I didn't need to be sent," he said, a low growl to his tone. "But the sire is helping me rescue you. Jason is here."

"The spymaster?" Legs shaky, she sat down on the bed. "You *both* got in?" She couldn't imagine how; she had a headache from trying and failing to work out a successful escape route. "No one's meant to have ever infiltrated the citadel. How did you do it?"

Naasir came to crouch in front of her. Reaching up, he flicked her nose. "It wouldn't be a secret if we told you and you wrote it down in your history books." Rising to his haunches, he leaned in close to her face. "Don't put this in your books."

"I won't," she whispered, fascinated by this wild, utterly beautiful creature who had come to rescue *her*.

She wasn't a woman who touched easily, having been rarely touched herself, but she found herself reaching up to cradle his cheek with one hand. Turning his head, he rubbed himself against her. His skin was smooth, without stubble, and the contact sent a shiver over her; when the sleek strands of his hair ran across the back of her hand, she wanted desperately to weave her fingers into the thick silk.

"Later," he said, his eyes heavy lidded. "First we have to escape." He rose, held out a hand.

Taking it without hesitation, she allowed him to haul her up, hope and excitement bubbling inside her. "Wait," she said when he would've headed to the door. Retrieving her knives, she dug out and unrolled a drawing of the citadel Suyin had surreptitiously made for her, then told him about a gate the architect said she'd hidden in the outer wall. "I don't think she's lying."

Naasir folded the sketch and put it into a pocket of his khaki-colored cargo pants. "I'll tell Jason, but we'll escape another way." He took her hand again after she transferred both knives to one hand.

She stood stubbornly in place. "What about Suyin?"

Naasir looked back at her, silver eyes glinting. "It'll be difficult enough to get you out—we can't take another person."

"She's my friend." Andromeda was willing to take the risk that Lijuan's niece was no spy but another captive. If she was wrong, she'd live—or die—on that mistake, but she couldn't walk away; the memory of Suyin's sorrow would haunt her always. "She's been held prisoner for thousands of years."

A harshly primal sound rumbled out of Naasir's chest. "Where?" he asked, the grit in his tone making it an erotic kiss over her skin.

Fighting back a responsive shiver, she described the location of Suyin's suite.

"Go to her," he told her after she was done. "Walk there as if you can't sleep and want company. Wait for me inside her quarters."

About to step out, she turned back to him and smoothed out a wrinkle she'd made in his T-shirt when she pulled him inside. The instant she'd heard that scratch, she'd *known*. "Thank you for coming for me."

Naasir's smile was feral. "I'm going to find the Grimoire, so be ready to rut with me."

That quickly, her fear at what they were about to attempt melted into flustered heat. "Keep your mind on escape."

"I am. I'm looking forward to my reward."

Coming from another man, those words might've made her uncomfortable, as if he was trying to put her in his debt. From Naasir, the statement was so honest, so open that she was only flattered, her blood hot. "I'll see you soon."

"Go."

She stepped out of the room and, leaving the door open, began to stroll to Suyin's suite. She knew she was being watched, but she didn't look around, focusing her attention on the artwork on the walls.

Suyin was awake.

"I rarely sleep," the other woman told her from her favorite sofa, an odd scent akin to seared flesh lingering in the air of the room.

Skin creeping at the realization that something horrible had occurred since they spoke just three hours earlier, Andromeda zeroed in on the new lines around Suyin's mouth. She went to kneel by her friend, took Suyin's slightly clammy hand in her own. "You're in pain."

A faint smile. "Xi came after you left. He believed my wing was regenerating too fast, so he ordered it be excised to the inner curve."

Hands fisted and teeth gritted so hard a muscle jumped in her jaw, Andromeda checked the freshly cauterized wound. The pain had to be excruciating. Knowing there was nothing she could do about that now, she swallowed her rage and took in Suyin's ethereal white gown. "Do you have a tunic and pants like mine?"

Suyin's pain-dulled expression sharpened. "Yes, but if you're planning an escape, don't try to take me. I'll only hold you back." Bright, wet eyes. "My aunt won't kill me—I'm family after all."

Andromeda squeezed Suyin's hand, the bones so fine, the skin delicate. "I won't go without you." She put steel in her tone. "So you must change because if you don't, your dress will hamper your movements."

Suyin's lips trembled, but her words held a resolute strength. "I have only one wing, youngling." She patted Andromeda's cheek with her free hand. "I treasure your loyalty, but I won't take advantage of it. I cannot fly, will be but a burden."

"We won't be flying," Andromeda said, thinking of the wild creature she'd left in her room, the one who'd come into enemy territory for her. For *her*. "We'll go as the tigers go." It was the first image that came to mind when she thought of Naasir: a tiger, deadly and stealthy.

"Tigers?"

"You'll see. Now change."

Suyin didn't argue any further, though her expression made it clear she thought this a foolish risk. Disappearing into another part of her suite, she returned dressed in dark blue leggings paired with a tunic in a slightly paler shade of blue. She touched her hand to the deep brown scarf with which she'd covered her hair. "I wore the darkest things I could find."

Thunder rolled across the sky just then, right before rain began to fall outside in a hard beat. "The dogs can't track in this," Andromeda said with a teeth-baring smile. "We're clearly meant to escape tonight."

The words had barely left her mouth when Naasir slipped into the room. Eyes huge, Suyin's hand lifted to her mouth as Naasir took her in and said, "You have one wing. Does it affect your balance?"

The blunt question made Suyin blink and blurt out an answer. "Yes. It'll also drag me down should I need to run."

Naasir's eyes met Andromeda's and she felt her entire body tense. Looking to Suyin, she knew Naasir's silent solution was the right one, but it would brutalize the other woman when she deserved so much better.

Suyin's next words proved she'd also worked out what needed to happen. "I'll bleed too much or I'd already have cut off my remaining wing and tried to escape via the ground," she said without any hint of self-pity. "The pain from excision is intense and will likely cause me to lose consciousness for an hour at least. The blood loss will render me weak for much longer."

Anger was a burn in Andromeda's blood, but she forced herself to think. "We can break your wing." That, too, would hurt, but it shouldn't cause unconsciousness or the kind of blood loss that came with excision.

Andromeda had experienced a broken wing herself as a much younger angel, after being caught in a sudden draft that slammed her into the gorge wall, understood the resulting level of pain—and from what she'd seen, Suyin had developed a much higher pain threshold as a result of the repeated wing excisions. "Once it's broken," Andromeda added, "we can strap it tight to your back." Like a folded-in fan, so it wouldn't gather air.

Suyin took a deep breath, nodded. "Bones heal."

Naasir closed the distance to her on that soft permission. Picking up a small cushion that had been lying on one of the sofas, he gave it to her. "Muffle your pain."

While Naasir did the horrible task and Suyin bore it, Andromeda stepped onto a chair and removed the swords mounted on the wall. They may have been intended to taunt and terrorize Suyin, but they had razored edges and handled well. Conscious she'd need a scabbard if she was to carry both, she reluctantly left one behind.

As for her knives, she set them aside for Suyin; the other angel had no training with the sword, would find it unwieldy. Knives, however, were instinctive to use.

That done, she took the sword to the unfortunately white sheets on Suyin's bed. By the time she'd finished slicing them up, Naasir had also completed his grim chore. Suyin's wing hung limp, and though the angel's face was as bone white as her hair, she'd held on to consciousness. Using the long strips of cloth, Andromeda and Naasir together strapped the broken-and-folded wing to Suyin's body. "We're almost done," she reassured Suyin when the other woman's body shuddered.

Wrapping the final strip of fabric around Suyin's ribs, she tied it off. "Done." She didn't stop to think—she enclosed the much older angel gently in her arms and held her, rocking softly until Suyin drew in a shaky breath and pulled back.

"You were strong," Naasir said, approval in his tone as he slid away what looked like a small phone. "Is your balance better?"

Taking the knives Andromeda handed her, Suyin walked, then ran quietly around the suite. "Yes, but I'm not used to heavy exercise."

"We won't be running hard." Naasir came over to Andromeda to tug at her braid. "Ready?"

She held up the sword. Its deadly edge gleamed in the light.

Naasir grinned as Suyin smiled in angry satisfaction. "What a beautiful irony that the instrument of my torture will now help us escape."

"I've contacted Jason," Naasir told them both, and suddenly, he was the dangerous man who was part of an archangel's innermost circle. "He'll soon cause a disturbance in another section of the citadel—when he does, you must become my shadows." An order. "I am the alpha. You follow." His extraordinary eyes held Andromeda's. "Not for always. For this."

Andromeda was oddly pleased that he'd clarified his statement. "Until we escape," she agreed.

Naasir went silent, his head slightly bent. Then he grinned again, his teeth bright white against the lush dark of his skin. "Jason is very clever."

Andromeda didn't know what he'd heard, but the ground vibrated with the thunder of running feet seconds later. All were heading to the other side of the compound. Screams sounded soon afterward.

"Reborn," Naasir said with a feral smile. "Jason has driven them home." A deep breath that made his eyes glint. "And he's set a fire." Opening the door, he said, "There is no one here now. Let's play."

14

Let's play.

The statement should've sounded dismissive given the level of danger, but it made Andromeda grin. When she glanced at Suyin, she saw the other woman was also smiling—an astonished, startled kind of a smile. Naasir had that effect. Together, the three of them moved quickly down the corridor. Naasir made no noise; Andromeda and Suyin weren't as quiet, but they did their best.

When Naasir held up a hand, she froze and caught Suyin when the wounded angel would've stumbled. Lifting a finger to his lips, Naasir jumped. He was on the ceiling before Andromeda knew what was happening. Her mouth dried up. Watching him make his way around the corner, she had to force herself not to follow on foot, her protective instincts bristling.

He returned not long afterward. When they turned the corner, she saw one of her vampiric escorts propped up against the wall. "Is he—"

"Alive," Naasir said, and without warning, opened a door. "Inside."

They ducked inside and he followed them in. Shutting the

door, he put his ear to the wood, eyes gleaming liquid silver in the darkness. "Xi has sent people to check on you and Suyin." Opening the door, he stepped out.

This time, Andromeda followed.

Naasir had already incapacitated one guard, and as she watched, he put his forearm around the neck of another and twisted. Clean and efficient, with no desire to cause unnecessary pain, his actions were honest in a way that spoke to the warrior in her.

Returning to the room, she brought out Suyin, and the three of them moved as fast as possible down the corridor. They had to slide into another room to escape a patrol and while in there, Suyin suddenly said, "I know this room. I built a special entrance to the tunnel in here."

They both stared at her.

"What tunnel?" Andromeda said, wondering if her instincts had led her wrong after all. "You said there were no other escape routes but the secret gate in the wall."

Suyin's delicate face was so sheepish it couldn't be disbelieved. "I forget things," she admitted. "The Sleep has that effect, as I'm never awake long enough to truly recover." Walking to an elegant sofa with curved wooden legs, she said, "I think the trapdoor lies beneath."

Naasir moved the sofa and pushed the rug aside to expose a smooth, flawless floor. "Where?"

Tucking the knives into the strips of fabric that bound her wing to her body, Suyin went to bend down. Andromeda caught her arm. "Careful," she whispered. "Don't bend your back; use your knees."

Even that made pain lines flare out from the corners of Suyin's eyes, but her fingers were sure on the wood of the floor as she began to touch what must be pressure points. Andromeda took the opportunity to block the door into this room by propping a chair under the handle. Behind her, the trapdoor opened on a puff of dust.

Waving a hand in front of her face after stifling a sneeze that made her muscles wrench and her eyes tear up, Suyin looked down. "The tunnel goes to the outside. It was built as an escape route of last resort for Lijuan's people."

Naasir dropped down into the hole, then pulled himself back

out with a lithe strength that made Andromeda want to simply watch him. "We won't go that way," he said definitively.

Disappointed, but not that surprised, Andromeda said, "It's a trap?"

"Yes. It stinks of fresh scat and of reborn." His lips lifted to reveal his fangs.

"I didn't know." Suyin's throat moved, her fingers trembling as she rubbed them on her thighs. "On my honor."

"You don't stink of lies." Naasir glanced down at the tunnel again. "It's a trap, but we can turn it on those who set it." Pulling down the trapdoor, he got up and looked at the rug and sofa they'd pushed aside. "Now we hide."

Andromeda wasn't sure that was a good idea, but she'd promised to trust Naasir, so she followed him into the walk-in closet on one side of the room, and there the three of them stood. They didn't have to wait long. Thudding bangs on the door announced either boots or shoulders hitting it, but the end result was the door breaking open and guards pouring in.

Shouts followed, then came the sound of the trapdoor being thrown back.

Andromeda took Suyin's hand when she felt the other woman begin to shake. Suyin had to be so scared of what Lijuan would do to her should they be discovered. When she felt Naasir put his arm around the wounded angel, she wasn't surprised. Naasir might be feral and uncivilized in his true skin, but he was good in a way Xi would never be.

The general's voice sliced through the air at that instant. "Go after them. *Now.* Do not allow the reborn to get to the scholar." Swearing low under his breath, he gave further orders. "Make sure the opposite end of the tunnel is watched, on the low chance they make it out."

"Sir."

All went quiet soon after that.

Sliding out only once Naasir confirmed no one remained in the room, the three of them headed toward an exit. This time, they encountered no one in the corridors. Stepping out into the rain-lashed night, Andromeda glimpsed a tongue of hot yellow flame shoot from a window in a distant section of the citadel.

Rain couldn't put out a fire on the inside. Yes, the spymaster was clever.

When Naasir held out a hand to her, she took it at once. Since her other hand was wrapped around the hilt of the sword, she told Suyin to grip the waist of her pants under the tunic.

The world was an opaque, punishing blackness but Naasir navigated it like he'd been born for it.

When Suyin stumbled, her legs threatening to collapse, Naasir and Andromeda put her between them and wrapped one arm each around her waist, careful not to apply too much pressure. As they helped her to a door in the inner wall, Andromeda saw a flicker of movement to her right. She acted without hesitation, slicing out with the sword to almost decapitate a vampire.

He fell gurgling to the ground.

It was the first time she'd ever truly hurt someone and part of her flinched, bile rising in her throat. That part bore the name of the girl she'd been, the one who'd run from a home where brutality was an everyday affair and kindness considered a laughable weakness. The rest of her understood this wasn't violence for violence's sake. It was about survival. Not just her own but Suyin's and Naasir's. There would be no mercy should they be caught; these same guards would mete out base torture if so ordered.

Naasir's eyes gleamed at her through the pounding rain. "Stop playing. We have to leave."

She went to scowl, realized he was the one who was playing—with her. So she wouldn't think about the blood she'd just spilled. Wanting to kiss him, she instead helped Suyin through the inner wall gate as the rain washed the scarlet stain from her sword.

That was when their luck ran out.

Three sentries came around the corner almost at once and the men were looking right at their small group. Naasir was on them a split second later but it was three against one. Leaving Suyin leaning against the wall, Andromeda swung into the fight. The sentries could not be allowed to send up an alarm.

Her target was trained, but he wasn't expecting her skill. She cut his throat, left him trying to clamp his hand over the bleeding orifice. By the time she turned toward Naasir, he'd already taken care of the other two. Seeing her sentry, he reached out and hit the man on the side of his head, slamming him into unconsciousness. "He could've seen our direction from here, betrayed us to others."

"Sorry. I was worried about you."

He tilted his head to the side, rain rolling down his skin. Then he smiled and went to pick a shaky Suyin up in his arms. Sticking to his side, Andromeda watched their backs as they ran to a small servant's gate in the outer wall. This time, no one spotted them and they were soon outside, but hardly free.

The area directly around the stronghold was grass currently being flattened by the wind and the rain, offering no hiding places. It seemed an interminable distance to the cover of the trees when winged sentries flew constantly across the sky. "How do we do this?" she asked Naasir.

"Go low and let the wind bend the grass over you." He put Suyin on the ground, then gently rubbed dirt over the bandages on her back to make them less white. "On your bellies. Be the cat creeping up on its prey."

"My wings?"

"Hold them as tight as you can. No big movements. Go!"

The ground was wet and muddy, but Andromeda did exactly what Naasir had ordered, the three of them spread out enough that from above, each one would be nothing other than another muddy patch of grass. It was hard and relentless and they had to go motionless more than once when an angel flew too close overhead. Breath coming harsh and low, Suyin did her best, but she lost consciousness halfway through.

Andromeda helped put her on Naasir's back and he took the hurt angel the rest of the way.

By the time they reached the trees, Andromeda's muscles were quivering and the front of her body coated in mud. Using the rain dripping from her hair to wipe off her face, she saw Naasir had already placed Suyin in a seated position against a tree.

"I can't believe that worked." Turning into the rain in the hope it would wash off more of the mud, Andromeda looked out over the distance they'd covered.

"The rain helped. Otherwise, we'd have had to hide and wait for another chance." Picking up Suyin after that short break, he led Andromeda through the trees that didn't do much to hold back the rain. "Jason probably drove out most of the reborn, but their scent is still thick, so one or more may remain."

Sword held at the ready as the rain continued to thunder down, Andromeda kept her eyes on alert for the shambling half corpses that were the reborn. When Naasir hissed and said, "Left," she pivoted, sword already coming up.

A severed head rolled to the ground seconds later. The reborn's body gushed blood as it fell, but Andromeda stepped out of the way of the spray just quickly enough. "Thank you for the warning." Again, the rain washed her blade clean.

As it had her father's when he methodically cut a vampire to pieces once.

Naasir's gaze searched her face, as if he could sense how disturbed she was at her unhesitating ruthlessness. "It's us or them. You aren't torturing or harming the reborn without cause—you are fighting for your survival. That is the right of any creature."

Andromeda jerked her head in a nod. "Yes." The reborn may have been innocent prior to their transformation, but they were an abomination now. As for the guards, they would've killed Naasir given the slightest chance.

Her jaw firmed, hand tightening on the hilt of the sword. "I won't let anyone hurt you."

Instead of laughing at what must seem a ridiculous statement when it came to a man so dangerous and capable of looking after himself, Naasir's lips curved in a satisfied smile. "I knew you liked me."

Surprised into a soft laugh, Andromeda reached out to check Suyin's pulse. It was even shallower than she'd expected. "She could fall into *anshara*." Normally, the semiconscious healing sleep was a helpful thing, but it could be a serious handicap if Naasir had to carry Suyin the entire way.

"Angels would be much more efficient if they could drink blood," Naasir said conversationally.

"Well . . . I suppose that's true." A feed would've given Suyin an immediate jolt of energy. "Do you ever feed anyone?"

Naasir shot her an intrigued look. "Do you want to taste me?"

She wasn't put off by that question as any civilized scholar should've been. "No," she said at last, and had the feeling she was telling a lie.

"*I* want to taste you." A wicked smile. "Will you feed me if I need it?"

"Of course," she said, trying to sound pragmatic when the idea of Naasir feeding from her made her insides turn molten. "You're my only hope of getting out of here."

He growled at her and didn't say anything else for the next ten minutes as they made their way through the forest. Finally, she couldn't stand it anymore. "Stop sulking."

Another rumbling growl. Turning, he snapped his teeth at her.

She jumped even though she'd thought she was ready for an aggressive reaction. Teeth gritted, she glared at his infuriating face. "Growl at me again and I'll bite you." She didn't know where the words came from, probably from aggravation.

Staring at her, he went as if to speak. His nostrils flared. "Reborn," he said, and placed Suyin against a tree with a wide-enough trunk that her back was fully protected.

Andromeda didn't need to be told where to stand; she stood with Naasir behind her, Suyin to her left. His back pressed into her wings, but she knew he wasn't being provocative for once.

"Be careful of your wings."

She suddenly remembered his bare hands. "Do you have weapons?"

A joyous laugh. "Yes."

And then there was no more time to talk. The slavering, blank-eyed and ferociously hungry creatures who were Lijuan's reborn boiled out of the woods around them.

15

Naasir drew deep on the primal heart of his nature. His claws released and his canines elongated, his vision a knife blade through the dark and his sense of smell acute. All trappings of civilization gone, he wanted to turn and nuzzle at the neck of the woman who smelled like his mate, but that had to wait.

First, he had to kill the foul creatures howling toward them.

They were shambling and laughingly slow in comparison to his speed, but their infectiousness made them a threat against which he couldn't risk using his teeth. From all evidence to date, it appeared the reborn needed to kill their victim for that victim to become reborn, but Naasir wasn't going to take the risk that the creatures hadn't mutated and become strong enough to infect living flesh.

His teeth might be out, but he utilized his claws like blades, slicing and ripping and tearing. At his back, he could feel Andromeda moving with a fighter's grace, her sword slicing through the air on a deadly whistle of sound.

Heads rolled to the leaf-strewn earth around him.

"Naasir?"

He growled in answer at the concern in her tone. He couldn't speak quickly when living in this skin that was another aspect of his nature, but he was pleased she was thinking about him.

A clean slice of sound as her sword moved again, blood spraying the air.

He clenched his teeth against the putrid smell and reached out to rip a reborn's head from its shoulders. That emptied more blood around them, splattering him, but it was worth it to get rid of the tainted creatures. Kicking out with clawed feet, he disemboweled one while decapitating another. He didn't like to cause the reborn unnecessary pain—Lijuan had likely used innocent villagers as her fodder—but he couldn't rip off two heads at once.

Behind him, he could hear Andromeda breathing hard. She leaned against him. "Are they all dead?"

He took care of the one he'd disemboweled and thought hard about the words he'd been taught as a child after Raphael carried him to the Refuge. "Yes." It came out a growl so deep, he knew he didn't sound human.

Shifting to face Andromeda, he gripped her jaw with a clawed and bloody hand. He turned her head—gently—to one side then the other before checking her neck and body. Her wings were bloodied, but it was from spray. "You're not hurt," he got out just as part of him realized he'd probably scared her.

Women didn't like his claws, didn't like the way his eyes glowed after a hunt.

Andromeda pushed off his hand and grabbed his jaw. He was so surprised he let her pull him forward and turn his face this way and that. Releasing him, she walked around to his back and pushed up his T-shirt, then came around to do the same to the blood-soaked front.

"You're not hurt either." She looked down at his feet. "Did you get cut or bitten there?"

He snorted at the ridiculousness of her question. Dropping her hand from his T-shirt, she scowled at him. "Are those things all dead or do you think we'll run into more?"

Thinking about it, about words and how they worked, he said, "They would've come toward the scent of blood."

"Good." She knelt down to look at Suyin. "Can you carry her the whole way?"

"Yes." It would slow them down, but he didn't leave helpless people behind to be eaten by monsters or imprisoned by Lijuan.

Andromeda rose to her feet as Naasir bent to pick Suyin up with an effortlessness that betrayed his strength. He was splattered with blood, his silver hair streaked with it. She wanted to scrub it all away; Naasir was as real and honest as the reborn were unnatural abominations.

At least the rain washed off the worst of it as they walked.

"Why did you decide to study the Sleeping archangels?" Naasir asked some time later.

She noted that his voice was less growly now—she liked it either way. The only voice she didn't like was the cold, cultured tone he'd used when she'd first made him angry. "I'm just fascinated by the idea of all these powerful beings resting in hidden places on and in the earth."

"How many?"

"No one knows. The Ancestors are stories we tell children, but there are more credible legends of Ancients who've Slept so long that they, too, have become myth." She bit her lip and admitted her secret wish. "Jessamy says Alexander could sometimes be coaxed to speak of times of myth. They are his memories. With him and Caliane both in the world, we could find out so much."

"Caliane speaks to you?"

"No—to Jessamy. Even then it's not often, but Jessamy visited her soon after you left Amanat; she said Caliane was most gracious and generous." Andromeda knew the Historian, her wing twisted and unable to take her aloft, remained highly conscious of not being glimpsed by ordinary mortals, for angelkind could not be seen to be weak in such a way, but that wasn't an issue in Amanat.

When Jessamy wanted to view things in more populated environs, she skimmed the landscape in a light plane or in a helicopter modified to fit angelic wings while hiding the occupants from view. Usually the occupant was a single slender angel. Jessamy had quietly learned to operate both those vehicles.

Andromeda saw in Jessamy's determination a woman who was her hero. The other angel had survived thousands of years before inventors gave her a way to take to the skies on her own. Andromeda could survive five hundred years in a court devoid of hope.

"According to Caliane," she said, setting aside the inevitable for this night, "counting Alexander, there are seven archangels who Sleep."

"What if they all wake up at once?"

"It would be catastrophic." Archangels couldn't be in close proximity for long periods without a dangerous rise in their aggression. Ten was the perfect number spread out across the world. One or two more could be accommodated, but after that . . . "We'd end up with back-to-back wars until the balance was restored."

"Natural law," Naasir said bluntly. "Nature will always seek to maintain balance."

"Yes." She checked on Suyin again, shook her head when Naasir looked at her. "No improvement."

Face set in harsh lines, Naasir kept on walking.

"I don't only study Sleeping archangels," Andromeda said in an effort to keep their minds off the bleak situation. "If you promise not to laugh, I'll tell you about my other studies."

Open curiosity. "Tell me."

"Promise you won't laugh first."

Lips curving, Naasir snapped his teeth playfully at her. "How can you ask me to make the promise after that?"

She glared because he'd made her jump again, but told him. "I study creatures," she said, waiting for the condescending amusement she saw so often on the faces of her colleagues. "Like shape-shifters," she continued when he just listened, "mermen and mermaids, griffins, chimera, walkers . . . things like that."

"Why study the impossible?"

"Because the stories must've begun *somewhere*. And . . . I like to think there remain mysteries in the world."

"I think mermen and mermaids make sense."

"You do?" She narrowed her eyes but he didn't look like he was making fun of her. "Why?"

"The world is covered in water. Why shouldn't a species have evolved to live in that water?" A silver-eyed glance. "You should ask the Primary. Maybe the Legion are the truth behind the legend. They did live an eon in the deep."

The hairs rose on her arms. "I've been desperate to speak to them," she whispered, her historian's heart overflowing. "I know Jessamy's had some contact with the Primary, but I didn't want to ask for his time for my little subspecialty."

"I'll introduce you when you're ready," Naasir said. "I'll even sneak you into their new green home."

Andromeda almost danced on the spot, forgetting for a moment that she wouldn't have the freedom to do such things soon. "What about griffins?"

He took time to think before speaking. "I think the stories must come from large birds of prey in primordial times."

"That's my theory, too." Childishly happy to discover that his mind was so open, she said, "Skinwalkers?"

"No. But, I knew a medicine man once who walked with a spirit guide. He understood the land and all its creatures better than anyone I've ever since met." His tone held unvarnished respect. "Mortals die too quickly. The medicine man was wiser than many an immortal, but he was gone almost before I knew him."

"You miss him," Andromeda said softly.

"He was my friend."

Her throat grew thick. "Will you tell me about him?"

"Yes, later." A curl of his lip over his fangs. "My friend was a man who lived on the plains under an open sky. He does not belong in this forest tainted with reborn. What other creatures are on your list?"

"Chupacabra."

"I hope it exists. It has the best name."

Andromeda giggled. "Chimera?"

"A snake-tailed animal with a lion's body and a goat's head attached to its spine?" He snorted. "His goat head would unbalance him before he ever took a step, and he'd immediately get eaten by something bigger. And wouldn't the lion head constantly be trying to eat the goat head?"

Andromeda had to agree, fascinating though such a creature might've been. "I never could figure out how that would work." She tapped her chin. "But what a strange thing for people to imagine. Just like the karakasa-obake."

"I don't know that one."

So, as the rain tapered off into a fine mist, she told him

about the talking umbrella with one eye and one leg, and they kept on walking.

Naasir was having fun talking with Andromeda, playing with her—though she didn't know it yet—when he smelled black lightning. A shadow passed overhead and then a piece of the night was separating out to land in front of them. Taking in their bloodied state, Jason said, "You eradicated the remnants of the nest."

"Yes."

Jason walked forward. "Suyin."

Naasir was unsurprised the spymaster knew the identity of the woman in his hold; as far as Naasir could work out, Jason knew everything. "She needs to go to Keir. Xi ordered one of her wings be excised, the other I had to break."

Holding out his arms, Jason said, "I'll take her. With her wing strapped down, she's easy enough cargo—I'll go to Amanat and ask Keir to travel there." He looked to Andromeda. "You'll have to stay grounded. You can't fly high enough to avoid the squadrons, but Naasir can get you out."

"Understood." She touched her hand gently to Suyin's shoulder. "Please take care of her. She's been trapped a long time."

"I will," the spymaster said, holding Suyin with arms Naasir knew wouldn't permit her to fall.

"Stay safe." Stepping back on those words, Jason flared out his wings and made a flawless vertical takeoff. He was lost in the night within three wingbeats. Naasir knew no one would ever spot him.

"Incredible," Andromeda breathed, her head turned upward.

Naasir scowled. "Jason doesn't have claws." He showed her his.

Andromeda looked at the claws, then at him, a slow smile lighting up her eyes. "Those are very sharp. Why didn't you cut me when you grabbed me?"

"I didn't want to cut you." He growled at the question that shouldn't have been asked.

"We need to find some water," said the woman who was acting and sounding more and more like his mate. "I hate being dirty and bloody."

"The water here isn't good. Tainted."

She made a face. "Then let's leave."

Deciding no further conversation was needed, Naasir began to lead them out of the forest. Squadrons flew overhead, but none landed. Naasir thought they'd dismissed him—if they even knew his identity yet. And they clearly believed Andromeda was in the sky. Stupid.

She kept up with the pace he set for the next three hours. It was slow for him, but he knew he was pushing her—angels weren't meant to cover this much ground on foot. Their power was in the air. On the ground, their wings became an extra weight that created considerable drag.

Andromeda was also wearing flimsy slippers that tore halfway through.

"It's surface pain," she said to him when he stopped to check her feet. "The cuts will heal when we stop."

Naasir didn't like seeing her feet bruised and bloody, but he knew she was tough, would make it. Still, he took care to choose a path with few rocks and stones. Finally out of the formerly reborn-infested forest, he led her to a valley between two mountains. It took another hour for him to locate a spring-fed pond, but the deep water within was crystal clear and icy cold under the now-rainless night sky.

"Bathe," he said to her, taking in the exhaustion she was trying to hide but that had made her wings begin to droop. "We can't be out in the open at dawn."

Andromeda placed her sword carefully on the grass. "Turn your back."

"I want to be clean, too." The scent of the reborn was ugly.

"I'll watch for threats while you bathe if you do the same for me." She folded her arms and stood in place. "I'm not stripping off unless you turn your back."

He bared his teeth at her, but did as she asked. Dmitri had taught him that he must never take what a woman didn't want to give.

Do not steal what only has value if freely given.

Naasir had needed to hear that. He wasn't a bad person inside, but though he could put on a cultured skin that fooled people, inside, he sometimes still didn't know how to behave. When he'd been younger and first starting to feel the urge to rut with females—and before he'd grown up to the point where many of the opposite sex found him irresistible—he'd tried to court girls by bringing them meat and shiny things.

It turned out he'd scared them.

"Most women and girls," Dmitri had told him, "don't know what to do when a man drops a hunk of raw meat in their hands."

He'd learned that lesson after the girls screamed, dropping perfectly good meat he'd spent time hunting and skinning. When he'd come back with the shiny things, they'd looked at him with huge eyes and he'd smelled fear-stink. It had angered him and confused him and so he'd gone back to Dmitri.

"I'm not going to hurt them."

"Unfortunately, they see you as a threat now. Start with the shiny things next time and skip the meat. If you smell fear on a woman, back off and don't return."

Dmitri's advice had worked. Some women liked the shiny things and they liked to be naked with him, but then he'd scared them in bed. Apparently, biting wasn't always allowed, and pounding into a woman's wetness wasn't always acceptable. Those women had pushed him off and screamed that he should be "gentle" and "courteous" and not "a feral beast." Irritated, he'd found others who didn't mind if he pounded or bit.

Today, many women said he was a good lover. What they didn't know was that ever since he'd realized what was and wasn't acceptable, he no longer unleashed his full desire, even with the women who didn't mind if he was rough: they couldn't take it. And with Andromeda . . . he was so deeply sexually hungry that he wanted to turn around and pounce on her, do *all* the sexual things he'd never before permitted himself.

A splash sounded behind him, accompanied by a startled little squeak-scream.

Grinning, he turned around and went to crouch at the water's edge.

16

"Hey!" Andromeda splashed water at him. "You're supposed to keep your back turned."

"I won't look under the water," he promised her as he got up to prowl along the edge of the pond. "Are you cold?"

Her teeth clattered as she said, "Fr-freezing. But the b-blood. Want it off. Rain wasn't enough."

Finding what he needed, he tore up a clump and went back to her. "Come here and I'll wash your hair."

Giving him a suspicious look, she nonetheless came over so that her back was braced against the edge. He knelt behind her and tapped her shoulder with a single claw. "Here. This grass will help you be clean." The smell was sharp, lemony.

"Oh!" She looked up and smiled at him and he felt good.

Crushing the grass he still held, he retracted his claws, then unraveled her braid and used the grass like a soap. He did it quickly because she was shivering so hard her bones were almost clattering against one another. "Angels are built for cold." For the icy places high above the earth.

"Just because we can stand it doesn't mean we all like it," she said, sounding grumpy.

"Go under and rinse your hair."

Taking a deep breath, she went under and stayed under for long enough to come back up with sleek, shining hair. "I hate the cold. I hate the cold. I hate the cold."

He looked around at the clothes she'd taken off. "Your clothes are all bloody." And there was nowhere for him to steal her more.

"Let's wash them. I don't mind wearing wet clothes. The reborn stink is horrible."

He found more of the lemony grass and mashed it up with her tunic before throwing it to her so she could wash it. He did the same with her pants and with the tiny panties that didn't smell like reborn, but like her. Warm and musky and feminine and making him want to lick her.

"Take off your T-shirt and I'll do that, too," she said as she rinsed out the clothes.

Ripping it off, he handed it to her while taking her wet things and throwing them over the branches of the trees around them. Then, deciding there was no reason to keep on his pants, he began to strip them off. It was as he went to empty his pockets that he realized his phone was gone, likely having fallen out during the fight with the reborn.

His family would worry if he didn't make contact; he'd do so at the first opportunity.

"Naasir!"

"Close your eyes." He growled without really meaning it. "There are no threats here and I want to be clean."

Her wings faced him as she said, "Yes, I'm sorry. I shouldn't have made you wait so long."

Leaving his pants on the bank with a hunk of the grass, he dove naked into the pond. The icy temperature made him grit his teeth, but he loved being in water itself, loved the cool slide of it against his skin. Breaking the surface, he pushed back his hair and saw Andromeda's eyes on him. He grinned and swam over to her. "You're looking."

"I can't see in the dark." She tried to frown at him, but he could smell the heat on her skin, as if her blood had rushed to it. "Where are your pants?"

"On the bank," he said lazily, stealing some of the grass she was holding so he could scrub off the reborn stink.

"Turn around."

When he obeyed, she rewarded him by working the crushed grass through his hair. He leaned back, a deep sound rumbling in his chest. He felt her pause, but she started again a heartbeat later, her strong, clever fingers massaging his scalp. When she moved her hands to rub the grass over his shoulders and back, he felt his already-hard cock throb.

It was a good thing she couldn't see in the dark or she'd probably leave.

He didn't want her to leave; he wanted to play with her.

"Down." She pushed at his shoulders.

Going under, he washed out the grass from his hair. This time when he came back up, she was paddling over to grab his pants so she could wash them out. Her wings were spread out on the water, the blood having sluiced off, and he really, really, *really* wanted to touch. Sidling closer, he ran one hand over her primaries.

She jerked and shot him a look over her shoulder. "You know that's bad behavior."

Heading to the bank, he reached up and grabbing his wet but clean T-shirt, threw it at a tree. It hooked on a branch and opened out. The night air would dry it a little at least. "I'm often bad," he said honestly. "I like your wings."

Instead of continuing on the topic, her skin suddenly flushed red hot. "Um, here are your pants. I rinsed them out."

"Thank you." He knew it was polite to say that when someone did a nice thing for you. "Why are you red?"

She swam away instead of answering. Throwing his jeans toward a tree and managing to get them hanging over a branch, he swam after her, his pulse racing. Was she playing with him? But when he came up beside her after having dived under the water, she gasped. "You said you wouldn't look!"

"I didn't. I closed my eyes." It had been tempting to break his promise, but promises were to be kept. It was one of the first things Dmitri had taught him—by keeping his own promises.

"I'll bring you the cured meat you want when I return."

"Promise?"

"Yes."

Dmitri had been gone a long time in the child's mind—it must've been three months at least. Naasir hadn't forgotten the promise, but he hadn't really expected Dmitri to remember.

He'd just been excited at the return of the man he saw as his father.

"Dmitri!" He pelted out the door, escaping the hapless vampire set to watch over him. "Dmitri! Dmitri!"

Strong arms grabbing him tight and lifting him off the ground, Dmitri's dark eyes sad even though his mouth smiled. Naasir didn't know why Dmitri was sad but he'd seen the way Dmitri's eyes began to warm after they were together for a while, so he knew he wasn't what made Dmitri sad.

"Have you been behaving, Naasir?"

Naasir ducked his head. "No." He'd eaten the school's pet bunny. He hadn't meant to—but it was right there in front of him and he'd been so hungry. "I'm in big trouble."

"Ah." Deep male laughter that made him look up and bare his teeth in a feral smile because he could see Dmitri wasn't angry. "You can tell me about it while you eat this."

Naasir took the package and tore it open to find the gift for which he'd asked. "You remembered!"

Sadness in his eyes again, Dmitri ruffled his hair. "A man keeps his promises, Naasir."

"Naasir?"

He shook off the memory of childhood to hold Andromeda's pretty, sparkly gaze. "I didn't look," he repeated. "If I look, it'll be because you invite me."

Cheeks hot, she smiled at him. "Want to race?"

"I'll beat you," he warned. "Your wings will slow you down."

"Give me a head start to make it competitive. You don't start until I'm halfway across."

Delighted at the idea of a private game with her, he nodded. "Okay." Elena had told him cheating was allowed when one party was weaker than the other in some way. As when they'd sparred, Andromeda was cheating, but it was the good kind of cheating. It meant they could play together.

When Andromeda struck out for the opposite end of the pond, he saw she was more graceful and faster than he'd expected. His mate had been keeping more secrets. Laughing inside at her trickiness, he waited until she was at the halfway point, then began to slice through the water. He'd been born knowing how to swim.

Having reached Andromeda, he could've overtaken her at

any point, but he did something sneaky. He lowered his speed as if tired, so he could swim with her. And when they reached the end of the pond, he let her lunge out and grab the bank first. "I win!" she said, her whole face alight. "You owe me a forfeit."

"What do you want?" he asked, bracing his arms on the bank as she did the same beside him. "I have a treasure of shiny things."

"Really?" Her eyes widened but she shook her head. "I don't want a shiny thing this time—maybe next time I win."

Naasir liked the idea of more games.

"I want you to do something for me," she said.

"What?" He moved surreptitiously closer, so that her wing brushed his arm.

"Go with me to a dinner held by my parents."

Naasir blinked. Women liked to rut with him, but he'd never been invited home for dinner, and since Andromeda didn't want to lie with him, he didn't understand her request. Unless . . . "Do you want to shock your parents?" Naasir was different and unique. Many in the world wanted him for his skills, but he was also deeply *other*.

He accepted himself. His mate would have to accept him, too, not treat him as a freak.

Andromeda laughed as if he'd told a great joke.

Scowling, he began to get out of the water.

Seeing the water sluicing off Naasir's muscular body, Andromeda lost her mind for a second. Only when the upper curve of his buttocks was exposed did she squeak, and, placing a hand on the taut strength of his arm, hauled him back down. "You're naked!" she reminded him.

He shrugged, looking at her with silver eyes that glowed white-hot. "I don't care."

"Well, I do." Her heart was still racing at the sight of him. He was built like the most beautiful statue she'd ever seen, only he was flesh and blood.

"I'm cold. I want to be out."

She'd forgotten the cold, she'd been having so much fun with him. "Oh." Disappointment a lead weight in her stomach, she closed her eyes. "You can get out."

He didn't move. "Why did you laugh?"

"What?" Her eyes flicked open at his harsh tone.

Seeing the anger he made no effort to hide, she belatedly realized he'd taken her laughter in the wrong way. "My parents are incapable of being shocked," she admitted with a shrug that hid the echoes of childhood hurt. "Ever."

Expression altering to disbelieving fascination, Naasir leaned in close. "Even by me?"

"Even by you," she assured him. "If there is a debauched thing on this earth, they've indulged in it." Sex, brutal violence, rare narcotic substances, that was Lailah and Cato's way of life, their compulsive desire to do more, *feel* more, endless. "They'll probably proposition you."

Frown lines on his forehead. "But I would be with you."

"They have no boundaries." She thought of the young angel with whom she'd been in puppy love, of how she'd walked into the great living room one day to find him and her mother naked and in the midst of copulating. Her father had been sitting in an armchair watching while a male vampire sucked on his erect penis.

Her gorge rising, Andromeda had to go under the water to wash off the memory. Some things no child should ever have to see. The awful thing was that the nauseating incident had been far from the first or the only one. Andromeda had too many such images stored in her mind, images that she resolutely refused to think about, but that would not fade.

Taking position beside Naasir again after wiping the water off her face with one hand, she went too close. So close that her arm pressed into his and her wing touched his back . . . but he didn't push her away, instead looking at her with those wild eyes that were suddenly painfully incisive.

"I will not rut with your parents." A solemn promise. "That would hurt you and I will not hurt you."

Her eyes stung, her throat thick. She couldn't speak for a long time. When she did, her voice came out husky. "The dinner is technically in my honor. It's mandatory for those of my blood to return home on our four-hundredth birthday."

She knew she should tell him she wouldn't leave again for five hundred years, but the words stuck in her chest, hard and taunting. "I thought you'd make the dinner more fun."

Naasir's cheeks creased, his eyes glinting. "We'll have fun," he promised. "I'll bring your parents a present."

Her instincts shouted an alert. "Ah, Naasir—"

Laughing at her dubious tone, he pulled himself up and out of the water without warning. She saw the hard curve of his buttocks, the strong muscle of his thighs, the sleek strength of him as he stood on the bank and shook himself dry like a big cat. His silver hair glittered even in the darkness.

He began to turn toward her.

Skin so hot it seared her from the inside out, she forced herself to shut her eyes and go under the icy water, staying there until she was no longer in danger of combusting. When she came back up, she saw Naasir had pulled on his wet pants. He didn't look happy about it, though. Nostrils flaring, he picked up a couple of things he must've left on the ground and slid them back into his pockets, then examined his T-shirt and finally started to pull it on, no doubt figuring it'd dry faster on his body.

"I won't look," he told her, keeping his eyes scrupulously on the trees in front of him.

Trusting him, she got out of the water and found her things. She stared at her panties, belatedly realizing he must've handled them earlier. Also remembering that he'd had no underwear. Skin hot again and breasts aching, she pulled on her heavily damp tunic. It hit her several inches below her butt, saving her modesty.

"I don't want to wear the rest," she admitted aloud.

Naasir glanced over, taking her words as permission. "Don't. I'll carry your things since you have the sword, and we can dry them in the sun after dawn."

"Do you really want to wear your T-shirt?"

It was as if he'd just been waiting for her words. Stripping off the T-shirt to reveal a chest that threatened to make her a breaker of vows, he watched as she, blush furious, tied her pants and panties, as well as his T-shirt, into a small bundle. Taking it, he said, "You must wear the slippers. They protect your feet at least a little."

Nodding, she slipped her feet into them; they were falling apart, but as Naasir had said, they did provide a faint measure of protection for her tender and bruised feet. As they began to move again, air kissed her most private places, her nipples rubbing against wet silk. She felt scandalous and wild and adventurous.

Beside her, Naasir prowled along at what was clearly a lazy pace for him. They didn't speak as the world turned from black to gray. Wet and half-naked . . . and she'd never been as comfortable with someone in her entire life.

Until he glanced over and reached out a hand to bounce the tight spirals of her hair on his palm. "I like this better than your braid."

Her stomach dropped . . . but then she realized it no longer mattered if someone saw her and was immediately reminded of Lailah, daughter of Charisemnon; her mother had the same distinctive gold-streaked brown curls and facial bones. Though instead of Andromeda's freckles, Lailah had smooth, silken skin perhaps two shades darker than Andromeda's.

Lailah's curls also never frizzed like her daughter's, were always glossy and perfect.

Those differences made Lailah a beauty many a man had coveted, Andromeda the far more ordinary child. One who'd known from childhood that people looked at her and saw an inferior imitation of the original. "Really?" she whispered, wondering if Naasir would compare them, too. "My hair is totally out of control."

A grin from the wild creature next to her.

The tight band easing from around her chest, she laughed and they continued on.

"We stop here," Naasir said as dawn's fingers stroked the horizon. "There's too much activity in the sky. Villagers will also have been alerted to be on the lookout."

"We'll travel only at night?"

A nod. "I have an advantage at night and they won't expect a scholar to seek the darkness."

"I'm tired, too," she admitted, Galen and Dahariel both having taught her to be honest with any partner in battle—and this was a kind of battle. "Being grounded and having to hold up my wings while walking for such long distances is straining my wing muscles."

Naasir went as if to reach out and ease her muscles, stopped halfway, obviously recalling the intimacy of such a touch. Brushing part of a wing was one thing—squeezing the arches and other muscles far, far different. "We'll rest," he said, then cocked his head. "Wait here. Don't get caught."

"I'll do my best," she said dryly, holding up the sword.

A sharp flash of teeth against that flawless, pettable skin, and he was gone, so adept at disappearing into the trees that she didn't see him vanish.

17

Raphael wasn't expecting to be called into a Cadre meeting anytime in the future, so when the call came—especially when it came from Titus—he knew it must be deadly serious. He cut an over-sea night-training drill short the instant Aodhan relayed the message, and headed to the Tower communications room.

Sirens rose up from the streets as he winged his way past lit-up high-rises, a yellow cab rear-ended another, and tugs on the Hudson sounded warning horns. All familiar sights and sounds, his city back in one piece.

That didn't mean the war had been won.

Elena, he said after landing on the Tower roof, aware she was in the Tower helping young Izak with his physical therapy. *I'm about to speak with the Cadre.* He folded in his wings and strode forward. *I want you to listen in.* Not only did Elena need to understand the political climate, his hunter had a sharp mind and an acute gaze.

On my way.

He didn't wait for her, but knew when she slipped into the room out of sight of the cameras that linked him to the others. He glimpsed the lightweight crossbow strapped to her thigh and the blades in her forearm sheaths before the screen in front of him split to display Favashi, Titus, Astaad, Elijah, Michaela, Neha, and Caliane.

Missing were Lijuan and Charisemnon.

Lijuan's absence was no surprise, but since Raphael's ascension, Charisemnon hadn't missed a meeting regardless of wars and battles. It gave credence to the theory that the Archangel of Northern Africa had been ravaged by the very disease he'd created—he wouldn't appear in public again until he was in full health.

"Titus," Neha said, her hair swept off her face into a soft bun at her nape, and her body clad in a sari of gold-shot green silk. "What is the emergency?"

When the archangel who controlled the southern half of the African continent began to speak, his voice wasn't the tempered quiet he usually used in meetings. It was a booming bass that vibrated with raw anger. "One of my scouts has long been a friend of Jariel and was invited to his home for a stay. He arrived to find Jariel's people massacred, and Jariel's head placed in the center of the entranceway, a pile of ash the only evidence of what may have happened to his body."

Onyx eyes glittering and muscles bulging under the jet of his skin, Titus slammed down a glass jar. It cracked to spill black ash over the wooden surface on which the Archangel of Southern Africa had slammed it. "We all know ordinary fire does not create a neat pile of ash in a defined area. It also does not destroy the brain while leaving the rest of the head untouched."

A stunned silence.

Archangel?

Jariel was believed to be on the cusp of becoming an archangel, Raphael told his consort. *Perhaps in the next two decades.*

"You're certain?" Astaad asked Titus, his black goatee neat against the sunless white of his skin. "We must be certain."

Titus's nostrils flared. "My man will send images, but I am dead certain. From the condition of the other remains, it was done at least a week ago, more likely ten days."

Not long before Andromeda's abduction, Elena said, her mind clearly walking the same path as his. *Coincidence?*

I don't believe in such a lethal coincidence.

Someone sucked in a breath as the images Titus had promised began to scroll across their screens. Jariel's decaying head looked at them with sightless eyes filmed over with white. Images of the rest of his home showed dead vampiric retainers and broken angels with crumpled wings. All killed in ways that were final even for those seen as immortal by the humans.

It was Michaela who said it, the piercing green of her eyes focused on the ash. "There is only one way to confirm."

Titus silently scooped up the black ash and held it close to the camera on his end. Ash created by a fire, and ash created by an archangelic ability might appear identical to the naked eye, but look closely enough at the latter and sparks of power lingered within it for up to a month afterward.

"So." Neha's voice was a blade, the Archangel of India's view on the massacre unmistakable. "It was one of the Cadre."

They were the only beings on the planet who could incinerate with that much power. It didn't even necessarily require angelfire, not if the archangel was close to the target—a simple discharge of concentrated archangelic power would equal the same end.

"Why?" Astaad shook his head, clearly deeply disturbed. "He wasn't Cadre yet, had no say in our politics."

Raphael thought again of the scholar's abduction and of Lijuan's plans for Alexander. "Perhaps someone decided to get rid of a competitor before he reached maturity," he said, careful not to give away too much—alliances were fluid things and someone in this meeting could well have formed one with Lijuan.

"If that's the case," Neha said in a silky whisper that dripped venom, "you had better watch your Bluebell to make sure his head remains attached to his body."

"I'll take that under advisement," he said in a bland tone that betrayed nothing.

Elijah stirred, stroking his hand over a small puma—perhaps a cub—who'd just climbed up to settle on his desk. "Only one of us is capable of such a heinous act."

"You speak too soon, Elijah," Favashi said in her soft, steely tone. "Any one of us could be taking advantage of Lijuan's notoriety to make a power play." She locked gazes with Michaela, who only smiled coldly. "Any one of us."

They spoke for another ten minutes without coming to a consensus on the identity of the perpetrator. They did however make the decision to warn seven other angels who were the most powerful in the world once you took the Cadre out of the equation. Illium wasn't on that list . . . but he should've been. Despite Neha's acerbic comment, the others hadn't yet realized the intensity of the spike in his power levels.

Switching off the connection after spending an extra few minutes in conversation with his mother, Raphael turned to Elena. She walked over to join him, the near-white of her hair pulled back into a ponytail and a blade moving through her fingers as she stared at the image he'd frozen on the screens— that of the spark-filled black ash in Titus's hand.

"Favashi is right," she said, slipping away the blade. "It could've been any of you, though personally I'd eliminate you from the suspect list." Rising on tiptoe, she claimed a kiss that poured mortal warmth through him, melting the ice that had formed over the course of the meeting. "I'd also eliminate Caliane because your mom just wants to be left alone with her people."

Raphael cupped her jaw, running his thumb over her cheekbone. "Elijah and I have been in nearly daily contact of late." The two of them had decided to work together to defend this region against any further attacks. "Quite aside from the fact that my instincts say he is too honorable for such a cowardly act, I know he never left his territory."

Stepping closer, Elena put one hand on his chest. "I don't see Astaad and Neha doing this either."

"Astaad prefers to stay out of conflict when he can, so I agree." The Archangel of the Pacific Isles had only joined the coalition against Lijuan when the Archangel of China dared fly her reborn over his territory. "As for Neha . . . yes, she is a queen. She wouldn't consider it honorable to ambush a weaker, younger angel in his home."

"Michaela is looking surprisingly normal." Elena's eyes narrowed. "I expected her to have grown horns or something, the way she's kept her head down." She frowned. "Only . . ." Breaking contact, she turned to the main screen. "Does this thing record?"

"Of course." He showed her how to bring up the recording. "You want Michaela?"

"Yes." She watched the loop two times. "*Shit*." It came out almost soundless. "She's got the same fragile thing going on that Beth had when she was pregnant."

Since Elena's sister was terrified of him, Raphael had spent little time with her, but he had seen other pregnant mortals and immortals in his lifetime. And now that Elena had pointed it out, he noted the new delicacy of Michaela's skin—and the fact that though she was a woman who used her body as a weapon, she'd shown none of it today, her image cut off below the shoulders.

"Michaela may actually be with child," he said slowly.

"Holy hell." Elena whistled. "Do you think she was just laying the groundwork when she lied to us? So no one would believe it when it happened?"

Raphael shook his head. "Immortal pregnancies are too rare to be predicted with any accuracy. There is a second possibility." He thought of how he'd found a wounded Michaela with a glowing red fireball in the bloody cavity where her heart should've been. "Whatever it is that Uram did to her, it may be starting to show on the surface."

"Can we confirm either way?" Elena shook her head almost before the words were out. "If she's hiding because she's vulnerable, let's leave her be." His consort's throat moved in a convulsive movement. "I'll never forget how she looked that night in the Refuge when Sam was taken. I've always wondered if it was losing a child that made her so mercenary and heartless."

Raphael's heart wasn't as soft as his consort's, and he didn't think motherhood had or would change Michaela, but if she was in fact with child, he hoped the infant would escape being warped by Uram's poison. "If she is pregnant, it may be another Cascade event," he said, his mind on Illium's struggle to hold the deadly levels of power building up in his body.

Elena blew out a breath and leaned against him. "Have you heard from Jason or Naasir?"

Spreading his wing to slide over hers, Raphael nodded. "Jason is safely out of Lijuan's territory and is carrying a wounded hostage." A woman who'd been thought long dead. "No word from Naasir and the scholar."

Elena's hand curled around his. "It's Naasir. He can get out of anything." Fierce belief, but below it was a dark worry.

Thinking of the black ash in Titus's hand, Raphael knew she was right to worry. Naasir was strong and fast and highly intelligent, but he was currently trapped in the heart of enemy territory, and that enemy did not fight according to any known rules of war.

18

Naasir followed the faint smell of mortal food to a tiny settlement on a riverbank. Only three houses, all spaced generously apart, two with small fishing boats moored to rickety docks in front of the houses.

The farthest house had smoke coming out of the chimney and a neatly tended garden. That house was the source of the cooking and food smells. An old man and woman sat eating from small bowls on the porch of the house next to it. Both were wrinkled like walnuts and appeared as if they'd laughed for a lifetime.

Naasir smiled at seeing them. He would like to laugh a lifetime with his mate.

Turning his attention to the third house, he drew in a breath, caught no fresh scents.

Prowling around the backs of the houses, out of sight of the mortals, he listened at the door of the third house and heard only silence. No breathing within, no heartbeats. When he turned the handle, it opened without resistance. Walking in, he saw it was empty but clean. There was a bed and he found sheets in one cupboard, plates, cups, and utensils in another, but saw no signs of recent habitation. No food anywhere, no towels hung out, the fireplace neatly swept out and cold to the touch.

It was probably a hunting or fishing cottage, he thought, catching faint traces of old animal and fish blood on a table on the back porch when he ventured out again. The other two with their thriving gardens looked like permanent homes, but this one had an empty yard overgrown with grasses and weeds. A little more investigation and he found a small boat garaged neatly in a tin shed, as if its owner had put it away for the season.

Deciding it would be a safe enough hiding place since he'd hear anyone who attempted to come in, he prowled away as soundlessly as he'd arrived and made his way back to Andromeda. He couldn't see her at first, but he could scent her. Grinning because she was smart, he looked up and there she was, sitting on a branch. "I've found us a hide," he said.

She jumped off, using her wings to balance herself. "I might need some food," she said apologetically. "I'm burning more energy than I usually do, and I'm too young to go without food for long."

He'd already worked that out. If she didn't feed, she'd start to weaken, her body cannibalizing itself from the inside out. "I have a plan." He waved at her to follow him. "Be a shadow."

She was too noisy to be a shadow but it didn't matter. By the time they arrived, the two fishing boats were gone and all was quiet. He stealthily checked the houses to ensure no one had stayed behind—or had entered the empty house since his departure.

Only once he was certain all was clear did he take Andromeda to the house. "Stay here," he said, palming a small knife he'd earlier seen on the kitchen table. "I'll get food."

She shook her head. "We can't steal from these people—they look as if they have little enough as it is."

"I won't. Trust me."

A small nod. "I can see a fishing pole there. I might try with that while you're gone."

"No. You'll be too visible."

The skin around her mouth tightened, but she didn't argue. "Stay safe. I'll watch out for you."

Leaving her after doing another circuit to ensure no one else was around, he took off at high speed. It didn't take him long to get what he needed. It was only when he was at the door she'd opened that he realized he'd brought her meat. He'd been proud of being able to feed her, had forgotten he wasn't supposed to offer a woman meat.

Her eyes went to the rabbit he'd taken in the hunt. He'd been quick, merciful. He was always fast and he never hurt his prey. They fed him and for that, he was grateful. He was a predator. He had to eat. That was the natural order of the world. And he was careful never to take things of which there were a small number in the world. He didn't want them to disappear.

Today, however, he realized he should've tried fishing even if it was a far less efficient method of finding food—if fish could even be called food. Before he could speak and try to stop Andromeda from screaming, she said, "Oh, you caught something." A frown. "Do you think it's safe to light the fire in here? There doesn't seem to be any electricity."

Walking inside after her, he put his catch on the kitchen table. "There's no reason anyone should wonder about this cabin from the air," he said, treading carefully because he wasn't sure if Andromeda really wasn't angry he'd brought her meat. "The neighbors who know it's empty are gone."

"Great. I unearthed the firestarting tools." She laid the fire using the sticks and pieces of wood in a basket next to it, then started it with competent hands.

Since he'd already cleaned and prepared the results of his hunt before bringing it to her, all they had to do was put the meat to roast on the spit already set up in the fireplace. Naasir sighed at seeing perfectly good meat get seared, but he didn't say anything. He knew Andromeda wouldn't want to eat raw meat.

After placing their clothes near the fireplace so they'd dry, she sat and turned the spit as needed. "You were really quick."

"I didn't have to go far." He'd scented the existence of prey on his first sortie. "I took the old one in the group, the one whose time had come." Never did he take the young ones, for that would destroy the ecosystem of which he was a part.

"My thanks to the hunter, and my thanks to the creature that gave up its life so we can live."

Naasir looked at her profile. "You are a scholar."

Somehow, she understood what he was asking. "I didn't grow up a scholar. My parents are based in an untamed part of Charisemnon's territory." When Naasir bared his teeth at the sound of her grandfather's name, she nodded, her next words blunt. "Yes, he is a disgusting excuse for an archangel."

The ugly emotion in Andromeda's tone had him growling. "Did he touch you when you were a cub?" Naasir knew of Charisemnon's appetites, that he took those not yet full-grown to his bed.

Andromeda shuddered. "No . . . but he looked at me in a way that made it feel as if I had spiders crawling over my skin." She shook herself, clearly throwing off the memory of the sensation. "My parents control a remote sector for him and it's a sprawling place full of creatures wild and free."

Her tone changed, her love for her distant homeland a second heartbeat. "I saw nature at its fiercest and most ruthless growing up. There are predators and there are prey. The lion runs the antelope to ground, and the cheetah hunts the gazelle. It is the natural order of things. It's only those who hunt without need of food that upset that order."

Feeling more comfortable as his pants started to steam from the heat, drying out fully at last, and his bare chest heated from the fire, Naasir stretched out his legs. "I'm glad you're not a vegetarian." He knew scholars who only ate leafy things, found them to be fascinating creatures. Who could live on only leafy things?

A soft laugh from the woman beside him, the one who smelled more delicious than the meat and who had beautifully uncontrollable hair he wanted to rub his face against. "Do you need blood?"

He thought about it. He'd eat some of the meat even if it was cooked, and he'd fed well during the journey to Lijuan's stronghold. "No. Not yet." Looking at her, he allowed himself to turn his eyes to her pulse.

It jumped.

Forcing himself to look away when his cock started to swell and harden, he stared into the flames. "Not from you," he said, the words coming out rough; he wanted to pin her down and sink his fangs into her at the same time as his cock. "You need your strength. I'll find someone else."

She didn't say anything, but there was a new stiffness to her as they finished watching the meat cook. When it was done, they ate in silence. He gave her the best pieces but she still didn't talk to him as she had before. Unable to figure out what he'd done wrong, he decided to talk about something else.

"Did you take your vow because your parents can't control their need to rut?"

Her head jerked up. Going so pale that her freckles stood out stark against her skin, she finished the food on her plate and got up to wash it clean. Then she went to the bed she'd made up using sheets from the cupboard, and lay down.

Not wanting to hurt her by asking more questions, he finished his own food in silence before going to stand watch at the window so she could sleep in safety.

"It's part of it." A soft confession from the bed almost ten minutes later. "But it's not all of it."

He waited; he could be patient when it was needed. Sometimes, he didn't move for hours when hunting cunning prey.

Sitting up with her arms wrapped around raised knees, Andromeda met his eyes. "It's me," she said, her tone husky and one hand tight around the wrist of the other. "I have the same carnal drives as my mother."

"You want to rut with many people?" He tried not to growl those words, though they made him want to growl—he was going to keep his mate for himself. He'd satisfy her as many times as she wanted, but *no one* else would be touching her.

Andromeda swallowed. "I'm afraid that's exactly what I'll become if I give in to the need inside me."

Naasir struggled to understand. "Have you never lain with anyone?"

"No," Andromeda admitted, conscious he wouldn't understand her choice. He was a vibrant, rawly sexual creature. Being with him had made her own consciously dormant sexual instincts fight to awaken; she wanted to rub up against him, wanted to taste him and be tasted by him.

Frown turning into a scowl, Naasir came over to crouch down in front of her. She'd shifted position to sit with her legs over the edge of the bed, suddenly realized he'd be able to see straight between her thighs if she wasn't careful. Her panties were still near the fireplace, the thin fabric probably dry by now.

"Does it not hurt to be alone?" he asked her, his hair sliding to the side as he cocked his head in that way he had of doing. "I like being petted. Don't you need petting?"

His honesty demanded her own. "I've made myself not need it." It had been brutal when her natural inclination was to wallow in sensation. "It's why I first picked up the sword. To put my sexual energy into controlled violence." Rather than the sadistic kind practiced by her parents.

"Fighting *is* like rutting." Naasir's eyes gleamed. "Not the same, but it gets the blood pumping and it makes me ready."

When her eyes dropped instinctively, she had to force them back up. She had no business checking whether or not he was aroused. "Sexual pleasure is like a drug," she said to Naasir. "You become addicted to it until it takes over your life, until pleasure alone isn't enough and the search for novelty turns brutal. At least that's how it is with my family."

"Your parents rule a sector," Naasir pointed out. "They do other things."

"It's a far-off and not very important sector." Charisemnon might have deviant appetites, but he was still an archangel and no fool. He knew his daughter and her husband weren't capable of running a large sector, so had stuck them in a small, unimportant corner politically speaking.

"They also have two stewards who can run the territory without instruction, they've been doing it for so long." The twins had been there since long before either Andromeda's mother or father had even been born. "My parents are powerful enough to be dangerous when called upon to defend the territory, but otherwise . . ."

She gripped one of her hands with the other, squeezing tight to restrain the urge to reach out and play with the silken temptation of Naasir's hair. "They've been dissolute and jaded and sexually violent since they were young." She'd read stories of her parents' debauchery, their every move chronicled because of her mother's bloodline.

"The fact they can't control their urges makes them weak." Naasir's gaze was a lightning strike, as if he'd shatter light right through her, exposing all her secrets. "A woman who has fought her natural sensual instincts for hundreds of years is not weak."

Andromeda sucked in a breath, wanting to grab at his words and hoard them close. "It requires constant control."

A shrug. "I have to exercise the same not to act too inhuman."

"Don't," she found herself saying. "Don't act with me."

Snapping his teeth at her, he grinned at her little jump. "I thought you wanted me to act civilized."

"*Argh!* I said that *once* while I was mad." She pushed at the warm, bare skin of his shoulders when he laughed, wicked amusement in his eyes. "You make me want to act totally *un*civilized."

His eyes lit up. "Good." Rising to his feet, he said, "I must keep watch. Rest and think about choices."

She scowled at his back as he retook his position by the window. "Don't try to give me orders when we're not creeping about."

Glancing over his shoulder, he raised an eyebrow. "Sleep or you'll fall down when you lumber about. You haven't mastered creeping yet."

She threw a pillow at him.

Catching it, he laughed in unhidden delight, his claws apparent on the softness of the pillow. His unrepentant badness made her lips twitch as she fell back onto the bed and pulled up the sheet, programming her mind to wake in a few hours so Naasir, too, could rest. He was older and stronger than her, but he still needed rest. As he needed blood.

Her mood sank again as she thought of him feeding from another woman.

But that, too, was the natural order of things. Naasir was a sexual creature and women were drawn to him. There was no room in his life for a scholar who'd taken a vow of celibacy before she'd ever understood what it was to *need*, to so desperately want . . . to look into eyes of molten silver and see a future far more extraordinary than the one written in her blood.

Andromeda and Naasir left the cottage after nightfall, fully dressed in their dry clothes. Naasir had ordered her to cut up a sheet and use the strips to wrap up her feet, since her slippers had fallen apart during the final hours before dawn. She'd used the oldest sheet she could find, the one that looked as if it had been forgotten in the cupboard.

Rejuvenated by sleep and food, with her feet protected enough that stones didn't cut into her soles, she was able to trek for hours without flagging.

"Why did you rescue me?" she asked Naasir partway. "I gave Jessamy a copy of the details of my research for safe-keeping."

Silver eyes glinted at her. "Stop insulting me."

Scowling when he turned back around and kept on walking, she poked at his shoulder with the tip of her sword, being very careful not to break his gorgeous, strokable . . . pettable skin. "It was a perfectly reasonable question. I'm an apprentice, and I'm not part of any court." A lie, but it was a lie she'd chosen to live . . . would live for the days of freedom that remained.

"Jessamy belongs to no court and to every court and so do all who work for her." He snarled when she went to poke him again. "I'll bite you if you're not careful."

Thighs clenching, she tried to think cold, nonsensual thoughts. Except her discipline seemed to have deserted her. When she strode past him in an effort to outrun the desire crawling over her skin, he came up next to her, drew in a long, deep breath and smirked. She held up the sword before he could open his mouth. "Say a single word and I'll put this right through you."

"You'd hurt me?"

"You're a six-hundred-year-old vampire. You'd recover."

He flashed his fangs at her and they carried on walking. It took her what felt like an eon to get her body back under control, and even then, it was a shaky control at best. Every time she saw him move, every time his scent came to her nose, every time he said something in that low, growly voice that felt like a rough caress, the sensual part of her nature sat up in quivering attention.

She stepped up the pace, pushing herself to the edge.

Naasir spotted a vehicle three hours later, but there was no way her wings would fit in it, so they continued walking till dawn began to shimmer through the sky again. Hunkering down in the shadow of a mountain, they rested in turns while the sun burned overhead.

The search squadrons appeared to have turned back, but she and Naasir couldn't afford to lower their guard. Should they be spotted by villagers who reported it to their goddess, a citadel squadron would come at them from one side, while border squadrons would angle in from the other. They'd be caught in between with no way out.

Watching Naasir sleep while she sat guard, on watch for any other signs of life, Andromeda couldn't help herself. She bit her lower lip and reached out very, very, *very* carefully to touch his hair. It was cool silk and far softer than she'd imagined it might be. She wanted to—

He snapped up a hand to capture her wrist, his eyes still closed. "Andi, what are you doing?"

19

Andi?

It wasn't an angelic name, not at all . . . but she liked it. "Touching your hair," she admitted, since she'd been caught red-handed.

Yawning, he released her hand. "You can." Then he seemed to fall right back to sleep.

Not quite believing it, she reached out and wove her fingers through the lusciously soft strands. He didn't wake, didn't even stir, though she had the awareness that he was like a great big cat who slept with one eye figuratively open. He was even striped like a tiger.

What?

Blinking, she looked again at his arms and face. The illusion held. She glanced up, wondering if it was a particular combination of tree branches that was causing it, but saw nothing that could explain the shadowy pattern beneath the gold-stroked deep brown of his skin. "What are you?" she whispered, but he didn't wake this time—or if he heard her, he chose to keep his secrets.

She stroked his hair for a long time, her pleasure in the act bone-deep. It felt exactly like petting a wild animal who had decided to permit her close. He wasn't tame and anyone who made that mistake would regret it, but for now, he'd decided he liked her. She knew that would change the second she took up her enforced position in an enemy court, and that, too, was inevitable.

Her heart felt as if it was being crushed in a giant metal fist.

Naasir had to feed that night. Leaving Andromeda to wait in the thick stand of trees next to a small village, he walked in, found his prey, fed, and walked back out. The entire exercise took him six minutes at most, but even that felt too long. He knew Andromeda could defend herself, also knew that if he didn't feed, he'd no longer be able to protect her, but it still felt wrong to feed from another when she was in his life.

Andromeda wasn't where he'd left her when he returned. Not that it took him long to track her to a small stream nearby. Her body was stiff, pretty wings patterned like a bird's held off the ground. "Done?" she asked without turning around.

"Yes."

She fell in beside him to continue their journey, but he could feel the wrongness in the air. As he'd demonstrated to her, he could put on a civilized skin when necessary. Most of the women he'd taken to his bed had never once seen him in anything close to his real skin. They had seen only the cool, cultured avatar who made them shiver with a primal fear that heightened their sexual pleasure.

It was a game that wasn't a game but a kind of a lie, and it didn't come instinctively to him. He'd learned how to pull it off only after realizing women wouldn't otherwise allow him near their soft bodies and delicate skin.

Don't act with me.

Andromeda might jump when he playfully scared her, but she hadn't flinched once when it counted. She'd been happy he'd brought her meat, had let him touch her with his claws, hadn't looked at him with terrified abhorrence just because he wasn't like other men. No, she looked at him as if she wanted to pet him and bite him and play with him.

Except tonight. Tonight, she wouldn't look at him at all.

"I chose a man."

She stumbled over something in her path, righted herself. "Oh." A long pause before she said, "I didn't think you liked men that way." Her voice was tight, as if she wasn't breathing properly.

"Food is food." As long as it wasn't diseased like the blood that ran in the veins of Lijuan's reborn, it would keep him alive.

Andromeda shot him a knife-edged glance that made him happy his mate had claws—and angry she was using them on him when he hadn't done anything wrong. "I've heard the women in the Refuge talk about how sensual it is when you feed from them."

Naasir shrugged. "Cooperative food is better than noncooperative food." When he needed to hunt, he went after meat prey. For blood, he took no one who wasn't consenting. "But the Refuge food is too cooperative," he grumbled. "How much blood do they think I can drink?"

Mouth falling open, Andromeda shook her head. She'd braided her hair again so it was as restrained as possible, but her eyes sparkled with wildness. Then she began to laugh, clapping her hand over her mouth to stifle the sound. Fascinated, he just watched those bright, sparkling eyes. Every time she tried to speak, she started to laugh again, so he just let her until she'd tired herself out. And he enjoyed her pleasure.

"What's so funny?" he asked when she finally spluttered into giggles.

"All those women," she whispered, eyes crinkling up again. "They boast about how you feed from them, the implication being that you find each one deeply attractive—and you think of them as *food*!" She doubled over again, shoulders shaking as she tried futilely to stifle the sounds.

Not that it mattered; there was no one to hear but him.

Grinning at the wicked glee he'd glimpsed in her, he stroked his hand down the center of her wings in a petting gesture. "They have different-tasting blood," he told her. "I think it has to do with their diet. I like the variety. Like going to different restaurants."

She fell to the ground, she was laughing so hard by now. Tears leaked out of her eyes. "Stop it," she managed to say between her giggles before setting her sword on the grassy earth and clamping both hands over her mouth as she lay on her back.

Straddling his fierce, sparkling, delicious-smelling mate with his knees on either side of her thighs, he braced his body on his palms above her. "Shall I tell you a secret?"

Laughter still holding her captive, she shook her head, but he could tell she wanted to know.

He levered himself down until he was bare inches from the lush-lipped mouth over which she still had her hands. "If Dmitri hadn't taught me to be civilized," he whispered, "I'd probably have eaten some of the women by now."

When Andromeda's eyes went huge, he realized he'd made a mistake, shown her too much of his nature. About to push off her before she screamed or acted terrified because he wasn't sure he could handle the hurt, he was held in place by her grip on his T-shirt.

Hauling him down, she whispered, "Are you making fun?"

He knew he should lie, but he didn't want to be with anyone who expected him to hide himself. Janvier and Ashwini didn't hide themselves from each other. Honor knew all of Dmitri's secrets. "No," he said. "I'm fully capable of eating a person, but I'd have to hate them and be really hungry." He thought about telling her what he'd done to the angel who'd created him, decided to see how she took this first truth.

Tiny lines formed between her eyebrows. "Do you think of me as food?" It was a snarl.

"No." Muscles easing, he rubbed his nose over hers. "If I bite you, it'll be in play. And if I eat you up, it'll be because I have my tongue in your—"

She slammed her hand over his mouth.

Pulse racing, Andromeda looked into the eyes of the feral, beautiful creature who was shattering every barrier she'd created in an effort to live a life of honor and discipline where she didn't only use, but created and gave. He was so *pure*, with a core of primal honesty that drew her like a moth to a flame. She knew that she'd never again meet anyone like Naasir, not even should she live to be ten thousand years old.

Part of her wanted to accept his invitation, to be with him, to hoard the memories against what was to come. She was bound to serve in Charisemnon's court for five *hundred* years, and knowing her grandfather, those five hundred years would be one horror after another. Surely, whispered the desperation in her, surely she could have Naasir for just a little while?

And what happens when you join Charisemnon's court?

The cold reminder was a slap. The idea of Naasir hating her or himself after they'd been so painfully intimate, it made her feel as if she was spun glass that would break with a single wrong touch. "Remember my vow," she said after removing her hand from over his mouth, her voice husky with all the emotions she couldn't set free.

His expression turned icily serious without warning. "If you were mine, I wouldn't let you rut with others."

She didn't know if that was a threat or a promise.

Pushing off her, he rose to his feet before she could decide how to respond. A single tug when he offered her his hand and he pulled her to her feet. "Tell me about your stupid Grimoire book."

Stomach tight, she blew out a breath. "You can't find it." Her eyes burned because she *wanted* him to find it, even if it wouldn't change anything.

"I can find anything." His confidence was arrogant but in a way that made her want to kiss him. "How big is it? Where was it last seen?"

"That's just it," she confessed. "It hasn't been seen in the past hundred thousand years or more—before that, there are mentions of it in old stories that might as well be myths." That was the reason she'd chosen it as her escape key. To ensure the door would remain permanently locked.

Naasir scowled. "It's not a real thing?"

"No, it is." Just of incalculable age. "Caliane is actually responsible for the most reputable report of its existence. Long before she was an Ancient, she made a casual note of it in a letter to a friend." Somehow, that eons-old letter had survived and was kept in a special part of the Archives.

"Where did she see it?"

"In the house of an alchemist." At a time when even angels had believed in such things. "The alchemist is long dead, the city he lived in no longer exists, and scholars have spent thousands of years trying to track down the fabled Star Grimoire without success."

"Tell me all about it," he demanded again.

Stupidly happy at his stubborn determination, she gave in. "It's a book on fantastical creatures and hidden mysteries meant to have been written by an angel so long ago that her name has been lost from the Archives. Within its pages are said to be illustrations of utmost beauty hand-painted by the angel's most beloved concubine."

"What does it look like?"

"Leather bound, with a golden clasp." A frustratingly incomplete description. "No one ever seems to want to describe its physical appearance, just what apparently lies within."

Naasir looked at her so intently that she knew he wanted more. So she gave him more, and as she did, she learned that he liked listening to her tell stories of times long gone. He wasn't bored by the history she held in her head and quite often said something that made her look at things in a whole new light.

Yes, she would never forget Naasir. Not so long as she drew breath.

20

Elena walked into Raphael's Tower office to find the Primary there instead of her archangel. The leader of the Legion was staring at a screen that showed Jessamy's face. "Oh, sorry." She began to back out.

"Wait, Ellie," Jessamy called out as the Primary turned to pin her with those eerie, beautiful eyes, translucent but for the ring of mountain blue around the irises.

"Consort." His greeting was toneless, but all at once, she could hear seven hundred and seventy-seven voices whispering to her.

Braced for it, she nodded. "Hello."

The voices receded. *Thank God.* After a few hiccups, the Legion had come to understand that, unlike Raphael, she couldn't hold all their voices in her head. They'd also started to learn that she saw them as individuals, not a single entity. Whether they'd take that on board themselves was an unanswered question.

"Have you had contact with Amanat?" she asked, coming to stand beside the Primary.

Jessamy's soft brown eyes filled with sympathy. "Keir is there now. He says Suyin has fallen into *anshara* and it's for the best—the repeated wing excisions without enough time to truly heal in between had a cumulative effect."

Elena couldn't imagine the horror the other woman had survived. "None of Jason's people have made contact with Naasir," she told Jessamy, conscious the Historian had a deep bond with the silver-haired member of the Seven.

Jason himself had flown to Titus's territory, after hearing rumors of a border confrontation between Titus and Charisemnon that could break out into war. The spymaster had been confident Naasir would make it out safely now that he and the scholar had escaped the citadel, but Elena wouldn't be happy until she heard from the damn teasing tiger creature himself.

"He is a being of stealth and shadow; this is what he was born to do." The Primary had a way of being so motionless that it'd be easy to forget him, but when he spoke, he always spoke sense.

Jessamy's smile was shaky but real. "He'd agree with you. He loves nothing better than sneaking in and out of places." She nodded at the Primary. "We've been talking history. Or at least I have."

"Our memories of what we heard in our time of slumber are fading," the Primary told Elena. "It is a . . . side effect of being in the world."

"Yet he still won't tell me everything he does remember so I can record it."

"Some things are not meant to be remembered." The Primary's voice held echoes of countless others. "Life becomes meaningless if all is known. This we have learned."

"But we could learn from past mistakes, not make them again," Jessamy argued.

"Each generation, each Cascade has its own rhythm." The Primary's counterargument was without passion, but it was no less potent, the eerie sense of endless age that clung to him coloring every word. "You cannot predict the future by looking at the past."

Slipping out as the two continued to speak, Elena made her way to what had been the infirmary floor. Most of the injured were now gone. The few that remained were in a small section to the northeast.

She walked in to find the mini-infirmary empty but for one angel. Blond curls having grown back, a shirtless Izak was standing on trembling legs, determinedly lifting a heavy set of hand weights. The bones in his arms had been shattered into splinters in the Falling, but they'd fared better than the legs he'd lost below the thighs. Those legs had only just finished regenerating in a searing agony of sensation.

"Izzy," she said, striding quickly to the young angel. "You know you're not supposed to do that without a spotter."

He gave her a guilty but stubborn look. "I can't be in here much longer, Ellie." Not fighting when she tugged away and set the weights aside after seeing his biceps muscles quiver, he added, "I'll go mad."

Elena's heart clenched. Izak was the youngest angel to have survived the cowardly attack that had sent so many of New York's angels crashing to the earth, and the terrible nature of his injuries meant his road to this point had been a long and painful one. Charisemnon had a lot to answer for, and answer he would: Raphael would never forget this crime of war. Neither would any of his people.

"Izzy," she said, keeping her voice light, "you have an eight-pack that would be the envy of any man." She patted his abdomen, happy to feel warm, healthy skin where there had only been raw, bloody flesh.

Blushing, he didn't meet her eyes.

"I spoke to the healer in charge of you," she continued. "He says you're a remarkable patient who is recovering far quicker than anyone expected." Izzy was only a hundred and seventeen years old, a baby soldier in angelic terms. "Galen was so impressed with the healer's last report that he sent you homework."

"More?" Izak looked so horrified it was comical.

Giving in to his shuddering legs, he collapsed into a seated position on an infirmary bed, his wings spread out behind him. "I can barely do all the exercises he's already sent me."

Stifling her laugh lest his young heart take it the wrong way, Elena showed him the tablet she'd picked up on her way out of Raphael's office. "Not that kind of homework and it's not all from Galen. Some of it's from Jessamy."

"Jessamy?"

"Uh-huh." Sitting down beside him, their wings overlapping in an affectionate intimacy she knew would comfort him, she said, "Being in a consort's Guard isn't always about strength." Since she'd somehow ended up with a Guard, she was doing her best to understand how it worked. "Apparently, you have to understand all the courtesy stuff so you don't accidentally insult an archangel and, you know, start a war."

Izak gulped.

Patting him on the upper arm, she said, "Don't worry. If I can learn this stuff"—or at least enough not to stick her foot in it—"then you'll be an 'A' student."

"Can I rethink being in your Guard?"

"Funny." And because his small, mischievous smile was adorable, she kissed his cheek.

He went bright red.

"What's this? An orgy?" came a slow male voice that held a Cajun cadence. "Seems like we've been invited here under false pretenses, sugar."

Looking up, Elena saw Janvier and Ash in the doorway, both wearing leather jackets and holding a helmet in one hand. Ash's long black hair was unbound, the knives strapped to her thighs only the most visible of her weapons. "These two miscreants are your study buddies," she told Izak.

"Hey." Ashwini scowled, not shifting her lithely muscled dancer's body from the doorway when Elena moved toward it. "What about you?"

"I've been in remedial etiquette school since I became Raphael's consort. I'm way ahead of you."

Loud grumbling from Ash at her smug statement, but the other hunter's dark eyes weren't laughing. Everyone liked Naasir, but he, Janvier, and Ash were especially close. "No news," Elena said softly.

Janvier ran his free hand through the dark mahogany of his hair, a lopsided smile on his lips. "Don't worry, *cher*," he said, throwing his other arm, helmet and all, around Ash's shoulders. "Naasir once got the two of us out of an alligator-infested swamp in the middle of a raging hurricane at night, and had fun doing it. He'll be fine."

Elena and Ashwini both stared at the Cajun vampire. Fangs flashing and moss green eyes laughing, he gave a sinful grin that illustrated exactly why he was such good friends with Naasir. "I'll tell that tale when Naasir is here to tell it with me. He always says I forget the good parts."

"Yes," Ashwini said firmly. "It's Naasir."

Sneaky and strong and with the scent of a tiger on the hunt.

21

Even with the handicap of Andromeda's wings and the unexpected resumption of search squadrons that forced them to hide out for an entire five hours on the forest floor, Naasir got Andromeda to the nearest water border in the dark of night two days later.

Part of that was because at one point, he'd cleared her to fly at night while he ran below. She'd never seen anyone move that gracefully, that dangerously on the ground. Like a silver tiger shadowed with darker stripes.

Their arrival at the border was almost anticlimactic after the stealth required for the rest of the trip. She'd expected guards bristling with weapons and air squadrons crisscrossing the skies, but Lijuan's people were distracted, drawn to another part of the border. "Jason?"

"Or one of his people."

"How did they know when to act?"

"They didn't. I'm guessing there have been annoying incursions or manufactured dramas along this border for at least twenty-four hours." He lifted a finger to his lips as a harried guard ran past them to join in the melee in the distance. "Now," he said once the guard was clear, and held out his hand.

Taking it, she followed him to a battered barge which Naasir told her was run by vampires allied with Astaad. It appeared the Archangel of the Pacific Isles had chosen to fly his flag with Raphael's.

"Naasir," she said quietly after they were safely on board.

Her wings would've made her stand out, except that no one had seen her and Naasir board, and as soon as she was on deck, she moved so she was hidden from view of the bank. He didn't have to tell her that she could only take to the air once they were past the last of the aerial scouts.

"What is it?" Naasir asked, his eyes scanning the shore as the barge pulled away mere seconds later.

"I think we should go to Amanat, get supplies, and head to the most probable location."

"Did you tell Lijuan that location?"

She rolled her eyes. "Of course not. I lied." Being forced to witness Heng's torture at the teeth of the hounds had only strengthened her resolve. "Very convincingly, I might add. Xi is probably somewhere near Mount Kilimanjaro right now."

"I knew you were sneaky." Eyes glinting on that approving statement, Naasir wrapped an arm around her neck and hauled her close. This time, the snap of his teeth was playful. "You fly to Amanat once we're out of range of the sentries. I'll make it there on my own."

Her instincts and her heart both rebelled. "I'm not going to leave you alone."

"I'll be able to travel faster on my own once I hit land." He took something from his pocket. It was a heavy gold ring with the letter *N* engraved on it, the engraving embedded with diamonds. "This will get you into Amanat. Stay outside the shield until a sentry appears, then show this to him."

Taking the ring, she ran her thumb over the jewels. She wouldn't have thought this was his kind of jewelry—the identity bracelet he wore suited him much better. "Why are you carrying it instead of wearing it?"

He kept his arm around her and rubbed his jaw against her temple. "I like shiny things but not to wear. Caliane gave that to me as thanks for my help in protecting her city when it first woke."

"I'll keep it safe," she said, just as he reached out and unhooked the simple gold chain she always wore around her neck and that had survived all their adventures. Sliding the ring onto it, he hooked it back around her neck, his fingertips brushing her nape.

Her nipples tightened, a shiver rippling over her skin.

She should've protested the familiar handling, but it didn't feel wrong—as it hadn't felt wrong to stroke her fingers through his hair. Andromeda couldn't think too much about that or it started to hurt deep inside. "Is there someone I should ask for when I arrive in Amanat?" she asked instead, glancing away lest he see all she sought to hide.

"Isabel." Naasir pulled her back against the heated muscle of his body. "She was my partner during my time there and she has chosen to remain in the city."

Andromeda had no will to fight his hold. "I've seen her at the Refuge." A tall, competent warrior who chose to walk the path of an ascetic.

Four hours later, she flared out her wings in readiness for flight. "I'll wait for you." Nothing would be right until he was with her again. "Stay safe."

Naasir watched her soar into the sky, his silver hair bright in the light of the moon.

22

Having taken advantage of the renewed border aggression between Titus and Charisemnon to stealthily invade Titus's territory, Xi and his squadron had spent multiple days in and around Kilimanjaro, searching the demanding and often harsh landscape for any sign of Alexander. He'd flown up and down all three of the volcanic cones that made up Kilimanjaro, studied the cold, deep crater that scored one, walked on the glaciers, and far below, in the caves.

He'd found nothing, though if Alexander had gone beneath the earth like Caliane, that would be expected. Still, even the closest villagers had heard no whispers, guarded no legends. He knew they spoke the truth because they were too afraid to lie. While he would've ordinarily ignored such weak mortals, he couldn't permit these ones to live. If Titus discovered the intrusion, he might decide to launch a retaliatory attack and Lady Lijuan needed more time to return to her strength.

"Is it possible the scholar lied?" one of his lieutenants asked after another futile day's searching.

"No." He thought of how Andromeda had sat with Heng, how she'd stayed even after Xi told her it was a foolish thing she did. "Her courage is of the heart and the mind, not that of a warrior.

And she accepts this is the right path." The world was in chaos and needed Lijuan's millennia-deep wisdom to steady it.

Cassandra's prophecy made it clear Alexander was a threat to that future peace.

Xi would permit no threat to his lady. "However, the scholar may simply have been wrong in her estimation of Alexander's attachment to his land and to his son." Unlike Xi, Andromeda had never had any direct contact with Alexander, so the error was understandable.

"Love may have made a fool of even an Ancient." The extraordinary thing was that Xi understood Alexander's instincts because he was driven by the same. Despite the strategic weakness of such, should he ever go into Sleep, he would do so near his lady.

His lieutenant stirred. "We go to Favashi's territory?"

"Yes." To the home of Alexander's only and beloved son. "Leave two men here to carry on the search, on the chance the scholar was right. Ready the rest for flight."

23

Andromeda flew straight and true toward Amanat, her sense of aerial direction good enough that three hundred and twenty-five years earlier, she'd got herself to the Refuge while not yet an adult. With each wingbeat, she had to fight not to turn back, return to Naasir, make sure he was safe.

She knew her thoughts were irrational. Naasir was one of the Seven for a reason—he was strong and lethal. She'd seen that when they fought the reborn. He'd taken down three for every one of hers.

He was so beautiful to watch in motion, pure grace and wildness.

Riding a powerful sea wind, she dropped low enough to feel the salt air. Below her, the water was a sprawling emptiness in every direction. Not a single vessel, no birds, nothing but the night and the ocean. There was a deep peace to it, to feeling the wind push back her hair as her wings rode it.

She wondered if this was how Naasir felt when he set himself free and ran full tilt. She'd ask him, she thought with a smile that faded all too soon. The only good thing about Lijuan's insanity was that it had brought Naasir into her life, allowed her to spend her last days of freedom with a man so extraordinary she knew eternity with him would be a constant and wonderful surprise.

Her heart hurt.

Eternity with Naasir was beyond her reach, but she could help him stop a heinous crime. For Lijuan to attempt to murder Alexander while he Slept wouldn't only shatter one of the deepest taboos of the angelic race, it would destroy hundreds of thousands of years of history. Alexander carried that history in his bones, in his mind, in his memories.

Lijuan's plan *could not* be permitted to succeed.

Jaw clenched, she rode another strong wind . . . and thought again of the silver-haired vampire who wasn't a vampire who was her partner in this critical quest, and of how he made her feel heartbreakingly young and wild. This time, she didn't fight the fantasies that whispered at her, fantasies of an eternity where she could explore and play and tangle with him forever.

On this night as she flew alone over a midnight dark sea while the stars glittered overhead, it didn't matter. On this night, she was free and wild with a bloodline that was her own, unconnected in any way to that of a court built on pain and brutality and sexual acts devoid of love or even affection.

But of course the night, secret and sweet, couldn't last.

Dawn was a blush-pink kiss in the sky, the morning light cool as she flew over the thick, dark green forests of Kagoshima, Japan, heading in a straight line to a city that should not exist here. Fog whispered a sinuous lover around the treetops, the mountains covered in sleepy-appearing white clouds, but Andromeda herself wasn't the least drowsy; her breath caught in anticipation of seeing the lost city risen anew, of walking its ancient streets, of speaking to the people Caliane had taken with her into her Sleep.

Andromeda had read every one of the reports filed by others, pored over the sketches made by artists who'd visited. There were no photographs, for something in Amanat caused cameras to malfunction, perhaps the simple low hum of an Ancient's close proximity.

Regardless, nothing could've prepared her for her first sight of the legendary city.

It appeared out of the green like a mirage, a city of stone and flowers and curves protected by a shield of delicate blue-tinged light that warned against trespass. Mouth dry with thirst and with wonder, Andromeda brought herself to a passable landing directly outside the shield, her wings strained from the long flight after days of near-inactivity.

She only had to wait a matter of seconds before an auburn-haired angel stepped out from behind the shield to face her. "What is your purpose here?" His green eyes were as cool as his voice, his body clad in the combat leathers of a warrior.

She recognized him from the descriptions in the reports: Avi, one of Caliane's most trusted people, and an angel who had quietly returned to her side as soon as Caliane awoke. "My name is Andromeda," she said. "I'm a scholar recently escaped from Lijuan's citadel, thanks to Jason and Naasir." Lifting her hand to her neck, she pulled out the chain that held Naasir's ring. "I come to see Isabel."

"Naasir is not with you?" No cool mask now, Avi's concern darkening his gaze.

"He's coming overland." Andromeda's fingers curled into her hand, her worry for Naasir a constant echo at the back of her mind. "It made more sense for me to fly."

A small nod and the angel led her into the city after somehow causing the shield to part. Or perhaps it was his archangel who had parted the shield for him. "Suyin?" she asked.

"In *anshara*," Avi told her shortly.

Andromeda refused to be brushed off like a child. "She will be all right?" she asked, unable to forget the agonizing sorrow that marked Suyin's gaze.

Turning to pin her with those penetrating green eyes, Avi took his time to reply, but when he did, his tone was gentler. "Keir says it is the best thing for her. Her physical wounds will heal, and when she wakes, she'll do so in a city where she was often a treasured guest before her imprisonment." An unexpected touch on Andromeda's hair, as a father might do to a child. "Have no fear, young one, Suyin has friends here who will protect her and help her heal wounds not so visible."

Throat thick, Andromeda nodded. Dropping his hand from her hair, Avi led her deeper into Amanat. It took her a minute to get her emotions under enough control to see clearly, and then, she had to fight not to gawp like a fledgling.

To a historian, Amanat was a fever dream taken vivid form. With each one of her steps, she walked *in* history itself. The architecture, the ethereal carvings on the stone of the walls that made up the buildings, the mineral-veined cobblestones of the path on which she and Avi walked, the window gardens that spilled blooms in every direction, they all fought to capture her attention, but she focused first on the people who had Slept so long beside their archangel.

They were clothed in bright flowing gowns when it came to the non-warrior females, and embroidered tunics and pants for the non-warrior males. A rare few of the men wore flowing kaftan-like robes. In contrast, as with Avi, the warriors were dressed much the same as warriors anywhere in the world. They also had the same grim-eyed and alert appearance.

All in all, not so different from the men and women of Lijuan's court. Only here, no one avoided her gaze, and instead of glimpsing shivering fear on their faces, she heard laughter drifting through the streets, was gifted with smiles by those who weren't warriors, and curt nods of welcome by those who were.

And this in the home of an archangel once judged insane, an archangel who had sung the entire adult populations of two thriving cities into the sea. Bloated corpses had littered the beach in the aftermath, pecked at by birds, and found by motherless and fatherless children who'd been so traumatized by the horror that they'd curled up and died "of such sorrow as immortals will never know."

Keir's words, as recorded for the Histories by an equally heartbroken Jessamy.

Was it possible Lijuan, too, could one day become a better version of herself? Andromeda bit her lower lip, unable to see that future. Caliane had Slept away her madness while Lijuan was intent on feeding it on the lifeforce of her people.

"Scholar."

Pulled from the disturbing tenor of her thoughts, she saw they'd stopped in front of an archway.

"Isabel is within," Avi said. "I'll leave you to speak with her."

"Thank you." Walking through the archway, Andromeda found herself in a tree-shaded but still light-filled courtyard surrounded by dual-level homes and empty but for an angel going through a martial arts kata. The angel was tall and muscular in a toned, fluid way, her black hair pulled back into a neat braid and her wings white with a splash of delicate green at the primaries.

Instead of warrior leathers, she wore black jeans with boots of the same shade, her white top loose and long-sleeved, cuffed at the wrists. None of that altered the fact that she was a trained and dangerous fighter who moved with an economy of motion that told Andromeda Isabel wouldn't be flashy in a fight, but she'd be effective.

Despite her tiredness, Andromeda stayed back, loathe to interrupt; she knew how much it meant to find peace in such a quiet pattern of movement. Isabel was setting herself up for the day and to interrupt would be to shatter her center.

Andromeda found a measure of peace in simply watching the other woman.

Completing her kata several minutes later, Isabel took a moment of silence before looking up. Her smile was quiet but deep, her eyes a brown darker than the darkest chocolate, and her skin a tawny gold. Handsome rather than beautiful, Isabel had a regal confidence to her that said she could command armies and courts without breaking her stride.

"You must be Naasir's Andi."

Andromeda blinked. "How could you possibly know that?" Not her identity, but Naasir's pet name for her.

"Naasir borrowed a satellite phone from the captain of the barge after you left." Isabel's smile grew deeper. "It doesn't come naturally to him, but he's learned all about technology from Illium."

"He's smarter than most scholars." Andromeda tried not to sound too proud and possessive, wasn't sure she'd pulled it off when Isabel's eyes crinkled as if she was holding back laughter. "More perceptive, too," she added, unable to help herself.

Isabel's agreement was obvious.

"And yes," Andromeda said, "I'm Andi." She could be that woman here, that young and happily reckless scholar who had adventures with a wild, wonderful man who bore secret tiger stripes under his skin. "Has Naasir been in touch since then?" The knot in her stomach wouldn't dissolve until she could see him, touch him, draw in his scent.

"No," Isabel said. "But he will make it to Amanat in far less

time than it would take any other vampire, of this I'm certain."
The open affection in the other woman's tone belied the wagging tongues of those who said she was an automaton devoid of emotions. "Come. I'll show you where you can bathe and rest."

Andromeda wanted to ask Isabel what it was to live the life of an ascetic, asexual and serene, for so long, couldn't find the courage . . . because she knew her own resolve was at breaking point. "I'll need to gather supplies for our onward journey," she said instead, her voice rough with need and a dull, throbbing loneliness.

"Naasir mentioned it. Rest first, then you must pay your respects to Caliane. I'll put together the supplies in the interim."

Andromeda stumbled, barely hearing Isabel's last sentence. "What?"

"You are in her city," the warrior said gently. "It is a matter of form . . . though she is aware of your bloodline, so she may subject you to deeper scrutiny."

Andromeda's lungs strained. "I appreciate the warning."

Leading her to a set of steps on the far side of the courtyard, Isabel showed her to a second-floor apartment filled with sunlight. The windows were open, curtains of gauzy lace pushed aside to reveal flower boxes bursting with life; more flowers grew in the large planters set on the small balcony, which could be reached through a set of doors that had also been propped open.

A fresh wind blew the lace curtains into the air, until they almost touched the four-poster bed covered with exquisitely patterned white-on-white sheets. Beneath Andromeda's abused feet, the thick carpet was a deep blue. More flowers—a wildflower posy—sat in a little glass vase set atop a writing table.

That cheerful posy gave the elegant room an air of welcome and whimsy—as if someone had gone out and picked the blooms just for her. "It's lovely, thank you. Especially the flowers."

"Ah, but I can't take any credit." Arms loosely folded, Isabel leaned against the doorjamb. "I mentioned to one of the maidens that a friend of Naasir's was coming to stay and she took it upon herself to make you feel welcome. He's a favorite with the women."

Andromeda wanted to throw the stupid posy out the window. "Yet she welcomes me when she doesn't know if I may be a competitor?"

"They all accept that Naasir is too wild to be held by any one woman," Isabel said easily before pushing off the door-jamb. "I'll leave you to your ablutions. Once you've slept and are ready to see Caliane, you'll find me either at my home next door, or at the temple." A faint smile. "Caliane has instructed me to teach her maidens how to defend themselves."

Andromeda thought of the sweet-faced creatures, some prettily plump, others reed slender, that she'd seen on her walk through the city. "Oh."

Isabel chuckled, one hand on the hilt of the knife she wore at her hip. "Yes. It's a sometimes frustrating task, but they're so earnest that I can't be angry with them—especially after they spent so much time sewing up 'warrior clothes' for these sessions."

Andromeda's lips twitched despite herself at Isabel's suspiciously bland tone; she was curious to see the maidens' idea of warrior clothing. "Wait," she said when Isabel would've left. "Avi told me Suyin was in *anshara*. Did Keir say when she might wake?"

The humor faded from the other woman's expression. "It may be many weeks or even months—she is very fragile." A pause. "It appears immortals can die of sadness and loneliness, of an existence without hope. I never knew that."

Tears clogged Andromeda's throat. "Suyin . . ." She just shook her head, unable to put into words the pain she'd seen in the other woman's eyes.

Isabel's face reflected the knowledge Andromeda couldn't articulate. "Caliane says it is a kind of willing the self to end. It takes a long time, but Suyin has had millennia. She probably wouldn't have woken from her next Sleep." Leaving on those solemn words, Isabel pulled the door shut behind herself.

Her heart feeling as if it had a crushing weight on it, and the knot in her stomach a lump of stone, Andromeda didn't allow her gaze to linger on the bed but headed straight for the large bathing chamber. The already-filled and steaming pool of water to her left made her moan in want, but afraid she'd fall asleep, she indulged for a bare minute, then rose and washed under the shower.

As the fat droplets crashed onto her skin, she would've

done anything to be where she'd been the last time she'd taken a proper bath, in that icy pool in the valley. She could almost feel Naasir's strong fingers in her hair as he washed it, the sneaky touch of his hand on her feathers, the way he'd raced with her. "Hurry," she whispered, her hand reaching out as if she'd catch him through space and time itself. "I miss you."

24

Naasir wasn't surprised when Jason landed beside him soon after he hit the shores of Japan. The barge hadn't brought him all the way—he'd transferred onto another friendly and much faster vessel soon after Andromeda took flight. When he'd dived from the barge to swim across to the sleek little freighter, both crews' mouths had fallen open. Someone had screamed.

He didn't know why. It wasn't as if he couldn't swim.

"Andi?" he said to Jason as the two of them spoke on a deserted part of an otherwise busy dock.

"Isabel tells me she's safe inside Amanat." Lines of tiredness marked Jason's ordinarily impassive face. "I just returned from the border between Titus and Charisemnon."

"War?"

The black-winged angel shook his head. "A small skirmish neither side appeared to want to fan into full flame."

"That won't last." Titus and Charisemnon had disliked each other for centuries if not millennia, and with the world going to hell, that dislike would collide into all-out war sooner rather than later.

"No," Jason agreed as one of his feathers drifted to the

scarred and stained concrete of the dock. "But the region's stable enough right now that Raphael doesn't have to worry about any ripple effects."

Naasir had always liked Jason, but as he grew, he'd started to see that the strong, black-winged angel was lonely. Perhaps even lonelier than Naasir. He'd tried to draw Jason out, instinct telling him it wasn't good for the angel to exist so tightly within himself, but Jason had stayed contained and remote. No longer.

"Your mate must be missing you," he said. "You should go home."

Jason's dark eyes flickered the tiniest fraction but in that flicker, Naasir saw his friend's raw need to return to his princess. "You and Andromeda will require backup."

"If we do, I'll contact the Tower." Naasir had thought the plan through during his and Andromeda's escape, discussed it with her. "Locating Alexander isn't a sure thing." Andromeda had made it clear her expertise only went so far—no one could predict an archangel's actions with pinpoint accuracy.

"And it's better if it's a team of two," he added. "We'll have to move with stealth so no one spots us and alerts Lijuan's people that they're in the wrong place."

Jason stretched and resettled his wings in silence. "You know I have people scattered across the world. If you need immediate assistance, call me."

"I'll buy a new phone before I leave the country." He had money on a card stored in a thin waterproof case in his back pocket. At first when Illium had given him such a card, he'd spent hours staring at it, trying to figure out how it worked. He'd finally made his brain understand that the card was a kind of machine that moved money from one place to another.

When he used it in a shop, the card moved money from his own treasury to that of the shop's. Dmitri and Illium kept an eye on his money, so he didn't really have to think much about the mechanics of it all. What he did know was that he had plenty of funds. Raphael had always been more than fair toward his Seven, and Naasir was very good at hunting down treasures everyone thought lost.

Treasures like the stupid Grimoire book.

"Tell me what you know about a book called the Star Grimoire," he ordered Jason, because Jason knew everything.

A raised eyebrow. "It's a mythical book coveted by those who collect such things."

"Do you know where it is?"

Jason's eyes narrowed, his expression intent. "No . . . but two hundred years ago, I met an old one of our race who spoke of the Grimoire's red leather binding and golden edges." A pause, Jason's form motionless in a way Naasir had never seen another angel replicate.

He didn't interrupt. Immortals had long memories, but Jason's was near flawless. The other man just had to track down the right piece of it.

"And this book of mysteries untold had a golden clasp carved with the fearsome image of a crouching griffin." Jason's voice held a rhythm not his own.

Memory stirred in Naasir, hinting tantalizingly at a clue, but stayed annoyingly out of reach when he lunged for it. "Was there anything else unique about it?"

"Yes," Jason said after almost an entire minute of silence. "A mythical beast in gold, stamped or engraved in the leather on the front."

Memory whispered again, only to fade. No matter. Naasir had the bit between his teeth now. First he'd find Alexander, then he'd find the Grimoire. Because Andromeda was his mate and he wanted to claim her. She might not agree with him yet, but she smelled like his mate and she liked him in his true skin, and she was as fierce as his mate should be.

He liked everything about her except her vow of celibacy.

At least if he found the Grimoire, he could court her in truth. He wanted to seduce her, wanted to make her melt. Mostly, he just wanted to keep her.

Andromeda woke to skies streaked with the vivid violets and golds of sunset.

Still wearing the robe she'd discovered on the back of the bathroom door, she got up to find her wings rested and her feet no longer as sore. Maybe she was getting stronger now that she was nearly four hundred. Rubbing her eyes on that sleepy thought, she wandered into the bathing chamber and threw cold water on her face before drying off and going to explore the options in the closet.

There were four gowns in various rich shades, three tunic and pants sets, and even a pair of jeans and a shirt. She chose a black pants and tunic set, the stark lines of it offset by the delicate silver pattern painted around the neckline. It reminded her of the color of Naasir's eyes.

Where was he?

Dressing as that question pounded in her blood, she gathered up her crazy mass of hair—thanks to falling asleep while it was yet damp—and somehow tamed it into a braid, then slipped her feet into a pair of outdoor slippers. There were also boots in the closet in various sizes and she knew she'd be wearing a pair when she and Naasir departed Amanat.

Why wasn't he here yet?

Leaving her sword in the room—she didn't think Caliane would be impressed by a visitor who came to pay her respects wearing a blade—she stepped out to look for Isabel. The other woman wasn't in her home, so Andromeda stopped a passing man to ask for directions to the temple. She used the language she'd heard spoken when Avi showed her to Isabel's courtyard.

Beaming, the handsome ebony-skinned citizen of Amanat replied in the same tongue, offering to act as her escort to her destination. "Thank you," she said, "but I'd like to go slowly and fully absorb this wondrous city."

Cheeks creasing again, he gave her what she needed and she carried on.

The light show of sunset had begun to fade to a paler palette, but there was yet no need for the tall standing lamps that bordered the pathways. When she peered up, she saw that despite the weathered iron that gave the impression of having grown old apace with Amanat, the lights within were electric.

Amanat was clearly being upgraded for this century. Either Caliane was more forward-thinking than Andromeda had believed, or she had a forward-thinking advisor. Andromeda would bet on the latter. It was apt to be Avi's beloved Jelena. As loyal to Caliane as Avi, Jelena was keenly interested in new inventions and technologies, and had often come to the Library seeking access to manuals.

Carrying on down the path, Andromeda saw a small black puppy, his coat smooth and shiny, running toward her. When he flopped down in front of her as if exhausted, she laughed and picked him up—whereupon he regained his energy and was a wiggling, excited bundle determined to give her wet puppy kisses.

Andromeda held him for some time, his warm body and the fast beat of his heart a reassurance, something familiar in an unfamiliar place. Her childhood may have been unorthodox in ways that had scarred her, but it had also been joyous because of the myriad animals who'd been her refuge, her friends, and her companions. They didn't lie, didn't look at her in disappointment for her scholarly inclinations, never made her feel as if she was a mistake.

It was a good thing Andromeda was so clearly her mother's daughter—it avoided awkward questions about the other side of her bloodline. Andromeda had always wondered if Lailah had chosen Cato in part because he'd permit her to exercise her tendencies without limits. After all, he was exactly the same.

If you were mine, I wouldn't let you rut with others.

Her face flushed just as the puppy wriggled to be put down. Placing him on the ground, she watched him race away on stubby little legs, but her mind was on a predator with silver eyes.

Naasir was like the animals who'd kept her sane during her otherwise friendless childhood. She didn't think he'd take the comparison as an insult—not when he had the same honest core. He was far, far better than most "normal" people she'd met in her near–four hundred years of life.

"Andi!"

She jerked up her head at the call to find Isabel waving to her from in front of a set of wide doors that led into the temple carved into the side of a mountain. A number of exhausted-appearing young women flowed out of the temple and toward nearby homes.

Deep orange tunic and pants offset by a green fabric belt tied to the side, a bright pink *gi*-style top matched with wide-legged white pants, a vivid blue tunic that came to mid-thigh paired with black leggings, those were three of the more conservative outfits.

Biting back a laugh, Andromeda joined Isabel by the doors. "Warrior clothes?"

Affectionate amusement in Isabel's eyes. "I think they consider anything with pants, or that shows the legs, as scandalous and warrior-like." Unlike her drooping students, Isabel didn't appear as if she'd broken so much as a sweat. "Caliane is walking the orange grove at the other end of the city. We'll fly to her."

"An orange grove in this climate?" Andromeda said before she realized the shield around Amanat allowed Raphael's mother to control the temperature within. "Does she ever lower the shield?"

"Not since a maiden was killed by one of Charisemnon's diseases." Isabel's lips flattened into a thin line as Andromeda's stomach dropped. "He thought to use Kahla as a carrier, but she died before infecting anyone. It broke Caliane's heart."

"I'm so sorry," Andromeda said, nauseated at knowing the murder had been done by a member of her family . . . and terrified what Caliane would do to her for it.

"It wasn't your doing." Isabel squeezed her shoulder. "You are as innocent as Kahla."

Flaring out her wings on those quiet words, Isabel took off. Andromeda followed, knowing full well that Caliane might not be as forgiving.

Deep in the orange grove, the Ancient wasn't dressed in one of the flowing gowns in which she was so often depicted in scrolls and illustrated manuscripts. Instead, she wore faded brown leathers similar to Avi's, her midnight black hair pulled back in a braid much like Andromeda's.

"Isabel," Caliane said in greeting when the warrior-angel landed, her voice hauntingly pure. "Are my maidens improving?"

"Like snails, my Lady."

Caliane's smile was unexpected and startlingly beautiful, her lips soft pink against skin of pure cream. "You must be patient—they are hothouse flowers suddenly exposed to the wind and the rain." Her smile faded. "Would that it wasn't necessary to teach them thus, but the world is changing into a dark place where the innocent are no longer safe."

Isabel bowed her head slightly in a gesture of respect. "I bring you Andromeda. She is Naasir's friend, of whom I spoke to you earlier."

"Ah." The excruciatingly pure blue of Caliane's eyes, eyes

she'd bequeathed her son, locked with Andromeda's. "Charisemnon's grandchild." Daggers of ice in that voice that could be a
beautiful, horrifying weapon. "And yet you show the good taste
of escaping from Lijuan to help save Alexander's life."

"My Lady." Not sure what else to do or say, Andromeda
bowed deeply—unlike Isabel, she wasn't a trusted warrior but
a much younger guest.

"Is there a reason I shouldn't execute you this instant for
the crime done in my city?"

Blood a roar in her ears, Andromeda dared meet Caliane's
eyes. "If blood alone is what defines us, no child born is born
in freedom."

Caliane's wings glowed for an endless heartbeat before
subsiding. "Well said, fledgling. And do not look so terrified—
I am not in the habit of hurting children for the crimes of their
elders." The archangel glanced at Isabel while Andromeda
tried to keep from shaking. "Go, Isabel. I know you must do
your flight over the city."

"Lady." Isabel left with another small incline of her head.

"She watches over my city as diligently as if it is her own,"
Caliane said conversationally as she motioned for Andromeda to
join her in her walk amongst the rows of trees that made up the
grove. "I've told my son I will tempt her into staying with me, but
he is confident in the loyalty of his people." A glance at Andromeda. "Your wild friend could not wait to return to Raphael's side."

Andromeda took a moment to think. Some older angels could
take grave insult at a single wrong word, and she had no desire
to end up eviscerated. "Your city is astonishing," she said, doing
nothing to hide her wonder. "For me, it's like being shown a
treasure box." She could spend weeks just walking the streets of
Amanat, listening to the lilt of its people's voices. "But Naasir is
meant for wilder places and less civilized adventures."

"Like my son." Caliane's love for that son was a piercing
arrow to the heart. "Raphael collects the wild of heart to him."

"He is the archangel who is least stuck in time," Andromeda ventured to say. "Even Michaela, who so often plays to the
cameras, keeps a court that works much the same today as it
did a hundred years past."

The pure white of Caliane's wings seemed to glow even in
the muted light; Andromeda was grateful that they no longer

glowed in truth, because when an archangel glowed, people generally died.

"He is my son," Caliane said quietly. "And he is Nadiel's son. Together, we created a child who will one day fly higher than both of us."

Having the sense that Caliane was speaking more to herself than to Andromeda, Andromeda kept her silence.

"Now he makes me even prouder by seeking to protect Alexander." A cold tension in Caliane's regal features. "I Slept during that time, but Jelena tells me that Alexander once thought to raise an army against Raphael."

Andromeda took her life into her hands. "Yet he didn't in the end," she said. "I think he was tired and he saw Raphael as a young interloper. War was the easy answer to his need to find a reason to go on living in the world. In the end, he showed his wisdom and left the world to the young."

Caliane pinned Andromeda with eyes aflame with power.

Her throat dried up, her pulse a rabbit in her chest.

25

"As I did in my time," Caliane said at last, turning her attention back to the glossy green trees as they continued to walk. "Alexander was my compatriot, but we were never friends. He was a terror as a child, always breaking his bones and skinning his knee, while I was a girl who preferred to keep my dresses clean and to have civilized tea parties free of dirty boys."

Andromeda felt wonder unfurl in her. Caliane's memories came from a time so long ago that there was no one else awake in the world who knew them. "Is it lonely?" she asked impulsively. "To be the only Ancient in the world as Alexander once was? The only one with memories of times long gone?" Lijuan might believe herself an Ancient, but even if she was older than anyone knew, her age came nowhere close to Caliane's.

Caliane didn't strike her down for the impertinent question. Rather, the Ancient smiled. "I see why you are Naasir's friend, scholar. You are as recklessly courageous as my son's leashed tiger."

Naasir isn't leashed, Andromeda thought. He simply chose to give his loyalty to Raphael—and she had a feeling Raphael understood that. Their relationship wouldn't otherwise be so strong.

"Yes," Caliane said after a minute's quiet. "It would be a

pleasure to have a compatriot to speak with of times no one else remembers—perhaps I will invite Alexander to Amanat when he wakes. He grew up into a great general, and despite his foolishness in threatening my son, seems to have learned a modicum of civilized manners along the way."

Andromeda realized Caliane was saying more than her words told. There was a hidden undertone to her statement. Caliane and Alexander hadn't been friends, but instinct told Andromeda they'd been more than strangers. Not lovers; that wasn't it. It could be as simple as the fact they'd sat on the same Cadre—perhaps they had exchanged dry insults across a negotiating table, all the while conscious that in the end, only an Ancient could understand another Ancient.

"Do you know of any secret places lost in time where he might Sleep?" she asked, hope burning inside her. "Could he have hidden himself under the earth as you did?" If so, the Sleeping archangel was safe.

But Caliane shook her head. "No, Alexander didn't have an affinity for the earth."

Andromeda's brain clicked—despite having risen from the sea, the Legion, too, were rumored to be of the earth. Raphael must've inherited some of his mother's gift, though his had manifested in a different form. "If not earth—"

"Hush, child." A deep frown. "My memories are tangled skeins I must unravel."

It was over a half hour later, the world gray, that Caliane said, "Metal. Alexander's affinity was to metal. He could make iron flow like water and draw gold and silver out of the earth."

Andromeda's eyes widened. That fact was in none of the Histories.

"When he was a cocky youth, he pulled gold out of the earth in front of me and fashioned it into a bracelet." Caliane shook her head. "He and Nadiel had such a rivalry . . . but Alexander grieved with me when my love's heart no longer beat, and he remembered who Nadiel had once been."

Andromeda heard the thickness of grief in Caliane's voice even now. What must it have cost her to be forced to execute her insane mate? Andromeda couldn't imagine the depth of her pain. About to gently excuse herself and leave Caliane to her private memories, she heard the Ancient draw in a breath.

"If I know Alexander, he will have built himself a vault of metal in a hidden place." Caliane's voice was so confident it confirmed Andromeda's belief that the two Ancients had been closer than anyone realized. "It would've been impregnable to everything except angelfire when he went to Sleep, but Jelena has been teaching me about the new machines using hot light."

"Lasers?" Andromeda guessed when Caliane paused.

"Yes. I think such a machine could cut through Alexander's metal, even if Lijuan was not there to use the poisonous black rain she spews from her hands."

It was news Andromeda didn't want to hear. "Will he wake when disturbed?"

"To wake from Sleep is normally a long and slow process," Caliane told her. "If Alexander's subconscious terms you a threat when you first disturb him, you may end up dead before you can explain anything. I would recommend you waste no time once you have his attention."

Andromeda swallowed, but felt no temptation to step back, attempt to hide. Far better that her last moments be spent with the most incredible man she had ever met, working to save the life of an Ancient, than to feel her soul shrivel away in her grandfather's court.

Naasir was climbing through the treetops of Kagoshima under early evening starlight, the resident monkeys chattering at him for invading their territory, and Amanat almost within sight, when everything went quiet. The monkeys in the trees, the wild horses below, the birds in the sky. Naasir.

Holding himself in position, not even a breath stirring the air, he listened. The hairs rose on the back of his neck, the early warning system one civilized beings had learned to ignore. Naasir didn't.

So he caught the unfamiliar scents on the breeze, heard the beat of wings snapping out to land. Turning very carefully, he made his way soundlessly through the trees. The monkeys didn't give him away—they might scold him bad-temperedly, but when it came to animal against *other*, they saw him as one of them.

They also knew who belonged this close to Caliane's territory and who didn't.

The wings Naasir could see below definitely didn't. It appeared he'd underestimated Lijuan's generals—it was pure luck the light squadron had arrived too late to pluck Andromeda from the sky. Pressing himself down along the branch, Naasir strained his senses to hear what the four angels were saying.

". . . go inside?"

"Negative." The tallest male sliced out a hand at the sole female angel's question. "We don't want to start hostilities. Philomena was clear that Lady Lijuan has other priorities. Our task is only to retrieve the scholar."

The angel on the left, the one who had skin as dark as Naasir's, nodded. "She must be here—the last sighting from one of our people in the country puts her above the southern end of Kumamoto. There's no other safe haven nearby, and she's too young to have the endurance to have continued flying."

"Agreed," said the final man, and though his dialect differed from the others, it was familiar enough in the basics.

When Naasir was yet a child, Dmitri had told him he must learn as many languages as possible, so no one could keep secrets from him. This wasn't the first time that advice had held Naasir in good stead.

"We watch and we wait," said the angel who seemed to be the leader. "She can't stay here indefinitely."

The woman appeared dubious. "Amanat is a jewel for any historian."

"But she has certain responsibilities in the Refuge. If she does decide to stay, we'll reconsider our options."

"Can we afford to wait?"

"Philomena wants her as soon as possible, but we can wait tonight. If she doesn't leave with the dawn, I'll contact the general."

Naasir listened further, learned the squadron intended to spread out around Amanat, covering one quadrant each. He thought about taking them down one at a time, but if they were used to checking in with one another within short periods of time, he'd betray his hand. Deciding to leave them to their surveillance and wanting to ensure the four didn't suspect he'd spotted them, he retraced his steps until he was about an hour out from Amanat, then ran toward the city openly.

Unlike Andromeda, he didn't have to wait for an escort to

enter Caliane's territory. The city shield knew him, opened automatically in a welcome that was a ripple of archangelic power over his skin. The only person who could revoke his access was Caliane.

He picked up Andromeda's scent the instant he hit the temperate air of Amanat; it was a shiny, delicious thread in the active mix of a thriving city.

"Naasir!"

He waved at the friend who'd called out to him from the second story of a nearby building, but didn't stop. Isabel's cool, clean scent crossed with Andromeda's at one point, then both scents ran parallel toward the walled courtyard Isabel used as a sparring ground.

He grinned when he heard the clash of swords.

Loping up a wall on one side of the sparring ground, he crouched on top and watched Isabel and Andromeda dance with blades. His former partner in Amanat was good . . . but Andromeda was better. He hadn't expected that. Neither, he saw, had Isabel. Naasir knew her, could read her expressions, tell when Andromeda's moves surprised her.

Because, Naasir realized, Andromeda fought instinctively.

Dahariel had given her an excellent grounding, but she adapted her moves to the flow of combat, causing Isabel to have to rethink her more classical style. His eyes narrowed. That wasn't just skill, not given Andromeda's age—the instinct came from within.

She was an archangel's granddaughter.

But where her mother wasted the strength that ran in her veins, Andromeda had honed it, made it her own. When she put her blade to Isabel's throat in a move that signaled a win, her chest heaving but her hand steady, he wanted to growl in pride. Instead, he waited until the women drew apart and raised their swords in front of their faces in the respectful bow of two warriors.

Jumping down to the ground, he saw Andromeda's head whip around. "Naasir!" She ran straight into his arms, sword thrust into a scabbard that hung alongside one of her thighs. He recognized it as one of Isabel's.

And then she was cupping his face in her hands and all he

could see was the clear brown of her irises, the golden star-burst around her pupils bright. "You're safe!"

Sliding his arms around her under her wings, he picked her up and spun her around. "You were worried about me." He could look after himself, but it seemed right that a mate should worry.

"Of course I was worried." Andromeda pretended to hit his shoulders as he held her up off the ground, but it was more a caress than censure. "You took your time getting here."

Really wanting to kiss her—*stupid* Grimoire—he put her on the ground and sneakily petted her wings.

She shot him a minatory look but her lips were tugging up at the corners, her eyes sparkling. Playing with him again. Their own secret game. When her fingers brushed his, he closed his hand over hers. "I had to avoid Lijuan's squadron," he told her and Isabel. "They're waiting for Andi to emerge from Amanat."

Hands on her hips, Isabel asked for further information. "Hmm," she said afterward. "Let them skulk about for now. We'll eliminate the four from the equation when you and Andi are ready to leave—we don't want to give Philomena a chance to send reinforcements or replacements."

"We can do it," he said, including both women in his statement.

Isabel shook her head. "Caliane's squadrons need the experience and the confidence that comes from defeating the enemy."

Naasir decided he could allow the squadron that; this prey wasn't very interesting. "I need to speak to Caliane." The Ancient would expect him. He wasn't hers, but she thought of him as hers while he was here, and regardless, she had his respect.

Caliane might be an archangel known for her grace and the haunting beauty of her voice, but she had the same killer instinct as Naasir—and the same devotion to family.

Andromeda was still giddy with relief an hour later when Naasir climbed up to her balcony and walked into her room through the open doors. He'd bathed somewhere, was dressed in clean jeans and a white collarless shirt with the sleeves rolled up to his elbows. Made of either a fine cotton or linen, it was washed soft and fit him so well that she knew it was his. He must've left clothes in Amanat.

Walking over to where she was sitting on the edge of her bed making notes on a small pad, he sat down beside her and nuzzled at her. She should've stopped him but she didn't. His warm breath, his warmer skin, his quintessentially masculine scent, the dampness of his freshly washed hair, it all felt too good, felt like the best thing she would ever feel.

"Did you feed?" she asked in a husky tone, having noticed the fine lines of strain on his face when he first arrived.

"Yes." He sprawled on the bed behind her—as if he had every right to just take over her space. "Have you seen the angel we rescued?"

Andromeda turned to sit with one leg bent and on the bed, curling her fingers into her palm to keep from reaching out and stroking the hard muscle of his thigh. "No, she's in *anshara*."

"She was brave," Naasir said, his tone matter-of-fact. "She'll survive."

"The body, yes, but I worry about her mind and her heart."

"When she wakes, she'll make a choice to live or to die while living." Starkly solemn words. "No one can make it for her."

That metal hand, it was back, crushing her chest. "Did you ever have to do that?" she whispered.

"Yes, when I was created. I decided to live and to be me."

It should've been a nonsensical statement, for what child remembered its birth? Yet she knew it for pure truth—Naasir didn't lie. "I'm glad," she said. "I like you."

A glint of silver under the curl of his lashes. "Lie down beside me."

Heart aching, she didn't fight her need or his. Going down on her side beside him, she propped her head on one hand . . . and spread a wing over his chest.

His smile held her captive, the hands with which he petted her feathers unexpectedly gentle. Though he stayed away from the highly sensitive areas, the caresses made her toes curl.

"Pretty feathers," he murmured, lashes lowered as he indulged himself. "Do you know you have bronze filaments that catch the sunlight?"

"No, I don't." Andromeda knew her wings weren't striking,

but they were strong and they took her to the freedom of the sky. It was more than enough.

Naasir smoothed out a feather. "Look."

When she did, she caught the faint glimmer of a bronze filament hidden among all the others on a middle primary covert. Wonder unfurled in her. "How did you notice that?"

"Because I notice you." With that comment that stole her breath, he began to stroke her wing again. "Alexander—tell me your thoughts."

Andromeda looked at the notepad she'd dropped on the bed by her breasts. She'd been using it to organize her thoughts. "I think there's a high chance he's in his former territory, but not beneath what was his palace."

She blew out a breath. "I tried to direct Lijuan's people away from the entire region, but I don't think Xi was convinced." The tightrope she'd walked in Lijuan's throne room made her breath turn shallow even now. "If he does go there, I'm certain he'll focus on the palace."

"Rohan is very strong—he'll delay them." Naasir bent his forearm behind his head. "Had you asked him, he'd have volunteered to be the first line of defense for his father."

"Should we warn him?"

Naasir took out a sleek black phone in answer. "Jelena had a spare," he told her before making a call to Raphael. "The sire will speak one-to-one with Rohan, tell him Lijuan's plans," he shared with her after a short conversation. "Rohan's loyalty to his father is an indelible part of him."

Trusting his judgment, she nodded. "What about Favashi?"

"She hasn't chosen a side—and if Alexander rises, it's near certain Favashi will no longer be the Archangel of Persia. Rohan won't risk telling her." With that frank summary, Naasir placed his hand flat on her wing, the touch possessive. "If not below the palace, then where?"

Wanting desperately to erase the distance between them, she picked up her notepad and showed him the crude map she'd drawn. "There's a highly complex cave system about a five-hour flight from the palace." More than distant and remote enough to offer total privacy.

"Parts of the cave system are so deep that no one has ever

successfully explored them, though many have attempted it. Most," she said, the tiny hairs on her arms standing up, "give up after suffering injuries. The others have disappeared without a trace."

"Alexander is Sleeping with one eye open?"

"He was a general." Giving in to need, she began to pet Naasir's hair. His rumbling purr made her thighs clench, her breasts feel as if they were swelling . . . and her heart threaten to break.

Forcing herself to speak past the lump in her throat, she said, "One mortal explorer who barely made it out said that at the far end of the caves, deep in the earth, there's a great chasm filled with molten lava." Andromeda hadn't been able to stop imagining the terrifyingly beautiful sight ever since she'd read the explorer's rambling, fragmented report.

"Most people discount his report because his sanity was broken by whatever it was he saw, but the report's full of too much detail for me to do the same. A number of the things he said line up exactly with how I imagine an Ancient might protect himself." About to tell Naasir more about what the explorer had stated, her mouth suddenly fell open.

She sat up in bed, eyes wide. "Maybe what the explorer saw wasn't lava at all, but molten metal—Caliane says Alexander had a strong affinity to it."

Silver eyes gleamed at her. Moving without warning, Naasir grabbed one of her arms and hauled her across his chest.

"Naasir!"

"To get to the metal-lava chasm," he said, totally ignoring her frown and holding her flush to the hard heat of his chest with one arm around her waist, "we'll have to infiltrate Favashi's territory."

Propping up her chin on her hands, the feel of his heart beating under her a deep pleasure, she surrendered to the indulgence of being so close to him. "You can sneak in anywhere. I'm the problem." She made a face.

"I need you." Blunt words that fell like a gift over her. "You carry knowledge about Alexander that could cause us to change our path midway."

"Yes." Her theory was based on historical records and instinct. There was no predicting the actuality. "I wouldn't let you go alone anyway. It's dangerous."

A slow smile that turned into a growl that made her skin go tight and her blood turn to honey. "That *stupid* Grimoire book." Gripping her chin, he bared his teeth at her. "I haven't forgotten your promise. I get to do anything I want to you after I find it."

Andromeda couldn't breathe. "Anything you want," she whispered, her voice husky and her breasts so swollen they ached. "Touching, licking, biting . . . anything."

The smile returned and this time it was so primal she knew that should he ever take her, he'd own her. Every inch, every drop, everything.

26

Illium flew over New York with a buoyant spirit. Jason and Naasir were both out of harm's way at present, and he'd spoken to his mother. Thanks to Raphael's call on the heels of his own, the Hummingbird had accepted an invitation to come to New York.

He was determined the anniversary wouldn't be so bad this year. He'd keep her too busy to think about what she'd left behind in the Refuge. Busy and happy enough that she wouldn't want to return quickly to her painful, soul-shredding vigil.

Seeing the shattered light of Aodhan's wings not far off in the afternoon sky, he smiled and angled up toward his friend. His mother loved Aodhan, and Illium knew Aodhan returned the affection. He'd spend hours with her if that was what she needed.

"Your mother has a great capacity to love," Aodhan had said to him once.

It was true—and it was also the Hummingbird's greatest weakness.

Putting two fingers between his teeth as he reached Aodhan's altitude, he whistled.

Aodhan glanced over, the faint smile on his face deeply welcome after two painful centuries when Illium hadn't been able to reach his friend, no matter how hard he tried. Aodhan's psychic scars might never fade, but he was rising past them in a show of grit and strength no one who didn't know what had been done to him could fully understand.

The twenty-three months Aodhan had been missing had been the most horrific period of Illium's life . . . worse than when he'd lost his mortal lover. He'd survived losing her. He didn't know if he could survive losing Aodhan.

Never before had he seen that truth so clearly and it shook him.

"What's wrong?" Aodhan called out from his position on Illium's left, their wingtips almost touching.

Illium went to shake his head, staggered by his realization and not ready to discuss it, when it felt as if his heart literally exploded from the inside out. The pain was excruciating.

Wings crumpling, he felt himself fall.

He'd played this trick a thousand times, pretending to plummet out-of-control from the sky, his wings tangled. Aodhan had stopped falling for it centuries ago, and, mind red with pain, Illium had no way to signal to him that this wasn't a trick. The high-rises of Manhattan rushed up at him at terminal velocity. Should the impact separate his head from his spine, his brain and internal organs pulverized, he wouldn't survive.

Not ready to die, and piercingly conscious the wound of his death would permanently break both his mother and Aodhan, he tried to stretch out his wings. A new blast of agonizing pain flooded his mouth with blood . . . and switched off the light on his consciousness.

Aodhan saw Illium's expression change right before his wings crumpled. So many times Illium had tricked him, but his instincts screamed this was no trick. Not stopping to think, he folded in his own wings and dropped like a stone toward Illium's rapidly diminishing form, those beautiful wings of silver-blue hanging uselessly as Illium tumbled toward metal and glass and concrete at deadly speed.

Sire! Illium is falling!

Even as he alerted Raphael, Aodhan knew his archangel wasn't close enough. He'd spotted Raphael's wings on the other side of the city not long before Illium whistled at him. Heart screaming as he willed himself to drop faster, he searched the air for any other help, but everything was moving by too fast, the wind burning his skin. His only advantage was that he was an aerodynamic bullet, while Illium's wings were causing drag, slowing his descent a minute fraction.

Aodhan didn't take his eyes from that falling blue form . . . and then he was passing it. He snapped out his wings less than two hundred meters from the roof of a high-rise and, back facing Illium, braced for impact.

It slammed through his bones, rattled his teeth, and sent him spiraling down in an uncontrollable fall. He could feel Illium sliding off his back, couldn't slow it down.

They were going to hit the roof at bone-breaking speed.

Aodhan wasn't sure either one of them would survive. *No*, he thought. *No*.

Managing to grab hold of Illium's wrist as his friend tumbled off him, he felt his arm wrench out of its socket. He refused to release his grip. And then he was seeing white fire in his vision, Raphael rising up from below and scooping Illium into his arms bare meters from the roof. *I have him*.

Aodhan let go.

Too close to the roof himself and with too much momentum to stop the collision, Aodhan braced himself for another hard landing when he'd only just recovered from the last one.

Having closed his eyes instinctively, he didn't know at first what hit him. He just knew he'd been rammed hard enough to crack several ribs. Eyes snapping open, he saw he'd been pushed into clear air.

Spreading his wings, he spiraled out of control a couple more times before finding his aerial balance. Sweat-soaked and with his heart racing what felt like a thousand beats a minute, he looked up to see Elena and the Primary flying toward him.

"Are you okay?" Elena yelled when she was close enough. "We couldn't catch you in time so we rammed you!"

"Thank you," he managed to get out, able to see a bruise already forming on Elena's face and upper arm. "Illium?"

Stark eyes. "I don't know."

The three of them turned as one to the Tower. Landing on the balcony outside the infirmary, he and Elena ran in while the

Primary waited outside. The senior Tower healer and Raphael were bent over Illium's limp form, the room otherwise empty.

Aodhan wasn't used to seeing his friend so still. Illium was never still. Even when he was lying down, his eyes sparked, his mouth laughed.

"Aodhan." Elena reached out a hand as if to take his, dropped it halfway. "He's alive," she said, her voice fierce. "You saved him."

Aodhan felt as if he was still falling. "There's blood on him." It came out a whisper.

Elena's breath trembled, and though she'd only known Illium a mere heartbeat in contrast to the centuries of memories in Aodhan's head, Aodhan knew she, too, was close to panic. Time made little difference; it was the heart that mattered, the ability to love. And Elena loved with a passion that had melted the ice-cold shields of an archangel.

Her unhidden fear for Illium made it easier for Aodhan to reach out and lock his hand with hers, to make voluntary contact with anyone other than his closest friend. The sensation would've been a shock at any other time; at this instant his mind and his soul had room for no other emotions but those already threatening to drown him.

Aodhan willed his friend to wake up, trying not to see the wings lying so limp on either side of Illium's body, the bloody tears smeared on his cheeks. If he lost Illium . . .

His hand clenched on Elena's.

27

Naasir stayed in touch with the Tower throughout the night. Dmitri had called all of the Seven outside New York minutes after Illium's fall, to ensure they heard the truth, not rumor.

"He hasn't woken," Dmitri told him two hours before his and Andromeda's planned departure. "But the healer says this is a natural sleep." Grim relief. "He'll likely wake while you're en route. I'll let you know the instant he does."

His own relief clawing at him, Naasir said, "The Hummingbird?" Naasir didn't have a mother, but he liked Illium's. She was soft and kind and even before she'd had her own son, she'd been gentle with Naasir.

During art lessons at school, she hadn't even minded if he used his hands to paint, or if he made a mess. "She'll be scared." The Hummingbird hadn't always been so fragile, but Naasir knew to be careful with her now; she was wounded inside.

"I had Jessamy tell her the news in person—she says it's been centuries since she saw the Hummingbird come so violently to life."

"Her cub is hurt."

"Yes. She's on her way to New York."

Hanging up so Dmitri could update Galen and Venom, Naasir told Andromeda the news. He'd snuck into her room after Dmitri's first call and woken her because he couldn't be alone while one of his family was hurt; taking one look at his face, she'd risen to give him a hug.

Now, she hugged him again, her embrace tight. "I'm so glad he's all right."

Holding her close, he rubbed his cheek against her hair and face, calming himself. She petted his back, making soft, soothing sounds that coaxed his muscles to relax. When she drew him to the bed, he went.

They slept the two hours till dawn with their hands entwined, face-to-face, one of Andromeda's wings warm silk over him.

He woke before her but stayed motionless and watched her sleep, counting the lashes on her eyes, the tiny freckles on her face, feeling the rhythm of her breath. After last night, he had not a single doubt in his mind that she was his mate. Even so far from his family at such a bad time, he hadn't felt angry and panicked and as if he was in the wrong skin.

Because Andromeda was here and because she understood him.

Though she'd only known him for a short time, she'd understood he'd come to her because he needed contact, needed someone to hold on to while he waited for news about Illium. She might play and fight with him in normal life but when it was serious, she was right there, her arms strong and her affection a passionately protective force.

He was going to win her, no matter what.

And he'd find that stupid Grimoire book so he could put his scent all over her, *inside* her.

Getting out of bed before he rolled her over onto her back, parted her thighs and sank inside her wet tightness, he tugged gently on the braid in which she insisted on taming her pretty hair. "Wake up. It's time."

Andromeda took in Naasir's expression the instant she woke, was happy to see that he looked more like his usual self. The painful hours since he'd woken her in the night had made it clear he cared deeply for his family . . . would care as deeply for the woman who was his. Andromeda wanted to be that woman so much it hurt.

Shoving down the need lest it paralyze her, she got ready. Isabel had found her some combat leathers that fit, the leather worn-in and the shade a dusty brown perfect for this mission. The pants hugged her legs, while the top—which she'd worn over a tank top modified for wings—left her arms bare but came up to her neck and fit snugly around her wings.

Soon after her meeting with Caliane, Andromeda had started wearing in the boots she'd found in the closet, and though they remained stiff, they were far better than flimsy slippers. As for the scabbard Isabel had given her, it was perfect. "I'm ready," she said, joining Naasir out on the balcony ten minutes after he'd woken her.

He was dressed in a sand-colored T-shirt and cargo pants of desert camouflage, boots on his feet.

While the two of them ate a quick breakfast, Avi and Isabel went out with a squadron and dealt with the four enemy lurkers. Since Amanat was Caliane's heart, it hadn't been built to house prisoners. Avi's only choice was either to execute the prisoners or send them elsewhere.

"He plans to place them on a prison ship once he's finished the interrogation," Isabel told Naasir and Andromeda after flying back to confirm things had gone exactly as planned. "It's anchored deep in the ocean, so even if Lijuan's people figure out where they are and mount a prison break, it won't put Amanat at risk."

"Thank you for the safe harbor," Andromeda said, touching both hands to Isabel's. "Please thank Lady Caliane too." Raphael's mother was with her maidens and not to be disturbed. "I hope we'll spar again one day, Isabel."

"Of course—I must reclaim my honor." A quiet smile. "Safe journey, my friends."

Andromeda and Naasir left quietly, slipping out into the early morning darkness like wraiths. They'd decided she couldn't afford to fly, not yet. Since this entire country had been part of Lijuan's territory before Caliane awoke, Lijuan had spies and loyalists throughout. Should Andromeda be spotted, the enemy might decide to shoot her down, or to take her in the air where Naasir couldn't back her up.

"It's so peaceful this time of day," she said as they walked through the forest outside Amanat. "Even the monkeys are asleep."

"They're not asleep—they're just not sure about you." Reaching out, he ran his hand down her back and over her wings. "Now they know you're mine."

She couldn't restrain her shiver. His eyes seemed to glow. "I'm going to find the Grimoire."

The low, deep promise sent a surge of pure *want* through her veins, temptation an ache in her breasts, tension in her abdomen, damp readiness between her thighs. "I'd break my vow for you," she whispered, heartbroken at the idea that she might never know him as intimately as a woman could know a man.

Fangs flashing, Naasir bent to her throat to breathe deep. But even as her eyes began to close, her blood honey, he pulled back and shook his head, the shaggy silver of his hair glinting in the faint light of dawn. "You must keep promises," he said. "Even those to yourself."

Her lower lip shook. "You see how bad my control is over my base urges," she whispered. "You're having to school me."

Naasir smiled as if she'd said something wonderful. "I don't see a problem. My mate should find me irresistible."

She wanted at once to kiss that wicked mouth with its sinful smile, and bare her teeth at him for his arrogance. "I'm not your mate." Could never be, her bloodline of the enemy and bound to that enemy.

Naasir growled. "I'll make you change your mind."

Andromeda wanted to play with him so badly that she did something unforgivable—she encouraged him to think they could have a future. "Oh? How?"

"Wait and see."

The monkeys started calling out then, one swinging upside down from a branch above to stare right into her face. When she cried out and jumped back, the monkey and Naasir both laughed. The others joined in, the sound raucous.

Scowling at her unrepentant partner, she pushed at his muscular arm. Undaunted, he grabbed her hand and held it possessively in his.

She curled her fingers around his palm, not challenging his right to touch her.

* * *

Two hours of walking brought them to the spot where Naasir had arranged for a large vehicle to be waiting for them, watched over by a vampire who saluted Naasir then took off in the direction of Amanat. Modified to transport injured angels if necessary, it had plenty of room for her wings and the rest of their journey to the airfield passed quickly.

Since Philomena likely had eyes on the airfield as well, they'd had to make a decision about whether to arrange a different jet, or to do the unexpected. Since it was unlikely they could arrange another jet as fast as those in Raphael's fleet, they went with the latter option. Driving the vehicle right to the jet in order to offset the chance of a surprise attack, they had the pilot file a flight plan that took them across Favashi's territory and deep into Michaela's.

Once Philomena passed on the information to Xi, he'd either follow them to their destination, or send a squadron after them while going with his own instincts—which would likely lead him to Rohan's palace. Regardless, he'd be at least a five-hour flight from Andromeda and Naasir's actual destination.

Once in the air, Andromeda settled in while Naasir prowled the aisles like a beast caged. "Come here," she said after ten minutes, having moved to an extra-wide seat meant to accommodate two angels who wanted to sit side by side.

He scowled but came. "I don't want to sit."

"Lie down and put your head in my lap."

Still scowling, he stretched out on the seat as she'd suggested. His tension remained unabated. When she began to stroke her fingers through the heavy silk of his hair, however, his eyes closed and he made a rumbling sound in his chest. Smiling, happy to simply be here in this moment with him, she continued to pet him until he fell asleep. Even then, she didn't stop, the pleasure in doing this for him a glowing warmth inside her.

When he stretched some time later and opened his eyes on a yawn, it was to look at her with a sleepy gaze and say, "This is a mate thing to do."

Yes, it was. "Is it?" She forced a teasing smile. "If I'm your mate, shouldn't you be doing it in return then?"

He reached up to place his hand on the back of her neck, his skin warm and a little rough. Her pulse thudded at the contact, her senses lost in the silver mysteries of his eyes.

"I wouldn't just pet your hair," he said. "I'd stroke your wings, especially the places I'm not allowed to touch yet."

"Naasir," she whispered, leaning so close to him that their breaths mingled. "Why did you not find me sooner?" They could've had centuries together instead of mere weeks.

"I wasn't full-grown." He ran the fingers of his free hand over her cheek. "I didn't yet have the understanding of what it meant to have a mate."

Lifting her head before she closed the final distance between them and stole a kiss, she tilted her head to the side. "But you're six hundred years old."

Sliding his hand from her neck, he insinuated his arm behind her waist, so that he was holding her under her wing. His body heat burned into her back and the upper part of his arm brushed against the inner surface of her wings. It was a deeply intimate hold.

And it felt unmistakably right.

"I'm not like other six-hundred-year-old immortals," Naasir said, his voice unexpectedly quiet and serious. "I'm not like anyone."

"I know." She ran her fingers through his hair again. "You're unique and wild and extraordinary."

"Sometimes I'm more animal than man."

She shrugged. "In my experience, animals are often far better than people." Massaging his nape when he tugged her hand down to it, she smiled. "You can't scare me off. I've stood face-to-face with monsters—I know you're the opposite."

His gaze darkened. "I really wish I could kill Lijuan."

Realizing he'd taken her reference to Charisemnon's court as being to Lijuan's, she nodded. "The mortals who seek immortality, do you think they ever consider the fact that immortality might mean being stuck with people you despise for centuries or even millennia?"

Naasir didn't answer, his eyes closed again. "Use your nails," he said lazily.

When she ran her nails over his nape, he purred. It made her body sing, her breath shallow. "Were you ever human or were you born as you are?" she asked when she could speak coherently, her need to know him endless.

His lashes lifted. "Most people ask who Made me."

She could see why—being Made by an angel was the only known way to become a vampire. "But you're not a vampire," she said definitively. "You have enough vampiric characteristics that it's easier for people to categorize you as a vampire than to accept the unknown, but I told you I like hunting secrets."

Naasir's lips curved in a playful smile. "Ellie calls me a tiger creature. It makes her crazy that Raphael won't tell her what I am and spoil my game."

Andromeda pulled at his hair a little. "You and your sire are clearly both as bad as one another."

His laughter filled the cabin. When he spoke again, he said, "I was once human . . . and I was not human. Then I became me."

She narrowed her eyes at the riddle. "I think Raphael's consort and I should join forces."

A grin. "It is a game."

"Give me another clue."

"I am a thing of more than one thing."

"You're not a thing," she said with a frown. "You are Naasir, a beautiful, dangerous man."

He sat up without warning, making her heart thud. Bracing one hand on the armrest on her left, his arm diagonally across her body and his face bare inches from hers, he said, "I am a person to you."

It wasn't a question but she felt compelled to reply. "You are the most fascinating, most wonderful, and most aggravating person I've ever met."

Bending his head with a grin at the last, he rubbed his nose over hers. "And you, Andi, are the smartest, most sparkling, most-delicious-smelling woman I've ever met."

Her thighs clenched at the memory of what he'd said he'd do to her should he ever sink his teeth into her. "I *will* figure out the mystery of you," she said, throwing down the gauntlet. "When I do, will you tell me of the adventures you had in your youth?"

"I can tell you a story now." Retaking his previous position with his head on her lap and his arm around her back, he bent one leg at the knee, the other stretched out on the seat. "When I first came to the Refuge, I was small, a boy like Sameon."

Andromeda tried to imagine him as a child, couldn't. To her, he was and would always be, a strong, deadly man.

"I didn't know I wasn't supposed to touch wings." He rubbed the back of his hand over the inner surface of her feathers, eyes going heavy-lidded when she shivered. "Even though Raphael had told me after I yanked out one of his feathers, I still didn't understand—I wasn't grown like another boy of the same size, and my mind couldn't understand things like that."

"But you could understand other things?"

A nod. "I knew who was a good person and who was a bad person. I knew never to be alone with certain people, and I knew I could play with the other children but that I mustn't hurt them with my fangs or my claws or I'd lose my friends. I was very careful with them—angel babies are very fragile."

"Yes, I suppose they are." Especially in comparison to a boy who had claws and fangs. "You said you were human and not human. When you were younger, were you more not human?"

A slow, sly smile. "You're clever, Andi."

She pulled his hair again. "Answer the question."

Baring his teeth at her, he said, "Yes, I was more not human. But I knew how to play with other children." A sudden darkness in his eyes. "I never played with angel or mortal children before I came to the Refuge. My before-friends were snow wolves. The other children were all dead. Ghosts."

28

The scholar in Andromeda wanted to follow that dark thread, but the woman who'd fallen so entirely for this man knew down that alley lay only hurt for him. "I'm sorry," she said gently. "Did you make good friends at the Refuge?"

"Yes." A flash of fangs. "Some parents said I was a bad influence, but the children liked me."

"Of course they did." Andromeda laughed. "Are you still friends with those children now?"

"Yes. Especially with two of them," Naasir said. "One works with Galen, the other is a scientist on a tropical island in Astaad's territory. When I visit, he gives me fish to eat." Naasir looked dubious. "I eat it to be polite, but I don't understand fish."

Her lips twitched. "You're a good friend." She could just imagine him eating the fish while trying to figure out why anyone would eat fish. "Tell me the rest of the story."

Fingers brushing over her hip, he grinned. "Because I didn't understand I wasn't supposed to touch wings, I'd do things like wait on top of bookshelves or cling to the ceiling and drop down on unsuspecting angels. Before they'd finished shrieking, I'd have torn off a feather and run away."

Andromeda's shoulders shook. "You were a little terror."

"Yes," he said proudly. "Then one day, I jumped on Michaela."

Andromeda's laughter dried up. "Did she hurt you?" The archangel renowned for her vivid green eyes and flawless skin the shade of milk chocolate, her beauty the muse of poets and artists through the ages, was not known for her patience.

"Michaela wasn't an archangel then, but she was dangerous all the same. Only her scent was . . . not what it has become." Naasir frowned, as if trying to figure out the change. "She was fast though. She caught me by the foot before I could run away and, holding me upside down with a grip on one ankle, her arm stretched out so I couldn't get her with my claws, she said, 'You are in trouble.'"

Andromeda swallowed. "What did you do?"

"I had one of her covert feathers in my hand and I offered it back to her. When she didn't take it, I growled and clawed and tried to get away."

Andromeda's heart was in her mouth, though Michaela clearly hadn't done Naasir any lasting harm if he was telling her this tale. "Did she take you to Raphael?"

"No. She carried me to Jessamy and told her I needed lessons in civilized manners."

"Did Jessamy make her let you go?"

Naasir shook his head. "I'd torn up all my schoolbooks the day before and eaten the schoolroom's pet bunny."

Andromeda knew she shouldn't, but she burst out laughing. "You *didn't*."

"It was there and I was hungry and no one told me I couldn't eat it," he said with an aggrieved look on his face. "Why would you put a bunny there if it wasn't for eating?"

"Poor Jessamy." Wiping away her tears, Andromeda shook her head. "What did she do?"

"She locked all the windows and doors in her study space in the Archives, then held on to me while Michaela slipped out and pulled the door shut behind her, making sure it locked. When Jessamy released me, I raged all around the room, tearing up things, clawing the furniture and even biting her."

Andromeda's smile faded. "You felt trapped."

"Jessamy didn't know all of my life before, didn't understand what it would do to me to be caged. As soon as she realized I wasn't just angry, but scared, she opened the door."

"And you ran?" she guessed, her heart hurting for that small, scared boy who didn't know how to be in an unfamiliar world.

Naasir's answer was a surprise. "Jessamy was crying. Even though I was scared, I knew that was bad, so I went over and patted her hand and said sorry for biting it."

Andromeda's own eyes turned hot.

"She went to her knees and told me that wasn't why she was crying. She was crying because she'd made me afraid when she'd just wanted a chance to talk to me without me running away when I got bored."

Andromeda could well imagine Jessamy's distress. The teacher of angelic young had a heart so huge, she loved each one of her charges as if that child was her own. "You decided to stay, didn't you?"

"I didn't like Jessamy crying—she was always nice to me, even when I tore up her books. I put my hand in hers and we went for a walk to a place with gardens, where she took a seat on a stone bench, put me on her lap, and started to teach me what I needed to know so I could live in the world without people being angry with me all the time."

The ache inside Andromeda, it was so deep now, for the boy he'd been. "How long did Jessamy teach you such things?"

"For years." Naasir's tone held a deep vein of affection. "It took me time to learn but Jessamy is patient. Every afternoon, we'd sit in the garden and she'd teach me things the other children already knew. Like how I shouldn't growl at people even if I didn't like them, and how bunnies and other animals in the Refuge weren't for eating."

He rubbed his fingers over her hip. "Dmitri taught me, too, but Dmitri didn't care if I ate pet bunnies or if I jumped out at him so he wasn't the best teacher on the topic."

Andromeda could well imagine that Raphael's deadly second had a far more laissez-faire attitude toward etiquette and behavior. When you were that dangerous, you made your own rules. "And now you can be so civilized it's scary."

A shrug. "I put on a different skin when it's necessary. Dmitri taught me that—he said I didn't have to change, but that my life would be easier if I could fool people into thinking I had at times."

"I'm so happy you never wear any skin but your own around me," Andromeda whispered, her heart wide open.

Silver eyes locked with hers. "I'll always be Naasir with you," he promised solemnly, then grinned. "Even if you ask me to act civilized for a minute."

She groaned and pretended to beat at him with her free hand. "You're never going to let me forget I said that, are you?"

"Maybe if you tell me a story of your childhood."

Naasir glimpsed many expressions move across Andromeda's face in a matter of split seconds. He didn't catch all of them, but he saw pain, anger, shame, and finally joy.

None of it surprised him; immortality meant many experiences. Though the shame wasn't a usual thing—but then, Andromeda wasn't a hardened immortal. Her heart was tender. She probably felt shame for a transgression others would've long forgotten.

"I never went to the Refuge school," she began. "I didn't see the Refuge at all until I flew there myself just after my seventy-fifth birthday."

"Seventy-five is not full-grown for an angel." At that age, she would've been close to a fifteen-year-old human teenager. "You flew to the Refuge alone?"

"Yes." Her expression altered, the golden bursts in her eyes suddenly dark. "My body had started to curve early, my breasts lush. I no longer appeared the child I was and a number of my parents' guests were starting to look at me in a way that was distinctly predatory and sexual."

Naasir felt his claws prick at his skin, fought to keep them sheathed.

"I couldn't take it anymore. I knew as a princess of the court, I was probably safe, but the look in the guests' eyes . . . it made me feel dirty and small. And the way my parents and their friends brutally tortured others for pleasure . . ." She shook her head, stark echoes of fear and shock in her expression. "I told them my plans, then flew out."

A shuddering breath. "I think Mother and Father expected me to give up and return home. When I didn't, they washed their hands of me."

Andromeda was lying. Not about her flight to the Refuge, but about another part of her story. It made him want to bare his teeth and demand she tell the truth, but he'd do that later, when she didn't appear so fragile. "Who did you play with when you lived with your parents?"

"The animals." Joy chased out the shadows. "Once, while I was having dinner in my nursery, a baby giraffe poked his head in the window and ate the fruit right off my plate."

Naasir grinned. "Truth?"

She nodded. "It came back, too. I used to make up a plate especially for him until my nanny caught me—and even after that, I waited until she wasn't paying attention and opened the window so the giraffe could slide its head and neck inside."

Delighted at the idea of her dining with a giraffe, Naasir said, "Did the other animals also join you for meals?"

A shake of her head. "With the cheetahs, we'd race. I'd be in the air, the cheetahs on the ground." She blew out a breath. "They're *fast*."

"I'll race you," Naasir said. "When we're free of Lijuan's spies."

"Deal."

As the plane flew onward and the world turned, she told him more stories of her childhood. It betrayed a total lack of other children. Not even any mortal playmates. Andromeda appeared to have had no one but her animals. Maybe that was why she understood him so well, accepted his wildness without hesitation. He was happy about that, but he didn't like to think of her so alone.

A chime sounded in the air a minute after heavy turbulence that threatened to throw them both around the cabin.

"That must be our signal," Andromeda said.

Naasir got up to look out a window. "Yes." Grabbing the pack lying on another seat, he put it on and snapped on the straps across his chest before pulling on a thin and tight knit cap that would stop his hair from glittering in the sunlight. "Ready?"

She grinned. "Oh, yes."

The co-pilot exited the cockpit right then. "Two things. First, Illium's awake and fine—message literally just came in, is probably on your phone, too." His smile matched their own. "Second, we couldn't stabilize over the initial drop point. Can you go through the oasis?"

"Yes," Naasir said, following the bearded male to the back of the plane. "Bad air?"

"This spot is notorious for it—unpredictable air currents, like the sky is telling you to get the fuck out."

Naasir met Andromeda's gaze as the co-pilot attached himself to the wall using a strap. "I think we're in the right place, Andi."

The co-pilot opened the wide door built for this purpose before she could reply, air screaming into the cabin. Pushing out two packs, he nodded at Naasir. "Good luck!" The wind almost ripped away his words.

Giving him a thumbs-up, Naasir jumped with one final grin in Andromeda's direction. With a descent this finely calculated, he had to get out at precisely the right altitude for the parachute to function safely. Opening the chute the instant he was clear of the plane, he whooped at the sensation of flight, the air, cold at this altitude, rushing past him.

He heard laughter nearby and when he glanced over, there was Andromeda, snapping out pretty wings patterned like a bird's. Grinning, he rode the late-afternoon winds all the way to his planned landing spot in the desert landscape, mentally marking the splashes of color that denoted the landing spots of the small chutes that had deployed with their supply packs.

He began to gather up the chute the instant he was on the ground, while Andromeda swept left toward the first supply pack. It only took him a matter of minutes to fold the chute back in. Instead of abandoning it on the sand, he took the time to bury it so it wouldn't arouse suspicion, or act as a beacon to any searchers in the air.

He finished just as Andromeda returned with the second supply pack, having already dropped the first near him. Naasir packed away the small chutes into special compartments, then pulled on the heavier pack and helped her strap on the smaller one. It was designed to be worn in the front. He hadn't wanted her to jump with it because the unaccustomed weight might've thrown her off.

"Comfortable?" he asked after fixing the final strap.

She nodded. "We should get off the sand. I feel so exposed here."

Agreeing, he told her to fly ahead to the date palms that sprawled in the far distance, part of an oasis inhabited by a small number of villagers. "Stay at the level of the tree line."

Rising into the air, she called out, "Race you!"

He took off. He preferred bare feet, but he'd worn boots for this mission, since they'd be climbing through cave systems. Those boots were soon covered in dust as he ran across the sand to the trees.

They both stayed on the same path and he ran in the shadow of Andromeda's wings for much of the race, their pace neck and neck, but he pulled away at the end, his chest heaving as he sucked in air. Tearing off the cap now that he was in the trees, he shoved it into a pocket of his pants.

Andromeda came down beside him in a rush of wind, her own breathing uneven. "I need to sprint more."

"We can do it together." Taking a bottle of water from the side of his pack, he gave it to her to drink, then drank himself. "No more flying for now," he said after putting away the water. "It'll just take one sighting by the wrong person to give away our location." According to Andromeda's research, this oasis was owned by a tribe not known for its hospitality.

Andromeda glanced around at the pomegranate and fig trees visible below the date palms. "This must be the tribe's source of income."

"Which means we can't guarantee there aren't people around checking their crops."

They went forward with care. It wasn't until an hour later that Andromeda said, "What if I'm wrong, Naasir?" Her voice was small. "What if Lijuan's people reach Alexander first and she murders him?"

"Then she's proved her evil once again." He ran his hand down her wing. "Lijuan is not your fault." And because he understood the thoughts that haunted her, he added, "As your parents' choice to hurt people for their own pleasure isn't your fault."

Face stark, Andromeda faced him. "Find the Grimoire." It was a command . . . but her voice, it trembled. "I need you to find it."

"I will." Then he would claim her and keep her—and order her to tell him all her secrets, especially the one that made her hurt so much each time she looked at him.

29

"Dmitri just heard from the pilot," Raphael told Elena as the two of them stood atop the roof of the Legion building, Manhattan draped in early morning darkness around them. "Naasir and Andromeda are safely away."

"I didn't doubt it." Elena tightened her ponytail, her hair gleaming white in the lights of the city. "Will we join them once they locate Alexander?"

"We?"

His consort raised an eyebrow, her gaze flinty. "Don't try that Archangel tone on me."

"I am an archangel."

Lips tilting up at the corners, his hunter spread her wings so that the white gold of her primaries brushed his. "You're also mine and I will hurt you if you dare go up against Lijuan on your own." She slid out her crossbow. "Don't mess with me."

Pulling her close, the crossbow flat against his chest, he took her mouth. He'd fallen for her because she was a warrior, and over the time since they'd come together, he'd learned to accept that she would never stand on the sidelines. But this time—*I need you to remain in the city, help hold it while I'm gone.*

Elena broke off the kiss, scowled. "Dmitri is plenty tough enough to do that."

"But you, *hbeebti*, are no longer just a hunter," he said, speaking the word "beloved" in the language his consort's grandmother had brought with her from a distant land. "You are a symbol—even if I am missed, so long as people can see you in the air, they'll feel safe." *Because everyone knows I would not leave my consort in a city I didn't feel was protected against all harm.*

"Shit," Elena muttered. "I hate it when you make sense." Strapping her crossbow to her thigh once again, she walked to the edge of the roof and waited for him to come up beside her. "Symbols are necessary right now, aren't they?"

Raphael answered by sliding his wing over hers, both of them aware the world was perched on a precipice that could give way without warning. Wind riffling through his hair, he looked toward the Tower, saw Dmitri step out onto a balcony with Aodhan. "I should only be away from the city for a short time, just long enough to protect Alexander during the most vulnerable part of his waking."

Elena nodded, her eyes turned in the same direction as Raphael's. "We going to talk about how you made it to Illium so fast? That was an impossible distance to cross even for you, Archangel."

Raphael watched the light glitter off Aodhan, shards sparking in the air, and thought of that moment when he'd seen Illium drop from the sky. He'd thought it a game until Aodhan's cry for help. "The Hummingbird can't lose him. He's her only link to a tenuous sanity." Raphael loved Illium's mother, had great respect for her, but he also understood that she was broken inside.

A slightly rough-skinned hand closing over his, his warrior-consort's fingers strong. "You can't lose him either." Her eyes held knowledge of him that belied the briefness of their relationship in immortal terms. "He's the heart of the Seven."

Yes. Illium might be younger than several of the others and appear irreverent more often than not, but he was their glue, the piece that tied all the others to one another. "Before Mahiya, when Jason was yet lost in darkness, the only time I saw him close to a smile was after Illium challenged him to an old-fashioned duel."

Raphael could see his spymaster's impassive face in his

mind, remember how Jason's eyes had warmed from within. "Your Bluebell was a stripling whom Jason easily defeated, but Illium just laughed and asked if he could have a longer rapier next time so he could poke at Jason from a distance."

Elena's lips twitched. "That sounds like Illium." Though he'd woken an hour past and appeared fine but for a little residual dizziness, terror still bled through her at what she'd witnessed that afternoon. It was pure chance she'd been close enough to help—she and the Primary had been flying toward the Legion building when she'd glimpsed the wild blue and shattered light of Illium and Aodhan high in the sky.

She'd smiled, remembering something Aodhan had said to her.

It was worth the risk to play a game with my friend again. Until I threw that ball at Illium over the river, I didn't understand I hadn't felt alive for over two hundred years.

When Illium had fallen, she'd shaken her head at what she'd believed to be a trick. Everything had changed the instant she saw Aodhan dive, heard Raphael's alert to every angel in the vicinity. Only no one was close enough—least of all Raphael. "Your wings were afire," she whispered, still unable to fully understand what she'd seen in those seconds stretched by horror into hours.

"Tell me what you saw," Raphael said. "I felt my speed increase, but I put it down to the urgency of the incident."

Blinking, Elena turned to face the archangel who'd branded her to the soul. The fact he didn't know hadn't occurred to her . . . but it had all happened so fast, his attention on saving Illium and Aodhan both. "The white fire that licks over your wings at times," she said, touching her fingers to the shimmering white gold of his feathers, "it took over. It was like you had no physical wings—as if your wings were pure white flame."

It had been a magnificent sight she'd only processed in the aftermath. "The effect disappeared as soon as you had Illium in your arms."

Spreading out his wings and curling first one inward, then the other, Raphael examined the feathers before folding them back in. "No evidence of it now, but what you're describing sounds almost like Lijuan's ability to go noncorporeal. On the same continuum at least."

Elena's skin chilled. "Yeah, I guess." Releasing his hand, she gripped the front of his white shirt and tugged him to her. "Don't you *dare* 'evolve' on me." She couldn't follow him into that other state, though she'd kill herself trying.

Raphael's lips curved. "Have no fear, *hbeebti*," he said. "I am too fond of the flesh." A caress of her hip, a luscious kiss.

Yet even as the crashing windswept sea of him infiltrated her senses, Elena knew even an archangel couldn't hold back the possibly catastrophic changes wrought by the Cascade. "I'll follow you," she whispered against his lips. "No matter where you go, I'll be right beside you."

Eyes of endless blue burned with an incandescent flame. "Together, Elena-mine. Always." Wrapping her in his wings, he held her until her heart calmed, the fear receding under a tide of furious determination: no one and nothing would steal her archangel from her.

"I heard a bit of gossip from Amanat," she said once she could speak again.

"How can you hear gossip from Amanat? Unless you and my mother have become the best of friends?"

She elbowed him. "Very funny." Elena and Caliane might have called a truce, but Caliane remained an Ancient and her freaking mother-in-law. "I made some other friends on our last visit." Including a smart, funny maiden who danced as gracefully as Elena's sister Belle had danced before a murderous vampire stole her life.

"Belle! Belle! Can I dance with you?"

"Come on, squirt. Stand like this."

Chest achingly tight at the memory of a loss she would carry with her forever, she said, "Apparently, there's a high chance Naasir and his scholar are no longer just colleagues."

He looks at her as I've never seen Naasir look at anyone. As if she is a treasure he wants to keep, wants to protect.

"You catch your consort by surprise," Raphael murmured. "Particularly as the scholar has taken a vow of celibacy."

"We're talking about Naasir here." Elena grinned. "He has a certain charm. Just like his archangel—I never planned to be naked with you, either." Deadly and inhuman, the Archangel of New York was not a man with whom Elena Deveraux, Guild Hunter, had ever intended to mess.

A glint in the eyes that held oceans, even in the darkness. "Plan it now," he said, lifting off with her still in his arms. "We have not danced in the sky for too long, and today, I feel a need to celebrate life." His jaw grew hard.

Stroking it as her skin turned electric, Elena pulled his head down to her own. "Life," she whispered before their lips met in a storm of sensation.

30

Two hours of hiking later, Andromeda and Naasir found themselves on the outskirts of the village that was the last bastion of civilization before the cave system, the homes built around what, from the air, was a startlingly clear blue-green lake. A small jewel in the ocean of sand that surrounded the oasis on every side, the lake wasn't a perfect sphere.

No, it was an elongated teardrop.

The village was based around the fat upper curve of the tear.

It would've been far easier had they been able to jump on the other side of the oasis, but not at the cost of crashing the plane.

Settling in to wait for the early evening to turn to full dark, they were careful not to alert the villagers of their presence.

The two of them ate the dried trail foods they'd bought, but Andromeda knew while that would sustain her, it wasn't enough for Naasir. "Sip on me," she said, lifting her wrist to his mouth.

He drew in a deep breath, eyes molten and fangs flashing. "I'll drink you up." It was a rough warning.

"No, you won't." She knew exactly how protective he was. "Drink or I'll start to think you don't like me."

Growl rumbling in his chest, he gripped her wrist when she

would've pulled it away, nuzzled her pulse point. It felt as if all her blood rushed to that spot, pouring toward him.

"Andromeda." It was a warm, luxurious purr before he scraped his fangs over her skin.

Secret inner muscles clenched, her breath catching as her breasts ached; jealousy captured her in vicious claws, dug into her desire. "Is this how you feed from others?"

He licked her skin. "I'm not feeding." Another lick, a hot breath. "I'm seducing you."

Yes, he was. Slowly and with primal patience. When he scraped his fangs over the delicate skin of her inner wrist again, she shivered and leaned closer, her wings curling around them to create a shadowed, private enclave.

The bite was a bright pain that shuddered into searing pleasure. Barely stifling her cry, she wove her fingers into his hair and held him to her, but he raised his head too soon, licking over the bite location with small, playful flicks of his tongue until the tiny wounds were closed and all that remained was a faint bruise.

"Did you take enough?" The question came out husky.

Hair brushing her skin in a thousand tiny caresses, he pressed a kiss to her pulse point before lifting his head. His eyes glowed. "For now," he said, stroking his hand up her arm to cup her elbow. "You're delicious."

Goose bumps broke out over her skin. Raising her hand, she placed it against his cheek and bent until their foreheads touched and their breaths mingled. "Am I food?"

Hand closing over her nape, he nipped at her lower lip. "You are mine." Words that didn't sound wholly human.

"Naasir." A whispered plea.

He tumbled her against him as he leaned his back on a tree trunk. Then he . . . petted her. Long lazy strokes of his hand over her wings, his fingers through the hair he'd pulled out of its braid.

She slept with her head against his shoulder and his arm around her below her wings. She'd never slept with anyone before—even as a child, she'd always slept alone. Feeling him warm and strong against her, his heart beating steadily, it gave her a sense of safety that dropped her into a deep, dreamless rest.

She could've kept on sleeping, snuggled up to him, but she'd set her body clock to wake after two hours. Naasir nuzzled at her when she lifted her lashes, the scent of him primal and sensual and familiar. "Sleep," he said. "We have another ninety minutes to two hours, depending on the villagers' habits, before the night is deep enough that we can get to the caves unobserved."

Running her fingers through his hair, she shook her head. "It's your turn to rest and don't argue—we both have to be at full strength if we're going to find Alexander."

He growled at her as the trees rustled in a sudden wind. She wanted to kiss him. Sitting up and taking position against a tree trunk, she tugged him to her. "Sleep."

His chest still rumbled, but he stretched out in his favorite position, his head in her lap, and closed his eyes. Quickly rebraiding her hair so she'd be ready to move when it was time, she kept watch, listening to the muted sounds of the last of the villagers going to sleep. More often than not, she petted his hair the way he liked, and just drank him in, determined to remember every tiny detail of their time together.

It was about forty minutes after everything went silent, the moon a spotlight in the sky, that she heard it. A low buzz that seemed to be getting closer. "Naasir."

His eyelids flicked up; he was on his haunches before she saw him move, his head turned toward the sound. "We have to run." Taking her hand, he hauled her up.

And they ran.

"Should I fly?" she gasped, her chest straining at the speed. "You'd be faster on the ground."

He shook his head, the silver of his hair flying. "They're in the air."

Swallowing, she wanted to go for the sword she hadn't removed even in sleep, but had a feeling that wouldn't help. Not with this. When she looked over her shoulder, she saw a deeper darkness against the sky. Memories of the recordings she'd seen of the Falling rolled over her—thousands of birds had fallen to the earth before the angels started to plummet. "Charisemnon."

Her left wing caught on a trailing branch. Biting back a cry of pain as she tore it free, she continued to run but the buzzing was getting closer and closer with every heartbeat.

Not birds. Bugs. Locusts? Bees?

Naasir halted without warning, looked back. "Not enough

time to get to shelter." Dropping her hand, he went to the ground and, using his claws, began to dig up the arid soil.

Andromeda began to dig beside him, all but able to feel the insects on her back. In normal circumstances, bugs might make her skin crawl, but they couldn't hurt her or Naasir. However, if this was Charisemnon's doing, these weren't normal bugs. The tiny creatures might be infected with the same disease that had taken down New York's angels.

The angels had been hurt because they fell from the sky onto the unforgiving city below, but the disease had *killed* vampires—and Naasir had vampiric characteristics. Even if she was safe, he wasn't.

She dug hard enough that her nails broke.

Sweat dripping down his temples, Naasir glanced back. "In." Grabbing her arm, he all but threw her in the hole. "Facedown!"

Andromeda went to tell him he was the more vulnerable one, but knew she didn't have time to argue. The faster she went in, the faster he could get to safety, too—because she knew he wouldn't do anything for himself until she was protected. That in mind, she obeyed his order, cupping her hands in front of her mouth and nose to create an air pocket—more for her own psychological need than because it was necessary.

Even extended lack of air wouldn't kill her, but it could leave her unconscious for hours or even days—in which time, anyone could cut off her head, dig out her heart and brain.

"Don't be afraid." That was her only warning before Naasir began to shove the soil back on her.

Being buried alive, her wings under the earth, was a terror, but she lay motionless and willed him to go faster. Her fear for him was viscous in her veins.

Then she was completely buried, the world hushed but for the roar of blood in her ears. A muted buzz surrounded her what felt like a heartbeat later. Panic stuttered in her lungs. Where was Naasir? Was he safe? Heart punching so violently it was painful, she listened as hard as she could, but all she could hear was the buzzing, as if the insects were right on top of her, determined to burrow through the soil.

But Naasir had spent precious time covering her up and the bugs finally seemed to give up. Though her heart screamed at her to get out, find him, she forced herself to stay under for ten more minutes; she would not cheapen his sacrifice by making herself a target.

When she did stir, she did so slowly. But the insects were gone, no buzzing in the air. Shaking off the soil that covered her, she rubbed away the dust on her face and looked for any sign of Naasir.

Nothing. No tracks, no glints of silver, nothing.

Breath coming shallow and hard, she thought of what he might've done. He hadn't had time to dig another hole, but he was fast. Really, *really* fast. He could keep up with her flight speed; that meant he could have made it to a small cave they'd passed on the way here.

She went to head toward the cave, hesitated. He'd probably want her to stay in place. "Hell, no," she muttered. If he was hurt, she had to find him. And if he wasn't hurt, he could track her easily enough.

Sword out of its scabbard and in her hand, she began to stride toward the cave. Ten minutes of walking later, she wasn't yet there and she'd seen no signs that Naasir had passed this way. Part of her said he couldn't have made it this far. Perhaps he'd gone toward the water instead.

She hesitated, caught exactly halfway between the possibilities. The cave would've provided shelter but it wouldn't have stopped the insects from getting in. The water on the other hand, *would* provide a shield—and Naasir was an almost-immortal. He didn't need to breathe for long periods, though the need to breathe was instinct.

She ran through a grove of peach trees toward the narrow end of the teardrop, the part hidden from the village. Her wings were heavy weights that created drag on the ground and scraped against branches and thorny bushes. She knew she was leaving a trail, ignored it. Chest painful, she tumbled out on the water's edge and looked frantically in both directions, the moon a spotlight that lit up the world in a soft wash of silvery gray.

Nothing.

A closer look showed her tiny corpses washed up on the rocks not far from her. As if the locusts—or whatever the bugs were—had tried to dive toward the water and drowned.

"Naasir," she called in a low tone that wouldn't carry beyond a short distance. "*Naasir.*"

Hearing no response, she slid away her sword and focused on the tiny insect corpses. They were gathered in a particular area, but the water had a quiet current. Walking her way upstream, she saw a spot on the edge where the grass was crushed and the soil disturbed—as if Naasir's heel had slid as he dived in.

She got on her knees and peered into the water, but couldn't see much. Everything was too churned up. There was only one option and Andromeda didn't hesitate to take it: leaving her sword on the bank, she kicked off her boots and dived in, searching the murky water using her arms and legs. Swimming on top of a body of water was one thing, diving quite another; she had to combat the buoyancy of her wings to go under and stay under.

She didn't find anything in the first pass, or in the second, but her right hand hit something that wasn't stone on the third pass. It was cloth over flesh.

Feeling her way up Naasir's body, she noted his head was hanging limply. Her muscles tensed to painful tightness—Naasir was old enough that he could survive a broken neck, but it depended on the intensity of the injury.

Fighting her instinct to breathe, she tried to pull him up but he wouldn't rise. She made herself let go. Searching all around his body using her hands, she finally discovered the large branch that was hooked into a tear in his pant leg.

Unhooking it, she managed to get him to the surface. She gasped in air and lightly slapped his cheek. "Naasir. Wake up."

No response.

Teeth clenched, she swallowed her panic and touched his neck with gentle fingers, trying to discern if it was broken. It didn't seem that way to her inexpert touch, but as she made her way upward, she felt a knot on the back of his head. Her eyes went to the large stones scattered amongst the grasses on the bank.

Naasir must've slipped and hit his head as he went into the water. That was survivable as long as his neck wasn't broken. Floating with him toward the bank, she kept on talking to him. She didn't want to risk wrenching his neck by trying to haul him out of the lake, so she stayed in it with him, holding him so his head remained clear of the water.

Her arms were starting to tire and her throat beginning to

choke with all the scared emotions she refused to allow free rein when she realized she was an idiot. Tilting back his head, she deliberately pressed her wrist against his mouth. No response. She looked around for something to break the flesh. Her sword was too far away, but she was just close enough to a sharp rock to graze the skin and bring a bare hint of blood to the surface.

Placing it against Naasir's mouth, she waited. Nothing.

"Drink, damn you." It came out a snarl.

His fangs burned into her flesh. There was no pleasure this time, just the suction of him drinking her blood.

Each time his throat moved as he swallowed, she felt her smile widen. Even when her head began to grow heavy, her blood surging into him, she didn't pull away her hand.

The suction suddenly stopped, Naasir's eyes flicking open in a blaze of silver as he lifted his head. "Your neck's not broken." Her voice came out slurred.

Naasir moved, hauling her out of the water with primal strength. Leaving her on the bank, he disappeared. She stared up at the blurry night sky, her mind trying to hold on to thoughts without success.

Then Naasir was beside her again. He had a pack with him. A pack. One of *their* packs, she realized dully. They'd left it behind when they ran from the swarm.

Opening it, he took out strips of jerky and said, "Eat!" When she just stared at him, he began to tear the jerky into tiny pieces and feed them to her.

She turned her head away after a few pieces of the cured meat. "Salty."

He hauled her back with a grip on her jaw, his fingers clawed. "Eat this or I'll hunt and make you eat raw meat."

She scowled at him but ate the jerky—there was a grimness on his face that told her he was dead serious. Waiting until he saw she was doing as ordered, he went and got some water from the lake, then dropped a cleansing tablet in it.

"We don't need that," she muttered as the water cleared, sick of jerky.

"It'll taste better." Helping her to sit braced against him, he brought the bottle to her lips and she drank. "Eat the rest."

She ate it, slowly able to feel her mind start to clear much as the water had done after he dropped in the tablet. When he handed her a fistful of high-energy candy, she ate that, too, drank more water. "Enough," she said. "I'm feeling better."

Coming around to face her, he stared at her for a long time before nodding. Then he picked up her wrist and licked over the bite marks and grazed skin to seal the wound. "You shouldn't have done that," he said afterward, tone harsh.

She rolled her eyes, fingers curling gently into her palm. "I should've let you drown?"

"Vampires can't drown."

"Are you sure?" She didn't know if the theory had ever been tested with long-term immersion. "And you're not a vampire."

He brushed the pad of his thumb over the bite bruise, his fangs flashing as he bared his teeth at her. "You almost drowned yourself."

"Do you know the words 'thank you'?"

A growl rumbled in his chest . . . but then he bent his head and pressed a soft and sweetly unexpected kiss on the bruise.

Her heart skipped a beat, fell right into his hands. "You're welcome," she whispered, and when he lifted his head, hugged him tight. "I was so afraid for you."

His arms came around her, his jaw nuzzling against her temple in a caress that was becoming intimately familiar. "I moved too fast because the bugs were almost on me." A squeeze. "We're both wet."

"At least we have dry clothes this time." No replacement leathers for her, but gear just as tough and durable.

They held on to each other for a long time before separating to dress after Naasir went and retrieved the second pack. "I hid our trails, too," he told her once they were both in dry clothes. "Buried your broken feathers." His eyebrows drew together. "How hurt are you?"

"Already healing—it hurt at the time, but the damage wasn't major." Leaving her still-braided hair as it was, Andromeda went to where the water had trapped the dead bugs against the rocks.

About to pick one up, she decided not to risk touching it with her fingers. Instead, she found two sticks and, while Naasir watched from a crouching position across from her, she used the sticks like chopsticks to pick up the insect.

It had a locust-like body and was a yellowish shade with faint blue-green markings—according to Naasir, since her own color perception was skewed by the moonlight. What she could see was that its wings were silver, a glittering shade as bright as Naasir's eyes and hair. And those wings looked as if they were formed of thin, *thin*, pieces of metal.

"Not Charisemnon," she whispered, feeling her eyes go huge. "Alexander?"

She nodded slowly after checking the other winged bodies she could see. All had the same metal wings. More than one was crumpled from the impact against the rocks, making their composition even clearer. "It must be some kind of a defense mechanism to drive off the too-curious."

"We said his name." Naasir peered at the bug she held between the sticks. "He heard."

It made sense. Alexander had been a master tactician after all. "If he is listening," she said, having to fight not to whisper, "I don't think it's conscious. We talked about Lijuan's plans during our walk in, about how we wanted to stop her, yet the defenses activated."

"They may be driven by a primal part of the brain."

"So more defenses could activate without warning." She put three of the bugs in a small plastic bag that had held trail mix. "I hope they survive the trip. I want to show Jessamy."

Naasir watched her store the insects in an inner pocket. "There is a silver lining to this."

Seeing his laughing eyes, she knew the pun had been intentional. "Yes?"

"We're definitely in the right place."

Andromeda's breath whooshed out of her; she'd been so focused on the minutiae that she'd missed the larger picture. "Yes." She swallowed. "Should we tell Raphael?" If Alexander Slept below lava—whether true lava or molten metal— only another archangel could get to him.

Nodding, Naasir took out the phone he'd stored in the front pocket of one of the packs—he hadn't wanted to risk losing it as he had his other phone during their escape from Lijuan's citadel. She was almost expecting his harsh imprecation.

"It doesn't work, does it?"

"It should work anywhere." Naasir pressed something on the screen, tried again. "Dead."

"Alexander's done something." She thought of the lack of

photographs of Amanat, of Caliane's sheer power. "It may not be on purpose."

Naasir slid away the phone. "It doesn't matter. If I don't check in, help will arrive." It was said with the confidence of a man who had absolute faith in his sire and his comrades. "We need to locate Alexander's exact Sleeping place before then, so Raphael doesn't have to be away from New York long." He rose to his feet and held out a hand. "Let's go annoy an Ancient archangel who has a distinct preference for age over youth."

Smiling, Andromeda slid her hand into his and let him tug her up. "No one else I'd rather do it with than you."

A wicked grin—followed by a mutter. "Stupid Grimoire book."

Xi was amassing his troops on the outskirts of Rohan's palace with the intention of taking it before Favashi was ever aware of the attack, when one of his commanders walked up to him with an urgent look on his face.

"What is it?"

"We're hearing rumors of a swarm of insects above an oasis in the east, about five hours on the wing from here."

Xi waited because the solid, stable man in front of him wouldn't come to his general with such a thing unless it had a bearing on their proposed plans.

"Our closest operative in the area caught the report from an angel who was passing by. He admits he only glimpsed it from a distance in the moonlight, but he says there was something unnatural about the swarm—according to him, they were too perfectly in formation."

It could, Xi thought, be a sign of Alexander's awakening. It could also be a clever distraction or a moon dream on the part of the angel. This location still made the most logical sense, regardless of Raphael's attempts to muddy the equation by putting the scholar on a jet to Michaela's territory.

According to Xi's people, the jet had been sitting on the

tarmac since it landed, all doors closed. No way to know if the scholar and Raphael's silver-eyed enigma were still inside. "Take half a squadron and check it out," he said, on the small chance that his instincts had led him wrong.

After his commander gave a crisp nod and went to gather his soldiers, Xi turned his attention back to the matter at hand: how to get into Rohan's home. Alexander's son had grown into himself in the past four hundred years and he'd absorbed the lessons of his father.

Rohan was now one of Favashi's most feared generals, having decided to give his loyalty to her when she became the Archangel of Persia. Prior to that, he'd technically been allied to no archangel and no one had challenged it, both because Rohan commanded the respect and affection of tens of thousands as a result of his bloodline, and because he was a powerful fighter and leader.

No archangel wanted to destroy an asset when he or she could win it to their side.

"Where is Favashi?" he asked the scout who'd just landed, because if Favashi was close, his plans would have to change accordingly.

"In Astaad's territory." The scout's chest heaved. "She accepted an invitation to attend a festival there."

Astaad's territory was on the other side of the world. Even if she left at the first sign of trouble, it would take her considerable time to return. "Prepare your squadrons to storm the palace," he ordered his commanders. "We'll take Rohan by surprise."

Decision made, he sent a message through to Lijuan. As he did so, he thought of the scholar with her translucent brown gold eyes and wings delicately patterned like a bird's, and of her question about how he could follow Lijuan after all she'd done. He hadn't punished Andromeda for the impudence of the question both because she was a scholar and as such, curiosity was expected, and because he'd found her intriguing as a woman.

Xi had always preferred intelligence over commonplace beauty. Had Andromeda not escaped, he'd intended to ask Lijuan leave to court her. He wouldn't have taken the scholar without the scholar's full consent—that was not the way of a true warrior . . . and it was a rule Lijuan had taught him when he first came into her service.

He'd been a scrawny boy who'd disappointed his warrior parents, Lijuan's the only court that would accept him. He'd expected to be placed in a minor position and forgotten, but Lijuan had taken an interest in him from the start because of the patriotic red and gray color of his wings, treating him almost as a son. She'd put him into training with the best trainers, into studies with gifted tutors, into etiquette lessons with high-ranking courtiers.

It had taken a hundred years, but by the end of it, he was a man and one respected by others. His loyalty to his lady was also etched in stone. She had changed over the past decade from the wise—if righteously arrogant—archangel he'd first known, into something *other*, but she continued to treat him with respect and she continued to share her new power.

Sometimes, when he was far from her, he questioned her newly warlike ways in the privacy of his own mind, but he had faith in her. Lijuan had plans for the world and she was a goddess. He couldn't hope to understand her vision. He could only follow, a loyal foot soldier.

Today, he spoke to his lady and said, "We prepare to take the palace." Lijuan was the only one who could actually eliminate the threat posed by Alexander, for only one archangel could kill another. "I can't yet confirm whether he lies within." Lijuan eschewed modern conveniences like jets, and was currently too weak to constantly travel long distances on her own, so Xi had suggested she wait until he'd confirmed Alexander's presence.

She'd accepted his advice when it came to Kilimanjaro, but today, her voice was steel. "I will come. You are right, Alexander would not leave his beloved homeland—I shouldn't have doubted your instincts and sent you to Titus's territory."

Her voice faded into eerie screams for an instant, returned pulsing with power. "If Alexander is not below the palace, he will be nearby." No screams now, only a voice so pure, it almost hurt. "Find him, Xi. I will do the rest."

Naasir climbed a tree tall enough that it allowed him to spy on the village that lay between them and the caves, but there was nothing to see. It was long past the midnight hour, the lights within the homes extinguished and the waters of the lake a whispering mirror under the moonlight. If the villagers had seen the swarm, they probably knew well enough to keep their shutters closed and stay within.

Climbing down rather than jumping, so as not to cause any unnecessary noise or vibrations, he took Andromeda's hand in his.

"If Alexander is Sleeping here," she whispered as they began to make their way past the village by skirting the far edge of it, "this can't be the first odd incident the villagers have witnessed."

Naasir had his senses focused on possible threats, but he saw where she was going. "You think they are loyal to Alexander and keep his secrets?"

"Like Caliane and the people of Amanat. She took them into Sleep with her, but Alexander could've simply brought this tribe with him, trusted them to watch over his Sleeping place."

"That would explain the number of strong vampires I sensed

in amongst the mortals." Vampires that old and powerful normally chose to work for the archangels, either managing small territories, or working directly in their strongholds.

It was where they found the most challenge.

One or two might decide on a simpler way of life, but Naasir had spotted far more than that when he and Andromeda first came upon the village. He'd figured this was a home village for a group of Favashi's soldiers who were on leave, but Andromeda's suggestion made more sense. "Mortals alone wouldn't have the physical strength to hold back Alexander's immortal enemies."

A dog barked at them from the backyard of a small, neat house that blended into its surroundings. When Naasir growled at it, the animal whimpered and went silent.

He felt bad. He usually tried not to scare smaller predators. He'd bring the dog some meat after it was all over; it was only doing what it was trained to do, looking out for intruders.

Turning to Andromeda, he lifted a finger to his lips.

They made it past the village in silence and without problems.

"Even if they are Alexander's guards," Naasir said once there was no chance their voices would give them away, "they aren't locked in time." He'd seen electronics and caught sight of clothing woven in modern ways.

"They must leave the village and interact with the wider world to keep an eye on things that might affect Alexander's Sleep." Andromeda thought of Caliane again. "If I had to guess, I'd say the fruit and other trees we've seen, exist to provide a front, stop awkward questions about how the tribe survives. Alexander will have left them funds enough to sustain the entire tribe for untold centuries." She bit her lower lip. "We didn't see any wings. Alexander had very loyal squadrons."

"Wings are highly visible," Naasir pointed out. "Vampires, on the other hand, can quietly relocate with no one paying attention, so long as the vampire in question doesn't hold a high-level position like Dmitri—or if his or her archangel is no longer in the world. Some do not want to serve any other."

"You're right." No takeoffs or landings to draw attention to this place; just a quiet village held by vampires who had withdrawn from life after their archangel chose to Sleep, and those who were likely descended from vampire-mortal matings, or who were family by blood.

Only the deeply trusted must live here, for that was the only way a secret this big could be kept. If a child was brought up as a warrior among warriors, and told he watched over an archangel, Andromeda didn't think that child would ever break the faith—for what greater honor was there in the world?

At that instant, Naasir once again lifted a finger to his lips. Andromeda went silent, ears straining, but she heard nothing beyond the normal noises of a moonlit night. A rustle of wind, the trees creaking slightly, the bark of another dog on the opposite side of the village. Naasir, however, remained on high alert as they continued on, his muscles bunched in readiness for an attack.

There was no attack. Not then. That came just before dawn, when the world was misty gray and they thought themselves safe. A crossbow bolt whipped by an inch from Andromeda's face—would've been embedded in that face if Naasir hadn't moved at the last second to push her out of the way.

Acting on instinct, she slammed behind a tree while Naasir dropped to the ground and crawled over to join her. "There are many of them."

Andromeda pointed to the quivering crossbow bolt embedded in the trunk of another tree. It was black with distinctive silver etchings. Silver had always been Alexander's color. "We're friends!" Andromeda called out, going with her gut and judging these were Alexander's people. "The enemy is coming!"

A hail of crossbow bolts was her answer. Pressing her back against the tree, her wings tightly curved in, she glanced at Naasir. "It was worth a try."

His eyes gleamed as bright a silver as that on the bolts, but more liquid, more *alive*. Even as she admired the wild beauty of him, the part of Andromeda that made her a scholar was wondering at the color that marked Naasir. Silver was a distinctive shade in terms of angelic wings. Illium had fine silver filaments in his wings and so did some other angels, but Alexander alone had borne wings of pure silver.

There was a feather in the Archives that came from Alexander and it was a glittering shade she'd seen in such concentrated form on no other living creature but Naasir. Not even on Rohan. Alexander's son's wings were a paler silver at the top that flowed into a charcoal gray; he'd inherited his coloration from both parents.

Where had Naasir inherited his coloration? If someone had
Made him, if there had even been an ordinary Making involved in his case, was it possible Alexander had something to
do with it? But if that was true, why would Naasir have grown
up in Raphael's stronghold?

And how *could* he have grown up if he'd been Made? Only
adults were Made, for not only did the transformation all but
freeze a person in time, children went insane or died. None
had ever survived an attempt—all of those attempts made by
angels who were themselves insane, or believed they could
flout angelic law without repercussions.

That repercussion was always death. None ever escaped it
and so it wasn't worth the risk. Alexander, however, was no ordinary angel. He could've done as he pleased and escaped exe-
cution, but had he Made a child, he would've still been
uniformly shunned by their people. There was no record of any
such shunning, and nothing Andromeda knew about Alexander
indicated he'd break such a fundamental rule of behavior.

Alexander believed in laws, in rules, in a society with a foundation of discipline.

The thoughts tumbled though her head in the split seconds
before Naasir reached up to grab hold of a branch and swung
himself onto the tree. Realizing what he planned to do, she
gave him enough time to get directly over Alexander's sentinels, then grabbed some of the crossbow bolts that had fallen
nearby and started to throw them at their attackers. As a distraction, it was a success.

Another hail of bolts.

Going to her knees to give the shooters less of a target, she
used her sword to deflect a few bolts that came too close, and
she hoped that Naasir was safe.

Naasir had climbed along the treetops soundlessly, heading toward the scents he could barely smell. The windless
dawn had kept the sentinels' secret, but the trajectory of their
crossbow strikes had given him a direction.

He couldn't have as effectively used the tree road had the
oasis been surrounded only by the tall spires of date palms, but
the villagers had planted and nurtured many kinds of trees,

including those with spreading branches. While Andromeda was right about the planting being used as a front to stave off the curious, the true reason had likely been to create shadows below, where the sentinels could mount an ambush.

He couldn't blame them for not worrying about a climbing foe.

Naasir was one of a kind after all.

He was on top of them now, but they were scattered far enough apart that no one could take them all at once. It also, however, meant he only needed to handle one at a time. Focusing on the desert camouflage–clad male directly below, his hair covered in a dusty brown scarf tied at the back of his head and dull brown and green stripes on his face from camo paint, Naasir didn't hesitate.

He dropped down, taking the sentinel to the ground with an arm pushed up against his throat so he couldn't cry out. "We are not the enemy," he said in the male's ear. "We are here to warn Alexander."

The man attempted to break free. Gritting his teeth, Naasir did the only thing he could and knocked him out. He did the same to two others before the sentinels suddenly realized they had a predator in their midst.

"Up!"

The order was vocal. Naasir crouched flat on his current branch . . . then realized they were reacting not to him, but to the wings beating in the distance. Moving with stealth, he angled his head just enough to look up.

The wings that came into view less than three seconds later were not ones he wanted to see. Below him, Alexander's sentinels crouched down, crossbows pointed up at the flyers clad in dark gray uniforms bearing red accents, but they didn't shoot.

Good.

If Lijuan's people were just doing a flyby—likely after someone spotted the swarm—then the best thing to do was to lie low and not give them a reason to believe the area was in any way interesting. The squadron did multiple passes, until well past the dawn. Naasir, Andromeda, and the sentinels remained silent and unmoving throughout.

Even when the squadron landed near the village, no one moved. The sentinels' family members were no doubt trained to act innocent under questioning or the secret would've never held so long—and if Naasir judged these men and women right, even the noncombatants would've been taught to fight well enough to protect themselves until the sentinels could get back to them. It was over an hour later, the morning sun bright in the sky, that the squadron finally took off, their wingbeats disappearing into the distance.

It left Naasir, Andromeda, and the sentinels in the same position they'd been in before the squadron's arrival.

Andromeda's voice rang out into the silence. "We're with Raphael! That squadron was wearing Lijuan's colors in case you missed it! Raphael's mortal enemy!"

The sentinels below Naasir didn't move, but a deep male voice came from the left. Speaking the same well-known local dialect as used by Andromeda, he said, "This land is forbidden to outsiders. *Leave.*"

"We can't. Lijuan is coming to kill your archangel."

A pause before the speaker's voice came again. "We will listen. Face-to-face."

"Swear on Alexander's honor that you will do us no harm!"

This time the pause was longer, more potent, but when the voice came, it was resolute. "On Alexander's honor."

Naasir had made it to the speaker by then, a tall and husky male vampire with tanned skin and hair hidden under the same kind of scarf as Naasir had noticed on several others. He dropped down right behind the man who had to be the leader of the sentinels, a deliberate choice to ensure the other male didn't attempt to treat them as prey.

The sentinel whirled around, pale gray eyes glinting and crossbow held up and pointed at Naasir's heart.

33

"The silver-eyed beast." Despite the description, the leader's voice held no insult as he lowered his weapon. "How many of my men did you kill?"

"None—there was no need." Naasir shrugged. "They'll have headaches when they wake if they haven't already. You should remind them never to forget to look up, even if there are no wings in the sky."

A slight incline of the leader's head. "A point well made."

Andromeda appeared out of the trees right then, her dark brown pants dusty and the paler brown of her fitted tunic bearing a streak of dirt. Her eyes went to Naasir, skimmed over him, the tense lines of her only easing once she'd taken in his uninjured state. Naasir wanted to preen at having a mate who cared, and he wanted to nuzzle at her to ease her worry. He also wanted to run his hands over every inch of her to confirm that she, too, was unhurt.

"So," she said, sword held out at her side and eyes on the sentinel leader, "we're all here and not attempting to kill one another. Why don't we go back to the village? I need some coffee."

Naasir didn't dispute her suggestion. Until they convinced the sentinels of their intent, they'd get exactly nowhere. "You know who I am," he said to the leader of the sentinels. "This is Andromeda."

"I am Tarek," the other man replied, his skin smooth over angular cheekbones and his jaw shadowed with dark stubble. "We will head to the village, but do any harm to the villagers and our agreement is void." When he pulled down the scarf to allow it to lie loosely around his neck, his hair proved to be not black but a dark brown threaded with gold.

"We have no cause to harm anyone," Andromeda said and the three of them walked back to the village, the other sentinels no doubt at their backs.

The villagers looked at them with wide eyes when they walked in, though a barefoot child with dark hair and skin not many shades lighter than Naasir's, ran straight for Tarek. "Grandpapa!"

The vampire, who looked no older than his third decade and yet who was likely not "grandpapa" but great-grandpapa many times removed, picked up the little girl without breaking his stride and held her with an ease that shouted familiarity. The child peered curiously at Naasir. Her eyes were the same light gray as those of her living ancestor.

Naasir smiled, flashing fangs; the child immediately dimpled and waved. Children liked him. They knew without being told that he wouldn't hurt them. It didn't matter if the child wore skin or fur or scales.

Osiris had taken and killed the young of many species without compunction. That was one of the many reasons he had to die. One of the many reasons why Alexander had to execute him.

The latter was a fact Naasir hadn't known until he was older. He'd always thought Raphael had done it, but Raphael hadn't been an archangel at the time, and Osiris had been an Ancient's brother.

"Whatever our later disagreements," Raphael had said to Naasir a hundred years earlier, "Alexander and I always agreed that Osiris had to die." A grim tone that echoed the hard line of his jaw. "Alexander's older brother wasn't insane. He was just wired wrong and he committed infanticide on a horrific level. Simply because he killed the children of mortals and animals didn't make his crimes any less terrible—he wiped out entire species in his obsession."

Naasir knew Osiris would've loved to have had an immortal child on whom to experiment—stronger, less apt to die on him—but he'd never been able to father one on the concubines he kept far from his stronghold and only rarely visited. And even he hadn't been arrogant enough to kidnap an angelic child.

Not then. Had he been allowed to live . . .

Calling out in a subdialect Andromeda didn't fully understand, Tarek led them to a clearing surrounded by houses on one side and the blue-green waters of the lake on the other. There was a table set up there by the time they arrived, benches on either side. Food and drink was being placed on it by fast-moving men and women.

Suspicion underlay the quick, curious glimpses to which Andromeda was subject, though she noticed the non-warrior women were sending Naasir some very come-hither smiles. Then she saw one of the male sentinels scan Naasir's body in an unobtrusive but admiring way and knew the interest wasn't confined to the noncombatants or to the female sex.

She couldn't blame them; there was simply something about the way Naasir moved that said he'd offer a lover great pleasure. The fact she'd chosen a life of celibacy hadn't made her blind to sexual attraction, or put her body into stasis, and Naasir . . . Just watching him walk or feeling his breath against her ear when he nuzzled at her aroused her to near-unbearable levels. As for seeing his nakedness when he'd come out of the pond in Lijuan's territory . . .

Her stomach fluttered, her skin hot.

Another woman gave him a flirtatious smile right in front of Andromeda. Her hand clenched on the hilt of her sword.

None of these doe-eyed beauties, she reminded herself, would last an hour with him in his real skin. He was too wild, too strong, too demanding, and too aggravating.

He was perfect.

While Andromeda was a fool, judging these other women when she, herself, was the most unsuitable of them all.

"We will break bread," Tarek said as he took a seat on one side of the table after handing off the girl in his arms to a mortal woman of about forty.

Andromeda and Naasir slid in on the opposite bench.

His troops, meanwhile, scattered around the village, but they didn't go far, clearly ready to go on the offensive the instant either Naasir or Andromeda made a threatening move.

A tiny, steaming cup of hot, strong coffee was placed in front of Andromeda, a fresh bowl of flatbread put in the center of the table. At the same time, a villager brought over two small glasses of blood for Tarek and Naasir, the condensation on the glasses showing the blood had been stored somewhere cold. Leaning in toward Naasir after placing his glass in front of him, the curvy and quite frankly beautiful woman whispered something in his ear, her face falling when he shook his head.

Andromeda knew it must've been an offer to feed him, found herself both pleased that he'd turned down the offer and angry because she'd soon be out of his life while countless other women wouldn't.

In front of her, Tarek lifted his glass after giving the lingering server a sharp look that had her hustling away. "To honor."

"To honor," Andromeda and Naasir said together and drank.

Placing her cup back on the table, Andromeda took a piece of the bread and tore off a small bite for Naasir. His consuming the ceremonial piece seemed to please the sentinel leader. Finishing off the blood in his glass then eating a small piece of bread himself, Tarek folded up the sleeves of his sand-colored shirt, the fabric shadowed with slightly darker blotches that allowed him and his men to blend into the landscape.

The tattoo on his left forearm, the lines inked in an impossible silver, caught Andromeda's eye.

A raven.

That wasn't a surprise. Alexander's symbol had been a raven. Legend said that on his ascension, a raven had flown high with him, only to die in the blaze of his power. To Alexander's people, the raven symbolized courage against all odds. But this particular stylized rendering of a raven . . .

Andromeda narrowed her eyes, sure she'd seen it before.

"You say you are friends," Tarek said into the quiet, "but you bring Lijuan's people with you."

Having caught Naasir's eye, Andromeda was the one who spoke. "Our task is to find and warn Alexander before the enemy locates him."

The sentinel's face grew austere. "In seeking Alexander you break a taboo so old, its origins are lost from memory."

Andromeda knew her next words could lose this man's trust and possibly endanger her and Naasir's lives. "Yes," she said. "We break a law, but if we don't, then Alexander will be helpless against Lijuan. You can't protect him against her." Even weak as she was, Lijuan could easily annihilate this village—if Xi didn't take care of that first.

"You *will* die if beheaded, and once you are gone, no one will stand between Lijuan and the Ancient." She held the man's gaze. "We cannot lose him from the world. He is the greatest angelic statesman who ever lived. He stopped wars and created cities that stand to this day. His battle strategies are taught to young soldiers and his political strategies studied by archangels themselves."

Tarek looked at her very carefully, the intensity of his gaze making the hairs rise on the back of her neck. "How do you know so much of Alexander?"

"I am a scholar."

The male's eyes went to Naasir. "I've been long from the Refuge, but I know you have never claimed to be a scholar."

Naasir's fangs flashed in the sunlight as he grinned. "I can read." Laughter in his voice. "I am a bloodhound and, like you, a guard dog."

"You're so much more," Andromeda said, unable to keep the words within. "You're extraordinary."

"Yes," Tarek agreed, his tone difficult to decipher. "There is no one else like you—the silver-eyed vampire who has hair and eyes the same unique shade as Alexander's wings."

Andromeda frowned at the explicit connection, her thoughts once more on that metallic feather in the Archives.

"Alexander didn't Make me," Naasir said, answering the unasked question. "It was his brother, Osiris."

Andromeda sucked in a breath as Tarek's expression turned deadly. "Osiris was purged from the family line, all traces of him erased."

"Except me," Naasir said unworriedly, accepting a second small glass of blood brought out by an older woman whose smile held simple courtesy.

"Except you." An unblinking gaze. "How did you survive the destruction of all that was Osiris?"

"I helped that destruction along," Naasir said before he drank from the glass. "I ate his liver and his heart." A sideways look at Andromeda. "Osiris kept me hungry to test my strength."

Andromeda closed her hand over his. "Then he was a stupid angel who deserved to get eaten."

Smile deep and wide, Naasir wove his fingers into hers and turned back to a grim-eyed Tarek. "I never called Osiris sire and I never would have even if Alexander hadn't executed him." Naasir's loyalty was Raphael's.

The sentinel stared at him. "Two hundred years ago, I ventured briefly to another part of the world and met a learned man. He told me there were rumors of a living legend, of a chimera with silver eyes who is not one but two, asked me if I knew the origins of it, for only Alexander and Osiris had eyes of true silver and both were gone from the world."

"Such things are myth." Naasir's eyes laughed when Andromeda glared at him.

Lifting her hand to his mouth, he kissed her knuckles, then tipped her gaping mouth shut.

She pursed her lips. "I am *not* talking to you." Turning to face the openly amused sentinel, she said, "If you don't believe we're here to oppose Lijuan, you should find out what's happening at Rohan's palace right now."

The amusement disappeared. "Is that a threat?"

She held her ground. "I had to tell Lijuan something when she kidnapped me and asked for Alexander's location. I tried to lead her away from this territory, but given the presence of that squadron, the distraction clearly didn't take."

"We got a warning to Rohan," Naasir added. "He won't have been caught unprepared."

"Rohan can look after himself." A confident statement from Tarek. "But even if you are here to oppose Lijuan, we can't break our vow and that vow is to hold the line."

"In that case," Naasir said, "I'll have to incapacitate you all." He sounded like he was joking but Andromeda knew he was dead serious.

"Even the silver-eyed beast can't take on the heart of the Wing Brotherhood."

Of course. That's where she'd seen the tattoo before. Usually on clean-shaven scalps.

Tarek must've seen her eyes flick to his hair because he said, "We all take the mark on our eighteenth birthday. Those who leave here shear their hair as a rite of passage, a reminder of the discipline and honor in which they have been forged."

"Your people have gone far from your homeland." The reclusive and deadly Wing Brotherhood worked on tasks for various individuals and groups, but always on a contract basis. Until now, no one had ever known from where they came—the guess had been that they belonged to an angel who preferred to stay in the shadows.

"Some of my younger brethren like to fly," Tarek said. "We do not stop them. All return eventually, for this is home. Often, they bring mates who understand our ways, and who rejuvenate our bloodlines."

"No one has spoken the secret in four hundred years?" Andromeda whispered. "How can that be?"

"Honor and loyalty and a crucible that does not forgive the weak of soul." He rose. "You can either fight us or you can leave. We will escort you out."

Naasir rose, hand linked to hers. "You need to think for today, not stand in the past."

The leader of the Wing Brotherhood didn't say anything, just put his hand on the butt of his crossbow. Polite, elegant skin suddenly on, Naasir glanced at Andromeda. "It appears we have worn out our welcome—and Alexander's guard hasn't fallen for my bluff."

She shrugged. "We had to make the attempt." Meeting Tarek's gaze, she said, "If you won't allow us to go to Alexander, then you must warn him yourself."

An impassive face. "The Ancient Sleeps. No living being can enter his chamber and survive."

"Not even Lijuan?"

No flicker in his expression. "She may style herself an Ancient, but she is no power in comparison to Alexander."

"You haven't seen her since the Cascade began," Andromeda said, but knew she was wasting her breath—Alexander's sentinel was too locked into the idea of what should be to see what was happening to the world today.

They walked out with a strong Brotherhood contingent as escort. It was an hour out from the village that Naasir let go of

her hand. Dropping her pack, Andromeda had her sword out
within the next two heartbeats but was still deathly slow in
comparison to him.

Using his claws, he took down three of the wing brothers
before they knew what was happening. There was blood but
no death, only incapacitation. Andromeda was hampered by
the fact she, too, didn't want to do real damage with the sword,
but she wasn't fast enough or nimble enough to fight the highly
trained wing brothers hand-to-hand.

Who, despite the name, were both male and female.

Wanting to ensure she didn't end up a hostage, she stayed
behind Naasir and acted as cleanup for the men and women
Naasir pushed off balance or otherwise slowed down; in the
end she managed to take down several by whacking their
heads with the hilt of her sword. Even in the midst of battle,
she took care to use less force with the mortals.

Alexander wouldn't forgive those who'd fatally harmed his
people.

"Andi, fly!"

Everything in her rebelled against the order, against leaving him surrounded by fighters with death in their eyes, but
she'd made a promise to obey him in such situations. Gritting
her teeth, she put her trust and faith in his skills and took off.

Crossbow bolts fired in her direction in a sharp whistle of air.

34

Naasir bared his teeth when he saw he'd slowed the Brotherhood just enough that none of the bolts reached Andromeda. The instant he'd confirmed she was safely out of range, he swung up into the trees and ran.

Bolts came up into the foliage but the wing brothers couldn't move as fast as he could and the bolts thudded in where he'd been seconds before. Trusting Andromeda to go in the same direction, he headed right back to the village. It was the fastest way through to the other side.

He wasn't arrogant, well aware the wing brothers were some of the most highly trained warriors in the world. The only reason this had worked was because they thought Andromeda a scholar despite her sword, and hadn't been watching her as carefully. The backup she'd offered had given him just enough of an edge—one more minute and the fight would've turned against them.

His heart pumping at full strength, he'd crossed the village using the trees on one side, well before the sentinels' cries alerted the fighters left within. He saw them mustering behind him, heading in the wrong direction, but he didn't drop his alert status; the wing brothers were scattered throughout this area, were no doubt also in the caves themselves.

His muscles were tight, his lungs burning but he kept going.

There were no trees in the final stretch to the caves, the sunlight bright on the fine desert sand. Even at his speed, a sniper positioned atop the cave system might take him out. *If* he ran in this skin. Not being stupid, he stripped and slipped into a skin that was his own, but that he hadn't yet shown Andromeda.

He wanted to surprise her.

To anyone watching, he was now a striped mirage they couldn't quite focus on. Thanks to the pack he decided not to abandon, a sniper did still spot him, but his aim was off by several feet. Naasir was never where he should be, the combination of his speed and the fact that his body was lower to the ground, not to mention his natural camouflage, making him the perfect predator.

He only stopped once he was on top of the mountain that hid the cave system, far from the frustrated sniper. Finding a supply of water by following his nose until he located a hidden stream, he threw some on his face before taking a drink, then pulled on his pants.

His senses cut out to below-human levels the next instant.

He had to wait for his heartbeat to settle before he could track Andromeda. It was frustrating, but at the pace he'd run, his body needed time to "recalibrate." Keir had said that to him when he grew old enough to understand such words and things—apparently, his unstable state after a sudden full-strength burn was a design flaw. But since the flip side was incredible speed unseen in any other terrestrial being, four-legged or two, Naasir didn't usually complain.

Today, he had to fight fury.

The instant his blood stopped rushing through his ears and his heartbeat settled, his senses flickered back to life. It took him mere seconds to catch Andromeda's scent.

Loping over the mountain's craggy surface in his secret skin and staying low again, he looked down to find her just below an outcrop. He grinned; his mate was clever. She was hidden from aerial view and she was nowhere near the cave mouth the wing brothers had to be watching.

About to jump down, he remembered Honor's shock that day he'd jumped onto her balcony, and looking around, found two small pebbles and threw gently. When they hit Andromeda's shoulders and she jerked up her head, her smile at seeing him was luminescent.

Jumping down to join her, he cupped her cheek with a clawed hand slightly chafed from his low-ground lope. "Did you get hit?"

She shook her head and threw her arms around him, holding on tight. He wrapped his own arms around her and squeezed, breathing in her scent. Her life.

Drawing back after a long time, she pushed at his shoulders. "A *chimera*? And you couldn't have told me? You pretended it was a ridiculous thing!"

"The one in the legends *is* ridiculous," he grumbled. "A lion with a goat's head on its back? What idiot thought that up?"

She glared at him, then blinked and shook her head. "You weren't an ordinary tiger, were you?" she whispered, seeming to notice his secret skin for the first time.

He realized at that instant that Andromeda saw *him*, regardless of the skin he wore.

Gentle fingers brushing over his chest, her honeyed skin dark against skin of a silvery white striped with black that made him all but impossible to spot in the glare of sunlight.

"A white tiger?" An even softer whisper.

He grinned as he allowed his usual skin to emerge. "It's a good skin for daylight, but I don't look 'human' when I wear it, so I normally wear my night skin." One came from the boy. One from the tiger cub. Both belonged to Naasir now.

"You are a walking, talking impossibility." In spite of the temper in her eyes, she kept stroking his hair, his shoulders.

"There's a reason for that, a reason my kind doesn't exist in nature." He made her spread her wings so he could confirm she hadn't been hit. Walking around to check the surface of her wings, he said, "I could as easily have been an insane beast or a crippled monster."

Pain and vicious fury tore through him so suddenly that he had to press his chest to Andromeda's back and bury his face against her neck. "There were many before me . . . my brothers and sisters in a way, though we were never alive together. I saw many of their twisted skeletons."

Andromeda's hands closed over his where he had them locked around her waist.

"Osiris executed all the others when they proved flawed. Of three thousand attempts, I was the only one who was physically whole and appeared sane."

Andromeda's fingers trembled. "He killed three thousand children?"

Nuzzling her, Naasir shook his head. "He killed *six* thousand children. Not all wore a human skin." Like the tiger cub who had given Naasir his secret daylight form. "To be a chimera requires two 'base' entities, one human, one other."

Tears rolled down Andromeda's face. "How? Why wasn't he stopped?"

Hugging her close, rocking a little, he said, "I will answer all your questions, Andi, but we must first complete our task."

Wiping away her tears as he went around to pull on his T-shirt, his mate nodded. "I saw a possible entry into the cave system when I flew over. It looks like it's relatively new, perhaps caused by a rockfall or a small earthquake, but it could still be a trap."

"Show me."

They crawled over the rough, craggy landscape, Naasir on alert for any wing brothers who might be posted this high, and Andromeda having to be careful not to get her wings caught. "There." She pointed up ahead.

"Watch our backs." Leaving the sole surviving pack with her, he went to the hole in the mountain.

The blazing sunlight made him wish he'd kept on his secret skin, but it worked best when he was naked, with nothing breaking the pattern. He didn't particularly want to be naked on craggy rocks that tore at his clothing and scratched his arms.

"So?" Andromeda asked when he returned.

"There are no scents around it from living creatures. The wing brothers apparently do not yet know of this new entrance."

Crawling with him to the hole, she winced. "It's going to be hell on my wings. Angels aren't meant to go through small holes into underground caverns."

He scowled at the idea of her being hurt. "Wait and I'll incapacitate the wing brothers inside, then you can walk in."

"That'll take too long—we have no idea how many of them are inside." A determined smile. "A few scrapes won't kill me. But you go first so you can cover me from below while I squeeze in. I think there's more risk down there than out here."

Naasir had to balance the known danger on top, with the unknown below; he finally decided she was right and the one below was more of a threat. Dropping the pack inside first, he jumped down to the sandy floor of the cavern, then stepped aside and pushed the pack out of the way so Andromeda wouldn't trip on it.

It took her at least three minutes to get in; her wings were badly scraped, feathers from darkest to palest brown falling around him by the time she succeeded.

Biting back his growl when he saw the extent of the damage and caught sight of the tears she was trying not to shed, Naasir made her stand in place in the light under the hole while he examined her.

"I'm immortal," she reminded him softly, though her voice was husky with withheld pain. "I'll heal."

He bit the tip of her ear. She jumped, then turned to take his face in her hands, her touch gentle. "I'm okay," she said softly. "Soon as this is over, we'll find a hot spring and relax."

She was lying. Naasir caught the minute change in her scent, the break in the rhythm of her pulse. What he didn't understand was why, but he'd pursue that once they'd completed their task and he'd gotten her to safety. For now, he took her hand and hooked her fingers lightly in the back of his pants after he'd pulled on the pack. "I can see in the dark." Even in places with zero ambient light.

A result of the mix between chimera and vampire.

"I won't let go."

Listening carefully to make certain the wing brothers hadn't detected them, he began to head down the corridor. When they reached a fork, he said, "Right or left?" At this point, he had no scents to use as a guide, so they had to rely on Andromeda's research.

"Right." Her wings rustled in the pitch-dark. "We're on a slight upward gradient—to get to Alexander, we need to head downward and to the north. That's the rumored location of the lava chasm."

Naasir kept her words in mind at the turns that followed.

"Can we talk?" Andromeda whispered after the third turn.

He understood what she was asking. "Yes. The caves and tunnels are structured in a way that sound won't travel if we keep our voices low."

"I feel trapped." Andromeda's fingers tightened their grip. "In a space this narrow and compact, I'm all but useless."

He thought of the wings that made her so beautiful in the sky and knew she was right. Here, those same wings were a serious handicap. "You'll still fight," he said, her courage an indelible part of her. "You won't allow your feelings of claustrophobia to trap you."

"No." She released a breath he felt ripple along the air currents. "Thanks, that helped."

Reaching behind him, he squeezed her wrist before dropping his hand. "Shall I tell you about Osiris and about how I came to be?"

A long pause. "No. Tell me in the light, under the sun and in a place that speaks to your soul."

He wanted to kiss her; his mate saw the wildness in his heart, understood that while he could navigate dark places, his choice was to live in the wind and the sun, the rain on his face and grass underfoot. "I have a special place I stay at near the Refuge," he told her. "About fifteen minutes' flight for you—it's in the forests that begin lower down the mountains." The Refuge itself was full of mountain wildflowers and other foliage, but had few tall trees.

"Really?" Andromeda's voice held a hunger to know him that was a verbal caress. "Did you build it in the trees?"

Yes, she understood him, his delicious-smelling mate. "Aodhan helped me design it." The angel was young to Naasir's way of thinking, but his mind saw in intricate patterns and shapes. "It's a house perched high in a tree and it opens out on all sides." Letting in the wind and the sun.

"There's a landing platform for my winged friends." He hadn't told many of his secret home, and all those who knew were careful never to give away its location. "The tree trunk is so straight and high, with so few lower branches that no one who isn't like me can climb it. If my vampire friends want to visit, I drop down a rope ladder."

"What about inside? Where do you sleep?"

"In the rain and snow, I make a nest inside, but when the sky is clear, I sleep in a hammock strung out between branches outside." Where he could look up at the stars and listen to the forest. "It's warm because Illium hid small panels near it that catch the sunlight and release it at night." He reached back to touch her wrist again. "I'll make the hammock bigger, big enough for your wings."

A sucked-in breath behind him, before Andromeda whispered, "I'd like to see your home."

"I'll take you, after." If she wanted to put her things there, he wouldn't say no. It was his territory, but he'd share it with her. He *wanted* her scent in his space, on his things. "I only have a few books," he admitted. "Things Jessamy gives me so I'll have knowledge—but I prefer to get my knowledge from listening to people."

"You must have an acute memory."

"Yes." It was apparently an inborn gift that came from the bloodline of the boy who was part of his self. "From the hammock, you can see the stars at night, so clear and bright, and sometimes, you can see the wings of passing squadrons."

"They don't spot you?"

"The hammock is too small to see from up high and the house itself is camouflaged in the branches, part of the tree." As if Aodhan had plucked the image straight out of Naasir's thoughts. "Aodhan says there is no other house like it in the world."

"He has such incredible talent." Andromeda's voice held a heavy vein of sadness. "Something terrible happened to him, didn't it?"

Naasir knew exactly what had happened to Aodhan. He'd helped Raphael track down the younger man—who he thought of as a cub in their family unit. That cub had been so badly damaged by the time they found him that Naasir had gone a little insane in vengeance. He wasn't sorry. No one touched Naasir's family and walked away unscathed.

"He's smiling again." It made Naasir happy to remember that and he knew it would make Andromeda happy, too. "He played a trick on Illium when Illium teased him too much."

"I've never seen Aodhan do anything like that."

Naasir grinned. "He's Illium's best friend for a reason." Naasir had been a hundred and twenty the first time he met the two. He still hadn't been full-grown, but he'd been old enough to know that two tiny angel cubs shouldn't be diving off a steep cliff into a pond below.

When he'd caught them by the scruffs of their necks, the two wet boys had wiggled like squirmy fish in an effort to get away. He'd growled and carried them straight to Jessamy. The memory was one Andromeda would like. He'd share it with her later, he thought, just as she said, "Tell me about Aodhan's trick."

Naasir wanted to laugh at the cleverness of it. "He snuck into Illium's room while Illium was asleep. Normally Illium would wake at once"—the squirmy cub had grown into a seasoned warrior— "but his mind would've known Aodhan was no threat, so he slept on." As Naasir would sleep on if Andromeda was in the room.

"Waiting until Illium turned over onto his front, Aodhan painted words on the outer surface of his wings with a special ink that soaked in but dried without leaving a sticky feeling. When Illium woke, he didn't notice anything."

Andromeda giggled. "What did Aodhan write?"

"Well, when Illium went out to join his squadron commanders for a drill, they patted him on the shoulder and said, 'Sorry, you're not my type'." Naasir had seen it all from his vantage point on a balcony.

"Don't keep me in suspense." Andromeda thumped him playfully on the shoulder.

Naasir grinned. *"Free Bluebell kisses on offer."*

Andromeda stifled a snort.

"The best part was that the ink didn't wash off, not for three days. Illium finally hunted Aodhan down and had him ink out the words so it just looked like he had splotches of black on his wings."

"Will Illium retaliate?"

"Of course." Illium's accident, Naasir knew, would've terrified Aodhan. "But they will always be friends, no matter what tricks they play on each other." Naasir had a feeling nothing would ever sever that bond. The two were incapable of betraying one another.

"Do you have a friend like that?" Andromeda asked, a wistfulness to her tone.

"I have family. I have friends." Far more than he'd ever imagined he might have when he'd been a feral boy who didn't understand what it meant to be civilized. "Janvier and Ashwini see me, understand me, are my friends." Like the others in the Seven, as well as Raphael, they had never asked him to be anything but

exactly what and who he was. "But they belong to each other
first." As it should be. "I will be always-friends with my mate."

Andromeda's voice was small. "She'll be a lucky woman."

He scowled; who did she think he was talking about? Before
he could challenge her, however, he caught the first traces of a
scent. "We have to be quiet now," he murmured. "This scent is
old but it means the wing brothers patrol here."

The tunnel widened soon after that point and Andromeda
was able to walk next to him, her hand in his. His eyes penetrated the darkness as if it was nothing, but he knew that for her,
it must be a stygian nothingness. Yet she walked into it without
flinching.

Lifting her hand to his mouth, he kissed her knuckles.

Her wing brushed over his back in a silent, affectionate
response just as the darkness of the tunnel became suffused
with a soft light.

Hearing nothing and scenting nothing fresh, Naasir continued on until they found the source of the light. It was inside
a large cave—part of the roof was slightly cracked. Not enough
to allow access, but enough for a shaft of sunlight to spear in.

"We're still far too high," Andromeda said, her lips brushing his ear. "We need to go deeper."

Nodding, Naasir did a careful scan of the cave. "That's the
easiest downward option." He pointed to the tunnel entrance
across the cave. "No fresh scents, but old ones are buried within."

"A trap?"

"My gut says yes." He and Andromeda walked across with
utmost care. He felt the minute change in the slope of the sand
beneath their feet an instant before Andromeda put her foot
forward.

35

Hauling her back before her foot could land, Naasir pinned her to his chest, her scraped and cut wings between them. "There's something beneath."

Fine white lines bracketed her mouth, but she just nodded. "I won't move."

Releasing her after making sure she had her balance, he crouched down and went to brush away the sand when he realized his fingers might create too much pressure.

"Here." Andromeda held out one of her feathers, this one a pale brown that turned dark at the tip. "It was about to fall off anyway."

He gently stroked her calf, knowing her wings had to be hurting. Being immortal didn't mean suffering no pain.

When he leaned forward, one hand still on her, and brushed away the sand, he found what he'd expected. "It's a pressure switch."

Andromeda's calf muscle tensed. "I don't think the ceiling cracks are accidental," she said slowly. "This cave is rigged to collapse."

"Burying all intruders with it." Naasir rose to his feet. "We can't risk crossing it—no way to know how many switches lie under the sand."

Making it safely back out into the tunnel by retracing their steps, it took them another thirty minutes to find a downward sloping tunnel again. It also brought them far too close to the entrance to the caves. So close that at one point, Naasir heard two wing brothers talking—a male and a female.

He immediately pressed a finger to Andromeda's lips so she'd know to be silent.

". . . in the caves."

"No sign so far, but if they are, they can't get past us." A gritty voice, holding a weight that spoke of experience. "All possible entry points to the chamber are tightly guarded."

"That explorer got in," said the first speaker, her youth apparent.

"Shavi was a new wing brother at the time. Green as grass. He fell for a distraction. Just as well the explorer went insane or we would've been knee deep in the curious and the dangerous."

A long pause. Naasir was about to move on when the younger wing brother said, "I always wondered about that." Her voice was diffident. "The others have told me he went in-side sane and cocky, came out screaming having clawed out his eyes. That that's why we didn't kill him—because it would've been dishonorable to kill a madman."

A chuckle. "They've been playing with you, girl. The part about why he was permitted to live is true, but the explorer didn't scream or claw out his eyes."

"Oh."

"He made it to the nearest city, thanks to the luck fate offers the mad and the stupid, but ended up catatonic in a hospital ward soon afterward. When he woke a year later, he had gaping holes in his memories and so rarely made sense that no one paid his ramblings any attention."

"The sire scrambled him?" An awed whisper.

"Simply because he Sleeps, it does not mean he isn't aware of the world around him." A thick clink that could've indicated a crossbow bolt being put back with others. "Remember, it is said Caliane rose before her time because she heard Lijuan plotting to kill her son."

That wasn't quite the truth, but the point was well made.

Naasir listened further but the two wing brothers moved on to talking about a man the female one wanted to approach. Silently wishing the hopeful wing brother good luck in her courtship, Naasir led Andromeda away from the entrance and to a space that felt safe, free of fresh scents and formed in a way that meant sound wouldn't carry.

Then, putting his lips to her ear, he told her what he'd heard. Having her so close, her warmth soft and female, it made him want to stop being civilized and sensible. He just wanted to take, to give in to the primal core of him that didn't understand why he should wait.

When she tugged him down so she could reply, he put his hand on an undamaged part of her wing in an effort to ease his need. *Stupid Grimoire book,* he thought, and again caught a flicker of memory—of a small red book with a drawing in gold on the cover.

His mind kept telling him he'd seen it. But *where*?

"It's true," Andromeda said, her lips brushing his ear and shocking jolts of pleasure over his skin. "The record from that explorer was disjointed and jerky. Almost like a delusion. The single reason I took it seriously was because I knew that as a very young angel, Alexander lived in the oasis."

That truth had become lost in time, buried by Alexander's ascension and eventual control of this entire territory. Andromeda had the knowledge because, a hundred years earlier, she'd tracked down Ancients still in the world and listened to them. Unlike Caliane and Alexander, these Ancients weren't powerful, but they were often wise.

The ones she'd spoken to were all once more Sleeping, having awakened together for half a century to "taste" the new world. Having decided against living in it, the three had told her they'd see her in another thousand years. "Save your other questions for then, child. It is quite lovely having young ears eager to listen to our tales."

One of the tales they'd told her had been of going to a newly adult Alexander's oasis home for a "warrior party" where mead was drink and the dancing was wild.

"He never forgot us," one of the Ancients had said. "Even when he became a powerful general, then an archangel, we still had an open welcome to his home—whether it be an arch-angelic palace or a hunting cabin—and he'd sit with us and drink a glass or five and laugh over old stories."

The others had nodded, their smiles holding a deep and true affection for an archangel who to them was a friend they'd grown up alongside. "I hope one day when we wake, he, too, is awake. I should like to share a drink with him and see what he makes of this world where metal machines fly in the air and an archangel keeps no court."

Thinking of all her conversations with the Ancients, she braced herself with a hand on Naasir's chest and said, "If Alexander is in some sense aware of people in this cave system, then we may be safe. He wasn't capricious or heedlessly cruel."

"But if it's an autonomous defense as with the locusts, then we could end up catatonic," Naasir completed in the low, slightly growly tone that she loved.

"Should we leave and attempt to get far enough away that the phone works?"

"I missed the check-in call—Raphael is already on his way." Naasir closed one warm, rough-skinned hand over the one she had on his chest. "But it'll take Alexander time to rise, and Lijuan has a shorter distance to travel than Raphael. We need to try to start the process so Alexander isn't helpless if Lijuan realizes this is his location and arrives first."

Andromeda thought of how Lijuan's physical form had faded in and out, of her thin face and missing limbs. The Archangel of China was clearly weak, but according to the news Andromeda had received from Jessamy while in Amanat, there was a chance Lijuan had killed Jariel—an angel rumored to have been strong enough that he might one day soon have become an archangel.

And Alexander was currently helpless should she strike.

"What are we waiting for?" she said to Naasir, her blood hot. "We have to go annoy an Ancient and hope he doesn't turn us into gibbering idiots."

Naasir's chuckle was soft, the teeth that grazed the tip of her ear sharp. "I knew you were my mate."

36

Lijuan had only gone a quarter of the way to Rohan's palace when her strength ran out. Heading to the ground before she fell out of the sky, her wings yet weak and useless appendages, she became corporeal.

Rage burned in her as she lay helpless on the earth, a torso with wings that barely moved when she attempted to flip herself over onto her front. Not that it would've mattered. She couldn't even crawl fast; her single fully regenerated arm was as weak as her wings, the muscles trembling at the least exertion.

Unable to contain the fury, she struck out with one red-tipped hand. Black shards erupted, demolishing the trees in front of her to dust. She jerked . . . and then she smiled. This humiliating weakness was bearable if her deadly abilities were returning to their full strength. A Sleeping Alexander would have no defense against them. She was a goddess, while he had spent the past four hundred years in stasis.

He might've beaten her in combat when she was an angel on the verge of becoming an archangel and Alexander already an Ancient, but she was stronger than him now. He wouldn't walk away from her this time, a tall golden-haired creature with silver wings who'd turned down what other men had coveted.

For a moment, she hesitated, echoes of that hopeful, sweet, smart girl in her soul. That girl had seen only wonder in the world. That girl had known Alexander was a piece of light that would burn through eternity, a man of war who had gained immeasurable wisdom over the ages he'd seen pass.

"My beautiful Zhou Lijuan." His fingers brushing her cheekbones, his silver eyes holding her in thrall. "So delicate and strong and full of such power."

Her palm tingled in a sudden sensory memory of closing over the thickness of his wrist. "Why won't you be with me?" He admired her, she could see that. "I can walk by your side, be your partner as you would be mine."

A gentle shake of his head. "You must grow on your own. Perhaps in seven thousand years, we can come together again. When you are in your power and we are equals. Now . . . I would crush you without meaning to, and you are destined for greatness."

Seven thousand years.

It had passed, she suddenly realized. Perhaps killing him wasn't the answer . . .

The rage rushed back in on a black roar. Not because Alexander had rejected her; she had forgotten that long ago, had fallen passionately in love with another man. For an eon, Alexander had been nothing but a sweet memory of her youth, one that caused her amused fondness. She'd been a pup in awe of a beautiful Ancient.

No, her rage came from the idea that Alexander, this silver-winged Sleeper of the prophecy, would one day seek to destroy her. *No one* had that right. And they weren't equals. No one was her equal. She was Zhou Lijuan and she would rule the world before this Cascade was done.

Throwing back her head, she laughed for the first time since Raphael had hurt her.

37

Naasir sensed two more booby traps over the next three hours. Andromeda caught another one, warned by a change in the air currents that he'd dismissed as natural. It turned out it was an ancient trick Andromeda had read of in a book.

"You should read more," she teased when he grumbled about missing the trap.

"You can read to me. I like listening to stories."

"I will."

Even in the darkness, he saw the sadness in her expression, knew she was once again hiding something from him. Frustrated he couldn't confront her about it right then, he leaned in and nipped her ear again.

She jumped, then pushed his chest. "Stop it." A scowl. "We'll discuss your biting habit later."

"The same time we discuss your habit of keeping secrets," he said and saw her face fall. "Tunnels are starting to go steadily downhill."

"If we run into a wing brother, don't kill or injure." Andromeda's voice was urgent. "If Alexander *is* watching on some level, that will immediately turn him against us."

Naasir scowled. "I'd planned to knock them out."

"We could tie them up and gag them. There's a T-shirt in the pack we can tear into strips."

Naasir wasn't convinced such measures would be effective against men and women as highly trained as the wing brothers, but knew she was right about not angering Alexander. Even gagging and tying up the sentinels could be read as an attack, but they had to take that risk.

He turned sideways, so the pack faced her. "Give me the T-shirt."

When she put it into his hand, he used his claws to silently tear it into strips that she stuffed in an easily reachable pocket of the pack, working by touch.

He wanted to kiss her again. He hated being down here and he could see in the dark. It had to be a hundred times worse for her, but she kept going. "Ready?"

"Let's go."

Hands linked, they carried on. There were more traps, including one that he had to spring in order for them to pass. A hundred crossbow bolts embedded into the opposite wall with deadly force a heartbeat after he triggered the mechanism and spun out of the way. Only after they were all expended did Naasir crawl underneath, making a worried Andromeda wait on the other side and pushing the pack ahead of him in case there were pressure switches embedded in the tunnel floor.

They took a short break afterward, drinking water from the bottle in the pack and eating more of the dried food. Thankfully, they'd stored food in both packs.

"No more jerky," Andromeda muttered, giving that to him. "I'm eating the nuts and fruits."

He decided that was okay, since she'd had jerky while they were above. Eating the leathery meat gave him no pleasure but it was fuel and it would keep him going without blood for a while.

Washing it down with water, he rose and tugged up his mate. "It won't be far now."

"I'm okay. Excited." A smile that lit up the darkest shadows. "We might be about to wake an Ancient. Right now, I don't even care that he might wake angry."

Nuzzling at her, he grinned. "Wild and fearless and a little bad. Perfect."

Eyes sparkling in the darkness, she bit down on her full lower lip as if stifling a laugh.

He wanted to growl.

Vows of celibacy should be outlawed as far as he was concerned. However, since Andromeda had taken one, he'd honor it because her honor was important and he wouldn't steal it from her. He would, however, happily end that vow by finding that stupid red book. "Let's finish this." So he could go hunt the Grimoire.

They continued to walk side by side until he scented a living being aside from him and Andromeda and the occasional large insect. He hadn't mentioned the latter to his mate—she was tough but he'd seen full-grown warriors, male and female, shudder at the thought of insects. He'd test Andromeda's tolerance later, when they weren't trapped underground and she couldn't see.

Releasing her hand, he touched her face to reassure her, then put the pack on the ground and moved forward on his own. The wing brother was standing at the entrance to a small cave, his eyes constantly scanning the tunnel and his crossbow held at the ready. No green youth this one.

By the time Naasir returned to Andromeda, her breathing was choppier than it had been, but she'd stayed in position. Hugging her, he cupped her nape and spoke directly into her ear. "There are two. One inside the cave, one at the entrance. I can take down the one outside relatively silently. You gag him and tie him up."

She nodded.

"If the one inside hears, I'll have to knock the first one unconscious and hope Alexander understands—our only advantage is surprise."

Andromeda touched her hand to his jaw, ran her fingers up to his eyes.

"Yes," he said. "They can see in the dark. Night vision goggles." He rubbed his face against the side of hers. "We'll steal you a pair. They'll get rescued soon enough."

She patted his chest in thanks and they separated to head toward the wing brothers after Andromeda pulled out some of the torn pieces of cloth.

* * *

It wasn't until after Naasir left her that Andromeda realized she wouldn't know if he'd taken down the wing brother and where, not without Naasir alerting her. And since the wing brothers were wearing night vision lenses, if she moved from this spot, she might give Naasir away. But she didn't want him alone out there.

Biting her lip, she focused and realized there was the barest touch of light coming from somewhere. Not enough to really allow her to see, but that might change if she got a little closer. About to slide out her sword and creep forward, she felt something hit her lightly on the chest. She missed catching it but when she went to her knees and felt around on the sandy floor, her fingers slid over the distinct smooth curves of goggles.

Wasting no time, she put them on. The world around her was suddenly tinged an unearthly green, but she could see clearly.

Naasir had hauled his captive around and somehow managed to keep the wing brother contained and silent while he threw the goggles to her. Closing the distance to them on silent feet, she helped gag and bind the wing brother, the muscular man's eyes furious with anger.

Task complete, Naasir jumped up onto the ceiling with such ease that she almost gasped. Winking at her, he went inside the cave. Creeping closer on foot, she watched as he dropped soundlessly from the ceiling and took down the wing brother, one hand over the other man's mouth and a clawed hand around his throat as he used his body weight to pin the armed male to the earth.

Darting in, Andromeda tied and gagged the wing brother. Afterward, she whispered, "I'm sorry," in his ear.

"Andi."

Getting up at that low call, she crossed the cave to join Naasir at the mouth of what appeared to be a downward sloping tunnel. When she pushed up her goggles for an instant, it was clear to her that this was the source of the faint ambient light—it seemed to be coming from the rough stone of the walls itself.

Goggles back down, she released a shaky breath. "Yes, this must be it."

"Start checking for traps. I'll retrieve the pack."

She was the one who finally found it, after five excruciatingly slow minutes that ended up with Naasir having to retie a wing brother who'd nearly escaped his bonds. In the ensuing scuffle, Naasir discovered the cave floor was a false one designed to collapse inward should the wing brothers activate the trap.

Depending on the depth of the fall, it would've surely broken any number of bones. That is, if the rockfall rigged to come down over the tunnel mouth didn't bury them first.

"I'm starting to feel sorry for all the cave explorers," Andromeda muttered, dusting off her arms after they stepped into the tunnel without setting off the booby trap, then deliberately collapsed the rockfall to impede pursuit by the wing brothers.

Alexander's sentinels surely had other ways in but at least she and Naasir wouldn't have to worry about danger at their backs—from that source at least. "I know they'll come after us, but I hope the wing brothers don't have to wait too long in the dark for rescue."

"You have a soft heart," Naasir said with an indulgent smile. "I'll have to make sure people don't take advantage of you."

She should've scowled at him, but her heart turned to mush. He sounded so happy to have the task. And since he expected her to fight beside him, used her skills where necessary, it wasn't as if he was being condescending. No, he was just being protective of the woman he wanted as his mate.

Her throat closed up, her face all stiff and hot. She was glad he'd turned his gaze forward and couldn't see her. She should tell him she couldn't be his mate, but the words kept getting stuck inside her, as if so long as she didn't say them, they wouldn't come true.

In front of her Naasir held up a hand. She halted.

But the wing brother had already spotted them. He gave a loud shout before they managed to subdue him. Pounding feet thundered in from several directions. Giving up on stealth, Andromeda and Naasir ran full-tilt, her wings getting badly bloodied and scraped in the narrow main passageway and Naasir's hand locked tight around hers.

When he hauled her into a small cave and indicated another rigged rockfall he'd made sure they skirted, she took out her sword and triggered it. The rocks came down in a noisy crash that sent up clouds of dust.

Coughing into her hand, her teeth gritty from the dust she'd breathed in, she looked to Naasir. "Where?" He wouldn't have asked her to trigger the rockfall if it would trap them; she knew enough of his senses to guess he'd seen, smelled, or heard something that had eluded her.

"This way."

She followed the imprint of his footsteps in the sand to find herself in front of another tunnel with rough stone walls that pulsed with that eerie glow. Only this time, the tunnel had so steep a downward incline it was near vertical, the floor slick and shiny in comparison to the walls and the roof. "Damn it," she muttered, sheathing her sword. "I'll go first. You can come after me and push me down if my wings get stuck."

Naasir shook his head. "No. I didn't realize the sheer gradient from a distance. We'll find another way out."

Hearing sounds from the cave entrance that told her the rockfall blockade would soon no longer exist, she blew out a breath and tucked flyaway curls of her hair behind her ears. "No way to do that without killing a large number of wing brothers—don't think they're in the mood to talk anymore."

"Your wings are already battered." It was a growl, his hand lifting to very gently touch an undamaged part. "You could break something."

A touch of her fingers to his jaw to reassure him. "It'll heal." Getting into the tunnel, she glanced once more at Naasir's beloved face, tucked her wings in as tight as they could possibly go, and released her grip on the outer edges.

Feathers and skin ripped off as she barreled down, blood scenting the air. Fighting back tears at the stabbing pain of the damage on such sensitive skin, she tumbled out feetfirst into a sandy pit of some kind and forced herself to roll to one side at once.

The pack thudded home seconds later, Naasir landing in a crouch beside it.

Running to where she lay on her stomach on the sand, trying to breathe past the agony, he touched the back of her head and bent down to nuzzle at her. "We are almost there."

Holding on to his affection, she got herself onto her hands and knees, then slowly sat up. She hadn't been able to fight back the tears at the end and could feel sand sticking to the wetness, her breath coming in short hiccups. It would've humiliated her to be seen this way by others . . . but not Naasir.

Naasir would never even think of using her pain to cause emotional wounds.

Taking her face in his hands, he rubbed his nose over hers. "You're very brave," he said, silver eyes glowing in the darkness and fierce pride in his tone.

"So are you." Her fingers trembled as she closed her hands around his wrists. "Alexander better not blast us after all this."

A feral grin as he got to his feet and held out a hand to pull her up. Once she steadied, the ice and fire of the damage to her wings—as interpreted by her exposed nerve endings—no longer threatening to make her crumple, she looked around. They were at the bottom of a smooth stone bowl that appeared to have no exits, the sides so obviously sheer even Naasir's claws would provide no purchase.

"I could fly up," she said, because while her wings were badly damaged, they'd still hold her aloft. "Try to see if there's an exit up top."

Naasir shook his head, that vivid metallic hair shifting like liquid mercury even through the green-tinged vision of the goggles. "The sound isn't right here." Crouching down, he placed one hand on the sand, the other on his thigh, and cocked his head.

Andromeda stayed motionless, but used her eyes to scan everything in her field of vision. When Naasir changed position, she took the chance to turn so she could see the walls behind her.

Her eyes widened. *"Naasir."*

"There is a way out of here," he muttered, head still cocked. "I can hear it."

Breaking position and the airflow, she ran over to the wall directly in front of her. "Do you see?"

Naasir came to join her. Leaning close, he ran his fingers over the thin lines dug into the stone. "It's a fragment of a larger design."

"Yes." She backed off to the far wall. Parts of the design

had been worn away, but she could still put it together. "A raven." Created of myriad intricate images that represented this land. "Alexander's chamber must be—"

The ground shook like a dog unwilling to release its prey.

Naasir hauled her into his arms as stone crumbled down around them . . . and then the ground was just gone and they were falling at a screaming pace.

"Snap out your wings!" Naasir yelled, his arms easing as if he'd release her.

She held on to him with a death grip. "I can't! Something is sucking us down." The pressure was intense, threatening to crush the small bones in her wings. Those bones were incredibly strong, designed as they were by nature to hold her aloft, but right now, she felt as if they were seconds away from buckling. "Don't let go!"

"I won't." Silver hair blowing back from his face, he tried to turn his head to scan the area, but the wind pressure was too strong to permit the movement.

Andromeda suddenly felt the air growing warmer around them. Understanding drying her throat, she managed to bend her head enough that she could look down. The movement was possible only because Naasir had kind of bent over her in an effort to protect.

At first, she didn't see anything and it was only then that she realized the goggles had been ripped off her face by the wind. But she'd been able to see Naasir . . . and it wasn't because of the luminescence from the walls.

A molten red glow came slowly into view, growing hotter with every split second of their descent. "The lava pit," she said, Naasir's ear close enough that she knew he'd hear.

"I see it." His breath on her skin, the sensation intense even with the wind. "Try your wings again, Andi."

She tried, so hard it felt as if she'd ruptured blood vessels in her eyes, but it was useless. When she shook her head, Naasir growled. "My mate is trying to save your fucking life, Archangel!"

The heat began to burn, though the cauldron was boiling far below. That was when Andromeda understood death would come long before they ever got close to the surface of the lava—or tempest of molten metal, whatever it was. The heat would liquefy their internal organs and melt the flesh from their bones before those bones cracked and turned to dust.

The disintegration would end them both, for total and absolute immortality was the province of myth. Given her resurrection, it was possible that Lijuan had reached that level of evolution. Andromeda was too young to survive even half of what was about to happen, while Naasir . . . She didn't know his limits, but she knew she couldn't watch him die.

"Alexander!" she cried in desperation. "You're meant to be a wise man!"

The bottoms of her boots melted, the feathers at the ends of her wings beginning to singe and burn, the air so hot and dry it threatened to sear the lungs.

"No, he's a stupid one!" Naasir snarled . . . and they jerked to a halt in midair.

38

Eyes wide, Andromeda stretched out her wings. They moved, but she knew without attempting it that should she try to fly out, she'd be sucked back down. Not that she would, not when she didn't have the strength to lift Naasir with her. Keeping her arms around the taut muscle of him, she looked around as he did the same.

There was nothing else in this tunnel of stone except Andromeda and Naasir and the bubbling, ravenous lava below. Heart a staccato beat and every breath an effort, she said, "I think you got his attention."

Naasir bared his teeth. "You're more civilized—you talk."

Molten geysers shot out of the lava, as if Alexander was getting impatient. "Archangel," she said, directing her words to the lava, though she knew Alexander could hear her regardless of where she pitched her voice. "The world is in the midst of a Cascade and the archangels of the current Cadre are spiking violently in power."

The lava bubbled and erupted with countless geysers as they fell another two feet.

The heat scorched her soles through her ruined boots.

Naasir's growl was more feral than she'd ever heard it, the

sound echoing off the stone to reverberate in her bones. "Lijuan wants to kill you in your Sleep, you stubborn old bastard! She believes she's a goddess!"

Andromeda winced. Alexander had been wise, but he'd also had a stormy temper.

The stone rumbled but they didn't drop again.

"He's laughing," Andromeda whispered incredulously. It pushed her over the edge. "Listen, damn you! Lijuan isn't who you remember! She's insane and she *can* kill you—while you've been Asleep, she's become the Archangel of Death."

She felt the heat of Naasir's skin as his temperature rose, smelled burning flesh. Not hers alone. No. *No.* "Even if you survive, your loyal sentinels won't!" As Naasir was Andromeda's, the Wing Brotherhood was Alexander's—worth dying for, worth fighting for. "Your men and women have held to their vows for four hundred years and they will die one by one in agony and suffering rather than leave you!"

She screamed as they fell again. The smell of burning feathers filled the air. It felt as if her blood was a heartbeat away from boiling, her eyes so hot she couldn't keep them open.

Naasir's voice was no longer in any way human, the words he spoke guttural. "I'll come back from death you ancient relic, hunt down your immortal ass if you harm my mate!"

"Brotherhood," Andromeda managed to whisper, sure Alexander's bond to his sentinels was their only hope of reaching him.

Naasir pressed his cheek to hers, trying to curve his body as much as possible around her own. "As for your sentinels, Lijuan might decide to make them reborn. Shambling, living dead who hunger for the flesh. You are no sire if you permit that!"

No warning before they were pushed up at the same suicidal rate they'd been pulled down. Up and up and up until the air was cool and they could breathe.

The voice, when it came, was everywhere.

I am waking. Prepare for battle.

Naasir and Andromeda found themselves shoved out of the wind tunnel and dumped on the sandy floor of the stone chamber again. The chasm that had sucked them in closed up so seamlessly that there was no sign it had ever been there.

Getting up with muscled, feline grace, Naasir crouched in front of her as she sat up. He ran his hand over her hair, then very gently over the arches of her wings—it was a highly sensitive area, the touch intimate, but she burrowed against his chest, needing the tenderness, wanting nothing more than to be close to him.

Death, she'd realized in that tunnel, could come at any instant.

"Kiss me," she said, lifting her face to the primal masculinity of his. "If death comes, I want to go having known your kiss."

He nipped sharply at her lower lip instead. "We'll kiss after I find your stupid Grimoire book."

Forehead scrunching up, Andromeda shook her head. "Forget the Grimoire."

Naasir gripped her chin, his eyes—so haunting and beautiful—locking with hers. "Your honor is important to you. It is as important as your heart. Kill one and I will kill the other."

She cried then, because he knew her heart. His arms came around her, his breath against her cheek as he rubbed the side of his face against her, but she knew they didn't have time for her sorrow. Stealing one more moment against the heat and strength and fierceness of him, she got to her feet.

Her soles were severely burned, causing excruciating agony, but she could already feel her body attempting to make the repairs. More important, she could still walk as long as she didn't focus on the throbbing pulse of pain. "My wings should hold me for short periods," she said, stretching them out. "I can fly up, search for a way out."

Naasir's eyes were flames of liquid silver as they took in her blackened and burnt feathers but he nodded. "Go. I'll look down here. There's still something about the air currents."

It was only when he turned that she saw his back. A pained cry leaving her mouth, she reached out instinctively before pulling back her hand lest she harm him with her touch. "Your back." Her voice shook with fury. "Alexander *hurt* you." His T-shirt had been almost totally burned away on that side of his body, leaving only exposed and charred skin.

Turning toward her, he cupped her cheek, his thumb scraping over her cheekbone. "It's only a minor burn. It'll be gone within hours."

Old and strong, she reminded herself. He was older and

stronger than her, and he was a legendary chimera. "Is it true that you can heal as well or sometimes even better than an angel?" That was a "fact" she'd just remembered, something she'd come across during her studies into mythical creatures.

"Yes." Leaning in, he rubbed his nose over hers as he'd done at the end of their tunnel ride. "I'll tell you all about chimeras after we get out."

She felt her lips twitch at his tone—as if he was offering her a treat. And the truth was, he was: she was a scholar, loved new information . . . and this wild chimera had figured that out because he looked at her and saw who she was. "I'll hold you to that."

Spreading her wounded wings on his smile, she rose into the air. Vertical takeoffs took more strength than a glide, but as a result of the training regimen Dahariel and Galen had taught her, she usually had no problems. Today, however, it felt as if a thousand thin spikes were stabbing into every inch of her wings, trying to hold her down.

Gritting her teeth and refusing to consider failure, she got aloft and began to circle around. Other than the impossible-to-climb chute down which they'd slid into this pit, there didn't seem to be any other fissures or tunnel mouths.

She flew higher.

Naasir watched to make sure Andromeda was steady on the wing before he pulled off the shreds of his useless boots and began to prowl around in search of an exit. The air currents in this room were stirring wrong against him, his skin rippling with stripes between one breath and the next. What wasn't visible unless someone stroked him at the exact right moment, was the fine, fine, *fine* layer of fur that occasionally appeared on his skin.

Maybe he wouldn't tell Andromeda about that part of him—he'd just let her discover it one day while they were playing naked. She wouldn't mind; he knew that about her now. She liked him despite the fact he wasn't in any way "normal." No, that wasn't right. Andromeda didn't like him despite his unusual nature. She just liked *him*.

Even when she scowled at him, she liked him.

Standing in different parts of the pit as that knowledge settled into his cells, he tuned into the air currents. When he felt Andromeda start to descend, he looked up. "Can you stay up a little longer?" Her landing would disturb the air that had settled after her takeoff.

She nodded and began to circle gently instead of staying in place. Realizing she was hurting too much to maintain a hover, her burnt feet and scorched wings making him want to snarl, he clenched his jaw and went toward a particular part of the wall. The air was fresher here, moved faster. "Andi."

Landing softly behind him when he gestured, she pulled off what remained of her own boots, and hobbled over to peer at the wall. "What do you see?" A sudden blink, her body motionless. "Why can *I* see?"

Naasir, able to see no matter the light, hadn't noticed the fact it was no longer pitch-black, the luminescence from the walls at a much higher intensity. "Alexander."

"I guess this means he liked us after all."

"Not enough to lead us out of here."

"Alexander was never known to be an easy archangel."

Grunting in acknowledgment, Naasir began to run his fingers along the lines where he'd felt the fresher air. "There's a door here."

Going to her knees below the outwardly unbroken stone, Andromeda began to feel around the wall at ground level. "Sometimes the pressure point is hidden lower, where people are less apt to—" Her fingers slid over a faint, shallow indent. "Naasir."

He came down beside her, confirmed he could also feel it. Fitting a finger against the indent, he pushed.

No door. No effect at all.

"I think we need to find two," Andromeda said, thinking back to an ancient door she'd read about in a history book. "Let's hope it's not a code which requires the application of pressure in a precise rhythm."

"Alexander can just drop those he doesn't like into a boiling pit," Naasir pointed out with a shrug. "Anyone allowed to stay alive must be given a way out."

"Good point." Andromeda felt for the second dent alongside Naasir.

"Got it."

Touching the spot Naasir indicated, she nodded. "I'll push here and you push there."

When nothing happened, her heart squeezed, the idea of being entombed a nightmare.

A harsh groan split the air the next second, motes of dust shining in the luminescence.

Rising to stand on marginally less painful feet, she took Naasir's hand and they backed away in case the mechanism swung outward, but when the ancient door finally moved, it was inward. The tunnel within was gray with thick cobwebs that made it clear no one had traversed it for centuries, but the walls glowed with the same luminescence as the central chamber.

"I hate cobwebs." They stuck stubbornly to her feathers and this thick, they might even affect her ability to fly once they made it out.

Again that smile from Naasir, the affectionate one that hit her right in the solar plexus. "I'll go first and clear the way for you." Stepping in, he started using his claws to rip away the sticky mass.

Sword in hand, she got the bits that he missed and together, they managed to keep her wings mostly unsticky. "I'm trying very hard not to think about the spiders who built these, or about what just crawled over my foot." She shuddered.

"You don't like bugs?"

"Not ones with more than six legs. Or shells. Or antennae."

Naasir chuckled and they carried on. It felt as if they walked for two hours on their burnt feet before the tunnel spilled them out into a small cave illuminated with the same luminescence that had lit their path this far. Given the lack of natural light, it was clear they were still deep inside the cave system.

Where they might permanently remain, courtesy of the angry wing brothers waiting for them, their crossbows pointed and primed.

Three hours after the tense meeting outside Alexander's chamber, night had fallen over the oasis and the wing brothers knew what was coming. The fact their archangel was waking had caused wide-eyed awe among the younger members of the Brotherhood, grim joy in the older.

"I am happy to know I will see the sire again." The tautly held emotion in Tarek's tone was a testament to the loyalty Alexander inspired in his people. "I only wish his Sleep hadn't been so precipitously interrupted. He did not plan to wake for thousands of years."

The leader of the Brotherhood was sharing a meal with Naasir and Andromeda under the starlight. She went to speak, ask him about his long service, when a long-range scout ran in. It turned out the wing brothers' phones didn't work here, either—they had a hidden communications bunker a considerable distance out from the oasis.

It was of no use right now. All communications systems had gone down not long after Alexander told Naasir and Andromeda he was about to wake. As far as the Brotherhood had been able to ascertain, it had affected the entire territory, perhaps farther. All information was currently being passed through a relay of runners and old signal beacons that utilized a Brotherhood code.

"The fighting continues at the palace." Accepting a bottle of water, the scout gulped it down. "It seems Rohan called in all his squadrons and ground troops prior to the attack."

"Your warning," Tarek said, and it wasn't a question.

Naasir's eyes gleamed in the dark. "Who is winning?"

"Rohan and Xi are evenly matched. Stalemate."

That, Andromeda knew, wouldn't last. "Lijuan will tip the balance unless Favashi returns home in time." The Archangel of Persia had to know about the assault, as it had begun prior to the communications blackout.

A blood vessel pulsed in Tarek's temple, his hand fisted on the table. "We can't leave our post to go to his aid and I do not think Rohan would wish it."

"Let's hope Lijuan is too weak to arrive anytime soon." The fact the Archangel of China wasn't already here was a good sign. "The storm you mentioned—would it be enough to delay Raphael?"

Naasir had expected his sire to arrive tonight.

"According to the last report we had before everything went dark," Tarek said, "the lightning storm is pummeling every part of the world except this territory, and the strikes are violent enough that all planes and angels have been grounded.

Your sire may have been forced to land midway—or he was hit and needs to recover."

"He'll be here." Dressed in a loose linen shirt he'd put on over his ravaged back after one of the wing brothers offered to replace his ruined tee, Naasir put another piece of meat from his own plate onto hers.

She smiled and ate the offering; it was nice to have someone who wanted to take care of her. She intended to do the same for him—the wing brothers had provided bottled blood, but she could tell he didn't like the taste. If she ate well, he'd have no excuse not to feed from her.

The ground rumbled at that instant, the night sky above suddenly awash with a silvery aurora that rippled like water. It was breathtaking, and it spanned the sky as far as the eye could see.

"The sire." The leader of the Brotherhood looked up, his throat moving and his voice thick.

Andromeda's own soul ached at witnessing the eerie beauty and incandescent power of an event that might never be repeated in her immortal lifetime. "As long as the aurora covers the entire territory, Lijuan's people won't be able to pinpoint the oasis or the caves."

"We should take advantage of tonight." Naasir's tone was far more pragmatic than either hers or Tarek's. "Leave scouts on watch and rest as many of your people as you can," he said to Tarek. "If you have a place to hide your vulnerable, do it. Lijuan will not spare them."

The other man's face turned harsh, his love for his sire replaced by brutal protectiveness. "Come." Showing Andromeda and Naasir to a small house on the edge of the village, he said, "You have excellent senses," to Naasir. "I may as well use you."

"I'll sound an alert if I sense intruders."

Saying good night to the wing brother, the two of them walked in to find the home was a simple one-bedroom space furnished with a bed large enough to accommodate Andromeda's wings. There was also a small table set with extra food and drink, and a separate section for the facilities.

As Naasir went and opened the large window not far from the bed, Andromeda walked into the bathroom and cleaned up. The wing brothers had retrieved the pack she'd abandoned during their escape this morning, and though she'd have rather changed into the loose sleep clothing given her by a villager, she put on the last clean set of her own gear.

If battle came to them in the middle of the night, she wanted to be ready.

Naasir brushed past her as she walked out and he walked in, his smile letting her know it had been deliberate. Like a cat rubbing past her. Smiling, she waited until after his shower, then made him turn around so she could examine his back.

His hair damp, he was dressed in a clean white tee she'd found in the pack, and a borrowed pair of dark brown cargos that hung low on his hips. Stripping off the tee, he threw it on a chair and stood still for her worried appraisal. Her breath caught; his skin was warm and rich and flawless, the muscles beneath liquid strength. No mystery why women fought to stroke him.

But beautiful as he was, that wasn't her primary focus at this instant. "You do heal fast." There were no scars, no sign that he'd come to within inches of being burned alive. "Does anything hurt?"

"No." Shifting on his heel, he took her shoulders and ordering her to face the window, examined her wings with slow, methodical care. "Parts of your wings have been scraped down to the tendon." The growl was deep. "Be careful when you sleep."

Andromeda nodded, able to feel the stretching, throbbing pain that denoted healing tissue.

"Your feet?"

"Healed." Usually, all energy would be directed to the wings, but her body had clearly decided the feet were a minor enough wound to deal with quickly.

Getting into bed, she lay on her stomach. When Naasir slipped in beside her, she lifted her wing to put it over him. He petted her gently over the uninjured sections. "Can I have one of your smaller feathers when it sheds? Don't pull it out." The last was an order.

The gritty roughness of his voice made her toes curl. "The one under your index finger—I can't feel it." An angel's feathers were another organ in a sense, the awareness of them bone-deep. "I think it's detached."

Naasir touched it with care, and when it slid away, he took it and, getting out of bed, went to their single surviving pack. He returned with a fine strip of rawhide in hand, the kind men sometimes used to tie back their hair. As she watched, he sat on the bed and tied the feather neatly to the rawhide, then wove the strip of leather into a thin braid on one side of his head, tying it off with a clever twist at the end.

"There," he said with satisfied pleasure, and turned over onto his stomach beside her.

Heart so melted it was just this warm thick honey in her chest, she draped her wing over him once again. "You need to feed."

"I'll drink the rest of the bottle."

Andromeda ran her nails over his nape, to his heavy-lidded groan. "Drink from me. I ate well." She slid the wrist of her other hand under his mouth when he lifted his head.

His soft, astonishing hair brushing over it, the damp strands a cool caress, he pressed a kiss to her pulse. It jumped. Nostrils flaring, he licked over the skin but didn't bite. "One day, I'll sip from you while my cock is snug inside your tight sheath, and it'll be slow and deep and long."

Breathing suddenly became a difficult task.

"But on this night, your body needs all its energy to heal the damage to your wings." Another kiss, this one so tender, it made her lower lip quiver and her eyes well.

How could she possibly survive five hundred years without him?

39

Andromeda woke to the crash of thunder. Naasir was already awake. Lying on his back, one of his arms curved around her as she used his shoulder for a pillow, he was petting her wing as he watched the lightning storm beyond the window. The strikes glittered as bright as Naasir's hair, no rain to soften their harsh brilliance.

"How long did we sleep?" she asked, snuggling closer to the furnace-like warmth of his body.

"It's early morning." A boom of thunder almost drowned out his words.

"I've never seen the sky that color." A dark, roiling purple that threw shadows on the earth and sparked with shards of lightning. "It's beautiful." As wild as the chimera who held her so affectionately. "This must be the same storm that's already covered the rest of the world."

"I didn't say anything in front of Tarek, but Raphael can fly above lightning."

Andromeda's eyes widened. "Yes, no archangel should've had any problem avoiding it." Yet, unless something had changed in the night, neither Raphael, nor Lijuan, nor Favashi had made it here. That wasn't coincidence. "It's said that when an archangel ascends, the world changes in inexplicable ways. It might be the same for the waking of an Ancient."

"This lightning isn't normal," Naasir agreed. "Caliane's waking was violent, but not to this extent."

"Alexander was a general, Caliane an angel known for her grace and her song."

"She's also a trained warrior who rose to protect her son," Naasir reminded her. "I think the Cascade must be getting stronger."

Hairs rising on the back of her neck at what that might mean, Andromeda shivered. "The good news is that I don't think Lijuan would risk her noncorporeal form to a strike."

Naasir's chest rumbled under her hand. "Perhaps the storm will do the world a favor and burn Lijuan from existence."

Both of them conscious such a gift was unlikely, they lay in silence until Andromeda said, "Do you remember being two before you became one?" It didn't seem wrong to ask about that here, not with the ferocity of nature so close.

"Yes. The human boy played with the tiger cub." His words held a smile. "They were best friends in a place with no other living beings but Osiris and the wolves he kept as pets . . . and when Osiris forced them into one, the friendship between boy and cub kept the chimera I became stable."

Six thousand dead. The cub and the boy could've been two more casualties . . . and she might've never known Naasir.

Violently repudiating the thought, she listened to his heart, and she reminded herself he was very much strong and alive.

"The two parts didn't fight for supremacy but worked together for survival," he added, his arm tightening around her. "It's why my form isn't twisted or crippled. And now, there is only one. I am me. I am Naasir."

The simplicity of his declaration made it all the more powerful. "Did you choose your name?" There was no doubt in her mind that even if Osiris had called him by a name, it wasn't one Naasir would've kept.

"No," he told her. "Dmitri gave it to me, in honor of a friend who perished in a battle where he saved Dmitri's life." Unhidden emotion in his tone. "I'm proud to bear it, to know Dmitri always believed I would do justice to such an honorable name—and that I would be strong enough to make it my own."

"No one can dispute that," Andromeda said. "You are Naasir,

a legend across continents and through time." Under her hand, she felt the formation of a layer of fur so fine and so soft that she couldn't see it, only feel the texture. What she could see were the tiger stripes on his skin. Rising on her elbow beside him, she whispered, "I am so happy to know you."

He bared his teeth at her. "What secrets are you keeping from me?"

"I'll tell you after the dinner at my parents' estate. You'll still come?" The question held an edge of desperation she hoped he didn't hear.

"I've been thinking of a gift for your parents," he said in response, his tone solemn. "When I was in New York, I saw a television show about dolls that look human and are fully anatomically correct. They would be the perfect tireless concubines."

Snorting with laughter, she tried to appear stern. "Don't you dare."

His grin was unrepentant. "I gave Ellie a carnivorous plant. She liked it."

"Should I be jealous?" She'd heard how he spoke about his sire's consort—with admiration and affection both.

Quicksilver fast, he tugged her down with a grip in her hair, holding her so close that she could count each individual lash over his eyes. "Elena is Raphael's consort and a sparring partner for me." His voice had fallen into the guttural range. "She is not you. *No one* will ever be what you are to me."

Her heart broke. Into a million tiny pieces.

40

Lijuan arrived at Rohan's stronghold long after she should have. It infuriated her that the unmistakable sign of Alexander's awakening had forced her to ground herself for long periods; instinct had whispered that those silver lightning strikes could do serious damage to her yet healing body.

It appeared Favashi, too, had been delayed, for Rohan had no archangelic backup.

Good. Also good was the fact the swiftness of the storm indicated Alexander was forcing himself to wake at rapid speed; he'd be weak, while she could feel her strength returning to her with each hour that passed. Even her wings now felt strong enough for short flights. And, unlike Raphael, Alexander wouldn't have developed any defenses against her black rain—if she could hit his heart, she could kill him.

The best option, however, remained to execute him before he rose.

Lijuan wasn't about to discount Alexander until he was dead.

She spoke to Xi from her chair inside his battle tent. "You need to break this siege." Lijuan could use her abilities to turn the tide, but that would mean dipping into her power reserves.

"Rohan is not his father and you're a seasoned general. Why is this taking so long?" The lightning was dangerous but it was no longer constant.

"Rohan is better prepared and has a larger number of troops garrisoned here than reported by our advance scouts—I believe he had warning." Despite the fact he'd been fighting for hours, Xi's expression was as cool and intelligent as always. "He's also improved the palace with new technologies that are hindering our troops. The passion with which he fights appears to confirm that Alexander lies within."

"Yes. The boy was always devoted to his father." Lijuan considered her options, decided the expenditure of energy was justifiable; the earlier and faster she got to Alexander, the easier it would be to kill him.

Waiting only until her strength was at full capacity—though that capacity was paltry in comparison to what it would be once she healed totally—she rose into the air during a break in the lightning, and blasted the palace with her black rain. The attack vaporized part of the buildings, creating a large gap in Rohan's defenses. Leaving Xi to take advantage of that, Lijuan invaded the palace in her noncorporeal form.

She escaped a lightning strike by mere millimeters.

It was a waste of precious energy to maintain her noncorporeal form when the palace was a ghost town, everyone at the defenses, but she had no legs and using her wings would attract too much attention.

She saw no signs of Alexander's presence. Even when she sank below the earth, she sensed nothing of the silver-winged Ancient. Rising to the surface just before her noncorporeal form solidified humiliatingly into flesh and blood on the tiled floor of the palace, she knew there was only one option.

Because Zhou Lijuan did not crawl.

Before she could order Xi to bring her a sacrifice, her eye fell on an old retainer shuffling along a back passageway. Snapping out her wings to sweep through the wide corridors designed for angels, she grabbed him in silence and, cutting his throat with his own ceremonial knife, lapped at the blood that bubbled up. It was a poor substitute to directly sucking up his lifeforce, and blood tasted vile to Lijuan, but it transferred enough of his life energy to her that she was temporarily rejuvenated. If she felt weak again, she'd take another life. There were always warm bodies available to a goddess.

Ready for this to end so she could concentrate on her healing, she waited for the lightning to stutter, then rose above the palace and blanketed it with her black rain. *Xi, find Rohan. I want him alive.*

In took another forty minutes and two more inefficient feedings before Xi succeeded in overwhelming the defenders, and captured Alexander's son. The palace lay half in ruins by then, Rohan's fighters mostly dead, along with a large number of noncombatants who'd been hiding in a room that had fallen under Lijuan's archangelic power.

Lijuan hadn't done the latter on purpose—a goddess didn't worry about weaponless ants—but neither did she feel any guilt. Rohan should've surrendered the instant he saw he was up against an archangel. He had to have known there was no way he could win.

Yet, even now, when he stood in the charred ruins of what must've been his great room, his hands bound behind him and his wings half cut off and cauterized by fire, while she sat on a chair in front of him, Alexander's son was defiant.

"I do not know where my father Sleeps," he said with an insolent laugh. "Do you truly think he would be so foolish as to leave the information with his *son*? It would make me a target. Neither would he remain in this territory, which is the first place a stupid enemy would look."

"Do not forget you speak to an archangel," Lijuan warned him. "And swallow your lies, for we both know your father loved his people and would not leave them."

Lijuan had long thought that love a foolishness on his part. Raphael shared the same failing, as did Elijah, Titus, and Astaad. Even Neha, for all her ruthlessness, would shed her own blood to protect her people. Lijuan wasn't so sure about Favashi, and Michaela put herself first, as had Uram. Charisemnon alone, of them all, thought like Lijuan.

To be an archangel was to be a god. Lijuan cared for her people by making sure they were safe and that they had enough to eat, but she did not love them. She would use them in her wars as necessary. They were disposable. More would spawn and fill the world.

Alexander hadn't thought in such a way. He'd created orphanages in his land that still provided shelter and education for urchin children to this day. He'd been so proud of those homes and of the schools he'd founded. "Every child in my land," he'd said to her once, his hands on the railings of the top balcony of this very palace, "will have the chance to become better than a lost piece of flotsam on the street."

She'd laughed and shaken her head. "You are a fool, Alexander." The amused, affectionate words of a friend. "Mortals are born and die in a mere glimmer of time. What use is it to waste your resources and your emotions on them?"

Alexander, his golden hair afire in the sunlight, had smiled. "Did you not admire the tapestry in the hall? It was designed and created by a mortal. The work of a lifetime and more beautiful than any such work I've seen completed by immortal hands."

Laughing again at how neatly he'd trapped her, Lijuan had conceded the point that very occasionally a particular mortal had his or her value. Most, however, were nothing. Insects to step on.

She hadn't put it that way then. Only a thousand years into being an archangel and she'd been . . . soft. And for all their disagreements, she'd still admired Alexander, hadn't wanted to disappoint him. But that time was long gone. She now saw him for the weak creature he'd been, driven by emotion and heart rather than the cold pragmatism of a god. That would be his downfall.

"You know something," she said to the son Alexander had shown her when Rohan was a mere day old.

Lijuan had congratulated him, but in that tiny, squirming bundle she'd seen only a chink in his armor, a living vulnerability. Lijuan had long ago killed the mortal who had made her heart stir, and who could've become her own living vulnerability had she not taken preemptive action. Chaoxiang had been as dark as Alexander was fair, and he'd laughed as much as Raphael's blue-winged commander did now.

"Beloved" he'd called her, eyes dancing.

Those eyes had held hers as she stabbed a dagger into his heart. There had been no recrimination in their black depths, only piercing love and forgiveness. His last word had been a whisper. *"Lijuan."*

That day marked her true ascension, when she became invulnerable.

Unlike Alexander.

"If you do not speak," she said to Rohan, "I will annihilate what remains of this palace and of your squadrons, as well as the surrounding villages and towns. I will kill tens of thousands."

Rohan's eyes, a deep ebony rather than Alexander's silver, glittered. "You are a monster." The words were spat out, his pale brown skin hot with rage.

"I am evolution." Gripping his neck while she hovered using her wings, she lifted him off his feet. She'd fed again in the inefficient fashion that nonetheless gave her a power boost, and now she burned with it.

Bound as he was, Rohan couldn't fight her, but his eyes remained unyielding. "My people stand with me and my father," he said. "All know that if you come to power, the world will drown in death."

"The world will be purified." All weakness burned away. "Speak, or die."

"You would go to war with Favashi for this?"

"Favashi is young." Now that she could feed again even in a limited fashion, Lijuan knew she could kill the much younger archangel should Favashi be so foolish as to get in her way. "Where is your father, Rohan?"

Alexander's son, the babe she had once held, looked at her without flinching. "I am Rohan, proud son of the greatest archangel ever to live, and you are an abomination who will never break my will."

"Insolent fool!" Crushing his neck until his head lolled forward, she dropped him to the floor. He'd live—he was a strong angel of enough age to heal those injuries.

"My men have sacked the palace but there is no sign of Alexander," Xi told her. "If he is like Caliane and able to hide deep in the earth, we may not find him in time."

Alexander loved his people. He loved his only son even more.

Lijuan's eyes went to Rohan's already healing form. Her lips curved. "Then we make Alexander come to us," she whispered, and waited the minutes it took for Rohan to heal enough to open his eyes. "Your father will wake at reckless speed to avenge you."

Her words made Rohan's jaw go tight, but Alexander's son didn't beg, didn't scream as her black knives plunged into him. He went to his death with the stoic and defiant pride of a true warrior.

Part of Lijuan could admire that, and had it been possible, she'd have ordered that Rohan be given a warrior's burial. But it wasn't possible—her black death had caused his body to disintegrate into ash of the same shade.

Rohan was gone.

The world screamed, lurching under Xi's feet.

41

Naasir and Andromeda were out of bed and about to head out to speak to Tarek when the land bucked with violent fury. Struggling out of the small house, they went to their knees outside. The shaking seemed to go on forever.

"Naasir!"

Following her pointing finger, Naasir looked to the horizon.

Sand spouts burst out of the ground to spiral to the sky, burning a destructive path through the landscape, the lightning so electric and bright that it hurt the eye as it hit over and over and over again.

The shaking stopped with a spine-wrenching jolt, but the clouds above had turned a silvery black that boiled across the sky, turning morning once more into midnight. In the distance, the land cracked, the lava that poured out of it a molten and angry red that crawled across the ground at impossible speed.

Andromeda felt her heart slam into her ribs, but her fear wasn't enough to make her miss a simple fact. "The village!" she yelled to Naasir over the sounds of the violence. "No lightning strikes within! No sand spouts!" Even the earthquake hadn't collapsed any buildings.

"Inside!" he yelled and they both retreated.

Shutting the window to cut down the noise, he shoved a hand through his hair. "Something has angered Alexander, but even in his rage, he hasn't forgotten the wing brothers who protected him these many centuries."

"Alexander was meant to love his people." Andromeda's fingers trembled as she fixed her braid. "Do you think he's killing them?"

"We'll have to wait until after this is all over to find out." Naasir suddenly hissed out a breath. "In protecting this village, he's put a beacon right over it. Lijuan will know to head for the eye of the storm, will be aware Alexander must be nearby."

Andromeda picked up her sword. "We should go, see how we can help the wing brothers."

Nodding, Naasir opened the door again and they walked out into the fierce dust-swirled wind. It didn't take them long to find the Brotherhood—they were gathered in the large central meeting hall. Since they'd spotted no one else on their way here, not even a face at a window, it appeared the noncombatants had already been moved to safety.

"These are the portents for which we were told to watch," Tarek informed them. "But it was meant to begin far more gently and be a process that took a year."

Andromeda considered if she should take another weapon from the wing brothers' stockpile, decided on a relatively light crossbow. "The enforced speed of the Ancient's waking means he's going to be far weaker than he should be when he rises."

Tarek's hand fisted.

"If we can distract Lijuan's troops," Naasir began, right as the wind and the lightning dropped without warning, the ensuing stillness eerie.

Shaking his head, Naasir started again. "If we can distract Lijuan's troops, it'll give him a little more time at least."

Andromeda didn't say anything, but they both knew Alexander would still be at a catastrophic disadvantage. From what Andromeda had read in the Archives, when an archangel rose this quickly, he or she was at less than half strength, with little endurance. Lijuan simply had to outlast him and she could kill him when he fell.

"Hide your men and women in the trees and shoot up," Naasir said. "This assault is all about speed, about reaching

Alexander before he gathers his strength—Xi won't bother waiting for ground troops. It's going to be nothing but air squadrons."

"We have weapons for the air." Tarek's tone was ruthless. "Buried in the lands around the caves and the village. I didn't want to activate the weapons with the sands twisting and the ground shaking, but it takes two hours for them to power up."

Naasir chose his words with care, aware he was talking to a man who was used to running a lethal group. But Naasir had spent centuries working at the side of an archangel; he knew the value of the knowledge in his head. "I'd recommend you do it," he said, holding the other man's gaze. "I say that as someone who was in the battle in New York—I know how to fight a winged enemy from the ground if necessary."

Naasir's respect for Tarek grew when the leader of the Wing Brotherhood just gave a curt nod before ordering one of his men to start the process to activate the weapons. Turning back to Naasir, the other man said, "Tell us what else you know of fighting against angels."

Naasir focused on how the wing brothers could maximize their assets—skill, knowledge of the terrain, and the element of surprise. He also told them to utilize their agility by rigging trap lines in the trees using wires so thin they were nearly invisible. Any angel who tried to land would get caught up in it, like an insect in a spider's web.

"We stand a higher chance of success if we can keep them in the air, especially since you have ground-to-air weapons," he said once Tarek agreed to the traps. "On the ground, you'll be fighting one-to-one and Lijuan's squadrons are full of old angels with unknown and dangerous abilities. Too old to be hampered by their wings."

"If they do land," Tarek told his men and women, "shoot for the heart or the head. No warnings. We have to incapacitate as fast as possible."

"You do have one winged fighter," Andromeda pointed out.

Naasir glanced at her. At that instant, he was more the experienced and honed commander of an archangel and less a primal chimera. It was a little intimidating.

"Your injuries?" he asked, and though his expression didn't change, he touched a gentle hand to her primaries.

He was still Naasir, she realized on a wave of love. This was no false skin, just another aspect of his personality. "Healed enough to not be a problem." Especially if they only wanted her aloft for short bursts. "I'm good with a sword in the air, but I won't be able to do much damage on my own."

"You'll take out the stragglers we manage to corner off." The feather he'd woven into his hair in a silent, powerful declaration fell forward as he leaned in to cup her jaw and cheek. "Or you'll drive them down into the booby traps." His voice took on the faintest edge of a growl. "In between, you stay grounded."

A sense of urgency beating at her, Andromeda wanted to rise to her toes, press her mouth to his. "How long do you think we have?"

A dusty scout, his cheeks burned by the driving sand, tumbled into the room on the heels of her question. "I've been to the waypoint," he gasped, hands on his knees. "The message was garbled because so many of the signal mirrors have been broken, but two things were clear: Lijuan has murdered Rohan, and she is on her way here."

Andromeda's gut went cold. Children were sacred to angelkind, and though Rohan was no longer a child, he had been the only and beloved son of an archangel.

Around her, the wing brothers—jaws clenched and muscles bunched—lowered their heads in silent respect for Rohan. When they looked up afterward, it was with fury in their eyes and blood on their mind. A cold-voiced Tarek's questions to the scout elicited a chilling detail: Xi's squadron was a bare four hours away. "No one's spotted Lijuan," the scout added. "But . . . part of the message said something about blood sacrifices."

Andromeda's hand clenched on the hilt of her knife as Naasir growled. "She feeds on the lifeforce of others to strengthen herself." In his voice was firsthand knowledge. "Has there been any sign of Raphael?"

The scout shook his head. "Nothing. Parts of the beacon chain in some directions are broken, but messages are still getting through—he hasn't been spotted anywhere in the territory."

"Go," Tarek ordered the wing brothers. "Set up the traps while I make sure the ground-to-air weapons are powering up as they should. Then find your positions and stay there." He paused, held each wing brother's gaze in turn. "Today, we fight for our archangel, do what we pledged to do four hundred years ago. If we fall, it will be in honor and we will wake at our archangel's side when it is his time to leave this world. That time is *not* today."

The wing brothers uttered a battle cry that made Naasir's eyes gleam wild. When they scattered, Naasir and Andromeda went with them and helped to set the traps in place. Andromeda also had to memorize the exact positions of those traps for when she had to drive winged fighters into them. The time raced by as if it was falling from an open hand, until she looked to the west while in the air, and glimpsed the smudge of a large winged presence on the horizon.

Calling out a warning to the others, Andromeda went to the ground, her borrowed crossbow in hand and her sword hung off her belt. She wasn't as good with the crossbow as she was with the sword, but so outnumbered by enemy forces, it would be safer and more effective for her to keep her distance if she could.

When Naasir jumped down beside her, she saw a kind of feral joy in him at the prospect of battle, but below that primal emotion was another. "You don't think we can win without Raphael," she whispered.

He shook his head, silver strands sliding against one another. "Alexander left these men here not to fight a battle, but so that when the time came for him to rise, he would do so with those he trusted, be able to rest in unhurried quiet as he grew in strength." He examined her remaining injuries as he spoke. "The Brotherhood's task was to protect the caves from the curious, not hold them against an enemy archangel and her squadron. They're brave beyond measure, but they'll be slaughtered."

Andromeda didn't want to think of that future, a future where Tarek lay with blood on his face, his mind and his heart lost to the world. "Do you think Raphael is far?"

"I can't hear him." Naasir touched his temple and Andromeda realized he must have the honor of speaking to his sire mind-to-mind. "I can hear the sire from far enough away that I can estimate distances. If I can't hear him still, then he won't make it in time." Grim words. "It's possible Lijuan spotted him and sent a group of her powerful commanders to slow him down."

A cold knot in her gut, Andromeda put her hand on Naasir's cheek. "Whatever happens today, know this: I would have been *so* proud to be your mate. Nothing would have given me more joy."

His claws dug into her without cutting as he hauled her close. "Let's fight, mate." The wild gleam was back. "Then I'll find your stupid Grimoire book and we can rut and you can pet me while I'm naked."

He made her cheeks go red and her mouth laugh at the same time. Giving her one final squeeze, he disappeared up into the trees, while she held position where she was. Everything was quiet now, no lightning, no thunder, no sand spouts. It wasn't, however, a peaceful silence—no, this silence held too much portentous tension.

Like a wave about to crash.

And then it did, Lijuan's squadrons swarming over the area, Lijuan in her physical form at the front. She immediately directed her incongruously beautiful black rain onto the village, each shard a piece of living onyx that gleamed with blue, black, and deepest green highlights.

None of the defenders moved.

There were no longer any living beings in the village—even the animals had been spirited away. Let the Archangel of China waste her energy.

All too soon, however, the enemy began to head as one toward the caves, as if Lijuan had realized that was the likeliest possibility. The defenders had to act, keep the squadrons away from Alexander's place of Sleep. It would've been better had they been able to set up more than the odd sniper on the roof of the caves themselves, but as Andromeda and Naasir had discovered, there was little shelter there, barely any places to hide.

The first volley of crossbow shots took down at least ten of Lijuan's people. When the angels fell, they didn't rise again, the wing brothers hidden in the trees and on the ground efficient with knives and having no compunction against taking lethal force. Learning from that first surprise volley, the squadron flew higher, out of crossbow range.

Tarek fired the ground-to-air missiles.

It worked to scatter the ordinary angels, killing at least ten more, but Lijuan was an archangel. She sent her rain of jagged black shards down into the trees. Andromeda heard at least two bodies hit the ground near her, wing brothers who had been impacted directly by a blade of black. Even as she ran toward the sounds, the trees began to blacken and crumble around them, as if Lijuan's death was now so strong it withered the earth, too.

Realizing all their plans would be for naught if Lijuan destroyed the trees, Andromeda rose up in the air just enough to line up the Goddess of Death. Lijuan, in her arrogance, wasn't expecting such a blunt attack and the shot took her through the wing, sending her into an uncontrolled spiral. She recovered with killing speed. Screaming, she raised her hand as if to rain down the black shards again . . . and the sky erupted with glittering silver lightning that began to hammer her forces to the earth.

Wings crumpled and bones broken, angels began slamming into the trees and the ground at terminal velocity. Andromeda took the chance to run toward the fallen wing brothers. Both were just . . . gone. Ash.

Above, Lijuan turned away from the trees and put up a black shield that held off the lightning, her new flight path a direct route to the caves. She intended to destroy them, Andromeda realized. Even if she attacked only from above, her potent black poison could well seep in and kill Alexander . . . as well as all the noncombatants likely hidden within.

"Rise, Alexander!" Andromeda screamed as she ran out onto open ground from where she could see the caves; she wasn't sure anyone was listening but couldn't simply watch in horrified silence as Lijuan murdered an Ancient. "She will poison your home!"

The lightning stopped.

A heartbeat later, the stone above the caves cracked in a jagged fury that sounded like the earth screaming, and then an angel was rising out of them. His wings were pure metallic silver, his hair rich gold, and his skin a paler gold. His beauty was flawless. Like that of a statue carved out of marble. But this statue was born of rage, his hands full of silver fire.

That fire arced toward Lijuan like directed lightning.

Lijuan laughed when Alexander's fire didn't penetrate her shield, then she attacked with her deadly black rain. Alexander swept aside fast enough to avoid a direct hit, but he was sluggish. If Andromeda could see that, so could Lijuan.

The Archangel of Death beat her wings upward in a decisive move, and Andromeda knew she intended to rain down her death on Alexander from above. There was no way he could move fast enough to avoid it.

Naasir broke the neck of the angel who'd slammed into one of the booby traps when a lightning bolt fried part of his wing, then moved to check on a wing brother who'd fallen under Lijuan's rain. He was gone, only a smear of ash to mark his existence. Hissing out a breath, Naasir ran to make sure Andromeda was all right.

She wasn't on the ground.

He looked up, his heart painful it was beating so fast, and found his strong, courageous mate in the air. She was winging her way to Lijuan, and by some miracle, hadn't yet been spotted by the half of the squadron that had survived the lightning bolts. "Keep the angels busy!" he yelled to the wing brothers who could hear him and they renewed their efforts with the crossbows.

The snipers on the cave roof were trying to reach Lijuan with their bolts, but she stayed out of range. The longer-range missiles had ceased to be of any use as soon as Alexander rose; given his diminished strength, an aerial shockwave could take him down. As it would Andromeda.

Naasir bared his teeth and silently promised his mate he would punish her for this, but on the ground, he grabbed a portable missile launcher from the supplies they'd hidden throughout the area, and put it on his shoulder. The shock wave from this weapon should be far more contained. As Andromeda shot crossbow bolts at Lijuan's back in an effort to give Alexander a little more time to gather his strength, Naasir unleashed the missile.

Lijuan managed to avoid it, but the maneuver left her off-balance long enough that Andromeda was able to drop like a stone and arrow herself toward the trees. Naasir's blood pulsed in a roar as Lijuan spun around and tried to come after Andromeda, but Alexander hit her with his silver lightning again and this time, her shield was down.

Screaming high and shrill, she turned to throw that hard jewel-like black rain at Alexander. The Ancient couldn't avoid it this time. It hit, and where it hit, his skin grew black, as did his hair and his wings.

Alexander began to fall to the earth, as if those large, powerful wings no longer worked right.

Ice white hair turned a lustrous black and crackling with power, Lijuan threw back her head in laughter Naasir could see from the ground. As she raised her single regenerated hand to deliver the killing blow, Naasir loaded up a second missile, was about to shoot when he felt the crash of the rain, the fresh bite of the sea in his mind.

Focus on the squadron, Naasir. I will take care of Lijuan.

42

Raphael didn't bother with subtlety.

Falling through the heavy cloud layer in a controlled dive, he hit Lijuan hard and fast with the wildfire that came from inside him but was kissed by his hunter's mortal heart, and was the antithesis of Lijuan's deadly rain. She hadn't expected him, hadn't seen him, and so her body was totally unshielded.

His hands slammed into her back, right above her heart, and the wildfire crawled all over her, burrowing through her wings and clothing to touch skin as it fought to get to her internal organs. Though she screamed, he could tell she was fighting it off.

He hit her again.

This time, she turned and began to wing away. He had a choice at that moment—go after her and try to do fatal damage, or to save Alexander. It was one of the most difficult of his life. If he killed Lijuan, he could be saving tens of millions of lives. But if he allowed Alexander to die, he would lose a powerful ally who might help in the fight against Lijuan should she survive.

There was no guarantee the wildfire was strong enough to kill her—she'd survived his and Elena's last attempt to end her, and before she'd run today, he'd seen the way the black rain ate at the wildfire, seen how it had put up shields against the ravages. Whatever she'd become, Lijuan was no longer like the rest of the Cadre, and Raphael had the gut instinct that no one archangel would ever be able to execute her.

Dropping down toward Alexander while Naasir and the other defenders fired up at the squadron that had turned to follow Lijuan, he landed beside Alexander's fallen body. The Ancient, his clothing not so different from that of his fighters, had come down hard on the rough stone that covered the caves, some distance from the snipers Raphael had spotted.

Leave this place, he ordered those snipers. *Go assist your brethren.*

Alexander's left wing was crumpled under him, his right leg shattered so badly that had he been mortal, it would've been impossible to put him back together. Blood dripped from his mouth, but his eyes were open and they were pure obsidian.

Remembering his own blindness under Lijuan's attack, Raphael took the Ancient's hand. "Alexander, it is Raphael." He reached out with his mind, the interference that had stopped him from contacting Naasir—likely caused by Alexander's waking presence—no longer a problem. It had cut out as Alexander fell.

I'm sending something into your body to counter Lijuan's poison. Don't fight it. With that warning he hoped the stubborn warrior would heed, he released a tiny ball of white gold fire swirled with luminous blue, directly onto Alexander's wing.

The Ancient's body went rigid as the wildfire entered his system, tendons and muscles stretched and his hand crushing Raphael's, but Alexander made not a sound. He was a general, would suffer pain in silence. As Raphael watched, the black slowly receded from that part of his wing.

Breathing heavily, Alexander stared blindly toward Raphael. *Your cure is as bad as the disease.*

Raphael hadn't heard that deep voice with its touch of Ancient arrogance, in four hundred years. And though Alexander had been threatening to go to war against him at the time, he felt an unexpected welcome inside him for this man he'd always respected. *I must be careful. The wildfire may kill you if I use too much.* Any more than needed to counter the poison and it became a weapon in itself.

Alexander suffered excruciating pain throughout the operation. He bore it with the grace of a warrior and when his eyes cleared at last, he looked at Raphael and said, "Well, young Rafe. It's as well that I didn't kill you, isn't it?"

Raphael felt his lips curve at the name no one had ever called him—no one but an Alexander who refused to see the archangel he'd become. "Try to remember that, Xander."

Alexander's smile at the familiar address he permitted only intimates, was fleeting. "She took my son from this world." Rage boiled in every word. "I will not stop until I hunt her down and cut out her venomous heart."

That, Raphael thought, was what many people had forgotten about Alexander: he was wise and strong and a great peacemaker, but he'd begun life as a warrior and it was the bloodthirsty heart of a warrior that beat in his chest.

"I will be at your side." Raphael moved down Alexander's body to see if he could speed up the Ancient's healing. This much damage on the heels of an early waking could leave Alexander broken for days.

"What has become of Lijuan?" Confusion beneath the blood fury. "She was many times arrogant after her ascension, but she showed signs of greatness."

"That was true enough even a hundred years earlier." Raphael had found Lijuan disturbing at times, eerie more than once, but the old ones of their race were often a touch removed from the world. He'd asked her advice on countless matters over the centuries, received genuine responses.

After spending an eternity wondering if his parents' madness would one day claim him, Raphael saw Lijuan's devolution and couldn't help but consider if age alone was the killer of souls. Was it possible Lijuan had no choice in her evil, that eternity itself had betrayed her?

We are not your parents and you sure as hell aren't anything like Her Evilness. She killed her mortal lover, remember? You made your lover your consort. She had a choice. Elena's voice was as sharp and as annoyed as if she stood beside him. He knew it was exactly what she'd say should he articulate his thoughts.

The incipient cold inside him burned off by her fire, he spoke to Alexander. "I don't know what precipitated the change, but Lijuan has become a scourge upon the world. She believes herself a goddess—the rest of us are hindrances to her desire for omnipotent rule."

Alexander turned his head toward the destroyed village in the distance. "My people come. I do not want them here."

Raphael understood; it was why he'd told the snipers to go. Touching Naasir's mind, he said, *Naasir, tell the ones with you to prepare a place suitable to receive Alexander. He will come down in his own time. They are not to come to him.* No archangel would want to greet his people looking weak and broken.

I'll make them obey, Naasir said with the brutal honesty that was part of his nature.

"It is done," Raphael told Alexander.

"You are no longer the stripling I left behind."

Raphael had been more than a thousand years old when Alexander chose to Sleep. No stripling. Though, in the eyes of an Ancient who had lived countless eons, perhaps it was correct enough. "I am Cadre, Alexander, and I've held my own in battle against Lijuan. You would do well not to forget that." Raphael respected Alexander but he also knew the other man had a warrior's instincts—weakness was despised, strength admired.

"The feral creature who came to warn me," Alexander said as his bones began to knit together as a result of a combination of his own archangelic healing ability and Raphael's powers, "he was the wild thing you rescued from Osiris and adopted into your court."

"Naasir has become a warrior unlike any other." Fierce and loyal and with an unquenchable hunger for life.

"He has little respect for anyone."

Raphael raised an eyebrow. "He is one of mine."

Alexander laughed, the sound rusty. "Yes, you never did have enough respect for your elders either." Laughter fading, he stared out at the horizon. "My son is gone from this world, Raphael. The babe I held in my arms, the boy I taught to wield a sword, the man with whom I fought in battle, he is gone forever." Open grief in his voice, raw and endless.

Raphael said nothing, giving the other archangel time to mourn the son he would never again see. Rohan had made mistakes, most specifically when he'd attempted to hold Alexander's entire sprawling territory himself after his father chose to Sleep, but in the end, he'd proven himself.

"Your son was a man respected far and wide," he said a long time later, after Alexander's leg was nearly healed and the clouds above had begun to dissipate. "He held this section of territory for the archangel who came after you . . . and he sired a son of his own."

Alexander's eyes locked with Raphael's, happiness blazing out of the grief. "I have a grandchild?"

"Yes. He wasn't at the stronghold—Rohan fostered him with Titus so that he could learn from Titus's warriors. He is a stripling of two hundred. His name is Xander, after his grandfather."

Fierce joy in Alexander's expression. "Did Rohan take a mate?"

"Yes. He and Xander's mother were a pair, but she is likely gone. She lived in the palace with Rohan, would've fought beside him to the end." As Elena would with Raphael. "She loved him and together, they loved their son."

"The boy will have a home with me," Alexander said, his voice a passionate roughness of grief, joy, and rage. "And one day, he will have vengeance."

43

Andromeda and Naasir helped the wing brothers hurriedly pick up and set aside the broken pieces of their homes. Part of the village was just gone, crumbled into dust. What remained was nothing whole.

"We will have to greet the sire under the open sky," Tarek said, and though his expression and tone were controlled, the same couldn't be said for all his men and women. Their distress at being unable to show due honor to their archangel was clear.

Andromeda thought of everything she'd heard of Alexander. "The stories say that your sire preferred to drink mead with his warriors around a fire, rather than to sleep comfortably in a sumptuous tent."

The wing brothers visibly relaxed.

"Yes." Tarek nodded. "He's one of us."

Decision made, they cleared out the communal space near the lake, then one of the fleet-of-foot scouts was dispatched to fetch their vulnerable. To Andromeda's surprise, he went not in the direction of the caves, but toward the damaged trees. *Secrets, more secrets.*

Deliberately turning her back on the trees so she wouldn't

see this one and thus be able to betray it in Charisemnon's court—*a stabbing pain in her gut*—she continued to help pick up and stack shattered pieces of wood and glass and roofing material. When she started finding personal items, she made a neat pile of them inside a former home that had no roof but had three walls that had survived to about three feet off the ground.

It would work well enough as a storage space for now.

The noncombatants flowed into the village a half hour later, bubbling with excitement. Their dismay at seeing the broken state of the village was quickly overcome by half-terrified joy at playing host to not only their own archangel, but to a second one. Most people never came within close proximity to even one archangel their entire lives.

Nerves or not, the cooks were able to get a fire going and create a stew out of food items scavenged from the devastated homes, as well as flatbread. When a fridge was dug out of the debris, everyone clapped at the find of undamaged fruit within. Someone else discovered that their tins of dried fruits were dented but whole, and soon a newly washed and barely chipped plate was bearing a bounty of dried figs and other sweetmeats. A teenage boy placed it on the large wooden table that three of the wing brothers had put together with the materials at hand.

When Naasir dug out a bottle of mead that had been buried under the fallen beams of a house, a raucous cheer went up. Grinning, he passed it to Andromeda and went hunting for more supplies, his senses having made him a favorite of the cooks. Anytime they needed something, they'd tell him, and more often than not, he'd find it in amongst the debris.

The village was as neat as it could be by the time the sun streaked the sky the dark pink and rich orange of sunset. Not only were the villagers ready for Alexander, they'd created shelters for the young and the weak, and cleaned themselves up as much as possible. Aware Alexander had been injured, everyone was on tenterhooks.

As the sunset grew ever more dazzling before beginning to darken until the clouds glowed like rubies, the village went quieter and quieter.

"Papa! Angels!"

Following a small child's pointed finger, Andromeda looked

to the color-splashed sky above the caves to see wings of glittering silver side by side with wings of an astonishing white gold that seemed aflame.

Overwhelming power and magnificent beauty, the sight made her heart stop. "They aren't like us," she whispered to Naasir, feeling that understanding in her bones. "They are *nothing* like us." As different from her as she was from a mortal.

Arms wrapping around her shoulders from behind, Naasir nuzzled her temple. "They love as fiercely, Andi. And they fight as wildly."

His words made the difference in their growing-up years so clear. To him, Raphael wasn't a distant archangel who was a deadly member of the Cadre. Naasir saw Raphael as his sire and a warrior first, everything else second. She would've liked to have seen Raphael through his eyes over the years, gotten to know the blindingly powerful being who landed not far from them in a strong sweep of wings.

The power that burned off the two archangels made her eyes hurt.

As Alexander's people, young and old, knelt down in front of him in a silent and devoted fealty, Raphael walked to join Naasir and Andromeda. Having moved around to stand beside her, Naasir clasped the archangel's forearm in greeting when Raphael held it out, his own hand closing around Naasir's forearm.

"You did well, Naasir," the archangel said, his voice as pure as the searing blue of his eyes. "Alexander is of the opinion that you have no respect for anyone."

Naasir grinned. "Especially not for stubborn Ancients who refuse to listen to reason."

A slow smile before Raphael turned to Andromeda and held out his forearm. Her mouth dried up, her heart thundering. "I have a warrior as a consort, scholar," Raphael said at her frozen response. "I recognize one when I see her, even if she chooses to wield the pen more often than the sword."

Awed and astonished, she gripped his forearm, the power that lived in his body an almost painful ache in her bones. And yet his consort had been mortal before her transformation, was yet an angel newborn. Andromeda wanted desperately to meet Elena Deveraux at that moment, to know the woman who had the strength to hold her own against an archangel.

"Because of your and Naasir's courage and will," Raphael said after they broke contact, "Alexander lives today. He will not forget it."

Andromeda found her voice at last, and though it came out raspy, it did at least come out. "I'm glad an Ancient has not been lost from the world."

Raphael nodded and turned to watch as Alexander greeted his loyal sentinels one by one, having asked all his people to stand. "My mother will be happy to have a compatriot with whom to speak."

That was the moment Andromeda realized a staggering truth. "There are now eleven living archangels in the world, two of them Ancients."

The Cadre had, at rare times, been less than ten, but never more. *Never*.

"It appears the Cascade has changed the natural equilibrium of the world more deeply than anyone comprehends." Raphael looked up at the painted sky, but she knew he saw the battle that had broken its peace not long ago. "Ten has been enough to maintain balance throughout time. That apparently no longer holds. More Ancients may yet rise before this is over."

Because the Cascade was just beginning.

44

Raphael escorted Naasir and Andromeda safely out of Favashi's territory before he went to speak to the Archangel of Persia herself. Midnight had long fallen by then, and he found her standing in that starry darkness in the ruins of Rohan's palace. Her brown eyes were brittle, her bones stark against the golden cream of her skin.

Sweeping wings the shade of aged ivory touched the broken shards all around her.

"It's true then," she said, looking at him when he walked toward her through the ruins peopled by no others, as if Favashi had told them to leave her alone. "Alexander has woken and you battled Lijuan to protect him."

"Yes." He could understand her disbelief—there was so much impossibility in those events.

One: an Ancient had been Sleeping in the heart of her territory.

Two: that Ancient was now breathing aboveground.

Three: Lijuan had sought to kill a Sleeping archangel.

"Rohan was always loyal to his father," Favashi said to him, her voice elegant and cultured but the steel core of her exposed for once. "I knew that should Alexander ever rise, I would lose him, but until then, he was loyal to me." Midnight winds sifted through the luxuriant dark brown of her hair, creating a tangle she didn't bother to ease away. "I always knew I could trust him to watch my interests."

"He safeguarded the people in this area well."

When Favashi looked at him, he was surprised to see tears in her eyes. The Archangel of Persia might appear softly female, but she was as ruthless as any other member of the Cadre, the archetypal iron hand in a velvet glove. "He was my lover once, before my ascension." A sudden harsh rasp to her voice. "Strong and loyal. I should've taken him as mine, but I wanted someone with more power."

Someone like Dmitri, Raphael thought, aware Favashi had offered his second the position of consort. "I am sorry for that, Favashi." Had he not seen her tears, he wouldn't have believed her heart involved. But those tears were real, as was the twist of her face as she tried to fight them.

The other archangel drew in a shaky breath. "He used to make me laugh," she whispered. "Even after we went our separate ways and he found a mate, he remained my friend who could make me laugh. I never realized how much I needed that until this instant." She looked around, her eyes lost. "I should've made him mine," she repeated. "Now he is no more and no one will ever again make me laugh as he did."

A pregnant silence.

Then, hands fisted, Favashi took a deep breath, and when she turned to face Raphael again, the lost, heartbroken woman was gone. In her place stood a furious archangel with vengeance on her mind. "If Lijuan believes I will forgive her this crime, she is a fool."

Raphael wondered if Lijuan realized her arrogance may just have cost her an archangel who might've otherwise remained neutral in any future battle. "Lijuan's arrogance is dangerous, but worse are her growing powers."

Raphael hadn't missed the fact that the Archangel of China had gone noncorporeal as she fled. Paired with her vicious black rain, her capacity to rejuvenate herself from the lifeforce of others, as well as her ability to create infectious reborn, it made her the most dangerous being on the planet.

"She isn't the only one whose powers are growing," Favashi said, and suddenly, the winds were a tornado around them.

Those winds fell flat just as quickly, but the display confirmed rumors of Favashi's Cascade-born ability.

Considering the offensive uses of such a power, Raphael said,
"Alexander and you cannot exist in the same territory for long."

There was a reason archangelic territories were separated
by considerable distances. Two archangels could stay in close
proximity only for a limited time. The exact period depended
on the archangels involved. Sooner or later, their powers began
to shove against each other, creating tension that could erupt
easily into bloodshed. Even Raphael's parents hadn't always
been able to be together, though their deep love for one another
had significantly ameliorated the effect.

As if nature knew their hearts should not be forced apart.

"The Cadre will decide," Favashi said, spreading out her
wings. "For now, I will go and welcome him to the world."

Raphael rose into the night sky with her, showed her to the
village. And he warned Alexander of her impending arrival. The
Ancient was standing laughing with his sentinels when they
landed, nothing in his stance or expression to betray his vulnerability. He'd woken at far too high a speed, would need at least
six months to recover. Until then, he was at risk of a deadly
attack, but *only* if someone realized the extent of his weakness.

Raphael would've worried Lijuan would launch another
assault except that she'd retreated far too quickly from this
battle. According to what Andromeda had seen in Lijuan's
citadel, the Archangel of China had only been partially healed
when she'd decided on this mission. A second wildfire injury
on top of the first should take her out of the equation long
enough for Alexander to come to full strength.

"Can we kill her?" Favashi asked flatly once she and Alexander had completed the formal greeting. "While she's weak?"

Alexander frowned.

Raphael, knowing the Ancient's beliefs on honor and the
rules of battle, expected him to negate that option. But he'd
forgotten the rage now in Alexander's blood. "Any archangel
who attacks a Sleeper and murders his son is not worthy of
respect." Each word was a chip of ice. "I see no reason not to
strike at her while she's wounded."

"We considered it after she attacked my city," Raphael said,
"but Lijuan isn't stupid. Neither my spymaster, nor the spymas-

ters of my allies, were able to pinpoint the location where she went to ground." It hadn't, despite appearances, been her citadel.

Favashi's wings glowed. "Perhaps she has developed the ability to bury herself in the same way as Alexander and Caliane."

Alexander stirred, his jaw no longer held in a vicious line. "Caliane? She has woken?"

"Yes." Raphael met the other man's gaze. "She will be pleased to see you—I think I take no liberties in extending an invitation for you to visit her territory." Caliane would expect him to offer the invitation, for while he was Cadre, he was also her son.

Their relationship would never be simple or one-dimensional.

Alexander inclined his head in gracious acceptance of the offer before returning his attention to Favashi. "This land was once mine and still sings to my blood. Yet you have held it safe since your ascension." The implication was clear: Alexander wanted his territory back.

Favashi didn't back down. "As always, the Cadre's decision will be law."

"Agreed."

"However," Favashi added, "until the Cadre meets, the section of my territory which fell under Rohan's aegis is yours." Grief thickened her voice. "He always said he was looking after it as you would've wished."

Alexander's eyes sharpened. "You mourn my son."

"Yes." White lines bracketing her mouth, Favashi spread her wings. "I leave for my stronghold," she said to Alexander. "Rohan's palace—your old home—is badly damaged, but I can send a team to help repair it should you wish to use it."

"No." Alexander's voice was subtly gentler. "I thank you, but my people and I will do what is needed."

Favashi left without further words, but her mind reached out to Raphael's as she flew toward the stars. *I thank you for not allowing such an evil act to occur on my soil, Raphael. I have stood on the sidelines long enough—from this day forth, consider me your ally.*

Raphael acknowledged her words, but he didn't take them as unfiltered truth. Favashi played a deep game; he couldn't trust that this wasn't a great double cross, for the fact she mourned Rohan didn't mean she didn't want Alexander dead.

As the Ancient had just proven, he wouldn't stand aside when it came to matters of territory—and in this land, loyalty to Alexander ran deep. Favashi had garnered respect in the short time she'd ruled, but even amongst mortals, the legend of the archangel with silver wings was talked of with awe and wonder.

Alexander had held this land for millennia before his Sleep.

As such, Favashi must've always known that if Alexander rose, she'd lose either all or a massive percentage of her current territory, face having to start all over again. The Cadre's decision was a mere formality.

"Raphael."

"Yes?"

"My squadrons will return to me," Alexander said with a confidence that betrayed his own arrogance. "They'll sever their contracts and fly home from every corner of this earth, but for now, I have no one who can fly to Titus's territory."

Raphael heard the unspoken request. "I must return to my own territory." He had people to protect, too, and a consort who'd worry until she saw him safe. "However, I'll fly through Titus's territory and ask him to send Xander home with an escort. You can trust Titus. He is as he always was."

"Blunt and honest." Alexander nodded. "Tell him I will speak to him personally once I have things in order here." He stared out at the caves under which he'd Slept. "A son should not have to mourn his father when his father is in the prime of his life, and a father should never have to mourn his son, but Xander and I will do this. We will give Rohan life in death and in vengeance."

45

After everything that had happened, the trip back to the Refuge seemed to go by at the speed of light. Andromeda and Naasir flew in the jet as far as it was possible to fly that way, their time together beyond precious to her. Upon landing, Naasir picked up a small pack of cold-weather clothing Galen had left for him at the airport, and told her to take the skyroad while he straddled the motorcycle the mechanic had retrieved for him.

"Your wings need rest to heal properly," he told her with a scowl. "The distance you'd have to fly to follow my overland path will only put more pressure on them."

She didn't want to be separated from him, but knew he was right. So she flew high in the sky, the ticking clock inside her growing louder with each wingbeat. She understood now that Naasir would never reject her—he wasn't built that way. He'd claimed her and he'd keep her no matter what. But he couldn't fight an eon of tradition, tradition that kept everyone safe. If she defected to another territory and the archangel in question didn't return her to Charisemnon, it would break a visceral taboo.

Even enemies did not steal children from one another. It was simply *not* acceptable.

Her tears whipped away by the wind, she flew until her wings ached, the sky around her starry velvet. She reached the mountains of the Refuge sometime in the hours between dark and dawn. Flying low, she tried to search for Naasir's secret home in the forests below, but it was too well hidden, a place he alone could show her.

She landed with stealth once in the Refuge itself, made her way not to her suite in Raphael's stronghold, but to the aerie she had along the cliff edge. Everything in her body ached, but the worst pain was in her heart. Already, she missed Naasir. Even with his ferocious speed, it would take him at least a day to arrive overland.

Drawing a bath, she sat in it with her arms locked tightly around her knees, trying desperately to think of a way out of the trap in which she was stuck. Nothing. Freedom could come only at Charisemnon's hand.

Her mouth twisted: Charisemnon expected his blood to do its "duty."

Getting out on that bleak truth, she dried off, then forced herself to sleep. She didn't want to waste a minute she could have with Naasir, wanted to be strong and rested when he arrived.

Her enforced rest took her through to midday.

So many hours yet to pass.

Unwilling to speak to anyone else, she stayed in her suite and did the painful task of cataloging any outstanding projects. It would make it easier for Jessamy when Andromeda left, not to return for five hundred years.

Time passed at a snail's pace when she wanted it to race.

Night fell at long last, whispered past midnight into the quietness when the entire world seemed asleep.

Throat tight at the thought of seeing Naasir again, she changed into a pair of simple black pants and a pretty pink tunic embroidered with fine blue thread around the vee of the neckline. She left her hair to do what it would, just pushed it away from the sides of her face using two jeweled combs Jessamy had gifted her.

Naasir liked her hair down.

Walking to stand on the cliffs, she watched for a familiar prowling stride, for a glint of silver under starlight. Only after she'd been watching for two hours did she realize Naasir might go straight to his home rather than coming here.

Her stomach dropped.

They had so little time and if she missed tonight, there would be no more nights. Tomorrow, she had to leave for Africa. "Naasir," she whispered into the wind. "I'm waiting for you. Please come."

As if he'd heard, he appeared in the distance, loping easily over the stone of the mountain. Her nose grew stuffy, her eyes gritty. Seeing her, he lifted his arm before disappearing from sight. It didn't matter. She knew where he was going. Lifting off, she flew to the spot where a delicate stone bridge connected the two sides of the gorge.

He was already on it, and jumped dangerously high to catch her ankle and haul her down as she hovered above him. "Naasir!" Laughing, she wrapped her arms around his neck.

Drenched in sweat and with heat coming off his skin, he was wild and beautiful and she wanted him so very, very badly. "Are you sure you don't want to take me up on my offer?" she whispered in agonizing hope.

He rubbed his nose over hers. "I will. You owe me many bed favors for my frustration and patience." That last was said on an impatient growl. "But I will collect the right way."

"What if you don't find it in time?"

"I'm good at finding things." Snapping his teeth at her, he said, "I want to bathe."

Leading him to her aerie, she drew him inside and shut the door. She had a scholar's home, full of books and art, and he was a beautiful, not-at-all-tame creature who didn't appear to belong. Then he tugged off his jacket, sweater, and T-shirt, and threw them on a chair as he kicked off his boots and socks, and suddenly, it was as if he'd always lived here.

He found his way to the bathing room without her help, since she was too tongue-tied at seeing the sleek, muscled beauty of him to give him directions. Leaving the door open, he said, "You ran the water."

She could hear rustling as he got out of his jeans. "Yes." Her throat was so dry she had to cough to clear it. "It was two hours ago, but I ran it close to boiling, so you should only need a touch more hot water to warm it up."

A splash of sound as he got in. "It's warm enough. The stone keeps it that way."

About as able to resist him as a child could a sweet, she walked to the doorway and looked inside. He was dunking his head and when he came up, he shot her a sinful smile. "Come wash my back, Andi."

Andromeda didn't even attempt to deny him, deny them both. Not only did she run the soap over his back, she washed his hair, massaging his scalp until he purred, his eyes lazily closed. The stripes were visible under his skin again, fine fur delicate under her fingertips when she explored his nape and shoulders.

"What are you thinking?" His lashes snapped up, nostrils flaring. "Your smell changed."

Cheeks hot, Andromeda went to lie, stopped herself. If these were to be her last hours of freedom with him, she would tell him every truth she could. And she would try to seduce him. Honor be damned. "I was wondering what it would feel like to rub my naked body against yours."

His eyes gleamed. Closing one big, wet hand over her thigh where she sat on the edge of the stone bath, he hauled her closer, leaned forward until he was dangerously close to the pulsing, swollen flesh between her thighs . . . and bit her hard on her inner thigh. She yelped even as liquid heat pulsed between her legs. "You didn't like my idea?"

Growling up at her, he bared his teeth. "We can't have those thoughts. You took a vow. Be good."

Her mouth fell open. "I can't believe *you're* telling *me* to be good."

"I won't steal your honor," he said stubbornly. "I'm going to find your *very* stupid Grimoire book so we can rut without guilt."

Every time he said the word "rut" it made her entire body hum. It was such a carnal word, so raw and unashamed. "I want to know what you'd do to me," she whispered, leaning in until her lips were a bare inch from his. "Tell me."

A loud chest-rumbling growl was her only warning before he tumbled her into the water.

When she came up, spluttering and pushing her hair out of her eyes, he glared at her. "Behave or I'll turn on the cold water."

At the end of her rope, she bared her own teeth at him. "Try it and see what happens."

He laughed and pounced on her, dragging her over to his chest. Another rub of his nose against hers. When she threatened to bite him, he grinned even harder. "I always knew my mate would be as wild as me."

No one had ever called her wild; she decided she liked it.

When he kind of snuggled her against his naked body, her wet clothes sticking to her, she stayed. Because being held by him, being affectionately petted as they spoke about their adventure, it was so wonderful it made her aching heart pulse in unfiltered joy, her eyes burning until she had to shut them lest her tears fall and give her away.

Naasir left his mate three hours past dawn. "I'm going to find your stupid Grimoire book," he muttered with a scowl.

"Naasir, it's a legend." His smart, wild—though she pretended not to be—mate glared at him, her hands on her hips. "I told you I take back that idiotic vow!"

"You can't." Something inside his Andi was broken and he wouldn't help her hurt herself any more. "I'll see you in a week at your parents' estate for the dinner, and you'll tell me what you hide from me." It came out a snarl. "No more secrets."

Eyes stark and wide, she nodded. Then she ran to him, wrapping her arms around him in a fierce embrace. "Don't get hurt searching for the Grimoire. And don't be late. I'll be waiting for you at noon on the seventh day from today." She pressed her cheek to his. "I'll make us a picnic and I'll go to what was the old elephant watering hole on the estate—you can find it by following the flight of the herons. They like that spot."

Drawing deep of her delicious scent, he lifted her up and spun her around. "I'll be there," he promised when he put her down again. "Make sure you don't cook the meat."

Her fingers played through his hair, where he'd woven in a second feather. "I promise."

"You should know something," he said as they separated.

"Yes?"

"When we're mated, I won't go far like this again. We'll be together." Naasir didn't understand why anyone would have a mate and not be with that mate. "If I have to go to New York or another place, you'll come with me. If you can't because of your work, I'll ask Raphael to allow me to stay here—he won't say no. He likes being with his mate, too."

His words shattered Andromeda. Though he occupied a far higher position in the immortal hierarchy, he didn't just assume his wishes would come first. "I would go anywhere with you," she whispered, emotion a knot in her throat. "Go find the stupid Grimoire so we can do bad things together naked."

A feral smile and then he was running out of the Refuge. She watched him until she could no longer glean even a hint of silver, and then she turned to pick up her small bag for the flight to Africa, a land that sang to her as Alexander's territory did to him, and yet that was to be her prison.

46

Naasir hated the cold. *Hated* it. But he had to go into it to find the Grimoire. Everyone thought it was a legend, but during the flight home from Alexander's territory, he'd finally realized why it seemed familiar: he'd seen it.

It had been long, long, *long* ago, when he'd still been two. The tiger cub was the one who'd seen the red book with the golden etching on the front. It wasn't something that would've registered on the cub except that the chimera experiment had happened that night, the boy and the tiger forcefully merged into one. The tiger's memories had become the boy's and the boy's had become the tiger's, but because they were two such different species who should've never been one, nothing had made sense for a long time.

It had been a confusing, terrifying period and the chimera he'd become had long forgotten the book the tiger had seen. But when Jason had described the Grimoire, the memories had surfaced as all parts of him worked together to win his mate. So he knew where that book had once been and where it should still be. Unfortunately, that place was now buried under tons of ice and snow.

Running over the cold white stuff, his body protected by

thick clothing and his feet by insulated boots, Naasir growled at the snow that hit his face and wasn't the least surprised when a black-winged angel landed not far from him. He was at the end of the world, but it made perfect sense to him that Jason would be able to find him. That was what Jason did—know secrets.

"What are you doing in Antarctica?" Jason asked, folding back his wings. "How did you even get here?"

Naasir shrugged. "I jumped out a plane." Far, *far* from his actual destination on the continent, which was why he'd had to run so long and spend two nights on the ice. And because it was important to keep this secret, he'd asked Illium to make any eyes in the sky look away until he was out of here.

No one but his family and his mate could know of this place.

"You should've worn white clothing and dyed your wings," he pointed out to the member of his family standing in front of him. "You stick out in this place without shadows."

"There's no one to see me except you—and you hate the snow." Jason didn't budge. "So what are you doing here?"

"I'm going to get the stupid Grimoire book." He growled as a flake of snow touched his nose. Brushing it off, he looked to Jason and caught his sudden stillness—as close to betraying surprise as Jason ever got.

"You know where it is?" the spymaster asked.

"I know where it once was." And since Osiris had a habit of clinging to his possessions, and the entire stronghold had been buried as it was, it should still be there. "Do you want to come with me?" Jason was sneaky in ways Naasir appreciated—he might be able to think of a faster method to get under all that ice and snow. "Will your mate be angry?"

"Mahiya's the one who ordered me to go find you when Illium told us where you'd disappeared to. My princess likes you." The other man spread his wings in readiness for takeoff. "Why didn't you ask one of us? We would've come with you."

"Illium wanted to come, but the healers wouldn't let him, and I knew you'd find me." Jason had as much curiosity inside him as Naasir, only he hid it better.

A faint smile. "You understand people better than anyone realizes." He took off in a wash of cold wind that drove snow-flakes into Naasir's face. Gritting his teeth, Naasir growled up at him. He almost thought Jason laughed. That intrigued him because Jason never laughed.

Unless . . . he did it with his princess.

Making a note to visit Jason and Mahiya so he could catch Jason laughing, he began to run again, the pack on his back doing nothing to slow his speed. He had frozen blood in that pack. It hadn't started out frozen, but this place was a giant refrigerator. He hated frozen blood. Unfortunately, before Jason's arrival, there'd been no one around he could've fed from . . . and he didn't think Andromeda liked it when he took blood from others.

Because he was her territory.

He grinned. He *liked* being her territory. If she wanted him to feed only from her, he would feed only from her. Until then, he'd drink bottled blood—or eat the disgusting cold ice cubes currently in his pack. And he'd dream of feeding from her while his cock was snug inside her and he'd already come once so that she was sticky with him and had his smell deep in her skin.

Heart thumping both from his speed and his arousal, he carried on into the white.

"Are you lost?" Jason yelled down several hours later, Naasir having forced himself not to go at full-tilt because he couldn't afford to just stop to allow his body to recover.

"No!" he yelled back. It was as if he had a homing beacon inside him, leading him to the place where he'd been created. "Another hour!"

Jason rose up above the clouds again, no doubt escaping the light snow that was irritating Naasir. Andromeda had better pet him a great deal for this—he'd gone into *snow* for her.

Running on, his mind full of memories of the ways she played with him, he came to a stop almost exactly an hour later. Jason landed beside him. "There's nothing here. It looks just like any other part of the landscape."

"There was a house here once," Naasir told the other man. "A stronghold. The angel who lived in it liked the cold because it stopped his experiments going far if they escaped. Inside his stronghold, though, it was warm—because children and small animals die when it's too cold."

Jason's dark eyes held his, and in them, Naasir saw dawning realization. "Raphael buried it, didn't he?"

"No. Alexander did." While on the cusp, Raphael hadn't yet become an archangel; he'd been able to incapacitate Osiris, but he couldn't bury this place of horror. "Raphael told me Alexander sank it into the snow, but he left it whole." Naasir began to walk around. "Here." He scuffed his foot over a spot. "There is a door here. If I can get inside, I can get what I need."

"Step back."

Naasir scowled but did as asked. "I was going to dig down." His claws were very strong but he'd also brought sharp digging tools. "You can help me. It's far down." So far that no one would ever accidentally discover the buried stronghold in this landscape inhospitable to life.

"Or," Jason said, "I could do this." Black lightning came from the fingers of one hand.

Naasir had seen Jason's lightning before—it created shadows that could encompass anything within their depths, suffocating and killing if Jason wished. Today, he saw that Jason's lightning could also act like what it seemed.

The heat of it sizzled through the snow and ice as if it was nothing. It took Jason time only because he was being careful not to accidentally damage what lay beneath, but he drilled a tunnel to an incredible depth within the next ten minutes.

"Wait," Naasir said and took off his pack. "I'm going to go down, see if it's far enough." As he spoke, he took a small package from the pack and put it in a pocket of his snow jacket.

"If it is," Jason said, his eyes on the hole, "come back up enough to signal me so I know you haven't been buried in snow down there."

Making the promise, Naasir didn't jump down into the hole but climbed down, using his claws to get a good grip. If Jason had drilled too far, he would feel the door as he went down. As it was, it was still a few feet below, but he decided to dig that out with his hands, pressing the extra snow to the sides of Jason's tunnel.

Then he climbed back up so he could yell to Jason. "Throw down the ax in my pack! I need to hack through the ice in front of the door."

Finding the ax, Jason told him to hug the wall before the black-winged angel dropped the tool into the snow tunnel.

Naasir picked it up and began to hack away the snow and

ice that blocked him from the door on the other side. It took time, sweat rolling down his back under the layers of warm clothing. Even then, the door wouldn't open, it was frozen so hard. He used the ax again to chip at the ice, but he was careful not to destroy the seal.

When he left, he'd close it up again.

Because the reason Alexander had submerged rather than destroy this place was because it was a burial ground. Naasir's brethren, who he'd never met in life, wouldn't mind him coming in to take something. He was one of them. But no one else was welcome here, and he would permit no one to defile it.

A black feather drifted down.

Realizing Jason had to be growing concerned, he climbed back up so he could wave at the spymaster. Then he dropped down once more and, after a little more careful chipping, twisted the handle of the door and pushed as hard as he could. A creaking groan sounded. He slammed his shoulder against the door. Once, twice . . . and he was falling into the frigid place where he'd been born and where so many had died.

"It's only Naasir," he said to the ones who slept here in the stone coffins Osiris had created one by one around a small home, until they became the walls and the floor of a large stronghold. Each square block held a twisted child who was two, or broken bodies who were still one.

"I've come for a book," he said, able to sense them all around, curious and excited that he'd come. "It's red with a golden design on the front, and it has a lock stamped with the shape of a griffin. That's a kind of half bird, half lion." His breath frosted the air as he spoke, his claws having sliced out of his boots to grip at the ice that covered all surfaces.

Icicles dripped from the ceilings. Stalagmites grew from the floor.

It was a cold, desolate place, but Naasir felt no sense of danger or unease. Only his brethren lived here now. Alexander had incinerated Osiris and taken his ashes far from here before the Ancient buried this place. "I brought you something." Reaching inside his pocket, he pulled out a toy that made music and kept it in his hand as he walked down the iced-over stairs to the lower level.

There, in the laboratory, he placed his gift on the large table where, according to the notes Raphael had taken and held in trust until Naasir was ready to read them, Osiris had cut up countless misshapen and twisted bodies, many while they were still alive. "I have a mate," he told the others, thinking not of the evil things that had happened here, but of how it had been reclaimed. "The book is for her. She's a scholar."

A stalactite fell from the ceiling in the dim depths of the laboratory. Taking the cue, he went to the spot and discovered that everything was encased in ice. Going back upstairs, he found his ax and returned. He was careful as he chipped here, too.

The book lay on the floor in a block of ice.

Cutting through until he could pick it up, but while it still had a protective coat of ice, he held it in his gloved hands. "Thank you," he said to his friends. "One day, I'll bring my mate here. She has wings, but she's brave and she'll come down." He didn't think Andromeda would find it strange that he knew his friends were still here, happily playing among themselves—she understood him, knew that his mind wasn't the same as hers.

Another stalactite fell in a tinkling symphony.

Smiling, he turned and walked out. As he climbed the stairs, he heard the music start to play behind him and knew his toy was welcome. Tucking the iced-over book in his jacket, he closed the door and made sure the seal was tight. Then he spent time packing snow all around it.

Climbing to the surface, he said, "We have to fill the hole back up again. No one can know what lies here." His brethren had earned their peace.

"The falling snow will do that itself, but we can help it along."

Together, the two of them began to manually fill the hole using the extendable shovels Naasir had in his pack. Meanwhile, the icy book began to melt against Naasir's body heat. Realizing it might get damaged, he put it on top of the pack so it would remain cold.

Night fell and still they shoveled.

Even after the hole was no longer visible, they stayed, waiting to make sure they'd left behind no trace of their visit. By the time dawn whispered softly over the landscape, there was no sign anyone had ever been here but for Naasir's footprints as he walked away from the site. Those were quickly filled in by the fresh snow that fell in a gentle rain from the sky.

His friends were safe again.
And he had the Grimoire.

Andromeda didn't know how she'd survived the past five days. Her parents were exactly as she'd left them, their excesses changed only in the specifics. Lailah and Cato still indulged in vicious sexual torture with "willing" playmates who may simply have been too scared to protest, and every so often, they meted out violence just because it was a "fun" way to break the ennui that colored their every action.

Even today, a hapless young angel screamed in her mother's quarters while her father sat in the great living area dressed only in pants of red silk while two naked vampires danced for him. He'd invited her to sit with him, watch the show—Cato was so jaded that he'd forgotten what it was to be a father.

Andromeda had been barely beyond a toddler the first time she'd seen her father having sex with a woman not her mother. He'd been strangling the whipped and bleeding woman at the time. Shocked, she'd cried. That day, her father had stopped and carried her out of the room. He hadn't bothered the times afterward, and she'd learned not to come unannounced into any room in the stronghold.

As for Lailah, Andromeda's mother had met her on arrival, and told her she'd placed a special triptych in Andromeda's room. Immediately nauseous, Andromeda had hoped she was wrong. She wasn't. She'd found three naked men waiting in her bed.

An angel. A vampire. A mortal.

A triptych. Her mother's little joke.

Andromeda had ordered the three out on the point of a blade.

This noon, the sixth since her arrival and the seventh since she'd left the Refuge, she fisted her hands, her spine rigid at the idea of another five hundred years of an existence mired in bone-numbing fear, brutal violence, and empty indulgence. Unlike her parents, her grandfather would not accept defiance. And as Andromeda wouldn't mete out torture on his orders, he'd turn the violence on her, brutalize her until she was nothing but an empty doll.

"Let it go, Andi." She forced her fists to open, shoved aside her frustration and anger, and smiled, grimly determined not to allow the dark future to steal this day from her. "Today, you're Andi, and today, you'll be happy."

Picking up the basket of food she'd prepared, a picnic blanket already over her arm, she exited into the back courtyard and rose into the sky.

Her lungs expanded, clean air rushing into her body.

47

Not long afterward, she sat under the dusky, midday sun on a picnic blanket she'd spread under the distinctive umbrella-shaped canopy of a tree that had as many names as Africa had languages. Aqba, nyoswa, samor, umbrella thorn acacia . . . the name or the dialect didn't matter. What mattered was that these trees provided welcome shade on the rolling grasslands of the savanna.

From her position, she could see the herons fly over the old watering hole, their wings flashes of white. Now that the reeds around the water were no longer regularly trampled under the ponderous feet of elephants, they grew lush and green when, elsewhere, the savanna was the golden green color of a season when the rains had come.

Much as Andromeda liked the herons and the lush foliage around the watering hole, she missed the elephants. There was something so very wise and steady about the magnificent creatures. And the way they cared for their young? As a babe herself, she'd been so envious of those awkward elephant babies who'd splashed in the water, certain their parents would protect them from the lions who liked to prowl around here.

But the elephants had moved on for reasons of their own,

and though Andromeda knew their new favorite place, she didn't go there. She didn't want to inadvertently betray them to her parents' guests. She'd done that once, accidentally shown a group of guests where the black rhino walked.

The three monsters had butchered two of the majestic creatures in front of her as she screamed and begged and tried to stop them. They'd done it for fun.

For *fun*.

That horrific day marked the only time she had ever been proud of her parents. Livid at discovering the slaughter, Lailah and Cato had meted out near-lethal punishments on the spot. Andromeda's parents might torture and mutilate mortals and immortals without compunction, but they did not allow the abuse or senseless killing of animals.

Andromeda had asked once, why protect one and not the other? Her mother's answer had been simple: *Animals have no choice in whether or not to play the game.*

Do all your playmates? Andromeda had dared ask.

Enough to not be innocent as an animal is innocent.

As a result of their stance, Lailah and Cato's territory teemed with wildlife, was considered one of the most rich and diverse places on the continent when it came to fauna.

Yet despite the fact the aftermath of the rhino slaughter was well known to all who came here, Andromeda didn't take risks when it came to the animals. The herons could fly away if anyone came here, and they weren't usually targets in any case.

Where was Naasir?

She stood and walked up the slight rise behind the tree for the tenth time. It gave her an uninterrupted view of the savanna in every direction, but she saw no familiar feline stride, no glint of glittering silver.

Refusing to give up, she returned to the picnic blanket and checked the food she'd prepared by hand and with all of the love in her heart. She'd packed the meat in ice to protect it from the heat, then placed it in an insulated container, but it wouldn't last more than two hours, given the warm temperature. She loved that warmth against her skin, loved the dusty scents in the air, loved hearing the far-off roar of a lion, had missed it all desperately when she was in the Refuge.

An hour later and the herons had flown away, leaving her

with only the grasses for company. Even the light wind had fallen, the entire world in stasis. When she walked up the rise again, all was emptiness. "Naasir!" she yelled out to the mocking landscape. "If you don't get here soon, I'll eat all the meat!"

"Liar."

Heart slamming into her rib cage, she swiveled so fast on her heel that she almost unbalanced. And there he was, his breath harsh and his skin hot, his hair tumbled from the run. She jumped into his arms, those arms wide open for her. Grabbing her under her wings, as if they'd done this a million times before and he knew exactly how to hold her, he lifted her off her feet and spun her around.

Laughing and crying, she locked her arms around him. "You're late," she accused when he stopped the spin. "I've been waiting forever."

Cuddling her close, he rubbed his cheek against hers. "I'm hungry."

She pretended to punch his shoulder, but when he put her on her feet, tugged him to the picnic blanket . . . and there, in the middle of the tartan was a book that wasn't supposed to exist. Lips parting on a gasp, she fell on her knees. She reached for the book, snatched back her hand before her fingers could graze the gold-etched red leather.

The gold outlined the image of a fierce winged creature with fiery breath.

"You can touch it," Naasir said, sprawling on his side on the blanket. "I asked Jessamy what to do to thaw it safely."

"*Thaw* it?"

Naasir didn't answer. He'd flipped open the insulated container and found the seasoned meat. Grinning, he popped a cube into his mouth . . . and his chest rumbled in pleasure, eyes heavy lidded. "Who made this?"

She bit down on her lower lip. "Do you like it?"

"Yes. I hope you bought a lot." He ate several more cubes. Forgetting the Grimoire for a second, she beamed. "I made it. I used special spices you can only order from a shop in Marrakech—I had the package flown down so it'd arrive in time."

His eyes lit up, but his next words were a growl. "Open the book so you can be sure it's your stupid Grimoire."

Laughing at the way he always referred to the Star Grimoire, she picked it up with utmost care. The leather was in near-flawless condition, only a little creased on the spine. "How can this be so old and so perfect?"

"It was hidden away," Naasir said. "Maybe Osiris found it in the ice when he built the house that became his stronghold." A shrug. "Later, it returned to the ice."

"Will you tell me about your becoming?" Under a warm African sun where no darkness could linger.

He growled and, reaching over, grabbed the Grimoire. Undoing the lock with a rough quickness that made her squeak, he thrust it at her. "Is this it?"

Realizing he wasn't going to tell her anything until she'd confirmed whether or not this was in fact the Grimoire, she took it from him and, sitting cross-legged on the picnic blanket, opened it with care. The text flowed like water across the page, interrupted only by two squares of delicately detailed illustrations.

Gold and silver and green and red, the colors were brilliant, as if the lines had been drawn yesterday. The black ink of the writing was as dark. Turning the page, she found a full-page drawing of a griffin. The mythical creature's wings were gloriously arched, its body that of a lion and its eyes a hypnotic obsidian. Running her fingers carefully over the image, she felt her throat thicken.

"This is a jewel," she whispered to Naasir. "One of the Seven Lost Angelic Treasures." She rubbed away the tears rolling down her cheeks before the salt water could fall and damage the page.

Shifting to sit behind her so he could look over her shoulder, Naasir wrapped one strong arm around her waist. "Can you read the writing?"

"Yes. It's an ancient angelic tongue." Though angels were immortals, their languages had nonetheless drifted over the eons. "If I read it aloud, you'd understand large parts of it. It's just the writing of it that's changed so significantly."

Naasir's hair brushed her cheek as he leaned forward to turn the page, his body warm and strong around her. "So it's the book from your vow?"

"Yes."

"Good." Tugging the Grimoire out of her hands, he dropped it on the far side of the picnic blanket. When she turned to ask why he'd done that, he slammed his mouth against hers, his hand thrusting into her hair.

The shock of contact was blinding. Then came the hot, hard punch of violent pleasure. It *hurt*, she'd been needing him for so long. Moaning, she twisted in his embrace so that she could wrap her arms around his neck. He had other ideas.

A second later, she was on her back on the blanket, Naasir over her.

Weaving his hands through her own, he pinned them to either side of her head. His hair—one of her feathers still in place—fell around his face as he dipped his head toward her, his eyes silver bright. *Mercy but he was beautiful,* she thought and then his mouth was devouring hers, and her heart, it was thumping like a brutal hammer inside her chest.

She devoured him as he devoured her, her tongue licking against his, her teeth grazing his lips. He bit. Of course he bit. And that was okay, because this was Naasir and he was hers for this moment, this instant, this day.

He lowered his full weight on her, nudging apart her legs and grinding his erect cock against the swollen folds between her thighs. Inner muscles spasming as a ragged cry was ripped from her throat, she wrapped her legs around his waist and rocked against him. Growling into her mouth, he released one of her hands, reached down between them.

Claws grazed her skin.

She jerked as she felt her pants tear. He didn't stop there—he ripped and tore until there were only a few shreds hanging by her boots. Her panties disappeared as quickly and then his no-longer-clawed fingers were stroking her with a slick, wet intimacy that made her want to beg and to take and to give all at once. Shuddering, her breasts aching and her nipples painfully sensitive, she pushed up his T-shirt and, when he didn't cooperate, nipped hard at his jaw.

That got her a growl and a silver-eyed glance through lashes as beautiful.

"Take this off," she ordered.

He thrust a finger inside her instead.

Her spine arched as her mouth fell open on a silent scream, her breath lost and her body clenching down hard on the small, possessive invasion.

Naasir's lips brushed her throat.

She jerked at the scrape of fangs, but he didn't bite, every muscle in his body so tense it was as if he'd snap. Her mind was fuzzy but she knew instinctively what was wrong. Pushing her free hand into his hair to hold him to her, she gasped in enough air to speak. "Yes. You can feed from me. *Take me.*"

Tension dissipating into molten heat, he scraped his fangs over her needy flesh again and, withdrawing his finger from her body to her moan and the carnal, liquid sound of her readiness, moved his hand to the fly of his jeans . . . and a second later, the rigid length of him was demanding heat against her. Shoving up her thigh until her knee pressed into her breast, he began to push into her.

She'd expected him to thrust, had been prepared for inevitable discomfort, but he nuzzled and kissed at her as he went slowly. "You're very tight, mate."

Heart melted and in his hands, she just held on to him with a needy, hungry desperation. Her other hand remained locked with his as her body stretched to accommodate his girth and length. Kissing her, Naasir rocked forward another inch. She clawed at his back. Growling into the kiss, he rocked again.

And again, and again.

Until he was lodged fully in her, the ache of him inside her an erotic pain, and the feeling of belonging so deep tears pooled in her eyes. "*Naasir.*"

Keeping one hand under the back of her knee, he nuzzled his way down to her throat.

Her stomach fluttered.

Her breath hitched.

And then he sank his fangs into her right as he began to move his cock in slow, deep thrusts, each movement rasping over her aroused flesh.

The pleasure was a huge, raw crash over her senses. Naasir rode her through the first wave, ignited another by sucking her blood and rubbing his thumb against the throbbing nub between her thighs. The second one slayed her, leaving her limp and honey slick, her muscles quivering.

It was all she could do to keep her leg around his body.

Increasing the speed of his thrusts once her body stopped spasming around his cock, Naasir raised his head from her neck and took her mouth again as he pounded her into the picnic blanket. She felt taken, branded, loved with an honest, wild ferocity that called to her own primal nature.

Not fighting instinct, she bit down on his neck when he bent his mouth to her throat again. A deep, inhuman growl, his hand tightening its grip . . . and his fangs sinking into her as he thrust his cock home.

N aasir collapsed on top of his mate, his cock still snug inside her, and lazily stroked one silken thigh. He could hear her heart thundering beneath him, feel her body clenching in unexpected spasms that wrung pleasure from her limp form. Shocked surprise had dilated her pupils to dark moons.

Smiling smugly, he kissed her, then nuzzled his way down to lick closed the tiny wounds he'd made with his fangs. "You're delicious." He would feed from her often when they rutted.

Enjoying their combined slickness, and happy she was marked by him now, he stroked gently in and out of her. His cock was beginning to harden to full readiness again. "Do you hurt?"

"I ache." She ran her fingers over his lips, eyes heavy lidded. "You fill me up." A smile when he nipped at the tips of her fingers, followed by a shiver as he circled his hips in a sensual tease. "Don't stop."

Delighted, he slid his hand down her body to push it under her tunic and the tight tank top she wore to control her breasts. Her inner muscles clamped possessively on his cock when he closed his hand over the warm, soft globe and squeezed. He liked that, so he squeezed again.

Andromeda arched her neck in response. Dropping his head to lick and kiss at her neck, he began to move. Slower this time, but just as deep. He could keep this up for an hour, might just do it if she let him. Lazily licking at her neck as he rubbed his thumb over her nipple, he pretended to bite her when she put both her hands in his hair and tugged.

A harder pull. "I want a kiss."

Kissing his mate was no hardship. Stretched out on top of her, he playfully seduced her mouth until she pushed at his T-shirt again. "Help me get this off."

Sated enough to be more patient, he cooperated and soon the

warm air kissed the naked skin of his back. He went to rip off her tunic, too, but she grabbed his wrist. "I already don't have any pants." Reaching down to her waist, she pulled the tunic off over her head, then followed with the tank top, freeing her breasts, the plump mounds topped by dark brown nipples.

"Pretty," he purred.

Maneuvering so he was on his knees between her spread thighs, his cock still buried inside her, he palmed both breasts with possessive hands, watched her eyes flutter shut. Her teeth sank into her lower lip when he pricked her with his claws, the moan that left her throat making his balls draw up tight.

Patience evaporated.

He covered her body with his once more. He'd fondle and bite and suck on her pretty breasts later. Right now he wanted to rub up against her, inside her, wanted to drench her in his scent until no one else would ever dare make a claim on her.

Andi was his.

Her hands stroked up his ribs and over to his back, her body beginning to move in time with his lazy thrusts. "This is . . ." Another moan as he ground himself against her.

Sliding his hand under her, he clenched his fingers on her ass, tilting her up for even deeper penetration.

"Naasir . . ." Her nails dug into his shoulders, her wings restless on the picnic blanket.

Unable to resist, he bent his head to her neck and bit again.

She came hard and out of control around him. Growling because he was pleased his mate found him so irresistible, he tightened the hand he had on her ass and drew on her blood as he continued to rock in and out of her. The taste of her on his tongue was drugging, her nails on his skin dark pleasure, the aroused, sated scent of her the final straw.

His spine locked as he thrust so hard into her that his balls slapped against her body.

He heard her cry out, but it wasn't in pain, and so that was all right.

48

Lying lazily naked on his back afterward, having taken off his jeans so Andromeda could wear them with her tunic, Naasir watched his mate watch him. He didn't know why, but she was shy about being naked under the sky. He didn't mind her wearing clothes if that made her happy, since she let him strip her whenever he wanted.

But she seemed to like him naked.

Her eyes kept going to him, and she'd sigh and lean over and kiss him. Or she'd pet his chest. Or his thigh. It was having a predictable effect, but he could contain himself now that he'd satisfied the first bite of need. Eating the square of meat she'd fed him—that she'd *made* for him, he watched her pick up the Grimoire.

"It's so beautiful," she said, stroking the cover before opening the book to look at the pages again.

Moving until she was sitting with her back half-propped up against his side, one arm on his chest and her hair electric and wild from his loving, she read to him from the book, translating the words unknown to him as she went. "And it was said that the griffin was the mightiest of creatures, but that it had a madness inside it nothing could cure. It could not be tamed.

Blood drenched the ground where it walked and though it was a peerless fighter, it could not be controlled and was a wild creature that did not know the hand of man."

She turned the page. "Those who saw a griffin were forever marked by its regal appearance, for its violent and maddened heart was not visible on the surface. Its golden fur glinted in the sunlight and its wings took it aloft as high as angelkind. Even in its danger, it was too magnificent to kill."

Turning, she showed him an illustration of a griffin flying in the sky beside an angel. "Can you imagine?"

The anger of memory stirred in him. "Legends like this drove Osiris. He wanted to make them true." His claws sliced out. "Alexander's brother was a melder and he decided to meld living beings."

Putting down the Grimoire, Andromeda turned to fully face him. "I'm sorry," she said, voice trembling. "I'm so sorry. All this time, I talked about the Grimoire and I never considered how it might hurt you."

Naasir hadn't meant for his words to wound her. "Your thoughts and wonder about mysterious creatures don't hurt me," he said, tugging her down into his arms and tucking her head against his neck. "It's fun with you." A game.

"Really?"

"Yes." Andromeda's heart wasn't twisted, and she had no desire to cage or own any of these creatures. "I like hearing the things you have to say."

Then, because it was time, he told her of the evil that had taken place on the ice. "I didn't know about the Cascade before, but now that I do, I think Osiris must've gained his abilities in the last one. He was an Ancient like his brother, would've been alive then."

Andromeda's head moved against his chest as she nodded. "According to Jessamy's research, while the Cascade most significantly affects archangels, it can also have an impact on a small percentage of other angels." She stroked his chest, running her nails over his skin and the fine fur that striped it.

The petting made it bearable to go into the death and the dark. "Osiris had the ability to put two things together and make them one." An ability no one had paid much heed to, for it seemed so frivolous. "At first, he melded inanimate objects for his and others' amusement—a chair to a broom, or a sword to a stone. Then he decided to see if he could meld two living things together." It had all been in the diaries Raphael had saved for Naasir.

"He started with plants and it worked. He is responsible for many of the most extraordinary flowers in the world—flowers that aren't one color but many, or that are so unusual a hybrid, no one can work out how they ever cross-pollinated."

Andromeda's breath brushed his neck, her nuzzled kiss making his eyes close. "After Raphael first found me and took me to the Refuge, I used to rip the heads off all the flowers Osiris had created in front of me, but then after a while, I decided that they had beaten him and should be allowed to exist. Like me, the flowers lived where he didn't."

"At some point," Andromeda said, her hand fisting on his chest as her voice vibrated with rage, "he decided to move from plants to people, to children. How can anyone justify such evil?"

"According to his diaries, it began by chance—he found an urchin boy and brought him to his old laboratory in Alexander's territory. He intended for the boy to become a cleaner. Then his hunting dog ran into the room and he was struck by the idea of melding them. He called it a 'glorious moment of genius.'"

Naasir pulled up Andromeda's leg so it lay across his body. She turned a little farther and swept her wing over him. The heavy warmth, the scent of her, it anchored him to the joyous present where he had his mate in his arms and Osiris was long dead, never to commit his atrocities again.

"He tried to meld the boy and the dog then and there. The two died in a twisted mess of limbs and organs." Naasir's heart raged at the knowledge that that had been merely the start of Osiris's murderous reign. "The failure only fueled his ugly desires. He bought children from poor families, or simply abducted them, paid poachers and hunters to bring him the young of animals."

Lifting Andromeda's hand to his mouth, he kissed her palm and forced himself to remember the peace he'd felt under the ice. No sadness, no pain, no horror. "The boy who is part of me grew up alone until the tiger cub. Osiris either stole or bought the boy when he was a baby—I never found out which."

He ran his hand through Andromeda's hair, bunching it up in his hand, then letting it escape in a burst of color and life. *Pretty.* "In his diaries, he called us his hope." Such an ugly use of the word. "And though I wish he'd never had the satisfaction, he succeeded with the tiger cub and the boy. Osiris never worked out why and all I can tell you is that the tiger cub and the boy were best friends who helped one another survive." The instant of change was blurry in his memory, but he knew there had been pain, such agonizing pain.

Andromeda rose up and, expression stripped of all traces of civilization, said, "I'm glad he's dead."

He squeezed her waist with the arm he had around her. "I tried to kill him immediately after my transformation, but I was too weak." It had felt as if he was a broken doll, his limbs useless and his mind dull.

"It took me months and months to start thinking clearly again, though my thought patterns weren't 'human.' Neither were they animal." Rather, an amalgamation of the two. "I had to learn to walk again, talk again. Osiris wanted to know why I had two legs instead of four, why the boy's form had taken precedence over that of the tiger cub, so he did more experiments."

Andromeda's eyes glinted. "I'm glad he's dead," she repeated, "but I want to bring him back to life so I can hack out his black heart and feed it to him."

Naasir bared his teeth at her. "I knew you were my mate." He drew her close with a grip around her nape, parted her lips with his own and licked his tongue against hers until her wing fluttered over him and her thigh rubbed against his.

Sliding his hand under her tunic to palm her breast, he rolled her over onto her back. His nostrils flared at her scent. Moving his hand down her quivering abdomen, he slipped it under the loose waistband of the jeans and stroked two fingers through her slickness. When he raised his head, her lips were more swollen than before and her breath shallow.

"Any more questions?" Lashes shading his eyes as he watched the rise and fall of her chest, he circled his thumb around the slippery nub at the apex of her thighs.

Gripping his biceps with one hand, she tried to glare at him but pleasure kept rippling over her. "Beast."

He grinned. "Your beast." Nipping at her lower lip, he used his teeth to tug at the soft flesh while he moved his fingers with a playful dexterity that made her give a startled moan and orgasm in sweet little flutters he wanted to lick up with his tongue.

His mouth watered.

Putting his lips to her ear, he said, "You're going to be my dessert after dinner tonight. I'm going to lick you up like honey, sink my fangs into the delicate, plump flesh between your thighs."

Her body jerked, her thighs clenching on his hand. She didn't startle when his claws released, though he was holding flesh so soft and fragile. No surprise. His mate was as wild as him and she knew he would never hurt her.

Trembling fingers wove into his hair but her teeth on his jaw were sharp. "Not if I get my mouth on you first."

He growled and tore off her jeans and ten minutes later, Andromeda lay sweat-drenched and naked on his chest, while his heart pounded, his entire self stretched out under the sunshine in sated bliss.

When Andromeda finally pushed up on his chest to face him, she looked deliciously used, marked by his bite and by his kiss. And the affection in her eyes . . . He basked in it. "How long till we have to go in?" he asked.

"Hours yet." She pushed back his sweat-damp hair as his eyelids lowered. "Don't go to sleep yet. I do have one question."

Lazy, he didn't bother to open his eyes. "Hmm?"

"The fact you're a chimera doesn't explain your vampirism."

Naasir yawned. "Osiris was afraid I wasn't a true, immortal chimera, that I'd die before he'd unearthed his answers. He also wanted to keep me a child so I'd be easier to control." Especially after Naasir's last attack had left him with claw marks shredding his face.

"Not that it would've saved him had I stayed a child. The day Raphael found me—after hearing about what Osiris was doing from a courier who'd seen more than he should—I'd jumped on Osiris from the ceiling, clawed out his eyes and made him slip on the stairs. His skull cracked hard enough against the stone to leave him unconscious." At which point, Naasir had ripped out his throat and clawed open his chest cavity. "But that was Osiris's rationalization for Making me."

Horror and rage had his mate going stiff above him. "Making a child is strictly forbidden. Children go mad if Made. They *die.*"

"I came close to death, but perhaps because I was a chimera, I survived no more mad than when he began the process."

"You were never mad."

"I was feral."

"That's not madness." Kisses on his jaw.

He turned into them, shamelessly asking for more. Andromeda gave him what he wanted, her lips as gentle as her love was fierce.

Opening his eyes so he could see that fierce love in hers, he picked up her hand to nip and kiss at her fingertips. "Those who know I ate Osiris's heart say that perhaps I'm so strong, so immortal, because I ate the heart of an Ancient while I wasn't yet full-grown."

"Does that bother you?"

"No." Naasir bared his teeth. "I *like* the idea of having consumed my enemy and made his power my own."

"Me, too," said his smart, wild mate, her eyes glinting. "You grew despite the Making."

"Yes." No one had expected that, those who knew of him readying themselves to deal with the distress and pain of a child who never grew, but whose understanding might get steadily older. "My growth patterns mimicked those of angelic children."

No one knew why, but the prevailing theory was that as a chimera, he *was* already naturally immortal and as such, his body had fought the toxins of the Making. However, because he'd been small and weak, he hadn't totally won the fight and thus gained certain vampiric characteristics. "Like angelkind, I haven't measurably aged since I became an adult. We can be together for eternity."

Andromeda's face blanched, all happiness wiped away.

Growling, he tumbled her over onto her back and braced himself above her. "Enough, mate," he said in a tone that wasn't wholly human. "What are you hiding from me?"

Her throat moved, the words she spoke a harsh rasp. "Tomorrow, I must go to Charisemnon's court."

Naasir curled his lip over his teeth. "You must do a tribute to your archangel? I will go with you to protect you."

"No." Andromeda's breathing turned labored, as if she was finding it hard to draw air into her lungs. "I'm bound to serve five hundred years in his court."

Naasir went motionless above her. "Why are you enslaved?"

"A familial blood vow. It cannot be negotiated."

Naasir snarled at the finality in her tone. "No one likes

Charisemnon," he said. "Just ignore the obligation." He nipped at her lower lip, then did it again because she'd been hiding things from him that hurt her.

Nails digging into his shoulders, she narrowed her eyes. He ran a clawed hand over her cheek in warning. She didn't look scared at all. "I like your nails in me," he said with a grin. "Dig harder."

A distinct *grr* sound from his mate. "I can't just not turn up," she snapped. "You know what archangels are like—they might fight amongst themselves, but they won't support rebellion within each other's families."

"Things have changed." Naasir braced himself on his forearms. "Raphael hates Charisemnon for causing the Falling. He'll accept you into his protection." Because she was Naasir's, and Raphael backed his Seven.

Andromeda shook her head. "It may cost him the allegiance of those like Astaad who are more traditional."

Naasir growled, but he didn't argue—they both knew she was right. Astaad considered Charisemnon an enemy, but if Raphael broke such a deep angelic prohibition, it could fracture their alliance. And any infighting or serious disagreement between the allies would give Lijuan a weakness to exploit. But— "Jason took Mahiya away from Neha."

"Our situations are very different below the surface." Andromeda had hoped when she'd heard about the union, dug up everything she could about the princess. "The service requirement is specific to my grandfather's court."

"I hate vows," Naasir muttered. "Now that we're mated, you can't make any more."

"How about if I vow to love you forever?" A soft question.

"That one is allowed." He nipped at her nose. "I love you, too, even if you keep taking stupid vows I have to break."

She bared her teeth at him. "I didn't choose this one." Anger made her voice rough. "I don't *want* to go, but if I don't, Charisemnon will declare me an outcast with a price on my head. Even if Raphael doesn't care about the blood vow, *someone* will—or they'll just want the bounty. I'll be hunted the rest of my life." And Naasir would be hunted with her. "That's no kind of life."

"What about your father?"

"Cato would never go against his archangel."

Naasir's silver eyes locked with her own. "You know Cato

isn't your father in blood. Why are you pretending otherwise? Even had Dahariel not given you an uncommon amount of attention, your wings bear markings a step removed from his."

Andromeda looked away, but Naasir gripped her jaw, made her meet his gaze again. Surrendering, she admitted the truth. "I was so happy when I realized," she confessed. "I thought he was brave and strong and intelligent—and he is, but he's also capable of gross cruelty."

She took a ragged breath. "Ten years before I left for the Refuge, I walked into a room in my parents' home and saw him torturing a mortal boy who was barely of age." It had shattered Andromeda, left her heart in pieces on the floor, the hope inside her snuffed out. "He meant for me to know," she whispered. "He could see the stars in my eyes and he wanted to erase them, to show me his true colors." To teach her that though he wasn't lost in a compulsive search for sensation like her parents, he was as pitilessly jaded.

Andromeda had begged him to let the mortal go. The man who was her father in blood had simply raised an eyebrow and flicked the whip once more on the boy's back, making him whimper as blood trickled down his ravaged skin.

A soft heart can be a fatal weakness in the immortal world, a lure for the predators. If you want to survive, you'd do well to learn from my example.

Andromeda had thrown up instead.

"Dahariel is a bastard," Naasir agreed. "But he is also Astaad's second and can request sanctuary for you. No one will interfere as you are his child."

Andromeda knew he was right; the archangels and old angels would deem it a private family matter since Dahariel—and thus Astaad—had as much right to her as Charisemnon. "I asked him," she admitted in a small voice. "Fifty years ago." She'd been desperate enough to chance the humiliation, knowing that though Dahariel was cruel, Astaad's court was nothing like Charisemnon's.

Naasir's expression hardened. "He said no to his own cub? Angels love their children."

"I think he does love me in his own twisted way." That was what made his abandonment hurt all the more. "He told me he'd given me what he was capable of giving and that he'd continue to train me, but in every other way, I was on my own."

"A lot has changed in fifty years."

"Yet he's never made the offer, though I have seen him many times for our combat sessions." She stroked back Naasir's hair. "I don't think the bond ever formed deep enough for him to claim me as his own—he didn't realize I was his until almost fifty years after my birth, when my wings settled into their final adult pattern. By then . . . it was too late for him to see me as a babe." To feel the protective instincts of a parent.

"So you want me to wait five hundred years?"

Yes. "I can't demand that," she said aloud even as her soul tore in two.

He growled at her, so loud and angry that she startled. "Are you going to rut with others in Charisemnon's court?"

"No!" She pushed at his shoulders but he refused to move. "Why would you say such a horrible thing?"

"Why would you say I shouldn't wait for you?" It was a snarl. "If you're mine, you're mine. And I'm yours. Today, tomorrow, always."

Andromeda began to cry. Hard, gulping sobs that held all her pain, all her love, all her dreams. Rolling over onto his back, Naasir crushed her close and made purring sounds in his chest as he stroked her hair and her back. "I'm sorry I growled at you," he said, nuzzling at her. "I wouldn't hurt you."

"I know," she got out through her tears.

Sniffing away the last of the tears several minutes later, she just lay against him. "I wasn't crying because of that. I was crying because you're wonderful and I can't bear to think of leaving you."

"There must be a way."

"It's a blood vow."

"I'm a chimera who was made of a small, fierce boy and an equally small, equally fierce cat. I can think of a way out." He wasn't going to let his mate end up in the court of the Archangel of Plague and Disease.

49

A day later, however, he had to watch her leave for that very court.

"Five hundred years," she said, one hand on his chest, over the heart that beat for her. "Will you truly wait?"

"If I have to," he said, taking her mouth in a ravenous kiss. "But I won't. Watch for me. I'll be coming to get you." He fisted both hands in her hair. "Stay alive." He knew the ugly rules of Charisemnon's court, knew the horrors she'd face.

"I will," she promised, but in her eyes, he saw the knowledge that it might not be enough.

Death had many forms. Not all were of the body.

50

A week after that parting, Andromeda couldn't help looking out through the balcony doors of her bedroom and out over the landscape. She knew it was impossible for her wild chimera to find an answer to a blood vow owed an archangel, but she waited nonetheless. He'd sneak in to see her as soon as he could, that she knew beyond all doubt, though they'd had zero communication since they parted.

Andromeda didn't dare carry a phone. It could be taken from her, and once taken, Charisemnon would know Naasir was her heart, not a simple sexual dalliance. Her grandfather would find a way to use that, to twist the pure into the ugly.

Five hundred years.

She would fight to survive . . . but she might not come out the same on the other side.

Today, her grandfather had summoned her for a special task. She'd seen the vampire staked out in the courtyard, seen the implements of torture, knew she would not pick up those implements. So they would be turned against her.

Because she was a princess of the court, her naked body would be staked out in a dungeon, not in public. And her torture wouldn't be at inexpert hands, but at the hands of Charisemnon's

Master Torturer. The tall, thin angel's aim would be to break her piece by piece. Until she became like Cato, like Lailah.

Daughter and fosterling raised side by side.

Empty shells repainted in Charisemnon's image.

For the first time, she understood that perhaps her parents were together because no one else could understand what they'd survived. A broken kind of love, but love nonetheless.

Gut churning and skin going hot, then cold, she put on her uniform: dark brown pants and a lighter brown tunic with the pattern of a tree printed in black down the front left side—the same kind of tree under which she'd loved with Naasir. The memory a secret held inside her, she pulled her hair back into a tight braid and strapped on her sword.

No more time.

Naasir. Fight for Naasir. Don't allow them to steal him from you.

She stepped out, striding down the hallways into Charisemnon's inner court. The smell of alcohol, as well as of strong narcotic substances that had an effect on immortal physiology, lingered in the air, a number of courtiers still slumped over the tables where they'd been last night.

Wings trailed limply on the sticky floor, and a glutted vampire slept on a chaise longue with his arm possessively around a slender mortal boy who couldn't have been more than sixteen. Hearing a grunt, she looked up and saw one of her grandfather's angelic generals copulating with a female vampire who already bore bruises from his meaty grip, but who seemed to be enjoying being fucked on a dining table.

Carrying on through the court without stopping, skirting sleeping and fallen bodies and ignoring slurred propositions, she walked to the great doors beyond. Carved with exquisite care and inlaid with gold and precious stones, the doors were as striking as her grandfather's heart was rotten. The guards—sharp eyed and alert—opened them for her at once, and she continued on to the inner sanctum.

She swallowed her revulsion before pushing through the unguarded door at the end, having to fight her way through hanging silk curtains to the bedroom. Charisemnon lay in bed, his previously healthy and muscled body shriveled and marked with scars. The disease he'd spread had turned on him like a vicious dog. The fact he was regaining his health, regardless, was no surprise.

He was, after all, an archangel.

The scars would eventually fade. The rumpled mahogany silk of his thinned-out hair would thicken, his muscle mass return. He'd be a beautiful man on the outside again, a dark-haired archangel with skin of deep gold and eyes the same shade but for slivers of brown within, his flawlessly shaped lips lush with sensual promise.

Mortal and immortal alike did not always wear their ugliness on their skin.

Keeping her eyes scrupulously off the barely budded girls who lay naked around Charisemnon, Andromeda looked straight into her grandfather's face. "Sire," she said, the address sticking in her throat.

"Ah, my dear Andromeda," Charisemnon replied in a voice that had gone scratchy after his illness. "My steward tells me you are settling in."

"Yes, sire."

Charisemnon didn't immediately respond, distracted by a girl who'd awakened. Those girls, Charisemnon's young concubines, were so brainwashed that they would stab each other in the back to stay in his good graces.

When they became too old for his tastes, the girls became courtiers and ladies' maids who groomed other girls to take their place. It sickened Andromeda, but she could see no way to stop it. She'd tried speaking to the newer crop of girls, offered to find them a way out, but they'd laughed and told her they felt lucky to be in the court.

"If I serve the sire," one pretty child had said, "my value will increase when it comes time for marriage. My husband will be honored to marry me."

The sad thing was that she was right: Charisemnon had conditioned his people to accept his perversions as honor. All Andromeda could do was keep watch for any girl who didn't appear to be so willing. If and when that happened, she'd find a way to help her.

"I have a task for you, granddaughter," Charisemnon said, one hand on the newly blossoming breast of the child in bed with him.

Nausea twisted her gut. "Sire." All she had to do was stay

alive. If she was alive, there was hope. Naasir was fighting for her. She'd fight for him. Until her last breath, she'd fight and she'd hold on to her sanity and her soul.

"Hmm." Charisemnon's smile was twisted. "I had intended for you to prove your bloodline to the court this morning, for none of my line can be seen as weak."

"You have witnessed my skill with the sword."

Charisemnon waved that away. "You are known as a scholar. A princess of the court needs be more ruthless."

Sweat broke out along Andromeda's spine. "Yes, sire."

"As I say, that was my plan, but it'll have to wait for your return."

Andromeda didn't feel any relief at the reprieve, aware worse could be waiting. "My return?"

"It appears Alexander wishes to speak to you."

Too stunned and off-balance to hide it, she just stared at her grandfather.

Charisemnon's smile deepened, as if he enjoyed her shock. "He feels you deserve a reward for your part in saving him."

Chest tight and skin cold, Andromeda stepped carefully. "My actions did not have a deleterious effect on your relationship with the Archangel Lijuan?" She'd been waiting for that particular ax to fall since her return.

Charisemnon pushed away the girls. Trained and obedient, they slipped out of bed and headed out without anything to cover their naked flesh. Leaving the bed himself while she averted her eyes, Charisemnon pulled on a robe the color of aged merlot and turned to her.

"It could have and you will be disciplined for not clearing your actions with me," he said, and all at once, he was no longer a man with sickening appetites but an archangel, his power blinding. "However, as Alexander clearly has gentle feelings for you, there's no reason we can't capitalize on that."

"You wish for me to cultivate Alexander?" she asked, her expression polite and respectful, though she felt as if she was attempting to balance on a tightrope so thin, it cut into the soles of her feet. "Would that not anger Lijuan and threaten your alliance?"

"Alexander is an Ancient." Charisemnon poured himself a

drink from an opaque bottle. "If we can gain his favor, Lijuan becomes less important."

Andromeda didn't fool herself that her grandfather was taking her into his confidence. "Of course, sire."

Charisemnon's lips flattened after he put down the glass, his eyes chips of ice. "Lijuan should never have taken a child of my bloodline, and she should've informed me of her plans for Alexander."

Ah. Andromeda knew she meant nothing to Charisemnon as a person, but as a symbol of his rule, yes. Lijuan had crossed a line there. But even that, she suspected, wouldn't have been enough without the latter transgression.

Tightening the robe of his belt, Charisemnon sneered. "I would have been able to ensure the success of the mission. She was a fool to disregard me."

"Yes, sire." Andromeda waited to see if there was anything further, but Charisemnon dismissed her after stating that Alexander would be at her parents' home the next day and she was to fly there today in readiness.

Fighting not to throw up in relief at the temporary stay of torture, Andromeda left at once, turning down an offer of an escort from the Master of the Guard. She was a warrior scholar and the mate of a wild chimera; she could get herself from one side of the territory to the other without guards.

Taking off, she stayed below the white cotton-candy clouds, low enough that she could see the lands over which she flew. It took about thirty minutes to get out of the city at the center of which stood Charisemnon's sprawling stronghold, and into the wilderness of this awe-inspiring territory. A herd of antelope ran below her for at least a mile, as if racing her shadow, and she saw elephants walking with regal pomp, hippos swimming in the rivers, groups of baboons chattering and fighting below the widely spaced trees.

Her heart swelled.

It seemed so unjust that all this bounty lay in Charisemnon's disease-causing hands. If life were fair, he would have a land as barren as his soul, and Lijuan's black rain wouldn't manifest with the beauty of black diamonds glimmering with water.

Sweeping along an updraft, she forced her mind off that

dark path, instead filling her thoughts with Naasir's love for her homeland. He'd told her he snuck in as often as he could, just to run with the animals. She loved that, loved that someone so courageous and honorable and pure found pleasure in this land. *He* should be the one in charge of this territory—though he probably wouldn't want the job.

She stopped for a while on the shore of a small lake that rippled with sunlight, loathe to spend any more time in her parents' home than necessary. It was better than Charisemnon's court, but better was a matter of degrees. Her sympathy for Lailah and Cato's childhood didn't extend to the vileness they meted out.

Night had fallen by the time she finally arrived, and though she tried to sleep, she spent the night on the roof, staring up at the stars. "Naasir," she whispered, her faith in his love the foundation of her new existence. "I miss you, my heart."

He didn't appear out of the savanna this time, didn't tumble her to the earth.

There was only the night and the silence.

Early the next morning, she flew out to perch on a hill and watched the skies turn from whispering gray to light-shattered dawn, then to a dusty, soft blue seen nowhere else on this earth. If she could, she'd meet Alexander out here. But when the archangel appeared in the sky ninety minutes later, his wings glinting in the sunlight in a way that brought Naasir vividly to mind and choked her throat with longing, he dipped his wings to show he saw her, but carried on to her parents' stronghold.

Andromeda forced herself to do the same.

Unlike Andromeda's simple sea-green tunic and tapered black pants, Lailah and Cato had come out dressed in formal clothing. Andromeda made the introductions, hoping she was following the correct protocols. She'd never had reason to learn how to introduce an Ancient to other powerful angels, but since no one censured her, she must've muddled through it.

"Please," her mother said, leading Alexander into the formal receiving area, elegant and hung with priceless artworks.

It took Andromeda a few minutes to realize both Lailah and Cato were intimidated by Alexander.

"Your daughter put her life on the line to save mine," Alexander was saying, his body clad in the clothes of a warrior, the colors charcoal gray and stark black. "I'm not a man who forgets such things."

"She has always been strong, always had a will more formidable than many an adult."

Astonished and startled at the pride she heard in her mother's tone, Andromeda stared at her, but Lailah had already returned her attention to Alexander. Her face was fine boned in profile, her smooth skin of dark honey flawless, and her tightly curled hair worn in a graceful updo.

Beside Lailah, Cato appeared ghostly pale, his skin having never held the warmth of the sun and his eyes a washed-out blue that were nonetheless haunting in their beauty. Fine blond hair fell to his shoulders, his face one that many an artist had sketched. They always drew him as an innocent.

"Yes," Alexander said into the small quiet that had fallen. "Your child is strong for one of her age and has enough courage to shoot a crossbow at one archangel to save another." A faint smile. "It is for that reason I would like her in my new court."

Andromeda froze.

Naasir.

He'd done this. Somehow, her sneaky, smart mate had done this.

Across from Alexander, her parents' faces had gone slack. Her mother was the first to recover, her golden brown eyes huge. "You wish our daughter to be one of your courtiers?"

"I do not have courtiers as such." Alexander's tone was cool. "However, I do have warriors and scholars in my inner circle. And I must rebuild my court after so many of them were murdered fighting alongside my son."

A chill filled the room, Alexander's power suddenly an agonizing pressure against Andromeda's eardrums, his wings having taken on a glow no one wanted to witness. Not because it wasn't glorious—*oh, it was*—but because archangels generally glowed right before they meted out death, vicious and final.

"I am honored," Andromeda said when it appeared her parents had been struck dumb. "A position in an Ancient's court is usually never offered to an angel so young."

Alexander's lips curved, and at that instant, she could see the "beautiful warrior" written of in stories of his reign. But she couldn't see him as a man, for in his eyes, she saw such *age* that it threatened to crush. She didn't know what woman would ever be able to handle the sheer power of him. Caliane? But Caliane was famously still in love with the mate she'd been forced to execute.

No one else on the planet was Alexander's equal in power and age.

"Ah, but you are not usual, are you, scholar?" Alexander's eyes locked with hers. "Not many people would dare tell a Sleeping Ancient to 'Listen, damn you!'"

As her parents choked on appalled disbelief, Andromeda found herself smiling. "In my defense, I was trying to save your life and you were being terribly arrogant and bad-tempered."

Throwing back his head, Alexander laughed, the sound filling the room in a way that made her understand why he had a friendship with Titus. The Archangel of Southern Africa also laughed with such open and unalloyed delight when amused.

"Yes," Alexander said afterward, "you are not usual, Andromeda." Smile yet on his lips, he turned to her parents. "I'm informed your child is tied by a blood vow, that she cannot accept my offer."

"Oh," her father said in an awed tone. "If you would give us a moment, we will speak to the Archangel Charisemnon. He is the only one who can release her."

Neither Andromeda nor Alexander said a word while her parents were out of the room. For Andromeda, there was too much at stake, and the Ancient likely had other concerns on his mind. Like rebuilding his palace and reclaiming his territory. He didn't have time to come all this way to offer Andromeda a place in his court, no matter what role she'd played in saving his life. Not to mention it was a security risk, given his weakened state.

How had Naasir done this?

Stifling her curiosity and trying not to allow her hope to burn too bright, she waited. When her mother walked back into the room, Lailah said, "Andromeda, your grandfather would like to speak to you in the study."

Andromeda excused herself and went quickly to the room with the large screen that currently hosted Charisemnon's ravaged visage—shadowed in a way to make it seem he bore no scars. Her father left the instant she entered. "Sire," she said on a deep bow. "You have heard?"

"Yes." Charisemnon's eyes gleamed, avaricious and satisfied. "You must accept. To have one of my blood in Alexander's court is an unimaginable coup."

"I am bound by my blood vow."

Charisemnon waved a hand. "I release you from the vow."

Her blood thundered, her head spinning. Tensing her stomach and managing to keep her feet though her knees threatened to crumple, she met her grandfather's gaze. "I believe the Ancient will wish to hear you say so himself. He is of the old guard and apt to be traditional about such matters." She hoped Alexander would back her because she needed him as witness. No one would ever question his word. "Shall I fetch him?"

"Yes. I should like to speak to him."

Walking back into the receiving room on rubbery legs, she made the request. Alexander's eyes held an unexpected amusement as he got up and walked with her. "I thank you for your indulgence," the Ancient said to her grandfather when Charisemnon formally released her from the blood vow. "It is a loss to send such a grandchild to another's court."

"She will always be family," Charisemnon said, once more an archangel pulsing with power. "I hope this will lead to strong ties between our two courts."

Alexander inclined his head slightly and Charisemnon didn't seem to notice the Ancient hadn't actually agreed.

"Do you need to pack?" Alexander asked as soon as the conversation ended, his tone curt and businesslike.

"No. I can go now." She had her sword; everything else, she and Naasir would figure out later.

"Good. I must return to my territory." Striding back to farewell her still somewhat-bewildered parents, he gave her a minute to grab a small bag of high-energy dried food for the journey, then ordered her to follow him out.

Andromeda said a quick good-bye to Lailah and Cato, was startled when her mother hugged her close and whispered, "Fly free, my daughter. Be what I could never be and leave the cage forever."

Andromeda stared, the haunting words echoing inside her skull, but in front of her, Lailah was once more the cruel, beautiful mother she'd always known, and Alexander was in the air.

She lifted off.

51

There was no way Andromeda could keep up with Alexander, no matter if he wasn't at full strength. It was a physical impossibility for any young angel. However, the Ancient stayed with her to the border. The instant they reached the sea, he told her to find her way to his territory at her own pace, then flew high and fast, heading home to a people who needed him.

Andromeda didn't linger, beating her own wings as hard as she could to get to safe harbor. Unlike Alexander, she couldn't do the trip in one go. She had to rest and when she did, she chose isolated places. It took her more than thirty-six hours to reach Alexander's territory; the sun was beginning to set in the west, its golden rays lighting up the sky. Not sure where to go, she made her way to the Brotherhood village.

It remained in ruins.

The wing brothers must've all moved to the palace, she realized. About to turn that way, she saw that the home in which she and Naasir had stayed was upright and in good repair.

Andromeda was too relieved to question why that one building had been repaired. She needed a safe place to rest and to find her bearings, and this small home with its memories of Naasir would do. It was a pale substitute for the man she loved, but it was better than anything she'd had before Alexander's offer. Tomorrow morning, she'd locate the steward of his court, find out her duties.

And surely Alexander wouldn't mind if Naasir visited her.

Hope a flame in her heart, she pushed through the door of the house, went into the bathroom and found that the plumbing worked. Grateful, she stripped and washed away the dust and grit of her journey. When she turned off the water and got out after wringing her hair dry, her eyes went instinctively to the back of the bathroom door. The silky black robe hanging there looked new . . . and it had the Grimoire in one pocket.

Andromeda had given it to Naasir to take to Jessamy.

Shoving her arms into the sleeves, she tied it haphazardly and burst out into the room. Her grin cracked her face as she ran to jump on the bed and on the man who was lying nonchalantly on it. "How did you get in?"

Silver eyes glinted at her in mock insult. "Did you just ask me that question?" He took the Grimoire and threw it on a small table. "Stupid Grimoire book."

Laughing, she smothered his face in kisses. Naasir opened her robe and slipped his hands inside to lie against her wet skin as he held her close and turned his face so she could cover all of him with her kisses. "I missed you," she said between each kiss. "I missed you. I missed you."

His chest rumbled under her, his skin bearing tiger stripes. "You should miss me. I'm your mate."

He sounded so smug that she kissed him again. "Why didn't you come? I waited and waited!" Slapping her hand on his chest, she sat up on her knees. "I looked for you every night."

Scowling at her, he said, "I had to think of a way to get you out of Charisemnon's clutches." He bared his teeth. "Then I had to hunt down Alexander and point out that he owed you and me a very big favor."

Her mouth fell open. "Did you really say that to him?" It came out a squeaked whisper.

"Why not?" Hands behind his head, he shrugged. "Alexander was always known for his honor, and he likes you."

Still astonished that he'd brazenly gone up to an Ancient and demanded repayment, she shivered. "He could've killed you in anger." And she could've lost him forever.

"No. He likes me, too." Grinning, he pulled her down and flipped positions so that she was pinned under him. "He tried to steal me from Raphael but I can't be stolen."

Stroking his cheek and feeling that fine, near-invisible fur that sometimes appeared with the stripes, she felt her eyes burn. "I was so scared." A ragged confession.

Thunder in his expression. "Did anyone hurt you?"

"No." Her wild chimera had no need to know how close it had come—that one thing, she'd keep from him, because it would cause him pain for no reason. "I knew you'd come."

His eyes told her he saw her secrets anyway. "I knew you'd be strong, that you'd stay alive no matter what."

Eyes hot and wet, she held on to him, was held, for a long time.

When Naasir moved, it was to pull something out of his pocket. "This is for you."

Surprised by the way he'd ducked his head, as if shy, she looked down. Her hands flew to her mouth. "For me?"

"Mates wear amber." Tugging one hand away from her mouth, Naasir slipped on the ring of gold that bore the patina of great age.

Its heart was darkest amber.

"*Oh,*" she whispered, staring at it and sniffing and smiling. "You gave me amber." She touched the ring with the fingers of her other hand, made incoherent noises of naked joy. "It's so beautiful."

"It has a story, a history," Naasir told her, openly smug at her delight. "I thought you'd like it better than a new ring."

"I do. So much." She smothered his face in kisses again. "I designed a ring for you," she admitted shyly afterward. "I couldn't have it made yet." Too much risk her grandfather would hear, would learn she'd bonded that deeply with another. "It's going to have my name written on the inside," she added, daring him to argue.

Naasir's eyes glowed. "Because I'm your territory." A clawed hand caressed her cheek. "Possessive mate."

"Yes. Very." She snapped her teeth at him.

Laughing, he snapped back, and they tussled in the bed like two big cats. She was breathless by the time she ended up under him again. Blowing her hair off her face, she said, "Tell

me everything about how exactly you got Alexander to agree."
Brazen and courageous, her mate astonished her.

Naasir sighed. "Can we rut first?" Grinding his sizable
erection against her, he closed his hand over her bare breast.
"I want you."

Andromeda shivered. Spreading her thighs, she wrapped her
arms around his neck. He sank into her kiss as his fingers
stroked and petted her between her thighs. When he thrust his
fingers inside her, she arched her back, lifted herself for his
claiming, but he wasn't done. Kissing his way down her body,
he licked and sucked at her with a feline playfulness that had her
writhing on the bed, the robe she still wore twisting around her.

Hauling her lower body closer to his mouth with a powerful
grip under her thighs, he licked her between those thighs and
straight into a wrenching orgasm, then kept going. The graze
of fangs made her moan and grow even wetter, but he was only
playing. Playing with her like she was his favorite and most
delicious toy.

"Naasir."

A rumbling growl against her, a wet suck of her clitoris. Her
stomach tensed, her spine snapped into a hard curve and she
came all over again. Boneless, she moaned as he scraped his
fangs lightly at her inner thigh, then went back to his licking and
tasting and sucking. Her breathing was so harsh it almost hurt,
and the pleasure, it was the blood in her veins.

When he scraped his fangs over her inner thigh a second
time, she shivered.

And he bit.

Crying out, she clenched her hand in his hair and surrendered to the blood kiss of her mate.

Naasir drank his fill; there was no battle to fight this night
and he'd brought in a pack of food for his mate. Afterward, he'd
feed her, and pet her and talk with her. Now he drank from her
and she was intoxication. Her warm, musky, sated scent surrounded him, her blood hot on his tongue and her free leg
hooking around his back as he tugged strongly on her.

Shivering, she whispered his name again and it made his

cock throb. He stroked her thigh as he fed, enjoying the silken feel of her. She was so soft and yet there was such strength in her. He wanted to spar with her, wanted to cross blades with her, wanted to lie naked in bed with her and tease her.

Licking the tiny wounds closed after he was finally full, he rose up over her. She was heavy lidded, her lips plump and her breasts flushed. Raising her hand, she pulled him down to her as he lifted up her thigh and pushed his cock into her tight, slick channel. He kissed her as they rocked together and she held him throughout.

It wasn't how he'd imagined this act when he'd thought about being with his mate. He'd always thought it'd be hard and raw. This was hot and tender and he liked it. Stroking her thigh again as he moved, he kept on kissing her. Their tongues played with each other and when she pretended to bite his, he growled and she laughed.

Nipping at her nose, he squeezed her thigh.

Her smile deepened and she held him even more tightly, her legs locked around him. "I love you."

"I know."

Laughing again, her sparkly eyes full of sunshine, she claimed another kiss. And they kept on playing their sexy little game that made him happy deep inside. When she clamped down on him in a startled orgasm, he rode her through it before leaning down to suck and lick at her breasts until she moaned and tugged up his head.

He loved kissing her, so he cooperated with her silent demand. And when he orgasmed, he made her all sticky, until no part of her didn't smell of him. Rubbing his cheek against her at the end, he lay on her for a long time, making sure to keep his weight on one arm so as not to crush her. When he turned over onto his back at last, she made a sleepy, complaining sound.

He cuddled her onto his chest, her wings spreading out over the bed and across his chest. Yawning, he stroked her wing and said, "I negotiated for you to return to the Refuge."

"Hmm." She put her hand over his heart, her touch possessive—as a mate's should be. "Is Alexander setting up a stronghold there?"

"Yes. Technically, you'll be attached to that, but you're free to do your work in the Archives with Jessamy."

Rising up on her elbow, her hair all tumbled, she blinked several times as if to clear her head. "I can't believe you just asked Alexander for this and he gave it to you." A sudden, deep worry creased her brow. "Did you lose something in the bargain?"

Naasir used his thumb to rub away her frown. "We saved his life." Now that the Ancient had been in the world, he understood just how bad things had become with Lijuan and the Cascade. "He's grateful he's not locked in Sleep while his people need him. What I asked was little enough."

He played with Andromeda's hair. "Alexander offered to free you from his court altogether, but that could cause problems with the other archangels. So you'll remain an official part of his court, but you don't have to take up any duties within unless you want to."

"My grandfather won't be pleased that I'm not feeding him information."

"Do you care?"

"No. He repudiated the blood vow in front of Alexander—it doesn't matter what he wants." Her smile was gleeful. "It just matters what we want. Are you going to take me to your secret aerie?"

"We leave tomorrow for home."

"Home." Tears rolled down Andromeda's face. *"Home."* For the first time in her life, home would be a safe place where she was loved and cherished, and where she could be herself without any secrets or fears. "Home," she whispered again.

Turning them over so that he was braced over her, Naasir kissed away her tears, then began to playfully kiss her "spots" one by one. "Home," he rumbled when she started to smile and count along with him. "For me and my mate and our cubs."

"Yes," she whispered, her mind filling with tiny, wild children who'd drive her crazy and who she would love as fiercely as she loved their wonderful, beautiful chimera father. *"Yes."*

Epilogue

Raphael ended his conversation with Alexander and turned off the communications screen. The Ancient had done one of Raphael's Seven a great favor, and though Alexander had said there was no debt, Raphael had reached out to thank him regardless.

"Why make the call?" Elena asked. "Wouldn't it have been better to just let things lie?" she added as they walked out onto the cliffs behind their home. In front and below them, the Hudson was sluggish and dull under the cloud-laden sky, Manhattan shadowed enough by the ponderous weather that a number of the high-rises had switched on their lights, though it was only early afternoon.

"You must remember that though Alexander appears little older than me, he is hundreds of thousands of years older."

"He's like your mother—he expects certain courteous behavior?"

"You are becoming an ever-more-elegant and knowledgeable consort." His tone might have been a tease, but the words were truth; Elena had been forced to absorb an incredible depth of knowledge in a highly condensed span of time. "Soon you'll be hosting angelic balls with regularity."

"Hey, watch the insults." She pointed a knife at him before sliding it away. "It's a delicate thing though, isn't it? When you talk to Alexander, it's not like when you talk to Elijah or even Titus."

Raphael watched the distinctive figures of Legion fighters fly in and out of their home in the distance. "Come. We'll talk as we fly. You have to be at the Guild soon."

Spreading her wings, Elena took off in a low sweep over the Hudson before using the air currents to rise up. Raphael didn't need to do the same, but he did so they could fly wing to wing toward the city. *Titus helped train me when I was a stripling,* he said after they were both in position, *but once I ascended, he accepted that I was an archangel and his equal on the Cadre.*

Alexander, on the other hand, has always had trouble with the fact that I became an archangel at only a thousand years of age. It made Raphael the youngest angel to have ever become an archangel. *As a result, I can never allow him to treat me as a youth.* He could laugh with Titus and call him "old man" while the other archangel called him "pup," but such games would never happen with Alexander.

Right. Elena's braid slipped over her shoulder as she swept left with the wind, her joy in flight apparent. *He's like a father who can't accept that his child has grown up.*

A good analogy. Almost to Manhattan, he said, *Look.*

Elena's response was free of the worry that had twisted through it in the days immediately after Illium's fall. *Bluebell and Sparkle are having a competition again.*

Not far from the Tower, the two angels were racing in a straight vertical line into the clouds. As Raphael watched, Aodhan eked out a lead, Illium overtook him, only to be overtaken himself . . . and then everything went to hell.

Illium slammed into the stratosphere as the world suddenly shattered into a blue-gold rain. Hitting Elena beside him, it glimmered and stuck, streaking her skin and hair.

Raphael, what's happening?

He's ascending. Raphael's heart thundered. *Land. Now.* With that curt instruction he knew his intelligent consort wouldn't fight, not with the air currents already turbulent around them; he rose into the sky after Illium.

It wasn't done to interfere with an angel's ascension, but the boy was too young, hundreds of years too young. Right then, Raphael couldn't help but think of Illium as the boy he'd first met, the one who had followed him all over the Refuge telling him stories of his adventures. The small blue-winged boy who, with his quieter friend, Aodhan, had pulled more tricks than most other children combined.

At not much past five hundred, Illium's body simply wasn't physically strong enough to handle the power that lived in an archangel's veins every moment of every day. A thousand had been a stretch—Raphael had barely survived the transition, been able to feel his skin about to break when he landed following his ascension. It had taken every ounce of his will to hold himself together instead of flying apart.

Today, using that same violent power to cut through the unstable air currents that had sent other angels dropping onto the closest landing surfaces, he arrowed directly toward Illium. The younger male was glowing golden, so much power pouring out of him that it threatened to ignite and annihilate him. His body was bent backward, his wings hanging down limply though his hands were fisted, his jaw gritted.

Raphael didn't hesitate.

Punching through the golden blaze of power, he grabbed Illium with a grip on his upper arms. "Illium!"

The blue-winged angel's eyes met his, pure terror in golden depths full of a hot red fire. As if his blood was boiling inside him. "Sire." The sound was strained. "I can't—"

His head snapped back, light pouring out of his eyes, his mouth, his skin.

Refusing to see the jagged cracks appearing in Illium's flesh as raw power forced its way out of a body not built to hold it, Raphael "caught" that power with his own. He was running on blind instinct, had no reason to believe it would work. Though there were rumors and suspicions that Lijuan had gained the ability to siphon power from other archangels, from what Raphael had seen in the battle above New York, all she might be able to do was to feed on the Cadre much the same as she did with anyone else.

No archangel could capture another archangel's true *power.*

Only . . .

Illium's power surged up his arms and into his bloodstream.

He directed the excess into the sky, where it turned into shattered lightning. When the lightning tried to pour back into Illium, he held it back with a shield of blue licked with iridescent wildfire, and he continued to capture the new energy pouring out of Illium.

The power he'd dispersed pushed against his shield, but it was new, fragile. Sending his own energy out into it, he made it break apart. Again and again and again. The rain continued to be glittering blue gold around him, but Illium's breath began to come a little easier.

The golden light still pulsed below the surface of his skin, but it was no longer surging out through the fractures that didn't bleed but glowed. Raphael didn't know what would happen if he captured all the power, whether it would kill Illium or destroy his chance at ascension. He stopped.

"Can you fly down?" They were high enough up and had been encased in so much blinding light that no one could've seen what Raphael had done, but if Illium was to join the Cadre, he *could not* appear weak, least of all now.

His face drawn and eyes glowing a vivid gold, Illium gripped Raphael's arm hard as he spread out his wings. "Yes." Another strained word. "Not far."

"Follow me. Head to Aodhan." The Tower balcony on which he'd seen the other angel land was the closest viable point.

Then he dropped through the now dead-quiet air, having judged that Illium didn't have fine muscle control over his wings. The new energy inside the younger angel's body was overpowering him. He kept in mental touch with the other male throughout, making sure to land first so he could break Illium's fall if he crashed. But the blue-winged angel managed to land on his feet . . . barely.

Aodhan, his face stark, went to reach out, stopped.

Illium's eyes reflected a hundred different emotions as he stared at Raphael. "Sire." His voice was so full of power it was barely understandable. "I'm not ready." Blood bubbled out of his mouth, was washed away by a heavy rain no longer stained blue gold.

The power, Raphael realized, was crushing Illium's internal organs. Left alone, it would kill him in a matter of minutes. Grabbing the side of the younger male's neck, Raphael looked into his eyes and drew a touch more of the power into himself. He didn't want to steal what was Illium's birthright, but he would *not* let one of his Seven die.

"Focus on controlling it," he said just as Elena landed on the edge of the balcony. "Hold the power in a tight grip."

Illium clenched his jaw, stared into Raphael's eyes, but the blood kept bubbling out.

Aodhan was suddenly there, his arm wrapped around Illium's waist from behind as he held up his friend. "Focus," he ordered. "You *focus*!"

Not far from Raphael, Elena was on her cell phone. "Lady Caliane," she bit into the receiver. "No, I can't wait! Get her!"

Mere heartbeats later, Elena said, "Lady, I'm sorry to be so rude, but Illium has ascended and it's killing him."

Running over with that abrupt greeting, she put the phone next to Raphael's ear. "Mother," he said. "I can leach off his power, but I don't know what it'll do to him." As far as Raphael knew, no ascension had ever been halted or reversed, but compared to his mother, he'd lived but a firefly moment in time.

"The boy is bound to you?" Caliane said sharply. "By blood?"

"Yes." The bond had been made when Illium became one of his Seven. It was partly why all of his Seven could initialize mind-to-mind contact with him regardless of age and whether they were angel or vampire.

"Absorb the energy, *all* of it. Now, before it's too late."

Not arguing when Illium was choking on his own blood in front of him, Raphael opened up his senses and did what he'd done instinctively in the sky. Power slammed into him, golden and filled with a joie de vivre that was pure Illium. Yet it melded with Raphael's so flawlessly it was almost as if it had been meant for him.

It was strong . . . but young. Even so, the golden light bonded with Raphael's cells in a way that said it was making him stronger on a permanent level. As if another brace had been added to the foundation of his power.

Not just an increase in strength. Evolution that took seconds rather than eons.

Gasping in air, Illium swayed but Aodhan kept him upright as Raphael continued to do the impossible and absorb the power of another archangel. Only Illium wasn't Cadre. When two members of the Cadre stood next to one another, there was a faint repulsion effect, as if they were not meant to be so close. It was mild enough to ignore for short periods, but it was always present.

Raphael felt nothing akin to that with Illium.

"Yes," he heard Elena say behind him just as he drained the last drop of the new energy from Illium. "I think it worked." A pause. "Yes, I will." Hanging up, she said, "Let's get him inside."

Between Raphael and Aodhan, they managed to get Illium into the office off the balcony—which happened to be Honor's—and shut the door. Elena pushed the button that opaqued the windows and it was only then that Illium collapsed into the nearest chair, his wings spread out on either side. "What happened?" he said, his entire body shaking.

When Aodhan crouched in front of him and pushed back Illium's dripping hair, the blue-winged angel shuddered and leaned into the caress. It took time for him to stop trembling, and when he did, it was to raise his head to meet Raphael's gaze. "Sire, I am no archangel."

"No," Raphael agreed. "You might be one day, but your body and mind can't handle the power at this age." And with it living in Raphael now, Illium showed no signs of an ascension.

Having found a bottle of cold water, Elena gave it to her beloved Bluebell and, perching on the arm of his chair, gently patted his back, her fingertips brushing Illium's wings.

"Did my mother say anything else?" Raphael asked her.

The gray of Elena's eyes was dark, the ring of silver vivid. "She wants you to call."

Not waiting in case Illium began to glow with power again, Raphael used his consort's phone to make the call, putting it on speaker so all of them could hear what Caliane had to say. He expected to get the technician who monitored the communications system he'd had Illium organize for Amanat, but it was Caliane's face that filled the tiny screen.

"Son," she said, her expression drawn. "Is your city still standing?"

"Yes." Her worried question made him understand the staggering truth: if he hadn't been there to stop Illium's premature ascension, the young angel's death would've resulted in a catastrophic shock wave. "Have you seen this before, Mother?"

"Yes, in a Cascade at the very dawn of my existence. Before I was an archangel."

Raphael couldn't imagine that time—his mother had been a power his entire lifetime. "What happened?"

"An angel who was the commander of an archangel, ascended without warning. He was only seven hundred and his body could not hold the power." Sorrow in her at the loss of that long-ago angel. "He died in a thunderous fury and he took over twenty thousand people with him."

Blowing out a harsh breath, Illium rose to his feet. He was shaky but managed to make his way to Raphael's side to face Caliane. "Lady," he said, giving a deep bow. "You saved my life. I thank you."

Caliane inclined her head as Raphael grabbed Illium before he would've toppled backward as he straightened from the bow. "Sit, child," Raphael's mother ordered. "You are damaged."

Illium didn't argue.

"Damaged?" Elena's tone was sharp. "Is it something we need to worry about?"

"No. He should recover now that the power is out of him." Caliane leaned back in her seat, her hair pulled back in a braid and her body clad in old combat leathers much like Elena. "Though the angel in my youth died, there were rumors of another young angel who ascended too early but who survived because he had a bond of blood—and of trust—with his archangel. He was weak after the power transfer, but made a complete recovery."

She looked at Raphael. "The archangel, however, gained in strength."

Raphael felt his blood cool. "I don't intend to steal what is rightfully Illium's." He'd done what he had only to save Illium's life.

"You may have it, sire. I insist."

Ignoring Illium's slurred words, Raphael held his mother's gaze. "I can't forcefully stop his ascension if this is what he's meant to become."

"The sudden ascensions of the too young occur only during a Cascade," Caliane pointed out. "On all three occasions that I know of, the angel in question was either an archangel's second or otherwise in his innermost circle."

"You think the power transfer is the point." Coming over

so she could look at the screen, Elena stood with her body and her wings touching Raphael's in a quiet, potent intimacy. "But what if Raphael hadn't been here?"

"The Cascade is never predictable, Consort," Caliane said, a sense of crushing age in her voice. "There's no way to foretell if such an incident will reoccur, or if it was the only time and the boy is no longer in any danger." Her eyes held Raphael's. "All I can tell you is that if you don't take the power, he'll die and he'll take tens of thousands with him. There is no other possible outcome."

"The fact you can even absorb the power," Elena said slowly, "that's got to mean something, right?"

Caliane raised an eyebrow. "A salient point. A true ascension does not permit any interference, not even by the strongest Ancient."

They spoke further, but Caliane knew little else. Signing off, Raphael turned to find that Illium had struggled to his feet again. His face was stripped of all shields, suddenly unbearably young. "I'm not ready," he said again, his voice shaken. "I'm not ready to leave your Seven."

Grabbing him by the side of his neck as he had earlier, Raphael hauled him into his arms. "I'm not ready for you to go." His eyes met Elena's over Illium's head as the blue-winged angel held on tight. *My mother is right. Now is not his time.* Illium would become a power one day, but he had to grow into that strength, not have it forced into him by the violence of the Cascade.

Beside Elena stood a white-faced Aodhan. *He'll need you now more than ever, Aodhan,* Raphael said. *Keep him in the present, not in a future that may or may not happen.*

Eyes of fractured blue and crystalline green, the shards bursting outward from jet-black pupils met Raphael's. *Yes, sire.*

Releasing Illium only after the younger angel had stopped trembling, Raphael looked into eyes that were back to their usual bright gold, devoid of the dark red flame. "Go to your suite. Rest. We'll speak more when you wake—but know one thing. If this happens again, I'll be there."

"Lady Caliane said it's unpredictable."

"If the power transfer is the point as it seems to be," Raphael pointed out, "it'll occur while I'm nearby."

Illium's shuddering relief was suddenly overwhelmed by an emotion that drew his skin tight over his cheekbones. "My mother—"

"I've already told Dmitri to make sure the Hummingbird knows you're safe and that what happened today was a simple experiment to do with your abilities and mine, gone a little awry." Illium's mother was still in Raphael's territory, but she'd gone to visit with Jason and Mahiya today. "Jason will confirm and keep her away from any recordings that may have been captured."

The blue-winged angel's eyes shone wet. "Thank you, sire. She . . ."

"I will watch over her, Illium." Raphael would never be ungentle with the Hummingbird. "Now go."

Waiting until the younger angel left the room, Aodhan acting as his support, Raphael turned to Elena. "So long as Illium is safe, the Hummingbird will accept a vague explanation, but we need to find a way to explain this to the wider immortal world as something other than an ascension." Should any of the Cadre believe Illium a weak archangel, he'd become a target.

"I have an idea." Dmitri ran into the office. "I've been working on it since the instant I saw you fly toward Illium." Raphael's second thrust a hand through his hair, his black T-shirt stretching over his chest. "All anyone really saw was Illium and you speed up into the sky. The images taken via telescopes and satellites just show a blinding haze of light." He put several printed images on Honor's desk.

Each showed a glow painful enough to cause flickering afterimages on the retinas. No way to tell who was inside the light.

"I'll allow it to leak that you and Illium were testing a power transfer like Lijuan can do with her troops." Dmitri's tone was clear, his features grim. "I'll also let it drop that it went wrong and Illium lost the power in an uncontrolled surge that caused the rain and lightning. No one's going to forget the sheer fury of the incident—failed experiment or not, you're clearly no easy target." A short pause before his lips curved in a grim smile. "The belief that you've been running dangerous experiments with him will also answer the lingering questions about his earlier fall."

"Do it." Raphael had appreciated Dmitri's tactical mind many times over the centuries, but never more than today. "No one wants to accept that an angel barely over five hundred years old could ascend. All we have to do is provide an alternative explanation."

Elena picked up one of the photographs after Dmitri left. "Raphael, is it my imagination or are you stronger?"

Of course, his consort would feel the change. They were too intimately entwined for it to be otherwise. "What I drew from Illium didn't leach off. It's become woven into my body, an auxiliary generator of a kind."

Dropping the photograph, Elena faced him, her boots touching his. "If Caliane's power transfer theory is right, then Illium became *more* temporarily because you need more power than you can generate on your own." She spread one hand protectively over his heart, brushing the thumb of her other over his right temple, over the Legion mark. "Something bad is coming. Worse than before."

Enclosing her in his wings and his arms, Raphael didn't say anything. They both knew she was right.

Eleven archangels.

A dangerous near ascension that could've annihilated an entire city.

Two Ancients walking the earth.

An archangel who could give a twisted form of life.

The Cascade was gathering momentum.

Beijing was already gone. New York and Elijah's territory had barely survived. No one could predict how much of the world would be left standing when the Cascade ended.

"Together, *hbeebti.*"

"Always, Archangel."

Turn the page for an excerpt from

Slave to Sensation

the first book in Nalini Singh's
bestselling Psy-Changeling series.

And don't forget to visit her website and
join her newsletter for up-to-date information
on her next books,
as well as free short stories set
in the Guild Hunter and Psy-Changeling worlds.

Sascha Duncan couldn't read a single line of the report flickering across the screen of her handheld organizer. A haze of fear clouded her vision, insulating her from the cold efficiency of her mother's office. Even the sound of Nikita wrapping up a call barely penetrated her numbed mind.

She was terrified.

This morning, she'd woken to find herself curled up in bed, whimpering. Normal Psy did not whimper, did not show any emotion, did not feel. But Sascha had known since childhood that she wasn't normal. She'd successfully hidden her flaw for twenty-six years but now things were going wrong. Very, very wrong.

Her mind was deteriorating at such an accelerating rate that she'd begun experiencing physical side effects—muscle spasms, tremors, an abnormal heart rhythm, and those ragged tears after dreams she never recalled. It would soon become impossible to conceal her fractured psyche. The result of exposure would be incarceration at the Center. Of course no one called it a prison. Termed a "rehabilitation facility," it provided a brutally efficient way for the Psy to cull the weak from the herd.

After they were through with her, if she was lucky she'd end up a drooling mess with no mind to speak of. If she wasn't so fortunate, she'd retain enough of her thinking processes to become a drone in the vast business networks of the Psy, a robot with just enough neurons functioning to file the mail or sweep the floors.

The feel of her hand tightening on the organizer jolted her back to reality. If there was one place she couldn't break down, it was here, sitting across from her mother. Nikita Duncan might be her blood but she was also a member of the Psy Council. Sascha wasn't sure that if it came down to it, Nikita wouldn't sacrifice her daughter to keep her place on the most powerful body in the world.

With grim determination, she began to reinforce the psychic shields that protected the secret corridors of her mind. It was the one thing she excelled at and by the time her mother finished her call, Sascha exhibited as much emotion as a sculpture carved from arctic ice.

"We have a meeting with Lucas Hunter in ten minutes. Are you ready?" Nikita's almond-shaped eyes held nothing but cool interest.

"Of course, Mother." She forced herself to meet that direct gaze without flinching, trying not to wonder if her own was as unrevealing. It helped that, unlike Nikita, she had the night-sky eyes of a cardinal Psy—an endless field of black scattered with pinpricks of cold white fire.

"Hunter is an alpha changeling so don't underestimate him. He thinks like a Psy." Nikita turned to bring up her computer screen, a flat panel that slid up and out from the surface of her desk.

Sascha called up the relevant data on her organizer. The miniature computer held all the notes she could possibly need for the meeting and was compact enough to slip into her pocket. If Lucas Hunter stuck true to type, he'd turn up with paper hard copies of everything.

According to her information, Hunter had become the only ruling alpha in the DarkRiver leopard pack at twenty-three years of age. In the ten years since, DarkRiver had consolidated its hold over San Francisco and surrounding regions to the extent that they were now the dominant predators in the area. Outside changelings who wanted to work, live, or play in

DarkRiver territory had to receive their permission. If they didn't, changeling territorial law went into force and the outcome was savage.

What had made Sascha's eyes open wide in her first reading of this material was that DarkRiver had negotiated a mutual nonaggression pact with the SnowDancers, the wolf pack that controlled the rest of California. Since the SnowDancers were known to be vicious and unforgiving to anyone who dared rise to power in their territory, it made her wonder at DarkRiver's civilized image. No one survived the wolves by playing nice.

A soft chime sounded.

"Shall we go, Mother?" Nothing about Nikita's relationship to Sascha was, or had ever been, maternal, but protocol stated she was to be addressed by her family designation.

Nikita nodded and stood to her full height, a graceful five eight. Dressed in a black pantsuit teamed with a white shirt, she looked every inch the successful woman she was, her hair cut to just below her ears in a blunt style that suited her. She was beautiful. And she was lethal.

Sascha knew that when they walked side by side as they were doing now, no one would place them for mother and daughter. They were the same height but the resemblance ended there. Nikita had inherited her Asiatic eyes, arrow-straight hair, and porcelain skin from her half-Japanese mother. By the time the genes had been passed on to Sascha, all that had survived was the slightest tilt to the eyes.

Instead of Nikita's sheet of shimmering blue-black, she had rich ebony hair that absorbed light like ink and curled so wildly she was forced to pull it back into a severe plait every morning. Her skin was a dark honey rather than ivory, evidence of her unknown father's genes. Sascha's birth records had listed him as being of Anglo-Indian descent.

She dropped back a little as the door to the meeting room drew closer. She hated encounters with changelings and not because of the general Psy revulsion to their open emotionalism. It seemed to her that they *knew.* Somehow they could sense that she wasn't like the others, that she was flawed.

"Mr. Hunter."

She looked up at the sound of her mother's voice. And found herself within touching distance of the most dangerous male she'd ever seen. There was no other word to describe him. Well over six feet tall, he was built like the fighting machine he was in the wild, pure lean muscle and tensile strength.

His black hair brushed his shoulders but there was nothing soft about it. Instead, it hinted at unrestrained passion and the dark hunger of the leopard below the skin. She had no doubt she was in the presence of a predator.

Then he turned his head and she saw the right side of his face. Four jagged lines, reminiscent of the claw marks of some great beast, scored the muted gold of his skin. His eyes were a hypnotic green but it was those slashing markings that grabbed her attention. She'd never been this close to one of the changeling Hunters before.

"Ms. Duncan." His voice was low and a little rough, as if caught on the edge of a growl.

"This is my daughter, Sascha. She'll be the liaison for this project."

"A pleasure, Sascha." He tipped his head toward her, eyes lingering for a second longer than necessary.

"Likewise." Could he hear the jagged beat of her pulse? Was it true that changeling senses were far superior to those of any other race?

"Please." He gestured for them to take seats at the glass-topped table and remained standing until they'd done so. Then he chose a chair exactly opposite Sascha.

She forced herself to return his gaze, not fooled by the chivalry into dropping her guard. Hunters were trained to sniff out vulnerable prey. "We've looked at your offer," she began.

"What do you think?" His eyes were remarkably clear, as calm as the deepest ocean. But there was nothing cold or practical about him, nothing that belied her first impression of him as something wild barely leashed.

"You must know that Psy-changeling business alliances rarely work. Competing priorities." Nikita's voice sounded utterly toneless in comparison to Lucas's.

His responsive smile was so wicked, Sascha couldn't look away. "In this case, I think we have the same ones. You need help to plan and execute housing that'll appeal to changelings. I want an inside track on new Psy projects."

Sascha knew that that couldn't be all of it. They needed

him but he didn't need them, not when DarkRiver's business interests were extensive enough to rival their own. The world was changing under the noses of the Psy, the human and changeling races no longer content to be second best. It was a measure of their arrogance that most of her people continued to ignore the slow shift in power.

Sitting so close to the contained fury that was Lucas Hunter, she wondered at the blindness of her brethren. "If we deal with you, we'll expect the same level of reliability that we'd get if we went with a Psy construction and design firm."

Lucas looked across at the icy perfection of Sascha Duncan and wished he knew what it was about her that was bugging the hell out of him. His beast was snarling and pacing the cage of his mind, ready to pounce out and sniff at her sedate dark gray pantsuit. "Of course," he said, fascinated by the tiny flickers of white light that came and went in the darkness of her eyes.

He'd seldom been this close to a cardinal Psy. They were rare enough that they didn't mingle with the masses, being given high posts in the Psy Council as soon as they reached any kind of mature age. Sascha was young but there was nothing untried about her. She looked as ruthless as the rest of her race, as unfeeling and as cold.

She could be abetting a killer.

Any one of them could be. It was why DarkRiver had been stalking high-level Psy for months, looking for a way to penetrate their defenses. The Duncan project was an unbelievable chance. Not only was Nikita powerful in her own right, she was a member of the innermost circle—the Psy Council. Once Lucas was in, it would be his job to find out the identity of the sadistic Psy who'd stolen the life of one of DarkRiver's women . . . and execute him.

No mercy. No forgiveness.

In front of him, Sascha glanced at the slim organizer she held. "We're willing to offer seven million."

He'd take a penny if it would get him inside the secretive corridors of the Psy world but he couldn't afford to make them suspicious. "Ladies." He filled the single word with the sensuality that was as much a part of him as his beast.

Most changelings and humans would've reacted to the promise of pleasure implicit in his tones, but these two remained unmoved. "We both know the contract is worth nothing less than ten million. Let's not waste time." He could've sworn a light sparked in Sascha's night-sky eyes, a light that spoke of a challenge accepted. The panther inside him growled softly in response.

"Eight. And we want rights to approve each stage of the work from concept to construction."

"Ten." He kept his tone silky smooth. "Your request will cause considerable delay. I can't work efficiently if I have to traipse up here every time I want to make a minor change." Perhaps multiple visits might allow him to glean some information on the murderer's cold trail, but it was doubtful. Nikita was hardly likely to leave sensitive Council documents lying around.

"Give us a moment." The older woman looked at the younger.

The tiny hairs on the back of his neck rose. They always did that in the presence of Psy who were actively using their powers. Telepathy was just one of their many talents and one that he admitted came in very handy during business negotiations. But their abilities also blinded them. Changelings had long ago learned to take advantage of the Psy sense of superiority.

Almost a minute later, Sascha spoke to him. "It's important for us to have control at every stage."

"Your money, your time." He put his hands on the table and steepled his fingers, noting how her eyes went to them. Interesting. In his experience, the Psy never displayed any awareness of body language. It was as if they were completely cerebral, shut into the world of their minds. "But if you insist on that much involvement, I can't promise we'll hold to the timetable. In fact I'll guarantee we won't."

"We have a proposal to counter that." Night-sky eyes met his.

He raised a brow. "I'm listening." And so was the panther inside him. Both man and beast found Sascha Duncan captivating in a way that neither could understand. Part of him wanted to stroke her . . . and part of him wanted to bite.

"We'd like to work side by side with DarkRiver. To facilitate this, I request that you provide me with an office at your building."

Every nerve he had went taut. He'd just been granted access to a cardinal Psy almost twenty-four seven. "You want to be joined at the hip with me, darling? That's fine." His senses picked up a change in the atmosphere, but it was so subtle that it was gone before he could identify it. "Do you have authority to sign off on changes?"

"Yes. Even if I have to consult with Mother, I won't need to leave the site." It was a reminder that she was Psy, a member of a race that had sacrificed its humanity long ago.

"How far can a cardinal send?"

"Far enough." She pressed at something on her tiny screen. "So we'll settle at eight?"

He grinned at her attempt to catch him unawares, amused at the almost feline cunning. "Ten, or I walk out and you get something lower quality."

"You're not the only expert on changeling likes and dislikes out there." She leaned forward a fraction.

"Yes." Intrigued by this Psy who appeared to use her body as much as her mind, he deliberately echoed the movement. "But I'm the best."

"Nine."

He couldn't afford to let the Psy think of him as weak—they respected only the coldest, cruelest kind of strength. "Nine and a promise of another million if all the homes are presold by the time of the opening."

Another silence. The hairs on his nape lifted again. Inside his mind the beast batted at the air as if trying to catch the sparks of energy. Most changelings couldn't feel the electrical storms generated by the Psy, but it was a talent that had its uses.

"We agree," Sascha said. "I assume you have hard-copy contracts?"

"Of course." He flipped open a binder and slid across copies of the same document they undoubtedly had on their screens.

Sascha picked them up and passed one to her mother. "Electronic would be much more convenient."

He'd heard it a hundred times from a hundred different Psy. Part of the reason changelings hadn't followed the technological wave was sheer stubbornness; the other part was security—his race had been hacking into Psy databases for decades. "I like something I can hold, touch, and smell, something that pleases all my senses."

It was an innuendo he had no doubt she understood, but it

was her reaction he was looking for. Nothing. Sascha Duncan
was as cold a Psy as he'd ever met—he'd have to thaw her out
enough to gain information about whether the Psy were har-
boring a serial killer.

He found himself oddly attracted by the thought of tan-
gling with this particular Psy, though until that moment, he'd
considered them nothing but unfeeling machines. Then she
looked up to meet his gaze and the panther in him opened its
mouth in a wordless growl.

The hunt had begun. And Sascha Duncan was the prey.

Two hours later, Sascha closed the door to her apartment
and did a mental sweep of the premises. Nothing. Located in
the same building as her office, the apartment had excellent
security, but she'd used her skills at shielding to ring the rooms
with another level of protection. It took a lot of her meager
psychic strength but she needed to feel safe somewhere.

Satisfied that the apartment hadn't been breached, she sys-
tematically checked every one of her inner locks against the
vastness of the PsyNet. Functioning. No one could get into her
mind without her knowing about it.

Only then did she allow herself to collapse into a heap on
the ice-blue carpet, the cool color making her shiver. "Computer. Raise temperature five degrees."

"Complying." The voice was without inflection but that was
to be expected. It was nothing more than the mechanical response of the powerful computer that ran this building. The
houses she'd be building with Lucas Hunter would have no such
computer systems.

Lucas.

Her breath came out in a gasp as she allowed her mind to
cascade with all the emotions she'd had to bury during the
meeting.

Fear.

Amusement.

Hunger.

Lust.

Desire.

Need.

Unclipping the barrette at the end of her plait, she shoved her hands into the unfurling curls before tugging off her jacket and throwing it aside. Her breasts ached, straining against the cups of her bra. She wanted nothing more than to strip herself naked and rub up against something hot, hard, and male.

A whimper escaped her throat as she closed her eyes and rocked back and forth, trying to control the images pounding at her. This shouldn't be happening. No matter how far out of control she'd gone before, it had never been this bad, this sexual. The second she admitted it, the avalanche seemed to slow and she found enough strength to push her way out of the clawing grip of hunger.

Getting up off the floor, she walked to the kitchenette and poured herself a glass of water. As she swallowed, she caught her reflection in the ornamental mirror that hung beside her built-in cooler. It had been a gift from a changeling advisor on another project and she'd kept it despite her mother's raised brow. Her excuse had been that she was trying to understand the other race. In truth, she'd just liked the wildly colorful frame.

However, right now she wished she hadn't held on to it. It showed too clearly what she didn't want to see. The tangle of darkness that was her hair spoke of animal passion and desire, things no Psy should know about. Her face was flushed as if with fever, her cheeks streaked red, and her eyes . . . Lord have mercy, her eyes were pure midnight.

She put down the glass and pushed back her hair, searching. But she hadn't made a mistake. There was no light in the darkness of her pupils. This was only supposed to happen when a Psy was expending a large amount of psychic power.

It had never happened to her.

Her eyes might've marked her as a cardinal but her accessible powers were humiliatingly weak. So weak that she still hadn't been co-opted into the ranks of those who worked directly for the Council.

Her lack of any real psychic power had mystified the instructors who'd trained her. Everyone had always said that there was incredible raw potential inside her mind—more than enough for a cardinal—but that it had never manifested.

Until now.

She shook her head. No. She hadn't expended any psychic

energy so it had to be something else that had caused the darkness, something other Psy didn't know about because they didn't feel. Her eyes drifted to the communication console set into the wall beside the kitchenette. One thing was clear—she couldn't go out looking like this. Anyone who saw her would have her sent in for rehabilitation in a heartbeat.

Fear gripped her tight.

As long as she was on the outside, she might one day figure out a way to escape, a way to cut her link to the PsyNet without throwing her body into paralysis and death. Or she might even discover a way to fix the flaw that marked her. But the second she was admitted into the Center, her world would become darkness. Endless, silent darkness.

With careful hands, she pulled off the cover of the communication console and fiddled with the circuits. Only after she'd replaced the cover did she press in Nikita's code. Her mother lived in the penthouse several floors above.

The answer came seconds later. "Sascha, your screen is turned off."

"I didn't realize," Sascha lied. "Hold on." Pausing for effect, she took a careful breath. "I think it's a malfunction. I'll have a technician check it out."

"Why did you call?"

"I'm afraid I'll have to cancel our dinner. I've received some documents from Lucas Hunter that I'd like to start going through before I meet with him again."

"Prompt for a changeling. I'll see you tomorrow afternoon for a briefing. Good night."

"Good night, Mother." She was talking to dead air. Regardless of the fact that Nikita had been no more a mother to her than the computer that controlled this apartment, it hurt. But tonight that hurt was buried under far more dangerous emotions.

She'd barely started to relax when the console chimed an incoming call. Since the caller identification function had been disabled along with the screen, she had no way of knowing who it was. "Sascha Duncan," she said, trying not to panic that Nikita had changed her mind.

"Hello, Sascha."

Her knees almost buckled at the sound of that honey-smooth voice, more purr than growl now. "Mr. Hunter."

"Lucas. We're colleagues, after all."

"Why are you calling?" Harsh practicality was the only way she could deal with her roller-coaster emotions.

"I can't see you, Sascha."

"It's a screen malfunction."

"Not very efficient." Was that amusement she could hear?

"I assume you didn't call to chat."

"I wanted to invite you to a breakfast meeting with the design team tomorrow." His tone was pure silk.

Sascha didn't know if Lucas always sounded like an invitation to sin or whether he was doing it to unsettle her. *That* thought unsettled her. If he even suspected that there was something not quite right about her, then she might as well sign her death warrant. Internment at the Center was nothing less than a living death anyway.

"Time?" She wrapped her arms tight around her ribs and forced her voice to even out. The Psy were very, very careful that the world never saw their mistakes, their flawed ones. No one had ever successfully fought the Council after being slated for rehabilitation.

"Seven thirty. Is that good for you?"

How could he make the most businesslike of invitations sound like purest temptation? Maybe it was all in her mind— she was finally cracking. "Location?"

"My office. You know where that is?"

"Of course." DarkRiver had set up business camp near the chaotic bustle of Chinatown, taking over a medium-sized office building. "I'll be there."

"I'll be waiting."

To her heightened senses, that sounded more like a threat than a promise.

Nalini Singh was born in Fiji and raised in New Zealand. She spent three years living and working in Japan, and travelling around Asia before returning to New Zealand.

She has worked as a lawyer, a librarian, a candy factory general hand, a bank temp and an English teacher, not necessarily in that order.

Learn more about her and her novels at:
www.nalinisingh.com